About the **Author**

Hannah Lynn is an award-w
Amendments – a dark, dysto
has since gone on to write *The Afterlife of Walter Augustus* – a contemporary fiction novel with a supernatural twist – which won the 2018 Kindle Storyteller Award and the delightfully funny and poignant *Peas and Carrots series*.

While she freely moves between genres, her novels are recognisable for their character driven stories and wonderfully vivid description.

She is currently working on a YA Vampire series and a reimaging of a classic Greek myth.

Born in 1984, Hannah grew up in the Cotswolds, UK. After graduating from university, she spent ten years as a teacher of physics, first in the UK and then around Asia. It was during this time, inspired by the imaginations of the young people she taught, she began writing short stories for children, and later adult fiction Now as a teacher, writer, wife and mother, she is currently living in the Austrian Alps.

Praise for *Amendments*

"Beautifully written, moving, powerful and thoroughly chilling, this is one of the finest works of speculative fiction I've read in years."
Joel Hames, Author of *Dead North*

"A delightful read with an intricate and intriguing plot, lovable characters and quite simply un-put-down-able!"

"A very impressive and accomplished debut novel."

"Amendments is beautifully and eloquently written, with interesting and convincing characters. The concept at the heart of it brings up questions of fate, free will and how much control we have – or want- over our lives; really make you stop and think."

"Very much in the spirit of Aimee Bender and Kazuo Ishiguro, with a little of Margaret Atwood thrown in for good measure."

Also by Hannah Lynn

The Afterlife of Walter Augustus

The Peas and Carrots Series

Peas, Carrots and an Aston Martin
Peas, Carrots and a Red Feather Boa

Don't forget to sign-up for my newsletter and get some fantastic EXCLUSIVE bonus content for a deeper look into the world of Amendments plus news on the up-coming sequels totally **free**.

Details can be found at the end of the book.

Amendments

A novel by

Hannah Lynn

This story is a work of fiction. All names, characters, organizations, places, events and incidents are products of the author's imagination or are used fictitiously. Any resemblance to any persons, alive or dead, events or locals is entirely coincidental.

First published 2015
2nd Edition published 2018

ISBN: 9781980918912

Imprint: Independently published

Cover design by germancreative
Cover image by Victor Tongdee

For Lucy

Prologue

THE EARLY PART of the 21st century saw a world divided. Faced with an unending wave of extremism and media propaganda, nations witnessed the rise of nationalism like never before. Countries began closing their borders; treaties and alliances broke down and by 2050 almost all international relations had ceased. Isolated from the rest of the world, countries raced to find sustainable sources of energy.

It was at this time a catastrophic explosion at a small fusion research laboratory in the north of England changed everything. Scientists had unwittingly ripped and warped the fabric of time. Retrocausality became reality. This new, unthinkable, discovery allowed people to communicate with their past. Small envelopes, containing the wisdom of hindsight, could be sent back in time.

Not everyone believed in the good that could be harnessed from this new technology and groups of protesters and objectors, known as the Marchers, rose up against the system. Organised and uncompromising, they undermined the scientific progress in any way they could. The ensuing civil conflict led to the collapse of society and gave rise to a new nation. The Kingdom, helmed by the all-powerful Cabinet, and with the newly formed Guards at their disposal, quickly quashed the uprising. Through the careful social engineering of the Administration, the Cabinet took total control, placating the masses by bringing amendments into the lives of every citizen in the city of Unity.

There will always be those who disagree. Those who will fight to the death for their beliefs, whichever way they lie. But amidst them, there will always be ordinary people, living ordinary lives. Those who fight only for the love of those they hold dear, praying that each second chance really is a second chance at life.

Those like Emelia.

Part I

Chapter One

From the Book of Amendments

Rule 1. Every person residing in the Kingdom must register their right to amend on the day of their twenty-first birthday.

I PLACE A CUP of water on her bedside table and start to strip her of her vomit-soaked clothes. I manage her skirt with little difficulty, but I won't be able to remove her top without waking her. Not while she's clutching the envelope.

'Please Fi,' I say softly and try to prise it from her grip, but she moans and rolls over, burying it beneath her. I give it another tug, but it's no good. In the end, I step back and look for another approach.

The stench is overwhelming. Every surface is covered in clutter and grime. Outside is freezing, as is every other room in the flat. Not in here though. The sweat is pooling on my forehead. I contemplate opening a window and letting in some air, but it's almost impossible to find a path through the dirty clothes, improvised ashtrays and empty drinks bottles. Tentatively, I pick up a random top by my feet. With a sudden jerk I throw it away from me. I swear something moved.

While Fi continues to twist and groan I shuffle rubbish from one corner to another. Then, after one more failed attempt to roll her over, I leave, slamming the bedroom door a little too hard behind me. It rattles on its hinges and shakes the light fittings. When she's awake I will do some tidying, and wash some clothes. Give the whole place a proper sort out. It can't be easy for her, waking up to that each day. It can't make her want to carry on.

Gabe glances up at me from the kitchen floor. The pit of my stomach starts to flutter. Feeling the heat rising to my cheeks I look away, while internally cursing my drab pyjamas. I should probably ask him how he got in, but he might take my question the wrong way. If he hadn't kept visiting Fi, I don't know how we would have survived these past few months. Fi's list of friends has dwindled into oblivion since everything happened, and Gabe has stuck by her, by us.

The early morning chill makes me acutely aware of my need for proper clothes, but it hardly seems right to walk out and leave Gabe cleaning up the mess. After a moment's deliberation, I venture from the carpet onto the freezing tiles and join him in cleaning up the shards of broken glass and half-smoked cigarette butts. Last night was obviously a bad one. I seem to sleep through it all nowadays.

Together we work at the mess. I scrub at the sticky patches of liquid that have dribbled down the countertop and congealed on the floor while tossing glass and crushed cans into the rubbish. Tidying is a futile act. I'll straighten the flat this morning, like always, then the minute Fi wakes she will recommence her destruction of the place. She's like a hurricane and she doesn't see mess anymore. I don't think she sees anything.

When the floor is clear, Gabe moves to start on the dishes, throwing me a tea towel en route. The lather grows thick, bubbling to the top of the sink and chock-full of rainbows. Rainbows always used to inspire such a sense of hope that I always hated to burst them. Apparently Gabe does not hold the same sentiment – one by one they rupture and fade as the clean plates pile up.

Half way through the batch he holds out a chipped glass for me to dry. My insides lurch. As my mouth dries to parchment, I stand rooted to the spot, staring through the glass that hovers between us. I can't draw my eyes away. I've never seen his scars that clearly before. All three are there on his left palm, glistening and magnified through the curved surface. He clears his throat politely, and I hurriedly take the glass from him.

'Did you bring her home?' I ask, trying to seem casual.

He nods.

'Has she still got a job?'

'For now.'

'I'm sorry. I'll talk to her. She just needs a little more time. She's grieving.'

'It's fine.'

'Gabe, I'll —'

'Honestly, Em. It's fine.'

I avoid his eyes and get back to the job in hand.

I know what he's thinking. Why aren't I grieving? I lost my mother, too. What's wrong with me that I can just keep going? But it's not the same, and he should know that. I didn't use one of my amendments to try and save her. I didn't *have* an amendment I *could* use then. I don't deserve the right to grieve.

I continue to help him, even though I get under his feet as he sweeps and mops the floors. I'd suggest he leave, go home, relax, but he won't – not until he's seen Fi awake and conscious. A familiar sensation tightens around my gut. Even before all this, he would come around to the flat and wait, sometimes for hours, for her to come home. More often than not, he'd be brushed aside and dismissed as soon as she arrived, usually with a man. How she could have ignored him like that I have no idea. We would sit together on the sofa and joke about things Fi had done or said while we waited for her to return. It seems like a lifetime ago now.

By the time he's finished, everything, from the glasses to the tiles, gleams. It almost looks like a home again. Not that Fi will notice. Perhaps she'll slip on the floor; she'd have difficulty making her way to a bar with a broken leg. A flicker of guilt tugs at my insides, but only briefly. Guilt from thoughts like that are just grains of sand on the dune I've accumulated recently. I'm still racking up the guilt tally in my head when Gabe speaks.

'Do you need a lift to the Annex?' he says. 'It is today, right?'

He fills a glass with water and hands it to me. Once again I freeze. This time I stare at my own left palm, with its wrinkled skin, deep creases and small wiry tributaries that branch from them. It seems to have become today's theme, not taking glasses in order to study hands.

'It's today.'

Being my twenty-first birthday, today is the last day my hand will look like this: pink, crinkled, unbroken. In a few hours it will be scarred; marked with my right to amend. I should probably be excited. Most people would be. But I know from experience that amendments don't solve everything. My mother is a testament to that. Then again, I remind myself, she broke the rules. I swallow back the tears before memories force their way back in, then I take the glass from Gabe and swallow back the water in one.

In the early years of the Kingdom, when amending was first made available to everyone, there were no age restrictions. While you still only got two, you were registered at birth. As such you could perform your first amendment the moment you could write it down and could go back to the day you were born if you so wished. Naturally, people exploited the opportunity. Children were born simply so parents could use their amendments or else trade them for something else; money, food. Then the Cabinet stepped in. There were demonstrations and violent protests but in the end, they made the Administration raise the age of registering to twenty-one. I get it. It was a sensible thing to do. Still, I can't help and wonder how different my life would be if they'd decided on a lower age limit. I feel the tears start to well but suck them back before they escape. There is no time for tears right now. I want to get registered and back to Fi as soon as possible.

'A lift to the Annex would be great,' I say.

'Not until Fi's up, mind.'

Of course not.

By nine-thirty, Fi is out of bed. She's hardly eloquent, and her breath is a pungent blend of aniseed, cigarettes and vomit, but she's lucid and coherent – for now at least. Her choice of dress is somewhat eclectic, with baggy tracksuit bottoms and a sheer blouse over a lurid fluorescent bra. All the buttons and zips are undone, yet as always, she somehow manages to fix the tiny clasp of her bracelet.

I look at it with envy. It's a tradition in our part of the Kingdom for parents to give a piece of jewellery to their daughters or sons when they register. There's no one to uphold that tradition for me. Except of course Fi, but then she can barely uphold a basic dental hygiene routine most days. A lone tear forms in the corner of my eye. I wipe it away before she sees.

Fi's stomach is concave and her collarbones protrude at scarily irregular angles; as usual there's no food in the house to help rectify this. Gabe manages to coax some water down her as she slumps onto the sofa and turns the pages of a half-charcoaled photo album.

'I've got to go out now,' I say.

There's no reply, even though I know she can hear me.

'Fi? Are you listening to me? Finola?'

One eyebrow rises upwards, and I am given the most fleeting acknowledgement. I bite down on my tongue and hold my breath as I try to anticipate her next reaction. There's no point trying to force her to speak. Forcing Fi to do something never helps anyone. After another minute's mindless page turning, she drops the album, rises and saunters to the bathroom. That's as good a response as I'm likely to get.

As we leave, I hear her rifling through the medicine cabinet. A loud clattering is followed by louder cursing, as the contents of the cupboard spill onto the floor. A sadistic smile curls on my lips – she can search all she likes, but she won't find anything, not in there at least. Before I call goodbye, I hover pathetically by the front door, hoping that maybe, just maybe, she might remember what day it is and say something – after all it's only two words. Still, she offers nothing intelligible other than expletives. In the end, I slam the door shut to the sounds of retching and running taps. Gabe squeezes my hand, but I am too heartbroken to even register that properly.

The Annex is in the Central Section, a forty-minute journey away, although on the buses it would take me nearly double that, if not longer with all the snow, and that's assuming the buses are running.

'Do you want to get some lunch first?' Gabe says as the elevator announces its arrival on our floor. Elevators in our building are shoddy, piss-reeking cages. No doubt the Cabinet has better things to spend its money on than derelict tower blocks that should have been knocked down decades ago. I fear for my life a little every time I step inside one.

The doors open to reveal a bald man and his daughter. He's dressed in a miners' grey coverall with his name *Andjrez* stitched above the pocket. I'd guess the girl is about four – maybe younger, maybe older – I've never been good with ages. I've seen him a few times around the building, but I've never seen her. There's no disguising the likeness though. Her almond eyes are an exact replica of her father's, as is her narrow chin. Her hair, however, is long and strikingly dark, not dissimilar to Fi's and nothing like the mousey mop I inherited. The girl is gripping at his hand and staring at her rose-patterned shoes. Andjrez runs his eyes up and down me, clicking his tongue against the roof of his mouth. He sniffs loudly – seemingly oblivious to the fetid stench – and smears the back of his hand across his face. A shudder spreads upwards through my spine. I let Gabe get in first.

'Drey,' Gabe says to the man with a nod. The tone of his voice slightly too sharp to be impassive.

The man grunts his response.

'So?' Gabe says. It takes a second before I realise he is now talking to me.

'Sorry?'

'Food?' Gabe says. 'Before you register?'

The smell of the elevator is making me nauseated, and a knot is tightening itself around my intestines. 'I think I'd rather just get it over with.'

'It's not that bad. Besides, you probably need to eat something. They take a fair bit of blood.'

I can feel Andjrez listening, his eyes boring into the back of my skull, his clicking and sniffing still audible over the groan of the elevator. It stirs the hairs across the nape of my neck.

'What about time?' I say, trying to focus on Gabe.

'We can go to the afternoon ceremony instead,' he tells me. 'We're already pushing it to make the morning one and you need food. You don't want to pass out. Trust me.'

I concede and agree to lunch, mainly to stop the conversation and the bald man's eavesdropping. It wouldn't hurt to eat something. Fi has taunted me about the fainting ever since she registered, and I'd hate to give her the satisfaction.

By the time the elevator grinds to a stop, I have every muscle clenched against the clicking and sniffing, and my reduced breath intake against the smell has made me light headed. My skin prickles as the man brushes past me, pulling his daughter in tow. A tattoo crawls from the bottom of his wrist, leaves and vines delicately intertwined with the red petals and green thorns. It disappears under his sleeves only to reappear at the base of his neck. He is two steps out of the elevator when he turns and blocks my exit. His eyes lock onto mine, black and unblinking, so close I can taste the menthol-masked smoke and alcohol on his breath.

My pulse rockets as I wait for him to say something. His eyes remain unblinking, set solely on me. I continue to wait, paralysed with unjustified fear, my pulse drumming loudly in my ears. Gabe has moved protectively to my side.

The man's mouth twists, contorting into a narrow, slanted sneer. 'Tell your sister I said hi,' he says. With a shake of his head, he spins on his heels and staggers away, dragging his little girl with him. I stand fixed to the spot, my hands trembling.

'One of my less desirable patrons,' Gabe says.

We walk to the car in silence.

Today, we pass through the first checkpoint without so much as a question. One quick glance at my card and the guards wave us straight onto the roads. Registration must be the one day when they don't scrutinise every last detail of your existence and intentions; no doubt they know we have enough to deal with. Theoretically we can travel to any of the nine sections we want, but the guards tend to get a bit twitchy if people are too far from home. Not surprising really, with the number of Marchers on the rise.

Gabe is taking a different route than I expected. The Annex is in the Central Section, where all the biggest buildings and most ornate structures are, but the dull grey towers grow rapidly sparser, with grass and weeds appearing in place of trash and children on the roadside.

'Aren't we going the wrong way?' I say after another five minutes of diminishing architecture.

'We're going for food, remember?' he replies.

About twenty minutes into our journey, he turns off the road altogether and onto some small country lane. The car is low to the ground and bounces in the potholes. One particularly deep one sends my brick-like phone straight off my lap and into the foot well.

'Shit,' I swear whilst rummaging around by my feet. I grasp hold of the slippery plastic and shove it into the bottom of my bag.

'Sorry,' Gabe says.

We've hardly spoken today. My tongue always fumbles and flaps uselessly when it's just the two of us. I usually start mumbling so quietly I can hardly hear what I'm saying myself.

'It's only a short drive,' he tells me, still trying to make conversation.

I first thought I was in love with Gabe at fourteen, when he took Fi on at the bar. Even though he was only a couple of years older than her, he always had an air of someone who'd lived a much longer life, and, given that all of his scars were already used, he probably had. I knew I was in love with him the night after Fi's failed amendment.

She had sent her first envelope and received her second scar, all in an attempt to save our mother. It wasn't enough though. Rules had been broken and my mother had to pay the price. There was no way around it. Fi may has well have burned her envelope for all the good it did.

Gabe held her in his arms all night. He let her cry and swear and kick and scream – no judgment, no advice, no false attempts at consolation or trite, meaningless words that were meant to be comforting. He didn't tell her that everything would be all right or try to justify what our mother had done. He just held her with an overwhelming sense of calm. For a single moment, I had wished it was me there, but even remembering that memory makes me feel guilty. I don't think Fi would have made it through that night without him. I don't think I would have. I thought there must be something in it, some ulterior motive, but I couldn't figure out what. I still can't.

Chapter Two

From the Book of Amendments
Rule 2. Once registered, each person can receive up to, and not exceeding, two amendments.

WE DRIVE THROUGH a gap in the trees and into a small gravelled car park. A small building stands in front of us. Time has yellowed the whitish stones to a dirty ochre and muddy-coloured moss covers the tiles in corpulent mounds. A stout chimney emits a constant stream of smoke, grey and ugly against the cerulean sky. Of all the colours, it's the green that takes me by surprise. Vivid greens, new and spring-like, puncture the quilt of white snow. A hint of fresh air tingles on my tongue. This is more than just a token garden in the midst of the concrete, it's a miracle the Cabinet hasn't claimed the land already for something more efficient; space is a commodity.

Unity is what the Cabinet decided to call the megacity that grew out of the ashes, the new capital city of The Kingdom. The only city in The Kingdom. It doesn't take a genius to work out why. Some people think it's cliché; I can understand that, it's a pretty corny name to choose, but I like it. I like what it stands for, even if it's not always quite on point.

Originally, they divided the city into nine distinct sections. Now though, those sections have spread and bled into one another and if it wasn't for all the checkpoints no one would have any idea where one section ends and the next begins. They vary slightly, of course; the Central Section takes in the mouth of the river up until it becomes little more than a stream. The outer sections hold the mines and factories. It doesn't make any difference to amendments, though. You all get two, no matter where you're born or work, but you have to come to Unity to send your amendment and you have to be here to receive it. It's all to do with the radius of the retrocausality field.

Out of the corner of my eye, I catch something glinting. When I realise what it is my jaw falls open.

'A stream?' I say. Gabe grins at me.

'Clean water too,' he says. 'Come on, let's go sit down.' I continue to stare for a moment longer before following after him.

The bitterness of the January air is subdued slightly by the midday sun. It drenches the grass in pale light and glints off the morning frost. Gabe goes inside to order food while I take a seat at one of the rickety wooden benches and continue to gape at my surroundings.

He returns with mugs of tea.

'You ready?' he asks.

'For registering or amending?' I half laugh.

'Both.'

'Registering will be fine,' I say with an air of confidence I'm not sure I feel. 'Hopefully I won't need the amendments. Not just yet. I want to save them, you know, for when we really need them.' I remove my hands from the mug as my skin begins to redden and prickle from the heat.

'Sounds good,' Gabe says.

Yet another awkward pause infiltrates the conversation and I fight to fill it before he gives up trying to communicate with me altogether. Only one question springs to mind. I know it's a rude thing to ask, but I want to know and there's never going to be a right time to say it.

'So, what did you use your amendments on?' I ask trying to sound casual. 'I mean, you've used them both, haven't you?'

'I have,' he says.

Gabe's never been one to try to hide the scars, at least not as long as we've known him. All three are faded to a subtle silver. The first scar — the one that mimics the headline through the centre of your palm — is given at your registration and marks your right to amend. In a few hours' time, I will have mine. There is no time restraint on the other two. Some people wait until they're at death's door before stumbling to a centre to rewrite their history. Others do their first amendment substantially sooner. It's difficult to talk to someone new without looking down and trying to steal a quick glance. You always want to know what page they're on, so to speak.

I heard Gabe talking to Fi about his amendments a couple of

years ago, although I never asked her what he used them for either. I used to wish that one of his envelopes had told him to come back and marry me. I'd daydream that he'd show it to me one day while he is down on one knee, holding out a ring. I would leap into his arms and kiss him and accept without hesitation. Soppy I know, but I guess that's the kind of thing most of us like to think of an amendment being used for. I'd like to say I've outgrown those kinds of daydreams, but it would be a lie.

He blows the steam from his drink. It weaves up around the cup before losing its form in the air between us. After a long pause, he finally speaks.

'It was black,' he says. 'My first envelope was black.'

My jaw falls open. Gabe chuckles.

'What do you think happened?' I ask.

Gabe cools his tea with an extended blow, only to place it down without taking a sip, and starts to twist the ring on his finger

'I dunno,' he says. 'Part of me, part of me thinks I did something bad. That I killed someone. Deliberately, I mean. I don't know. It's just a feeling.'

'You can't know that. You can't feel something that never happened,' I tell him.

He shakes his head but shrugs away whatever he was considering saying. 'I can't explain it. Some days I wake up and it feels like the whole day is just a rerun of a previous episode.'

'Everyone has that. I have that and I've not even registered,' I try to joke.

'It's not the same. There were days when I first got that envelope that I couldn't face getting up because of the guilt. What else could I have done?'

Of course he thinks that's what happened. Everyone thinks the worst. You have to. You have to believe that your life would have been ruined forever if you hadn't made that amendment. You have to believe that before you got that envelope your life wasn't just miserable – it was unbearable, tortuous, unliveable. If you don't believe that, then what was the point in amending? Amendments are there to make our life better. If you don't believe that, you might as well join the Marchers.

'A black envelope doesn't mean you killed someone,' I say. 'You know that. It's just a myth. Besides, even if it's true, the fact that you got a black envelope means you stopped something terrible from happening, doesn't it? Nobody died this time around, did they? Someone's life was saved because your envelope was black.'

His lips purse. It's funny how I can say something with so much conviction to someone else. The matter is entirely different when you're on the other side. My passionate display has taken us back to the one topic of conversation we were desperately trying to avoid: Fi. That was black too and we both know no one's life was saved by her envelope. No amendment can save someone who's broken the rules, no matter which life they broke them in. We didn't realise that at the time of course.

I'd like to believe that it was worth it, that somehow everything was worse the first time around for Fi, for us. But I can't convince myself of that, let alone anyone else.

Gabe offers a feeble smile; I know he's thinking the same.

'She'll get better,' he says.

'Maybe,' I say, unconvincingly.

I run my finger around the rim of the mug, unable to think of anything else to add which will sound believable.

Food arrives. I pick at it with my fingers, over-chew a few mouthfuls and push the rest around my plate. My stomach is too knotted to contemplate eating, and even the smell — which is far more tempting than our usual fare — doesn't manage to change that. Neither of us attempts conversation; the only topics we have in mind are ones we'd rather not discuss. As we climb back into the car – plates left half full on the table – I make a mental snapshot of the view. On another day, I'd like to come back here.

Our flat is in section six, near the outskirts and Gabe's detour has taken us farther out still. As a result, there are a fair few checkpoints to go through before the Annex. This, combined with the weather, results in a journey that is tortuously slow. Having long since given up on the idea of conversation I have only my own thoughts to occupy the time. Fi's teasing and taunting about registration rattle continuously around my skull and by the time we reach the Central Section my palms are slicked with sweat. I didn't think I'd get so nervous about registering, but there's so much adrenaline coursing through me that my legs are trembling. Gabe slows down when the Annex comes into view.

'Can you see it?' he says.

Breathing down the nerves, I press my nose towards the glass and try to absorb everything I see.

The river coils around the perimeter of the building like a

protective moat, as still as a mirror and equally reflective. In the centre stands the Annex itself. I don't know where I should look; I want to see it all.

Wrought iron arches curve around heavy glass windows in a series of twists and curls, while copper inlays glint with all shades of red and orange, from deep mahogany to fiery apricot. There are statues and sculptures, sleek and modern yet timeless all at once, and one single spire, of white and gold, rises from the centre, reaching toe-to-tip, reaching for the clouds. It is dauntingly impressive and impressively daunting.

The site of the Annex is where, over a century ago, the old world discovered amendments. It didn't look like this then. Not even close. Back then it was some unassuming, nondescript laboratory, working on creating endless, clean energy. This tiny laboratory in the little town of Runcorn, set their sights on heavy atom fusion. However, their calculations weren't quite up to scratch. The effect was catastrophic. Tens of thousands died from the shock wave alone. Then overnight, retrocausality went from being a scientific impossibility to the headline story on every news channel in the world. That's when the United Kingdom became substantially less united.

They never did manage to master fusion, of any type of atom, but people don't seem so bothered about that anymore. The scientists took on a new role in this newly formed Kingdom. They started the Administration.

Now the site of that tiny laboratory is magnificent. It's a shame you only get to go inside once, unless you end up with a career in Administration, but that's not on the cards for me. The Administration requires a university degree at least and for that you need money. My mother worked in the factories; university was off the cards a long time ago.

The Annex used to be the sole point for amending, too, but realistically it was never practical. While it sat smack in the middle of the nine sections, even those in the Central Section have difficulty getting here at night when the buses don't run, not to mention during the winter. The journey here made amending itself a burden, which almost eliminated the point. Now we just come here to register and each section has at least a dozen centres for amending; I can walk to two from our flat. Every time I head past them, I wonder which one my mother used that night. Not that it matters. It's probably better that I don't know anyway.

A small crowd of marchers are gathered outside the entrance, waving placards. My throat tightens.

'Why don't the Guards arrest them?' I say as their chants penetrate the windows.

'Don't worry. They will if they need to,' Gabe says.

'But what if they hurt somebody?'

'They won't. Not here.'

After the attacks, they show the marchers who've been caught on television. They show them being given an injection. Their skin reddens then yellows, and they foam at the mouth while their body spasms on the metal table, the clanging of the wheels doing nothing to drown out their assiduous cries. I don't know what drug it is but I know it doesn't have to be like that. The cameras stay fixed until the body goes limp and the marchers' eyes roll around to the back of their heads. Then the foam turns red. They keep the cameras there until they're certain the marchers are dead. I've only seen it once; Fi and I snuck into the living room one night, having heard the other children talking about it at school.

It was a hooded figure that administered the injection. He stepped forward, cloak trailing on the ground, syringe in hand, awaiting his orders. A cold chill set the hair on my arms into prickles. Even in my pre-teens I recognised the man in charge. He stood at the edge of the room, his dark hair slicked over in a side parting and his skin pulled tight around a narrow jawline. Tall, slender and dressed in a light blue suit, overseeing the marchers' sentences fell to Nicholas Hall, head of the Cabinet. Hall watched on as the executioner stepped forward, showing no signs of emotion as the needle was plunged into the marcher's skin.

When we watched, the marcher they had caught was a young man. He howled in pain, thrashing beneath his restraints, but Hall stood straight backed, staring down the camera towards us, nothing but a cold look of apathy on his face. When it was over he stepped back and swept his hands across an invisible crease on his light blue suit. Order had been maintained.

I swear I could smell the acrid tang of corroding flesh through the screen, and even now, when I think about it, a bitter taste catches in my throat. After that, my mother removed the television from our house. She needn't have – I would've never turned it on again.

I am gazing out of the window, trying to repress the memories of blood-drenched mouths when a marcher looks directly at me.

At first, I think it is my imagination, but before I can open my mouth to speak she has broken from the group and is making a beeline for us.

'Gabe?' I say, suddenly dubious about the protective capabilities of his little car.

'Don't worry, I've seen her.'

The final checkpoint and entrance to the Annex is less than a hundred metres away and there's no room for Gabe to accelerate. The marcher picks up her pace and sprints towards us. Two others join her in chasing us down. My hands grip at the seat, still unable to take my eyes away. My heart is pounding so hard I can't even hear myself breathe. I am about to squeeze my eyes shut when four guards appear from nowhere, blocking the marcher's route. They pin her to the ground, clamping cuffs around her wrists and ankles before she can take another step. I go to breathe in relief, but it's not over yet. Behind her, one of the other marchers tries their luck and bolts towards us. Noticing the guards closing in on him, he makes a last-ditch attempt. I cover my face and cower just moments before something splatters against the car.

All I can hear is my rapid, thumping pulse.

'Well, you survived the first part,' Gabe says.

Gabe winds down the window and removes a handful of propaganda posters from the windscreen. He throws one of the posters on my lap.

'In case you need some light reading in your ceremony,' he jokes. I don't laugh. Instead I glance down at the poster on my lap.

How many lives will your amendment ruin?

Do you know all the consequences?

What was the cost of your happy ending?

Marchers have been around since the discovery. When the Cabinet came to power and allowed the Administration to proceed with offering people amendments, they became even more vocal. I scrunch the paper into a ball and throw it down by my feet. It's one conspiracy theory after the next with the Marchers, who are a nuisance at their best, and murderers at their worst. The attacks have died down in severity at the moment, but they'll escalate back up again soon – they always do and they always follow the same pattern.

The attacks always take place on the second of the month, always two centres are hit. Sometimes it's a graffitied wall or a Molotov cocktail through the window. Other times whole centres are set to burn. They don't think twice about the bodies insides. It's a pathetically artistic interpretation: two attacks for the two amendments, but with so many centres in the sections, two a month is barely even a scratch to the Administration. Mostly, it's discussed like weather – where to expect the next big one or how certain sections have been dry for ages.

Gabe finishes showing our cards at the final checkpoint and then drives the car down into the basement.

'I'll just wait here for you while you register,' he says.

'You don't have to,' I reply, although I don't make any further objections when he insists. He offers me one more encouraging smile, before I take a deep breath in and step outside the car.

It's a concrete mausoleum down here with low ceilings, dark grey pillars and the overly strong smell of car fumes and oil. The nervous churning in my stomach recommences with a new fury as I make my way through the other cars and call the elevator to take me to the ground floor. Like the outside of the building, the elevator is wrought iron with doors that you have to prise open and close manually. I push the button and wait. After a few minutes it still hasn't arrived. I glance around, the internal butterflies swelling, and consider that I may have to take another way up, but I can't see a stairwell anywhere. There's a group of people huddled together in a far corner of the car park. I move towards them then stop. Plainclothes guards. They are not interested in someone like me.

I try the lift again, this time hammering on the button with a closed fist. After a second's hesitation, it whirs into life. The metal clatters as I pull the doors apart, step inside then close them back around me. There is only one place to go. I grasp at the sides of the cage as it lurches upwards, rattling and shaking on its chains. The moment it stops I wrench the doors apart and leap onto the solid ground before me. I decide to find the stairs on the way back down.

Deep floral air fresheners do little to disguise the dank smell of young adults confined in the extended lobby that greets me. The place is a giant echo chamber. Each footstep, murmur and mutter is amplified, reverberating in the slate tiles and parallel windows. A flutter creeps upwards from my abdomen. The palpitations knock against my ribs and are only increased by the sight of more guards.

Once again plain-clothed, the guards try to be discreet and

look like normal people, but it doesn't work – their shoes are too clean, their glances too furtive and their casual flannel shirts, ironed to perfection, hang unnaturally untucked on one side. Plus, they're about twenty years too old to be registering. I shuffle farther into the room. The presence of so many guards here is no surprise. While the building is far too large and too well watched for a successful attack, that doesn't mean the Marchers wouldn't try.

The obvious thing to do is join one of the queues snaking across the room, and I choose the longest one. The girl in front turns and offers me a timid smile. Her lips move as well, though she doesn't emit any sound I can hear.

'Happy birthday,' I say.

She replies with a one-breath, chest-cough laugh. 'Everyone says the same thing when I ask them,' she starts talking at me. 'They all say '*it's fine, but they take quite a bit of blood*'. And '*try not to faint in the ceremony*'.' Her ears glisten; new earrings probably. My stomach constricts with undeniable jealousy. She obviously has a more stable home life than me.

'They *say* the same to me,' I tell her, trying to repress the bitterness in my voice. 'But I'm sure it's not that bad.'

She seems slightly reassured. Her eyes stare at me expectantly, bulging in a frog-like manner as she awaits more words of wisdom, but I don't have any. In the end, I just offer a weak smile. Finally, she turns away, drumming her fingers anxiously against her thighs and flitting her head from side to side, probably in search of someone of a better conversational calibre.

She's not the only one with energetic limbs. Down the row countless toes are tapping, hands wringing, feet shuffling, lips quivering, necks stretching and eyes watering. I catch sight of at least a dozen sparkling bracelets, along with necklaces, earrings, watches and rings. One girl sports a large gleaming stud through her nose. I'm guessing her parents don't work in the factories or mines.

I redirect my thoughts away from my home life, and back to the registration.

'Just you wait,' Fi had laughed. Apparently nearly half the people in her ceremony fainted. It seems wise not to tell the girl in front of me this, particularly with Fi's habit for exaggeration. I always take what she says with a ladle of salt. Not that she'd lie; she just likes to stretch the truth a little.

It was a good day when she registered. It felt like we were starting again, wiping the slate clean. Our mother even joined us for dinner that night. She got out all the baby photos she still had, even the ones including our father. We laughed at the matching outfits, dated fashions and haircuts. Then Fi's phone started ringing with people wanting her to go out to drink and celebrate. Fi said she didn't mind, she was happy to stay in, but my mother's face had already dropped and she'd packed everything away, complaining that she was too tired to look anymore anyway. Fi went out, I stayed in, and it was less than a month before our mother had her final scar. And then Fi had her second.

Unaware of my gradual progression along the line, I glance up and notice only a few people left in front of me. I spend a moment attempting to work out where the rest have disappeared to; no doubt it will become obvious soon enough.

Among the hushed whispers and subdued conversations, several voices at the front of the queue become distinctly louder. I shift my position, peering between heads and over shoulders to find the source. A set of clearly identical twins stand at the front, their auburn hair androgynously cut, as are their clothes. One is shouting at an administrator, tears streaming down her face, while the other clings to her sister's smock, with white knuckles and translucent skin. This goes on for several minutes until their pleas are disregarded and one is led away. The other is forced to wait alone, unable to stifle her sobs.

'They're obviously from the country,' the girl in front turns back to me. 'They should let someone come in with them. Don't you think?'

I nod in acknowledgement rather than agreement, but she's satisfied with my response. My eyes continue to hover on the remaining twin. The sections of Unity are hemmed in by hills and valleys to the North and East. Sea and mountains barricade the West, while to the South sits nothing but wasteland. While I know there are people who live beyond the city borders I've never actually seen them. A lot of them don't agree with amendments; that's why they're out there. Obviously, this family is different. How would they even amend? Without knowing when you needed to be in Unity to receive your envelope in advance, it seems impossible. So what's the point I wonder.

I'm still watching the lone twin when I reach the front of the queue.

I have to wait behind a yellow line while my new friend approaches the glass window in front. I strain to hear what's said, but even in the general hush of the hall I fail to make out any part of the conversation, my hearing undoubtedly hindered by the relentless pounding in my chest. After a few moments, the girl steps through a large door to right of the desk, firing a quick glance and wave over her shoulder towards me. My pulse rises yet another notch.

The administrator remains in front of me, head bowed, shuffling paperwork. I wait, my nerves close to exploding and toes teetering on the edge of the yellow line. The noise of the hall is now completely muted, drowned out by the incessant drumming which pummels inside my head to the point where I can no longer hear my own thoughts. I bite down on the inside of my cheeks and suck in air through my nose, chewing my bottom lip so hard it must be close to drawing blood. The administrator clears her throat, my eyes spring open and my feet cross over the thin, yellow line.

Chapter Three

From the Book of Amendments
Rule 3. Amendments can be sent to any date on or after a registered person's twenty-first birthday.

'NAME.'

The surface of the glass screen bows slightly, distorting the light and the face behind it.

'Emelia Evelyn Aaron,' I say. 'Emelia with an E.'

The administrator smiles in a way that displays far too many teeth for one mouth and pushes her over-rouged cheeks into perfect spheres. Her voice is a sickly, syrupy drawl, and she asks more questions, including date and place of birth, current address and education, all of which she clearly has the answers to on the screen in front of her. Though our eyes don't actually meet, the whole time her face stays fixed in a mannequin-esque smile that I feel forced to reciprocate. My cheek bones quickly start to ache.

I wonder how much she must enjoy her job here, repeating the same question to endless twenty-one-year-olds, day after day after day. After all, she must be intelligent. The Administration doesn't just oversee amending, they oversee the universities too. That way they get the pick of the bunch. Of course, the Cabinet has some say, they run the Kingdom, but they tend to keep their noses out where science is involved. Some things are better left to the experts.

She looks up at last. 'And your documents?' she says. Her eyebrows rise as I riffle through my bag, shuffling around the contents before finally pulling out half a dozen crumpled sheets of paper. It probably takes less than a minute for me to place them all through the opening, but her smile has tightened in a way that makes my insides cramp. I can feel the pounding migrating back towards my ears and an ulcer already forming inside my mouth.

She checks through the forms one by one, tracing each line with her finger. There can't be more than a hundred words on each of the papers, but she follows each one with her perfectly polished nails as the pulsating drums continue behind my eyeballs. Closing my eyes doesn't lessen it; it just draws my attention to my incessant swallowing.

'Excuse me?' The saccharine voice knocks me back into the room, though I have no idea what she's just asked me. She sighs, her pencilled eyebrows now at the apex of her forehead. 'Can you place any electronic devices through the partition?'

I fumble for my phone, and on following her instructions receive a numbered yellow disk.

'You can collect it at the end,' she says, dropping my items down beside her. 'You need to read and sign these, then hand them in.' She passes me a thin pile of forms. 'You can do it at the next station.' With that, she starts to sort the paper in front of her.

The exit from the foyer is just to the right of her and leads to a long corridor. The smell of wood varnish is overpowering, and I see no indication of where I am to go next. One side the wall is covered in faded anaglyptic wallpaper, the other lined with identical doors. After a few minutes a light above the fifth door pings on. I move forward and tentatively put my hand against it. It swings open at barely a touch. My pulse quickens. I am one step closer to my ceremony. One step closer to the freedom of amendments. I move inside and close the door behind me.

The slap of my shoes echoes loudly on the white tiled floor. I scan the room in front of me. It is a far cry from the wrought-iron grandeur I expected. Barely the size of our living room, everything is white and sterile. A caustically antiseptic aroma, bleachy and harsh fills the air, while some steel-legged furniture and a few fixed wall lights are all that fill the space. There are two doors other doors beside the one I have just come through, one of which I assume I will have to exit through. I see no mirrors or scales, no charts or 3D models of graphically displayed body parts, analytically labelled and described in excruciating and embarrassing detail. There are posters though; ones to match the papers in my hands.

I pull the chair out from the desk and a shrill screech of metal resonates around the small space. I shudder before sitting down to read and sign, grabbing a pen from a small pot on the desk as I do.

Nothing here is unfamiliar. The first page is a brief pledge, where I must sign to uphold the sanctity of the Kingdom, Cabinet and the Administration. The second requires me to sign that all my details are correct. I barely give them a second glance before adding my scrawl at the bottom. The third page holds my attention a fraction longer. The rules of Amending.

Rule 1. Every person residing in the Kingdom must register their right to amend on their twenty-first birthday.

Rule 2. Once registered, each person can receive up to, and not exceeding, two amendments.

As I read, the voice in my head adopts the deep tone of my second-grade History teacher. His envelopes were the first I ever saw and he's probably the only teacher I can really remember; a slight man in his early forties with large ears and an impressively long nose, although no one ever made fun of it. He was far too revered. Love life and do it all again. That was written on the inside of both his envelopes. He received them when he was still in his twenties. The pessimist in me suspects I won't be so lucky.

I shake my head clear of wooden desks and the smell of pencil shavings and scan a little lower.

Rule 5. Amendments must only be used as a direct influence on your own timeline and cannot be used to amend a previous amendment.

I don't need reminding of that one.

There are other rules too; one about being of sound mental health and another about only using amendments for an act directly linking to you, but I don't read them all. I've known them by heart for as long as I can remember and I know first-hand the effect of not sticking to them. That's not going to be me; I have no intention of following in my mother's footsteps.

I scribble my name next to each one of the rules, then set the papers aside.

Whether from nerves or hunger, the ache behind my eyes is now throbbing. I try to blink it away and focus on my surroundings as a distraction, but the brightness doesn't help. I slump down into the seat, cover my eyes and push my thumbs deep into my temples.

The throbbing isn't helped by a bulb by one of the other doors, just above eye level, which refuses to stop flickering. Even with my face covered, its blinking flares through my eyelids. I am sitting, my head cradled in my hand, when another administrator walks into the room.

She's young, maybe a few years older than Fi. Her mascara is smudged and bags hang sallow and heavy beneath her eyes. Her cheeks are unrouged and her smile fleeting. She's dressed in a medical smock which clings tightly to the bump beneath it. I find it hard to draw my eyes away. Joining the Administration means handing your life over to science. It's an honour to be asked, of course, but at the same time the cost is huge; no family ties beyond the Administration. No communication with people other than at centres or here at the Annex. I've never seen a male administrator before, but I guess this is confirmation that they exist.

Without speaking or sitting, she takes my papers, then retrieves a tray from a cabinet, grasps my left arm and tightens a tourniquet just above the elbow.

'We need four vials,' she tells me without looking up. She chews on the corner of her lip as she draws the blood.

Rapidly the first vessel fills, then the next and the next. She places them back into the tin tray with no apparent labelling. The fourth one is larger, much larger. It's more like the blood bags they use in hospitals. I've had blood taken before, of course, but it's usually been just a few drops. This is different though, this is to make a link.

The sections of Unity make up a sixty-mile radius outside of the Annex. Any farther beyond that and amendments can't reach. Even here they need some form of marker to make sure the envelopes end up in the right place. DNA is that marker, although right now I'm questioning exactly how much they need.

As the blood is siphoned off, the pulsing in my head subsides, while the flickering bulb is growing more and more irritating. When my arm is released, the young woman lowers herself into the chair and hands me a glass of water with some rust-coloured tablets.

'To replace the iron,' she says, rubbing her hand over her swollen belly. I swallow them without the drink and then gulp furiously at the powdery bitterness that clings to my teeth. Iron tablets are an enforced supplementary in the weeks preceding registration and I recognise the metallic twang well.

Without warning, the light ceases flashing and glares on full beam, joined by an ear-piercing continuous ringing that causes my chest to jolt in surprise. Unperturbed by the siren, the administrator sighs and looks at her watch.

'I would've liked to have given you some time to rest,' she says, 'but I'm afraid you need to go now.' She pushes herself up from the desk. 'It's either that or wait for the evening ceremony?'

Waiting means leaving Gabe stuck in the car park for a good few hours, and he's probably got somewhere far better to be.

'I'm fine,' I say and start to stand. The blood rushes away from my head, and my knees buckle before they have any chance to straighten. Through good luck, I manage to lean forward and steady myself on the table.

'You really can wait,' the administrator says, looking genuinely concerned.

I shake my head. 'I'll be fine.'

'Just try and sit still for a while. Hopefully you won't be announced too early on.' She looks dubious as she says this but walks across the room and holds one of the doors open.

The ringing becomes even louder. With a rapidly drying mouth, I nod my thanks and leave. A heady scent of incense smothers the air as I head off down a curved corridor dimly lit with electric candles. Voices can be heard from one end. I know where I'm heading. We all do.

Chapter Four

From the Book of Amendments
Rule 4. Amendments may be up to, but not exceeding, fifty characters in length.

I MUST HAVE seen a hundred different paintings of this place yet nothing and no one could have prepared me for this. For a moment, I forget to breathe. Then all my insides twist.

This was where my parents met. This very hall, almost twenty-eight years ago at their own registration. It was one of those stories that was recited continually; my parents were more than happy telling it to anyone who'd listen. I can't blame them; meeting at your registration is always going to be a good story. Shame it didn't have a happy ending.

Birds squeeze through unidentifiable gaps and flit from rafter to rafter. Below them, the light floods through the frosted glass of the arched windows and casts each person in a delicate glow. Simple images in tones of blue hang in lead frames on the white washed walls, and a planked wooden stage rises out from emerald marble flooring. It could almost be a cathedral, if religion still had any place in the Kingdom.

With each step farther in, the air becomes cleaner and crisper. Wooden pews are arranged forward facing. There must be three hundred people here, if not more and there are very few places are left. The twins, tear-stained but back together, sit with their heads propped against each other. Given that DNA is the link the envelopes need, I wonder how it works for these two? Identical twins mean identical DNA. The Administration will have found a way though. They always do. The girl from my queue is sitting a few rows from the back, a space open beside her. I accidentally catch her eye, and she beckons me over. My manners insist I oblige.

As I sit down, the girl grasps my hand, squeezing tightly.

'That was a lot of blood,' she says as I manage to tug my hand free. 'I wasn't expecting that. Are you okay? You look a bit pale? Did they give you the iron tablet? You have to take it. It's to replace the iron you lost when they took the blood. I've got some of my own in my bag if you need them?'

'Thanks, I'll be fine,' I tell her, unable to understand how she can say so much in one breath. 'I just didn't get much time to rest. It was pretty rushed.'

'I know, but at least we got to this ceremony.'

I offer what I hope is an encouraging smile as she squeezes my hand again. This time when she lets go I fold my arms.

Scanning the hall, I find one face I recognise. A boy from my school. I vaguely remember that we have the same birthday. He is laughing, head thrown back. Another boy slaps him squarely on the shoulder. I suppose laughing's one way to deal with the nerves.

The conversations dim as an administrator ascends the stairs to the stage in front. Walking seems an awful effort, and she leans heavily on the thin bannister as she climbs. She is dressed differently than the others, in ceremonial clothing, and for a second I think that maybe she is one of the Cabinet. I sit up straighter, trying to get a better view when I notice the ornate image embroidered on her collar; Margaret of Cortona, the Saint of Second Chances. The woman is undoubtedly an important administrator, Chief Science Officer perhaps, but she is an administrator nonetheless. I berate my own foolishness. Why would a Cabinet member be at a registration? The important administrator motions for the others to take their places before proceeding up to the podium. Soon the only noise comes from the ruffling feathers of the house martins.

'There was a time,' she begins her speech, 'that when we reached a fork in a road we had to decide which route to take. And that route was final, that decision irrevocable, its repercussions unavoidable.' She looks down at noteless hands with the slightest dip of her head. 'But we are human. We are human and, as such, we are not above errors. Sometimes the path we unknowingly place ourselves upon does not lead to the destination we desire or deserve. There was a time when our decisions caused us pain and torment and tempests beyond justification or understanding. But worse still, our judgments bought us regret.'

The last syllable of her words resounds around the pillars. Every breath in the room waits suspended.

'Regret is cancerous,' she continues. 'The *what-ifs*, the *if-onlys*, they eat away at man, they erode our spirit, dissolve away the most fundamental essence of our existence. Our hope. And without hope we, as a species, cannot thrive.'

The young congregation leans in, nodding and murmuring with hands clasped. They devour her sermon, lapping up every ounce, and I, too, feel myself leaning in to hear the rest. Her hand moves upwards in a clenched fist, and her voice quivers as it echoes perfectly around us.

'We were dissatisfied, discontent. Disillusioned and disappointed by our lives, but no longer. Life is no longer a road we must follow brick-by-brick,' she tells us. 'We carry our own tools now, and we make our own paths. We build bridges where we know a ravine will be. We pack a raincoat and dance in a storm. We do not have regrets. We have peace of mind. We do not have dissatisfaction. We have comfort, safe in the knowledge that, in the end, we made the right choice. For we are the blessed. We are the Kingdom and we have been given the right to amend.'

She flings her arms up into the air as we fly to our feet. There's cheering and clapping, whistles and cries of adulation that send the martins fleeing from the roosts and roaring through the air around us. My chest swells with a sense of pride I can't possibly place or have anticipated, and when I glance to my side, beside me the girl's eyes are glistening with tears. The administrator is right, we are part of something special here. We are part of the Kingdom and my ceremony has begun.

The administrator's speech has left me in awe. The hairs on my arms are returning to place, but a shivering cold lingers down the length of my spine long after she has motioned for us to sit.

She descends from the podium to the front of the stage, her eyes glancing briefly across whatever is placed on the stand in front of her.

'Zero-zero-zero-four. Peter Andrew Abbot.'

Every head in the hall turns, all eyes focused on this poor boy whose cheeks have drained to the colour of sour milk. His hands are trembling openly in front of him as he stands motionless, apparently unable to move any farther. His chest rises and falls in ragged rhythms. The butterflies in my stomach multiply for him. It's a long pause, but somehow he manages to bring himself back to the moment. He seizes a large gulp of air and strides towards the front of the hall. Each wooden step creaks beneath his weight. When he reaches the administrator, he stops and raises his arms. He waits, arms outstretched, palms offered.

'Zero-zero-zero-four. Peter Andrew Abbot,' she repeats. 'I hereby seal your right to amend; gifted by science, granted by your Cabinet and protected by all hands of the Administration. The divine right of all who reside within the Kingdom. Absolute from this day until the day of your last departure.'

A flash of silver darts between them both. Whispers erupt among the pews. With a nod, she directs him to the font.

He moves in a semi-stunned stagger across the stage, where he fleetingly submerges his hands into the font before proceeding down the steps to his seat. His left fist, now marked with a cut along the headline, is clenched and dripping. In a day's time it will be healed, a perfect silver scar, his right to amend clear for all the Kingdom to see. Peter Andrew Abbot's part in the ceremony is complete. The rest of us are all one name closer.

Next called is "zero-zero-two-eight. Elizabeth Katherine Price."

'What are the numbers?' my new friend mouths to me.

I shrug in reply. Now that the initial excitement is over, my adrenaline has dropped and the effect of the blood loss intensifies. I close my eyes, too lightheaded to focus, and let my mind drift away.

'Tell us how the stars are made. Please, please tell us,' we beg, bouncing our knees on the soft, springy mattress. We know the story; we could recite it word for word. We just wanted her to stay a little bit longer in the bedroom with us, filling the air with her warm vanilla scent, glittering eyes and illusory tales. She stood in the doorway, shaking her head and telling us to sleep before we threw off our blankets and dragged her over to the bed. She sighed with feigned exhaustion, but her smile was always wide and she always relented.

'Once,' she said, tucking the sheets back around us and sweeping the hair from our foreheads. 'Once the Sun had been very, very big. Much, much bigger than it is now. It was so bright, so dazzling that it filled the whole of the sky day and night, and everything the light landed on would sparkle and glitter like diamonds.'

'Tell us what happened! Tell us what happened then!'

'Well, beautiful things are delicate and fragile. And the Sun was very, very beautiful and very, very fragile. One day, a tiny hummingbird got lost. Whilst it was trying to find its way, it flew higher and higher up into the sky.'

'Then what?' we cried out.

My mother's expression turned sad and serious. 'Well, then the tiny hummingbird's wing brushed ever so lightly against the surface of the Sun. The beautiful Sun was so, so delicate that even the slightest touch from the gentlest feather caused it to shatter. The little hummingbird could only watch as the broken shards of the Sun were flung far across the sky. And that was how the stars came to be. They are the tiny scattered fragments of the broken Sun.'

Then she wrapped her arms around us both and pulled us in together. 'When you were both born,' she said, 'there were so many stars I thought the Sun was whole again.'

'But what happened to the hummingbird?' one of us cried when we thought she might leave.

'Well,' she said, kissing the top of our heads, 'The poor hummingbird tried as hard as he could to find all the pieces, but it's a very difficult job and he's still up there now, wandering through the sky, trying to collect every last bit.'

'Can we see him?'

'Sometimes. If you look up and see a shooting star, then you know he's managed to catch a piece and he's carrying it all the way back to the Sun.'

Without warning, I am back in the present, back in the hall.

'The time,' I say. 'The numbers are the time that we were born.'

On the stage, Elizabeth Katherine Price is slumped over the font, her skin ashen.

Along with the rest of the room I watch as she drags herself off the podium, dripping water, and makes her way back to her pew, sinking suspiciously low.

Next is 'zero-four-two-eight.' I figure I need at least another six people before I'll be stable enough to tackle the wooden steps, but I have no idea what time of day I was born, only that the stars were out.

'Do you think it will affect when we can go back to?' the girl said. 'I mean, if we're born late?' Her features are once again painted with fear.

'We can go back to any date starting from our twenty-first birthday,' I say. 'It's in the rules.'

She shakes her forehead clean of the furrows. 'Of course,' she says. 'I forgot.'

The nostalgic memory moment with the stars didn't help. I may be called any second, yet I may have to wait through another twenty hours. And that is assuming, of course, my mother's story contains some remnant of truth. Uncurling my toes, I fix my eyes on the moving lips of the administrator. That's when I hear my name.

Zero-five-five-six, a morning baby. My friend offers a smile of support as I stand, though I manage to move my hand swiftly and avoid any more unwanted squeezes. My legs continue to tremble as I approach the stage and tread slowly up the steps.

The administrator looks even older than her voice. The deep grooves of crow's feet splay out from the corners of her eyes, and the skin around her lips is puckered and dry. Some people think the administrators get an extra amendment in payment for the sacrifices. I don't though. I've seen first-hand the consequences of not following the rules. You only get two.

She nods discreetly, and I raise my hands, palms open, my legs still quivering beneath me.

'Zero-five-five-six. Emelia Evelyn Aaron,' she repeats. 'I hereby seal your right to amend; gifted by science, granted by your Cabinet and protected by all hands of the Administration. The divine right of all who reside within the Kingdom. Absolute from this day until the day of your last departure.'

The blade is tapered to a point and glints as she flicks her wrist. It flashes, severing the space between us, scoring painlessly through my skin and marking the path of my headline. My right to amend has been marked. She nods again, and I make my way to the font.

The blood pools. There's far more than I would have expected from such a thin cut and it seeps between my fingers and falls in drops onto the stark white porcelain font. The droplets flare and spread and run into the water. I lower my hands. The warm water drives the flow. A blast of nausea hits as I watch the crimson eddies diffuse to nothing on the surface of the water. The quivering in my muscles has grown to a more substantial shake. I consider leaning on the font, letting the stone take my weight, but I know people will be watching by now, raising eyebrows and trying to conceal their twitching smiles of satisfaction. I'm not going to let myself faint, though. Not a chance.

With a deep breath, I make my muscles move. My foot rises from the floor, and sighing with relief, I turn to the steps. My hand is dripping, my eyes blind to the water already pooled beneath me. My foot has barely touched the ground when it slides away from me. My chest falls forward and my arms flail in all directions, struggling to find some way to brace my landing, but I find nothing to hold onto. A collective gasp echoes around the hall, accompanied by the loud crack of my head meeting the solid edge of the basin.

For the remainder of the ceremony I sit in one of the pews near the front, blotting the cut on my head with the heel of my hand and wondering if anyone will believe I actually slipped rather than fainted. Slip or faint, I'm sure the outcome would have been the same – a blinding headache and unending looks of sympathy.

One-four-two-two, James Douglas Wright, obligingly relinquished his seat after lifting me down the steps with no help from the administrators. His clean shirt is now smeared with my bloody handprint. An administrator is assigned the job of cleaning the floor every half dozen or so people, the mop was suspiciously close at hand.

My infamy, though prolific, is short lived, as one-six-one-eight collapses before the blade even touches her hand, not even completing her registration. As an exceptionally tall girl, her head falls in slow motion before finally hitting the floor by the administrator's shoes. Looks are exchanged, but it's not until James Douglas Wright makes a noise from the back of the room that two administrators — one male, one female — amble onto the stage. They drag the girl down and place her slumped forward in the nearest available seat. Again, they are surprisingly unconcerned by her apparent unconsciousness and return to their corners immediately afterwards. I assume the girl will have to go to the evening ceremony. They'll want her to register today, one way or another.

My palm is still painless, leading me to wonder if there is something in the font other than just water. Throughout the ceremony I prod at the wound provokingly but still feel nothing; I can see I'm not the only one. Interest in the ceremony dwindles as time wears on, although at one point two names are called together. A second administrator appears, and the two are sliced simultaneously, hand movements in perfect unison with flawless choreography.

No more faintings or falls occur, and the last name to be called is at two-three-five-three, after which the administrator steps back up to the podium and invites us to stand.

'May you never know the reality of regret,' she says.

With that, we are dismissed and file out a door at the front of the hall.

Chapter Five

From the Book of Amendments

Rule 5. Amendments must only be used as a direct influence on your own timeline and cannot be used to amend a previous amendment.

GABE IS SITTING in the car nodding his head to music. When he sees me coming, he reaches over, opens the door and turns the stereo down. A muggy heat hits me from inside the car. I hurry inside to avoid letting it out. Before I'm seated, his hand is on my head. I wince while his fingers needle at my skin. A small twitch at the corners of his mouth breaks into a wide grin.

'I'm sorry,' he says, laughing as I flick his hand away.

'It's not funny.'

'It's a little bit funny.'

'It's not.'

'Were you the only one?'

'I didn't faint.'

'You didn't?' He looks doubtful.

'I slipped.'

He clenches his jaw for a second before throwing his head back. 'Oh, Em.' He laughs.

'It's not funny!' But the corners of my mouth are twitching, my lips desperately trying to curl. I bite down on my cheeks to stop them.

'You can smile, you know,' he says softly.

I don't though. I dodge his gaze and look at my hand and the smear of blood. That solved the problem; my lips don't want to move anymore.

'You know, you used to be able to choose where you got scarred,' Gabe continues, the moment of reflection forgotten.

'Really?' I fix my belt, appeasing him with a response.

'It's true. When they first discovered amendments they didn't care where you were scarred. As long as it was somewhere. All that's needed is a marker. It doesn't matter where it is.'

'So why make the rule if it doesn't matter?'

'Well, people got … adventurous.' His eyes glint as he tries to coerce even the smallest of smiles from me.

'We should get back to Fi,' I say.

He starts the car, and we head out silently. The roads are empty, the grey tarmac covered in the brown sludge of snow, which, for now, has stopped falling. Frost warnings have been out for weeks. They used to salt the roads in winter to make them safer, but the Cabinet quickly realised safer roads meant more people moving about. As for those few who had accidents on the ice, well, I'm sure it didn't happen the second time.

Gabe's eyes flicker from the road to me.

'You should go and celebrate,' he says. 'You only register once. I can drop you somewhere if you want. I'll go back and check on Fi.'

'It's fine. I don't really feel like celebrating.' Even if I did, it's not like hordes of people are queuing up to take me out and buy me drinks. I was only ever popular by proxy; I've always known that.

'How about just you and me then?' he says. 'One drink?'

'Fi —'

'Will still be there when we get back.' Gabe's eyes turn from the road to me as he waits for a response. 'So?'

I nod, my voice stolen by the butterflies that have crept upon me and snuck back inside.

'Mind if I choose where?' Gabe says.

'Okay.'

'Great. Then I'll need to get some gas.'

When we were still a family, one of our favourite things to do was head up to the flat roof of our tower block. On one side, through a gap in the drab concrete blocks and metal pylons, we could see the mountains, green, alive, insurmountable. Fi and I spent hours watching as the light dimmed and faded across them. We made up stories about the people who lived there. We told each other tales in which we imagined living a life among the flowers and trees and forest fairies. We imagined stumbling into other people, people from the outside, without scars or amendments. People who sailed ships, or flew planes or danced at balls in long flowing dresses. Together, Fi and I weaved a thousand worlds from just a slither of green. I wish I remembered more of them.

Often, we took food and blankets with us and stayed the whole day, drawing pictures, dancing without music and acting out mini-plays for our parents, who came and checked on us sporadically. Then one day, when I was about twelve, they didn't come and check on us at all. Fi and I spent the whole night out there, dreaming about what we would find if we ever made it to the mountains. After that, the shouting started and my dreams began to change.

Now Gabe and I are driving right towards them – right towards the mountains that I stared at for so long.

We stop for gas at a dilapidated station where only half the pumps work, which is still a higher working ratio than the staff, most of whom sit on upturned crates playing checkers with bottle tops. They will be on the books, they have to be. As long as you're on the books somewhere the Cabinet will leave you be. If you're not they'll find you work. Probably in one of the mines. There is always work in the mines. While Gabe fills the car, I study my palm.

'We got the last of it apparently,' Gabe says when he climbs back into the car. 'They've stopped delivering while the weather's this bad. We've got plenty though,' he adds when he sees my expression. 'Right, let's get going.'

It's a long drive up. The farthest I've ever gone, passing through all of the check points. When we reach the final one the guard gives Gabe a once over.

'Staying up there long?' the guard asks.

'No, just an hour or so.'

The guard mumbles something then signals to a colleague to check in the boot. Gabe pops the lock. When they're satisfied they wave us through, and out of the sections. For the first time in my twenty-one years, I am leaving Unity.

'I didn't even know we could leave that easily,' I say. Gabe doesn't respond.

My hand grips the door as Gabe takes us farther and farther away from civilization. We drive past barbed wire fences surrounding old factories and the occasional rusted carcasses of a playground, where broken swings now sway empty in the breeze. We pass houses, now derelict, children's bicycles left strewn on the ground. These are the closest reminders of life before the discovery that I have ever seen.

'Are you sure we're allowed up here?' I say to Gabe.

'The Guards know where we're heading. It's not a problem.'

'Do you know where we're heading?'

'I've got a vague idea,' he says.

'What if something happens to us?'

'It won't,' he says.

'But what if—'

'It won't,' he repeats.

I decide not to ask any more questions about where we are going. Once or twice I try to bring up the subject of Fi — why it's not her fault that she's the way she is or what I could try and do to help her more — but Gabe cuts me off with lines like 'she'll be fine,' or 'she's an adult.' Soon I stop talking altogether.

The roads grow narrower and steeper while the buildings shrink and the plant life gets taller. We travel up, farther and farther away from the pylons, playgrounds and factories and mines. We keep going even when copses grow too thick to see through. The car slows in protest against the snow, yet still Gabe pushes on. When we finally park, the snow must be eight inches deep, with fresh flakes already settling on the windscreen. Gabe leans behind onto the backseat and retrieves a pair of gloves.

'My de-icing ones, but they're better than nothing.'

'We're getting out?' I say.

He grins sheepishly and hands them to me. I pull them on.

'Also, I hope you don't mind,' he says, 'but I got you a present.'

For some reason, I pretend I haven't heard him and focus my attention on my hands, pulling unnecessarily at the gloves.

'Here, take this.' He thrusts a heavy paper bag into my hand.

The bottle inside has a silver topped cork.

'Thank you,' I say quietly.

Birthdays always used to be a big deal in my family: birthday breakfasts, birthday teas, parties, cakes, presents, candles, cards, songs, the works. No expense spared, despite how little we had. One year we made our mother a cake from a recipe torn out of an old magazine, although we didn't pay too much attention to the measurements. We doused the mixture with pink food colouring and baked it in a heart-shaped tin. Then we drenched the cooked monstrosity in equally pink icing which splodged down the sides in powdery clumps. The overall product was chewy, lumpy and teeth-achingly sweet. Fi and I watched our mother as she dutifully ate all we placed in front of her. Later, because 'pink cakes are the sparrows' favourite,' we gave them quite a lot, too.

'You okay? You look miles away.'

'Sorry.' I shake myself back and button my coat.

'Right, we're heading this way.' He points straight into the thicket of trees before reaching over to look at my feet. 'They should be fine. Ready?'

I nod.

'Don't forget the drink.'

My feet are covered in old leather ankle boots, which whilst looking fairly substantial, have worn as thin as silk on parts of the sole and offer no resistance to the wet snow that seeps in the moment I step outside. The air is full of snow, and every part of me shivers. More snow settles on the cuffs of my jeans, quickly melting and spreading damp dark tidal marks that soon reach as high as my knees. I find myself hoping for the cold to lead to numbness, undoubtedly preferable over this freezing damp. I can't even appreciate the pureness of the air; I'm too afraid it's forming icicles in my lungs.

Gabe guides me on an indistinct path through the undergrowth, moving farther ahead with every step. Somehow he seems to be walking normally, effortlessly, as though he is gliding, completely unaware of the two feet of snow through which we are now wading. I, however, am trudging. I stagger upwards, heaving my feet, my numb fingers barely able to hold onto the bottle in my hand. When I look back, my stomach sinks to see the car just a few metres below us. I let out a low involuntary sigh and yank my feet back up out of the sinking snow.

After a few minutes, Gabe stops and turns.

'Are you okay?' he calls down to me.

I try to nod, but my neck muscles appear to have frozen. After a quick inspection of a nearby tree, he snaps a long branch from the skeletal remains. He runs his hands down the stem and strips off the small brittle spines and then deftly rips off the more obstinate twigs.

'Swap,' he says striding back down toward me.

He takes the bottle and hands me the smoothed stick in return.

My thumb slips into the forked top.

'Better?' he asks.

'Let's see.'

Balancing my weight with the new su

plodding upwards. This time our paces are mo

although I suspect he has slowed a fair bit, too.

'You know the mountains?' I say, my breath condensing in a mist in front of me.

'A bit.'

'How well is a bit?'

'I know a few. This one, about a dozen other peaks in the range, others I guess.'

'That's a fair bit.'

'I suppose. My dad knew pretty much the whole ridge. He knew their old names, everything.'

'How is that possible?' I ask.

'We lived here. I lived here.'

'You did?'

My jaw hangs loose in surprise. Of course I knew people lived out here, away from the sections of Unity, but I never for a second imagined Gabe had been one of them. He's far too structured, too normal. And he's used both his amendments. Maybe, I realise, that is why he moved.

My mind wanders back to the twins at the Annex. Most of the land beyond the sections is inhospitable, decimated after the years of civil war that followed the discovery, but the mountains are supposed to be the harshest regions of all. I heard about a girl who went hiking on one once and got lost. It took nearly five weeks to find the body, and they had to identify her by what the animals had left. I remember thinking how sad it was that no one was able to amend for her.

Even with my stick the climb is still tough. I constantly catch my hair on low-hanging branches or stumble on concealed roots. Beads of perspiration roll down my skin, and despite the temperature, I find myself more concerned with overheating than freezing. Attempting small talk, even with the hope of somehow impressing Gabe, falls well down my list of priorities.

Gabe pauses ahead of me. He creates an archway in the thicket by holding back an array of sapling branches. With a final burst of energy, I stride towards it. When I join him, my feet are soaked in snow, my back in sweat and my lungs raw from the freezing air. I ve time to catch my breath before it is swept away from

plintered light floods through the fissure of the trees onto a ain of perfectly pristine powder where the refracted rays yield an infinite stream of colours. My sodden feet and painfully numb fingers are instantly forgotten, and I tread forward, the soft snow crunching with a wet hiss beneath my step.

'It's beautiful,' I whisper.

On one side are miles and miles of would-be horizons. Jagged mountain ridges align layer after layer, their peaks dissolving into clouds that graduate in colour from the purest of whites to the purplest of greys. In front of me, pockets of high-rises jut from the divots and crevices of the undulating earth, where swirls of black smoke mushroom and envelop the air above the mines. I take another step forward.

'On a clear day, you can see all nine sections,' Gabe tells me.

'The whole of Unity,' I whisper. I gaze out, drinking in the snow filled air. One city. It's bizarre to think that that is all that's left. From seventy million people to under twenty million in just over a century. The Cabinet still make reference to the ones that left. What a chance they gave up on, sacrificing amendments for the chaos of the rest of the dying world.

'Are we safe here?' I say, a sudden thought causing my pulse to burst into life.

'Safe? Why wouldn't we be?'

'The radiation. I thought it got worse when you were higher? That's why we can't use planes anymore, isn't it?'

Gabe wrinkles his nose.

'It's not a problem up here,' he says. 'Planes used to fly at a much higher altitude than this.'

'They did?'

He nods his head.

There are so many things about the old world that seem more like science fiction than history. Flying in giant metal cars across the sky is one. I can't imagine anyone risking something that dangerous anymore, even if they do have amendments. As it is, the Cabinet banned any attempts at redeveloping air flight. Amendments or not, radiation poisoning is not a way I'd like to go.

'Do you ever wonder what it's like,' I ask him, 'beyond the Kingdom?'

'I try not to.' He pauses. 'Look,' he says, his tone of voice reinforcing the change in topic. 'The tree line down there marks the boundary for section nine.'

We stand together, staring at the world beneath our feet.

Gabe has dumped the bottle of wine on the ground and now traipses around kicking up a flurry of snow until his feet find what they are looking for. He waves me over to join him. His lips are curled up in a smile as he stares at a decidedly ordinary looking, though rather high, mound of snow. Still grinning, he leans forward and uses the back of his arm to wipe away layer after layer. A few swipes later, he reveals a small wooden bench facing out.

'Seat?' he asks.

'It'll be soaking.'

'You can sit on my coat.'

'Then you'll be freezing.'

'I'll be fine.'

I decline his offer once again before sitting on the bare bench. The cold shoots through me with a blinding sensation. I let out a small gasp and rub my hands against my knees, determined not to move.

'Cold?' Gabe asks.

'I'm fine.' I grimace.

Gabe laughs and removes his coat for me to sit on.

'It's an amazing view,' I say.

'My favourite place on Earth. No matter what goes on elsewhere, I know they'll never change this.'

'You come here a lot?'

'It's been a while.' He leans back into the wood, the cold having no apparent effect on him. 'I built this bench.'

'Really? I never figured you as the building type.'

He nods. 'I used to be.'

'When was that?'

'A long time ago.' He cleans away more snow from the back of the bench and reveals a coarsely carved date. Below, a set of initials is etched in the same manner, barely recognizable as letters. Crinkles emerge on his brow, and his eyes drift briefly away to a place I can't reach. He remains there for only a moment before turning back to me and repositioning his lips into a smile. 'Shall we?' he says as he retrieves the bottle of wine.

The popped cork soars upwards, and I lose sight of it well

before it begins its descent. There is not even a rustle of branches to indicate where it lands.

'Sorry, I forgot glasses,' he says and hands me the bottle.

The wine is warm, though ice water would feel tepid right now. I take a sip and pass back the bottle. We sit wordlessly, staring out at the horizons as we continue to swap and swig the bottle between us. Barely a glass's worth has been drunk when Gabe places it on the ground and digs it back into the snow.

'Can I give you your present now?' he says. I stiffen.

'I thought the wine was my present?'

'It's part of it, but I got you something else, too. I hope that's okay?'

I nod. The warmth from the drink has flooded my face and the nuisance family of butterflies has reoccupied my insides. Gabe reaches inside his jacket pocket and pulls out a red velvet pouch, smaller than his palm and tied with a thick thread.

'Happy birthday,' he says and kisses me swiftly on the cheek.

I stare at the tiny pocket of fabric. My hands tremor with a mixture of trepidation and anticipation, and my cheeks radiate a heat I know will have caused them to glow. Prompted by Gabe's polite throat clearance, I briefly fumble with the strings before accepting the inevitable and removing my gloves. Eventually, I manage to loosen them with my frozen fingers and tip the contents of the pouch into my hand. I want to say something, but I can't. The words simply don't exist.

Chapter Six

From the Book of Amendments
Rule 6. Only those in a fit mental state and of sound mind will be allowed to amend.

MY MOTHER used her first amendment to try and save her marriage. I don't remember it being that bad, but then I was a child. What did I know?

The envelope arrived the same day Fi and I were left forgotten on the rooftop. My mother kept her scar hidden as we were ushered outside and out of the way, but it was there, I am certain, concealed within a clenched fist. The following morning, when we finally came downstairs, in search of parents and food, the flat was in disrepair. A broken vase, scattered books; evidence of the argument that had raged long into the night. I found the envelope half-burnt and red lying in its ashes in the waste paper basket. *Don't—* was all that was left of the message.

That's another problem with amending. How many times have people admitted to sins they have not yet committed? It shouldn't make you guilty, particularly when you're trying to make amends, but I guess that's not how my father saw it.

He left soon after.

I choke back the angry tears and focus on the bracelet in my hand. It is almost identical to theirs, to the bracelets that Fi and my mother were given when they registered.

'Can I?' Gabe says.

He takes the heavy knotted chain from my hand, then fixes the clasp around my wrist. Twisting it around shows the only difference, the addition of a single charm.

'Is it okay?' Gabe asks. 'I know it's not the same.'

The thank you I want to say is somewhere between the mammoth lump in my throat and the tears reforming in my eyes.

'Em? Are you okay?'

'It's beautiful.'

'You're sure?'

I nod.

'Where did you get it?' I say.

'It took a little hunting,' he admits.

Jewellery itself is not rare. There are enough pawn shops selling the pilfered belongings of the broken down old world, but to find something this similar to theirs? I don't know how long he must have searched. My mother took a solid month scouring for Fi's. I know, I was with her.

'I know Fi wanted to get you one, before, well, before everything,' Gabe says.

'It's perfect,' I manage to croak. I tilt the charm towards me, noting how the tiny silver envelope casts minute patterns on the snow.

'I know your Mum's and Fi's were different. I just wanted a little bit of me there, too,' he says.

Without thinking, I touch his face in an attempt to brush away the lines of insecurity that have appeared at the edges of his eyes.

I'm not sure if I go to kiss his cheek or not, but either way my lips find his, and once they're there they don't want to leave. The pressure of his mouth builds a warmth in my chest that diffuses down. I try to think of a reason to draw away, like the pounding against my ribcage or the growing heat that has consumed my body from the torso down, but he doesn't stop and neither do I. It is a perfect remedy to the cold.

Gabe pulls away first, wiping the tears from my face with his thumb.

'Not quite how I'd imagined our first kiss,' he says as he tucks a fallen strand of hair behind my ear.

Inside, an aching sensation surfaces and swells. This – Gabe and I – has been my dream for as long as I can remember, but I've learnt from past experience that making a dream real just gives life another place to aim when it kicks you.

I try to smile, and Gabe laughs at my attempt, creating long dimples in his cheeks.

'You'll get there,' he tells me as he kisses me again.

For a while, we sit on his bench looking out at the view. The sun smudges beneath the clouds and tints them with deceptively warm-looking orange hues. I wrap my damp feet under my sodden jeans and curl up against his shoulder, his arms around my hips, his lips on my neck.

I have another dream, besides me and Gabe and the one-kneed declaration of love. This dream stays buried so deeply I only allow myself half-glimpses, so even I can't disturb it or damage it. It's the only way I can avoid suffering the heart-wrenching realisation that it will never be, can never be, not now. In this dream I am content. What would it be like to be so happy you wish for nothing more in your life, to have fulfilled every one of your dreams and ambitions so that now, in the present day, you require and desire nothing? That is my dream; contentment. The warm holds, the kisses on the top of my head, the heated breaths that rattle in my ear and cause my pulse to soar, they are more than I could have wished for, but they aren't true happiness. They're a distraction.

'Are you happy?' I ask Gabe, as I tug the heavy gloves back on.

'Now? Yes, very.'

'No. In life generally?'

'Is anyone?'

I consider his answer as I tip the bottle up and subsequently choke on the onslaught of wine.

'Some people must be,' I tell him.

The wind has picked up speed, whipping the clouds fast across the sky and bringing a scent of burning wood from somewhere farther over on the peak.

The numbness is still there – in my fingers and toes and almost all my facial features – but it doesn't feel so bad now. I could quite happily fall asleep here. I yawn widely and sink my head into Gabe's shoulder.

'We should go,' he says but only moves as far as to kiss me.

'We should,' I say, responding to his lips.

As the wind continues to strengthen, we banter back and forth, trading kisses for words, half smiles from me for dimple-forming grins from Gabe until the sun starts to sink and even the burgeoning warmth of his body can't stave off the shivers.

When I go to stand, my legs fall away beneath me. I tumble towards the snow.

'Whoa, are you okay?'

I nod and manage to push my body upwards, but my balance is skewed. I stumble forward trying to correct my lilting steps, but I just end up staggering.

'You need to sit down,' Gabe tells me.

'I'll be fine,' I say. I prop myself against the bench, my hand slipping along the icy surface.

'Em, sit down.'

I can't even manage that. Everything is swaying, spiralling faster and faster, the view blurring as my head spins uncontrollably, and I struggle to stay upright. I wonder if it's a concussion from my fall at the Annex; after all, I hit my head hard. I converse inwardly with myself and decide emphatically this point is important enough to convey to Gabe. I manage to find my feet and brace myself against the bench to tell him, but when I actually speak, different words come out.

'I need to lie down,' I say. So I do. It feels better, warmer, snugger, submerged in the softness of the snow, the evening sun falling in sheaths through the branches and across my body.

I go to close my eyes, but Gabe grabs me by my arms.

'No, not a good idea. You need to get up. You'll freeze.' He tugs at my good hand.

'You can just lie down here with me and keep me warm,' I say.

'Not gonna do that. Up you get.'

He heaves me back to the bench, and the spinning in my head is joined by body-jolting nausea. I lean over my knees, putting my weight on them as I rock. Soon my hand is throbbing viciously, red seeping through the fabric of his gloves.

'Sorry,' I mumble. 'I'll get you a new pair.'

'It's fine. I told you they were old.' He kisses me on the forehead, his face steeped in concern. 'We need to get back. Are you okay to walk?' Gabe laughs at my head shake. 'It was a rhetorical question, I'm afraid. Here, you can lean on me.'

Still, we wait a few more minutes. The swaying lessens only slightly, but at least I don't feel the overwhelming urge to vomit. Gabe helps me to my feet and guides me back down the mountain, holding wayward branches away from my head and knocking away stray and concealed roots with his feet. This time he's the one trying to keep pace with the retreating light.

In the car the balmy heat and some water help my balance return, though my head is now pounding. I inspect the gash along my palm and feel a sharp pang with every prod – the numbing effects of the font water are most definitely wearing thin.

'I must have drunk more wine than I thought,' I say apologetically.

As Gabe looks at me, his eyes widen and lips press into a flat line. 'Actually Em, I think it may be my fault,' he says.

'It's hardly your fault I drank too much.'

'You didn't. There's still some left.'

'Are you sure?'

'Positive.'

'Then it's probably from when I hit my head. Don't look so worried, I'll be fine.'

He screws up his face as if in a desperate battle with his conscience. 'You got registration sickness.'

'Registration sickness?'

'It's a euphemism for getting drunk on the day you register. It happens really quick because of all the blood they took. It used to be quite a trendy thing to do. I should have thought. I own a bar for God's sake.'

His lips are now moving out of sync to his voice. I scrunch my eyes closed as I try to reconfigure my senses. 'Seriously?' I say, rubbing my thumbs into my temples. 'People did this deliberately?'

'Em —'

'Please stop apologising – honestly, stop worrying.' I lean forward to kiss him, but my head topples and I butt against his nose. The laugh escapes before I can stop myself; it's only a chuckle really, but it's more than has passed my lips in a long time. I clamp my mouth shut.

'It's good to see you smile,' Gabe says, kissing my hair. 'You used to smile so much, you know.'

I push myself up, wrapping my arms around his neck.

'Thank you,' I say. 'Thank you for everything.'

In a swift sweep, he lifts me up out of my seat and pulls me over onto his lap, kissing my neck and whispering into my ear. The last slivers of light fade into the trees as the layer of snow deepens on the windscreen.

We are interrupted by the buzz of a telephone trapped in my pocket between our thighs. Blushing and apologising, I shuffle around against his groin and try to retrieve it. When I do, I study the screen only briefly. I don't recognise the number, though it can only be one person, meaning she's lost or forgotten her phone again. A small part of me should be flattered that she can still remember my number, but in truth it's the small internal fluttering at the realisation she may have remembered my birthday that makes me answer.

'Em,' she bellows so loudly the use of a phone seems superfluous. 'Where are you? I've been trying to get hold of you for ages.' The screen of my phone is blank.

'You have?' I say. 'I must have been out of range.'

'Em, I need you to come and pick me up.'

My stomach sinks – no last-minute apologies then. 'Where are you?' I say flatly.

'At the bar. And Gabe's not here because, apparently, he's doing something with you.'

Something. Even with all the insinuations in the world she wouldn't get it. Gabe looks at me, his lips pursed and eyes saddened as he absentmindedly strokes my knee.

'It'll take us at least an hour to get to you,' I say. 'Maybe more.'

'Seriously? Where are you? Nowhere takes that long.'

'Do you want us to come and get you or not?' My words come out short and bitter. I don't want to sound like that. I want to show at least some level of composure with Gabe here, but over the past few months every word that comes out of Fi's mouth grates on me irrationally. Just watching her lips move is enough to set my teeth on edge some days.

There's no reply from the end of the line.

'Fi? Fi, are you still there?'

'It's fine. I'll get a lift home.'

'Really?'

'I'll be fine. I'm sure I've got lots of friends who can take me home.'

'Fi —' The end of the phone clatters against something. 'Fine.' I spit the word back, despite knowing the line's already dead. After a second's glance at the screen I throw the phone onto the dash.

'Today's a whole new day, remember?' Gabe says.

Can it really be a new day when it's already tainted and soiled by all the ones that have gone before? I wonder. Even now, even with amendments, I struggle to believe there's such a thing as a clean slate, no matter how much you scrub. You might wipe away the writing, but the little scratches are always there. Maybe all you can do is dim the lights and hope nobody notices.

I scoot back over to the passenger seat, and Gabe starts the engine. Our fingers are interlocked and my head rests against his shoulder. He fiddles with the radio until he finds some music, a lady singing blues with a rich and treacly voice that fills the car and sends soft shivers down my spine. She sings about the moon and the stars and a love which will conquer and triumph over everything. I close my eyes and let the sounds pervade me, trying to convince myself that not everything she's singing is a lie.

When I wake up, the radio is off and the road is lined with drab tower blocks. The vents are blasting hot air, and the condensation has caused a thin film of frost on the window which I scrape at with my nails. Gabe doesn't normally take the main roads – they're too expensive to start – but tonight I don't blame him. The lanes must be covered with ice.

I stretch and uncurl like a cat. Pain sears across my hand. I remove Gabe's glove and inspect the wound.

'How is it?'

'Sore. Red.'

'It'll go down.'

'What time is it?'

'Late,' he answers.

I was hoping for something slightly more concrete, but my brain is not yet awake enough to question any further.

'All the local lanes are shut,' Gabe says. 'Snow. We've had to come the long way round.'

A growl erupts from my stomach, rudely interrupting him. My face flushes with embarrassment. It's understandable though – neither of us has eaten since the sandwiches this morning.

'Do you want to stop somewhere?' he asks.

'Yes, but we should get home.'

'You sure?'

'I'll be fine.' Just as I say the words, my stomach growls again.

Gabe's eyebrows rise with a smirk.

'Maybe we should pick up a few things.'

I have a little of our mourner's money with me. My mother worked from the day she left school. That's your only option in the Kingdom if you want the benefits, which is fair enough, provided you can actually work. As factory workers, she and my father encouraged Fi and me to stay in school as long as possible. They didn't want us spending every daylight hour working ourselves to the bone just to make ends meet. But after my father left we needed money, so Fi dropped out of school to get a job. I don't think she was that upset about it. She had never been particularly enamoured with academic study. At first, she did a few jobs off-the-books until she got a letter from the Cabinet saying she had two weeks to find something officially or she would be allocated to one of the workhouses. I've never seen anyone move faster. It was half determination, half luck that she found Gabe and he agreed to take her on. It was even more fortuitous that she turned out to have a talent for bartending.

Two days after our mother died the cheque arrived in the post. It wasn't much, but it was helpful. Fi didn't ask about the money until a week or so after it arrived. I told her most of it had gone on funeral expenses, living costs, etcetera. I'm not convinced she believed me, though, so I'm careful not to leave it around the house where she'll be able to find it. Gabe can't keep Fi's job at the bar open indefinitely.

Again, I'm faced with the realisation that I have to find work. I always assumed I would get picked up for an apprenticeship, an actual profession that would help us move up in the world, like our parents had hoped. I'd had a few deluded ideas about medicine, becoming a doctor, but deep down I knew I didn't have the determination. Anyway, it's been a dying profession for a long time now. However, service jobs –electrician, car mechanic – those I should have been able to do. Not long ago, they had seemed like the backup options. Now they seem as unobtainable as a place on the Cabinet. Sooner or later I'm going to get a letter from them assigning me a position. They've given me a longer grace period than I expected since our mother died, I suspect because I'm young. I'll do what I'm told and go to wherever the Cabinet sends me. We have to survive somehow.

We pull up outside a store. The shutters are already pulled halfway down, and a pacing guard is fending off the cold. Suitably dressed in heavy-set boots and fur-lined gloves it seems like an odd place for him to be present, though I suppose there are a fair few centres nearby. I climb out the car and leave Gabe browsing the radio for songs. Outside, the cold is like needles stabbing through my damp clothes and in the few short metres to the store, my eyes begin to stream.

Inside, the store smells of age-dried meat. It's the kind of smell that makes you retch and infiltrates its way into everything in the vicinity, my hair and clothes included. I rush around and gather groceries in a basket, my breath held the entire time. I buy only basics now – things Fi will have to cook, rather than gorge her way through when her hangover lifts. When I have enough for food to last us a few days, I pay at the counter, handing my money to a woman who is picking food out from around a protruding snaggletooth.

Laden with brown bags, I hurry back to the car and empty my loaded arms onto the back seat. My hand and the small cut on my head are now throbbing intently, and the sudden hot air of the car stings almost as much as the cold did. I ponder the likelihood of infections; there's certainly enough crap in the air to make it plausible. I might get blood poisoning. Then what would happen? Would I have to use one of my amendments to go back to the ceremony and tell myself not to slip? I laugh internally at the thought.

'Gabe?' I ask him before we draw away. 'Why did you choose today?'

'What?'

'I mean us. You and me. Why did you decide to do something today?'

'I wasn't sure you felt the same.'

'You didn't answer my question. Why choose today?'

He studies me with a look that makes my skin buzz.

'I guess today felt different. Today felt like…' His sentence fades into nothing.

'Like what?' I press.

'I don't know. Like if maybe you regret this, wish it hadn't happened, you could always —'

'Amend it?'

His eyes stay locked on me and a sad half-smile toys contemplatively at the corner of his lips – it's not a real smile, though, just a defence mechanism. His eyes are telling the truth. I should say something, laugh off the last comment, but I can't draw my eyes away from his. How many decades have those eyes seen? More than three I'm sure, but four, five, ten even? Why not? He's used both his amendments. Two lives lived without a single memory of what happened. No wonder so many people go mad.

'Amending for kissing seems a little extreme, don't you think?' I say. 'It's more likely I'd just have slapped you.'

He grins again and his age drops a decade, if not more. It's bizarre seeing him like this. Seeing him vulnerable. It tugs my insides in ways I'd never imagined.

'Thank you for today,' I say. 'It's been a good day. Definitely no amending.'

'You'll have more good days, I promise.'

I almost believe him.

We park outside our tower block. It's not the nicest of places to live, but it's certainly not the worst. A while ago they closed one of the nearby factories and a whole lot of people went out of work. The Cabinet managed to relocate most them, but no one came to claim the empty homes, so it's easy to tell if Fi's at home or not. Tonight, light blazes from every window in the flat. Even without the money, she manages to waste it.

'Let's just stay here,' I say, nuzzling Gabe's neck.

'We can't. We'll run out of fuel and freeze.'

'But we'd be happy,' I joke. I pause. It seems strange to have to ask the next question. I do though. 'Are you coming up?' I say.

'Just to check on Fi, then I should probably go.'

My stomach jolts.

'Unless you want me to stay longer, of course.'

I kiss him by way of an answer. It's only because my cheeks are aching that I notice it. I'm smiling. Really smiling.

We dash through the cold. The brittle grass is littered with frozen puddles that challenge every step. I tread carefully with no intention of repeating my earlier escapade and falling flat on my face. How was that today? My registration, lunch by the river, it all seems a whole lifetime ago. How much has changed since this morning, when Fi was barely conscious and the miner's stale breath choked the elevator? Maybe it's not that much, not really. Then again, maybe it's everything.

'What should we tell her?' I say as we stand waiting for the elevator.

'About what?' The comment stings. Gabe realises as soon as he's said it. 'Tell her you're happy,' he says. 'Just tell her you're happy.'

It should be that easy, of course it should, but the closer the numbers get to our floor, the more my lungs tighten. Whether Gabe's are doing the same I can't tell, but he's unusually quiet.

'It'll be fine,' he says and pecks the top of my head, but he doesn't look at me. It's understandable. I can't look at him either.

A wall of heat hits us as we open the door. The air is scorching and dry and thick with the scent of roasting meat. I don't remember when Fi last cooked, if ever. My mouth salivates. This must be a good sign – Fi cooking, Fi in for the night – though my squirming insides don't seem to agree.

'Fi? Fi?'

Gabe closes the door. I wander through to the kitchen.

'Fi?'

The scene is so familiar, so reassuringly comforting, that it makes my heart race. Her dark hair is scruffily tied at the base of her neck, and she stands there wearing layers of mismatched woollens with the sleeves rolled up over her elbows and arms deep inside the oven. I half expect her to turn around with a freshly baked birthday cake in hand, shower me in attention and sing happy birthday tunelessly. I stand, anticipating the moment, but she doesn't move. Not a single muscle on her moves.

Gabe drops the shopping to the floor and drags her away from the oven. She yells in pain.

Plunging her blistering arms into the washing up bowl, Gabe holds her with force. Water sprays from the taps as she screams and squirms, steam rising from the sink.

'What have you done?' he screams.

Chapter Seven

From the Book of Amendments
Rule 7. Amendments must not contain numbers, dates, or be written in any language other than those approved by the Cabinet for use within the Kingdom.

'WHAT HAVE you done? What have you done?' Gabe keeps screaming, but he gets little by way of response.

'I'm cold. I'm so cold,' Fi gasps in shivery little breaths.

Her eyes are unfocussed and detached, wobbling back and forth in their sockets.

The oven is still humming, empty.

I march across and slam the oven door shut. Fi doesn't even flinch. 'I'm so cold. I just want to be warm. It's so cold,' she continues.

Her hair is matted, thick with dirt or blood. Below the charred sleeves of her submerged jumper, I can see the oozing blisters, coating the blackening skin that covers her arms. Her skin is scorched, a black line across her wrist.

I grab ice from an otherwise empty freezer and pour it over her arms. She quails as I try holding it in place, but it melts too quickly, sliding across her skin and slipping out of my hands. The coldness isn't a lie. Even in her chargrilled state she is shivering, her jaw chattering. The entire weight of her trembling body is supported by Gabe. When I look to him, a tear is running down his cheek. I know what he's thinking because I have the same thought, too: he's thinking she can't be saved.

'Fi, what happened? Please, I need to know, I need to help you.' I turn her chin to face me. 'Fi, what are you doing?'

'We should get her to a hospital,' Gabe says.

I pretend I don't hear him. 'Fi, please. What happened? Tell me what happened.'

‘I’m so cold,’ she says, staring down at the glassy water. ‘I was cold, I was just so cold.’

Gabe wraps her arms in an ice-filled poultice and takes her to the living room. I can do nothing but watch and pace.

‘Em, she needs help. She should go to the hospital,’ he says again, looking straight at me. He’s shaking too. His hands tremble as he tries to hold the poultice in place, and attempts to hold my gaze.

I look away. ‘No, no hospital. Not yet. Not like this. I can help her, I can sort her out. Let me try, please. If we take her like this there’ll never let her out. They’ll think she’s crazy. They’ll lock her up.’

‘Em, please.’

‘A bath?’ I say, my voice trembling. ‘A bath might help, right? A bath will help?’

‘Maybe.’

‘I’ll run her a bath. That’ll help, a bath will help. And pain killers. There are some in my room,’ I tell Gabe. ‘On the bookshelf, behind the old Atlas.’

The tub is half full already, but the water is tepid and grimy, probably her attempt to wash away this morning’s hangover. I pull out the plug before wiping it clean and refilling it with water only slightly warmer than I had just emptied.

Gabe brings Fi in. I ask him to leave as I start to strip her.

‘She wouldn’t like it,’ I tell him selfishly.

After casting one more look down at Fi, he leaves us.

I try to undress her, but the charcoaled wool disintegrates in my hand and she winces under the slightest pressure. Her eyes dart constantly across the room as she shifts and flinches in varying degrees of agony. In the end, I find a pair of nail scissors and cut away at the stitching of her top with gritted teeth. I am only grateful she is not dressed in trousers.

Fi’s naked body slumps against the cistern, her eyes focusing beyond the physical perimeters of the room. Her hushed whimpers are all but drowned out by the uncontrollable sobs from my lips. I’ve no idea where to look or where to start. My lungs feel as though the very threads that make them have fused together and every breath sears a deeper and deeper pain as it attempts to force them back apart. I don’t want to see this. I don’t want to be here. But I am.

I tentatively go to move her, but I hesitate, not wanting to cause more pain. Her body is marbled in hues of reds and purples, with hard swellings and grotesque lumps covering her left side; touching her is only going to make things worse. I try to make her move herself instead. She has fewer bruises on her legs, and after all, she must have walked from somewhere to get home.

'Fi, honey,' I say. 'Do you think you can stand?' No response. 'Fi, please. I need you to get up. Get into the bath.' Nothing. 'Can you hear me, Fi? I need you to stand up. Fi?'

My pleas become more desperate, but she doesn't react, not when I beg or cry or curse with the most vulgar language I can concoct. She doesn't even register I'm there. With deep shuddering breaths, I step back, close my eyes and suck in air through my nose.

'The bath will help,' I say firmly, but I'm not sure whom I'm speaking to.

Beads of sweat trickle down my forehead as I try to hoist her up into the bath, but whether through lack of strength or concern for hurting her, I can't get a decent hold. After a few failed attempts, I call for Gabe.

He doesn't flinch, not at the sight of Fi naked or at the unearthly mass of bruises and blisters that adorn her. He hooks his arms under her, sweeping and lifting her up and into the bath in one fluid movement. Then he kisses me on the head and asks if I want him to stay. I say I don't.

'I'll get the painkillers,' he says.

I'm as tender as I can be in cleaning her. I dab a flannel against the broken skin and scrub the dirt as forcefully as I dare. For all the bruising, I find only a little blood, and most of it seems to have come from a small cut on her head. I rummage through the cabinet and unearth a lidless tube of antiseptic cream. It's been squeezed almost dry, and the end is caked in a white chalky crust, but there's enough good cream in the bottom to smear on the cut. The rest I use on the most oozing of blisters. While Fi lies oblivious in her stupor, the water turns opaque. I empty the bath and turn the taps on, refilling the tub with clean, warm water. The bath will help.

Gabe has returned and is standing in the doorway staring intently at the ground, lost in his thoughts. His face is white.

'We have a problem,' he says.

Leaving Fi as she is, he leads me to her room, where bottles and buckets from this morning have been removed and the festering clothes pushed to the edges. Several honeysuckle-scented candles are dotted around the room on plates, an attempt to disguise, or at least overpower, the stench, but they have already burned out, thankfully. Her envelope has been placed seal-side up on the dressing table, and the heavy curtains waft under the slight breeze of the open window. I sigh in relief. Attempting to tidy is a good sign. She's trying. She'll get there.

Gabe angles my shoulders towards the corner of the room, where the shadow of the curtain ebbs and flows over the crumpled bed linen.

'What am I looking —'

Gabe silences me with a finger and points again at the bed.

The silhouette is so slight and small beneath the animated shadow of the curtains, but now I've seen it I can't draw my eyes away. The sheet rises and falls rhythmically. The longer I stare, the more my eyes adjust and faster my pulse becomes. The cover is pulled up tightly and tucked in under her feet the way our mother did with us when we were little. Thin strands of striking black hair fall across her face. In her arms is a stuffed creature that feels vaguely familiar.

'Do you know who she is?' Gabe says.

Unable to speak, I shake my head, but I don't avert my gaze. My heart is skipping sporadic beats, and the shadows from the curtains are toying with the image, making it impossible to see her clearly. I have to move closer.

My footsteps creak on the floor. As I approach, her breaths grow more rapid. At first it's just shallow wheezing, but soon her chest is heaving with desperate, heavy gasps. Her lips move constantly in silent, unreadable mutters, and pinpricks of sweat start glistening on her forehead. I can feel her body heat and see her eyes darting around beneath her eyelids. She clutches forcefully at the soft toy, and I edge nearer, now so close I can smell the sickly mixture of blood and grime that cling to the air around her.

Should I touch her or is it best to let her sleep? I wonder. Just as I make the conscious decision to leave her be, her breath falls silent. I wait. Nothing. The curtains flap with more force. Still nothing. Even Gabe's breathing behind me is loud and clanging. But nothing comes from the girl – no sounds, no movement of her lips, no rise and fall of the sheet. It is as though she is a corpse.

A vice clamps my chest. My own breath held until my lungs

tighten and burn. A lump swells in my throat, and I reach my hand out to touch the girl's neck. A second before I make contact, her eyes snap open. Her body turns rigid, her back arches, her mouth flies wide open and an ear-splitting scream fills the room. Spasms follow. Her body contorts and writhes as her scream fades to a gurgling whimper. Her eyes bulge white and the veins on her forehead look close to popping. Finally, her muscles turn limp and she drops back down to the mattress, eyes closed, face relaxed, utterly silent. It couldn't have lasted longer than a few seconds, but it doesn't feel that way.

I don't need to see anymore here. I turn to leave but Gabe catches me by the elbow.

'Do you know her?'

I shake my head, but force myself to look at her again, with her delicate features and dark lustrous hair. 'No,' I tell him, but I'm not so sure. I take a step closer, my pulse rising as I move. 'This morning. In the lift. It's her, isn't it?'

Gabe nods his head. 'Maybe,' he says. 'I thought so too.'

My head drops and there on the floor I see them; rose patterned shoes. I turn on my heel and go, the room suddenly short of oxygen.

I lean against the bathroom radiator and watch as Fi's marbled chest swells and falls. The water is stone cold again, but she doesn't seem to notice. She's still asleep. One of her hands lies limply over the side, her feet curled towards her knees as if to maintain a degree of modesty. The front door opens and closes. I don't know where Gabe has gone. I don't know if I want to.

I spin scenarios out of the ether and entwine them with the bare threads of my imagination in an attempt to build a script, a story, anything that will help me explain what has happened and how the pair ended up here. I offer myself a hundred explanations, but every one is weak and unsubstantiated. It's a futile game and I quickly stop. I will find no answers on my own.

'Fi. Fi, honey,' I say, hovering my hand above her shoulder. 'I need to talk to you.' When she doesn't respond, I tap her gently on the right side of the cheek – the side not covered in bruises.

She frowns and opens her eyes.

'Fi,' I say. 'The little girl, who is she? Where should she be?'

My sister looks at me with little recognition, her frown lines deepening as she scours her thoughts and sinks deeper down into the dank water.

'Fi, the girl,' I try again. 'Where's her father Fi, where is she meant to be? Please help me. I'm trying to help you. I promise I just want to help you.'

The confusion of my questioning draws shadows across her face. Her eyes flicker from side to side as she attempts to understand her surroundings. The whites of her eyes bulge as fear wrestles on her face. I lean in closer, but she recoils, her breathing quickening as she labours for air. She grapples at the side of the tub and tries to stand, but her hands slide against the smooth surface. Her legs flail as she splashes and sprays water, struggling to find traction anywhere against the side of the bath. She slips and falls backwards, screeching and spluttering as her head is submerged, all the while fighting to resist my help.

'Stop, Fi! Stop it! Please, I'm trying to help!'

The water foams and gargles from her water-logged lungs; her battered and burned limbs flap hopelessly, smacking against the ceramic tub as I frantically try to keep her above the surface.

The front door slams again and before I realise it Gabe shoves me out of the way and hoists Fi up by her armpits, lifting her clear from the water. He holds her firmly in place as she thrashes around, howling in pain.

'You're hurting her!' I scream, thumping his arm. 'You're hurting her!'

'Finola,' Gabe says, ignoring my remonstrations. 'Finola, stop it. You don't have to do this. Think. Think about where you are. Think, Fi. Think about where you are. It's only Em. Think about Em.'

Her eyes flicker between us both before they close, her nostrils flaring and teeth bared as Gabe repeats his mantra.

'Think about Em, think about Em.'

A veil of tears wells in her eyes. Her limbs tremble and lips shake as she sinks back down into the stagnant tub. 'Em,' she whispers.

I push Gabe off her and kneel on the drenched floor with her, burying her head in my chest. 'It's okay, Fi, I'm here. I'm here.'

'I'm so sorry, I'm so sorry.' She repeats her apology again and again, through ragged breaths, her wrinkled fingers clutching at my clothes.

Chapter Eight

From the Book of Amendments
Rule 8. Amendments must never be exchanged for gifts, services, monies or personal gain.

WHEN FI IS calm I attempt to dry her, but the towel is so thin it suffices only to push the water around her scorched skin and protruding ribs. Gabe watches from the door before disappearing. I don't try to move her again; if she needs to sleep here, she can. Gabe returns twice with glasses of water and painkillers as Fi and I talk. He doesn't speak or interrupt, doesn't even eavesdrop from what I can tell.

At first her words are little more than sounds and syllables – no coherence, no flow — and she struggles to respond to even the most basic questions. Every answer is laced in ambiguity, the details suppressed beneath the mental scar tissue that has already formed and, I suspect, a fair amount of alcohol. Still, some things, some moments – memories and images – prise their way through to her consciousness and allow me to weave together the pieces.

When her words slur and her eyelids are so heavy they refuse to stay open, I dress her in the loosest cotton nightgown I can find and lay her down on my bed. She offers no objection as I move her, though she flinches when my hands brush against her wounds. I close the door and leave the heating on full. Tomorrow it won't matter anyway.

Gabe doesn't speak. For a while he cradles me on his lap and strokes my hair the same way he did with Fi that time. I try to predict the effects of tonight's events. They'll already be rippling their way through to tomorrow, evolving and shackling me to a future beyond my control. There is not a fibre within me that doesn't ache. Every nerve, every emotion has been stripped dry and drained. Yet the tears still fall in cascades: tears for Fi, tears for my mother, and tears for the child whose cries and whimpering can be heard through her tightly shut door. But I don't lie to myself. Most of the tears aren't for them, they're for me.

'I called around. There was an accident,' Gabe says, finally breaking the silence. 'On one of the lanes. They found Andjrez's car.'

'And him? Did they find him too?'

Gabe nods. 'They did,' he says.

Silence falls between us yet again as a thousand images run through my mind. An accident could mean a hundred different things. Anything could have happened. Anything at all.

'Can I tell you something?' I say, staring at the family photos that sparsely decorate the mantelpiece.

'Of course.'

'I've always been glad that what happened with my mother happened when it did. I was grateful even that she did it then, that she didn't wait any longer.'

'Why?' He's still flattening my hair like I'm a child.

'Because I always thought that if it had been me, if I'd had to choose like Fi had, I wouldn't have gone back. I was the lucky one. I didn't have to make that choice.'

He's silent for a moment as we take in the confession I've finally admitted after nearly a year of concealment. I somehow thought it would be a relief, a release, and I suppose in some ways it is. In some ways it's the opposite.

'And now?' Gabe asks me. 'What do you think now?'

'Now? Now I realise Fi never had a choice.'

He pushes me off his lap and spins my shoulders around to face him.

'You don't have to do anything,' he says, wiping away escaped tears that run down my cheeks. 'You understand that, don't you? You don't have to do anything.'

My avoidance is my answer. I don't look at him. I can't. I don't want to see another thing I've got to lose. The unbearable ache swells through my chest, and my muscles begin to tremble as I attempt to restrain the sobs.

'Please, Em, I'll help you. We can get through this. Please, you don't have to do anything. Give it some time and see what happens. Let it play out.'

It sounds so simple, just to 'let it play out,' like it's a game of chess. And he's right. I could wait a few days. Wait a few years even; what difference would it make? I could carry on playing in this game – one of a battered sister, a screaming child and gradually disintegrating existence – until all my chess pieces are taken and all my moves done. Then I could send the envelope. I could turn around and change the rules, throw up the board, scatter the remains and start playing another game, a different game, only when I know I'm truly beaten. That's what Gabe wants me to do. That's what he's saying. And he's right; I should let it play out. But when did what's right and what we have to do ever coincide?

'I can't do that,' I say. 'I can't live with this.'

'You don't have to live with it forever, you know that. I'm just saying to give it some time.'

'How long, Gabe? How long should I give this?'

'I don't know, I don't, but please —'

He doesn't carry on.

'We could have picked her up,' I say quietly.

'You don't even know what happened.'

'I know she asked me to help —'

'Please, wait until the morning. See what she's like tomorrow.'

'Tomorrow?' I snort more harshly than I mean to. 'She took a girl, Gabe. Whether it was the right thing to do or not it doesn't matter. She's unstable. She had her arms inside the oven for God's sake. What normal person does that? What sane, human adult steals a child and burns her own flesh?'

'You don't know that she stole —'

'I don't know what the circumstances were, but I know you can't just take a child. There are laws, consequences. And even if she's not guilty of anything, I'll have to stand there and watch her be dragged away. I'll have to call the people to drag her away. I'm already losing her, you know that. If they take her, I won't be able to help her. They won't let her amend, not in that state. For crying out loud, she's worse than —'

The last word stays frozen between my lips. It hangs prodigiously in the air between us and causes the hairs on the back of my arms to rise.

'It's okay, Em. It's okay.'

Gabe pulls me into him, so close I can hear his heart beating, he draws my face up to look at him.

'I can't visit her in one of those places, Gabe,' I croak out through the tears. 'I can't. Not knowing I put her there. Not for a year, not for a day. You can't expect me to do that. You can't.'

'I know.'

He kisses me so gently it melts on my lips. I feel the muscles of my heart tear and rip one by one until they have been shred to nothing more than dust. Each second of his lips against mine is more painful than the last.

'I have to do this. You know I do.'

'In the morning then. I'll take you in the morning.'

'Please, Gabe.'

'In the morning,' he says again.

'In the morning,' I concede.

Gabe tries to speak again, but I press my fingers against his lips to silence him. There's nothing to talk about. With Fi in my bed, I lead him into my mother's empty room. I haven't been inside it since we emptied it. It should feel sad, morbid perhaps. But as I lie down next to Gabe, and he presses his lips against mine, it's no one's room but ours.

Chapter Nine

From the Book of Amendments
Rule 9. No amendment should ever be made in an attempt to undermine the sovereignty or rule of the Kingdom

I COULD HAVE let my mother go into a home – enough people do it and I thought about it often enough. I even visited a few, though none in our section – not that it would have made any difference. I never told Fi. I wanted to, but I never did. I don't know what I was more concerned about: that Fi might turn around and call me all the selfish, narcissistic names I probably deserved, or that she'd tell me I should have put our mother in a home where all the disinfectant and elevator music in the world couldn't cover up the stench of urine or the gut-wrenching screams of the residents. Besides, there had been rumblings in the rumour mill for years. The homes were too full, there weren't enough staff, there weren't enough resources to deal with the influx. So many people trying to bend the rules. So many people paying the price. There was talk of limiting the amount of time people could stay in them to just a few years – Proposition Six, it was called. What would happen to people when their time was up was never made clear – not that it would have mattered either way to our mother.

It might've been the tickling on my neck, but more likely it's the rubbish trucks with their incessant beeping that wake me. My eyelids are sealed closed from the gooey cake of sleep, and my vision returns clearly only after a fair amount of rubbing, prodding and probing. The room is in a dull half-light. The curtains, left open last night, are not the colour I expect. Nor are the walls. I attempt to stretch my legs and find them entangled, not with a sheet, but with another pair of legs.

My body freezes. Even when I realise where I am and the

wave of consciousness glides over me, my muscles remain tense. My heart beats in an unusually strong, thumping manner. Willing it to slow down has no effect, so I hold my breath instead, only to expel the air quickly in one large gasp. I silently pray to myself that Gabe is a deep sleeper. My head has found a spot in the night just below his collar bone, where it has nestled itself so snugly that it rises and falls with his breathing. I concentrate on that with a renewed sense of calm.

Then it all comes rushing back. My stomach plummets and pulse soars. I start to roll over, but Gabe's arm has me pinned. I wiggle myself out from under him, carelessly pushing him off my body. His yawn exposes a long line of white teeth, a random molar missing.

'Morning,' he says, reaching up to kiss me.

I turn my head so his lips land on my cheek. My stomach twinges as I watch his smile dissolve. His forehead furrows slightly.

'How did you sleep?' he says.

I grunt and drop my legs over the edge of the bed, turning my back to him. He grabs my hand and pulls me back down.

'Wait a second.'

'I need to check on Fi and the girl,' I say.

'They can wait. At least until you've woken up.'

I try to wrangle my way out of his grip, but he's not letting go.

'Gabe, I need —'

'If you're going to amend, five minutes won't make any difference.'

His face is fixed with resolve. I know I won't be able to budge him. I sigh and drop my wrist, then climb back into bed and pull the blanket up, wrapping my arms around my chest. Gabe wriggles up beside me, though I've not left much room. I don't make any extra either. The silence is palpable, embarrassingly so. I tug at the sheet to make sure every part of me is covered. Then I do the same thing a second time. And a third.

'Talk to me,' he says eventually.

'About what?'

'Anything.'

I dig my nails into my palm, but he stops me.

'Don't do that. Talk to me.' He raises my chin with the back of his fingers. 'Don't shut me out, Em. You don't have to do that.'

I brush his hand away. 'It's probably best if —'

'If what? You're being churlish. Is this about me? Us? Something I've done?'

'No,' I say hurriedly.

'Then you're going to need to give me some clues.' Sighing, he tucks a strand of hair behind my ear. His fingers follow the same path a second time, even though the hair is gone. 'It's going to be fine. In a minute we'll go and check on Fi and the little girl. And they'll tell us what happened. It's going to be fine.'

'And if it's not?'

'We'll find a way.'

'What if we don't?'

I consider telling him about my mother, but then he probably already knows most of what happened. Fi would've told him everything long before now. I want to tell him though. I've never spoken about what happened that day to anyone before, not even with Fi. Just the thought of people's reactions makes me want to curl up and cry.

My father left without fuss and without warning. I was fourteen at the time, Fi was just approaching her eighteenth birthday. One day he was with us, kissing us goodnight and teaching Fi how to drive with makeshift car pedals and a steering wheel at the dining room table. The next day my mother returned home to a half-empty wardrobe and hand-written note. She told us with red but steadfast eyes that he was gone, and she held it together, for a while.

It was a little over a year later that the obsessions started. One day we arrived home from school to find her sat at the kitchen table, spitting at the two silver lines on her palm in disgust. All she would talk about was that first envelope, and how she wished she'd never sent it. Fi and I exchanged glances. She'd had her moments of regret before, but somehow this felt different. Over time the episodes became longer and the space between them substantially diminished.

There have always been people who struggle to come to terms with their amendments and we knew that. For some, the concept alone is enough to drive them insane. It is difficult to reconcile with an idea of free will when you never know if a decision was actually your choice or just the convoluted ripple of a hundred amendments that have gone before you. Personally, I choose not to think that deeply about it. Still, it had been years since my mother received her first envelope and we thought the chance of her suffering from any amendment related afflictions were long gone. Now I know that's often the case. The longer you live, the harder it can be to reconcile with those decisions around which you plotted your destiny.

Next went cleanliness, then went her job at the factory. Still, we struggled through. I stopped going to school to stay home take care of her. Fi took more shifts at the bar; her presence in the house became less and less. It was a full three years later that my mother decided to take a risk and challenge the rules.

In a way, I can't blame her. It is true that we had all heard tales of the horrid things that happened when people tried to amend their amendments, but they were all just that: tales. There are other rumours that fly about too; people who run about with four scars on their palms and not a hint of the insanity, people who wake up with a new scar, but no new envelope. There had to be some flexibility in the rules; an element of luck or chance at least. That was what we all thought. In my mother's mind, when everything started to unravel, she knew exactly what day she needed to go back to. Again.

Breaking the rules affects everyone differently, or so I've heard. I can only assume the amendment never took, or otherwise things would have been different, our past invisibly changed and morphed into a new present. She staggered back from the centre, barely even coherent a fresh scar on her hand. Fi and I both knew what must have happened. I think deep down we may have even been expecting it. She lay on the bed writhing, clutching at her stomach and clawing at her skin until her nails snapped. I lifted the phone to call an ambulance, but Fi took it from me. After all, what could they tell us that we didn't already know? She'd tried to amend her amendment. The cost was her sanity and later, her life. There's a good chance it's cost me my sister's life, too.

I lie still in Gabe's arms for a while. Consciousness wicks heat away from the body in a way sleep never does.

'Can you check on the girl?' I say, pushing myself out of his hold. 'Please.'

This time he offers no objections.

Thick beads of condensation roll down the window and obscure the view from outside. Whatever heat is left in the flat drains through the walls. I wait for Gabe to leave before slipping on a T-shirt, pulling the curtains closed and checking that the windows are tight. The room still holds the faint scent of my mother, pressed into the worn carpet and yellow-wood furniture. I can see her here, sitting on the bed, staring at the scars on her hand. A heavy weight presses down on my chest; I've been in this room long enough.

It feels odd, to knock on my own bedroom door. I don't feel the need to wait for an answer, yet I stand there for a minute to steady myself with a few controlled breaths – in through the nose, out through the mouth. Or is that the wrong way around? It's not until I step inside that I realise I've had my eyes closed. When I open them, my jaw drops.

Fi is sitting on the window sill staring blankly at a peeling patch of paint on the wall. Her skin is covered with goose pimples and the bruises have bloomed purple and bleed into blue at the edges. The cut on her head has reopened and is trickling blood down the sides of her face, and the one eye that can open is glazed and unfocussed. It's the eyes that scare me the most.

'Fi,' I say.

She tilts her head and frowns, fixing in deep wrinkles above her brow.

'It's my fault,' she says matter-of-factly. 'He's dead and it's my fault.'

She twists away from me and gazes out the window. I cross the room, slowing my pace as I reach her.

'Who? Do you mean Andjrez?' I say softly. She doesn't reply. 'Fi, please, I want to help. What happened? Why is it your fault?'

She continues to stare at the wall.

'Poppy,' she says swivelling around, a sudden urgency in her voice. 'Is she okay?'

'Fi —'

'The girl, is she okay?'

'Fi, she's —'

'She wouldn't stop screaming. She screamed and screamed and screamed and then all of a sudden —'

'Fi, please. I need to know what happened.'

'He screamed, too.' Her voice drops to barely a whisper. 'He wouldn't stop. I thought he would. I thought that when… I thought when…'

'When what?'

She jerks her head around as if my presence is a surprise.

Glistening streaks weave down to her chin, rerouted by her trembling lips. She looks barely older than the child. The same look from last night flashes across her face – the look when she didn't recognise me. Her muscles tighten as I reach my hand out towards her.

'It's okay. It's me. It's Em.'

She nods slightly as her eyes return to the room and start welling up once again with tears. 'Poppy?' she utters.

'Gabe's checking on her.'

More tears tumble down. 'It was my fault.'

'What was?'

'He's dead. I could have stopped it. I knew the roads were closed… I wanted to get home. I should have done something —'

Her head flops against her shoulders, her good eye falling closed.

'Poppy's okay though?' she murmurs again.

'Fi?'

'That's good. At least I managed that.'

Gabe is sitting on the sofa, a limp body slung across his lap. It occasionally shudders as he furiously rubs her arms and legs. When he sees me he shakes his head.

'It must be the cold,' he says. 'I thought she was awake. She looked at me when I came into the room, then —'

'Nothing.'

'Yeah, nothing.' He continues to rub her goose-pimpled skin. 'We need to get her to a hospital.'

'No, we don't.'

He looks at me with feigned confusion. 'Em?'

'This is Fi's fault. Whatever happened.'

'You don't know that.'

'She told me.'

'Fi's sick. She doesn't know what she's saying.'

'All the more reason for me to do this now.'

I glance down at the girl. She could be four, seven, eight – I have no idea.

'Em?'

'What?'

He knows what I'm going to say. Gabe knows my decision, he always has. He stands, the girl in his arms, and carries her back to the bedroom. When he returns, his eyes are damp. I feel the heat begin to build up behind my own.

'Gabe —'

'No.' He presses his finger against my lips. 'This is my turn to speak.' He switches the radio on and soft music fills the room. 'Now, can I please have this dance?'

'Gabe.' I try to object.

He takes my hands and pulls me upright, interlocking his fingers behind my neck.

'Gabe.'

'My turn,' he says again.

My legs and hands are trembling and the inevitable well of tears breaks free and runs down my cheeks, wetting my skin. Still, I sigh and relent and rest my head against his shoulder. I never knew it was possible for a person to smell of warmth before.

'I know I can't stop you,' he says. 'Not if that's what you have to do. But can you promise me you'll try to remember one thing?'

'Gabe you know no one remembers —'

'Promise me you'll try?' He lifts my head away from his body. His eyes stare directly into mine.

'I'll try,' I say, staring back with the same intensity.

He lets my head fall back onto his shoulder. 'Try to remember that I love you,' he whispers into my ear. 'Because I do. I love you.'

My body shakes. I clench my jaw and try to stop the cascade of tears, but I can't. I want him to stop talking, stop him from making it so hard to do this. But he doesn't stop.

'I'm so sorry, Em,' he continues. 'I'm so sorry it took me so long. I'm so sorry I wasted so much time trying to pretend I didn't feel like this.'

'Gabe —'

'If I could make all this go away, if I had one of mine left, you know I'd let you have it. You know that, don't you?'

The song comes to an end, and we stand there, dancing with no music.

'We'll make it next time,' I tell him as he wipes the tears from my cheeks. 'I promise.'

He offers to come to the centre with me, but I insist he stays with Fi in the house. Having him there would make it harder to do. As I leave, he turns the radio down low; I don't look back. I can't.

Gabe is waiting by the door when I return. The flat is flooded with a dusky cinnamon coloured light. I didn't mean to stay our so long, but I couldn't come home. Instead I have been wandering the streets, unable to face what awaits me. Gabe doesn't say anything, or question my absence. The music is off. His eyes are bloodshot. He takes my hand and gently traces the two marks across my palm. Yesterday's curved line is faint against the new one, though I feel nothing. Not on my hand at least.

Part II

Chapter Ten

RETCHING SOUNDS are coming from Fi's room. I know I should go and check on her. She's probably lying there in that festering pit, drenched in her own vomit and clutching that fucking envelope until her palms bleed – but then who am I to judge her for that?

At first I thought it was a trick of the light. I had fallen asleep with surprising ease and even when the familiar sounds of morning wheedled their way through my bedroom windows I was less than willing to give that sleep up. I stirred in my bed, desperately trying to claim a few more moments, when something caught my eye. The winter sun had not yet broken the horizon, let alone stretched as far as my room, and I assumed the dark shadow to be nothing more than some misplaced book. I stretched my hand out from beneath the blanket to retrieve the item. That was when I saw what it was. I can't say how long ago that was. It feels as though I've been sitting like this for an eternity.

The lurid green envelope is sitting mockingly in my lap, while my nails dig more holes into my skin. Of course, to know what the thing says, I have to open it, but to do that means accepting it's actually here, and I'm not swayed that easily, even when the proof is so blatantly in the palm of my hand.

I stare at the thin line, barely begun to heal, yet flecked with silver threads as thin as hair and sliced left to right across my palm. It's definitely an amendment scar. Even without the envelope I'd know that. Registration lines go across your head line, — the groove in your palm that cuts across the centre — this one is lower and curves around my thumb along the life line; the line of the first amendment. I have amended my life. I wonder how long I got before I had to use it.

Studying the envelope for the hundredth time, I turn it over and over in my hand, rubbing the grain and running my fingers down each of the seals. It's pristine, as if the paper has been ironed. Perfectly smooth, perfectly folded, not a crease or a mark or a tear. It's got to be opened at some point – and I know I'm the only one who should do it – but I don't think I can right now, not even if I wanted to. Not the way my hands are shaking.

There's a knock on my door, and only one person I know knocks. Some of Fi's random friends used to get the wrong room, but even those types of friendships have dwindled to almost nothing recently. He knocks again, a little more firmly, making sure I can hear. His feet scuff on the creaking boards outside the door as he waits for a response, but my lips can't even manage to move. Eventually, he twists the handle and peers around the door, a glass of water in hand. His jaw plummets so fast it should be comical.

'But you haven't even registered yet,' Gabe says, placing the water on the table next to me.

'I know.'

'Fuck.'

'I know.'

He comes and sits on the end of the bed, and I show him the score along my palm. Despite the situation, my pulse still quickens when he takes my hand to examine it more closely.

'Have you seen it like this before? With just the amendment scar?' I ask. 'How is that possible? Surely I must have registered?'

'You must have done,' Gabe says, but he shakes his head as he speaks, his eyes still fixed on the solitary line. He is a dumbfounded as I am.

'What does it say?'

'I don't know, I can't open it.'

'I remember that feeling.' He smiles and places my hand back on my lap.

'What if I just don't open it?' I say. 'People do that, don't they? They just don't open them, let fate play out.'

'True, but you're not that kind of person.'

'How do you know?'

'You wouldn't have sent the envelope.'

'It's green. I don't suppose you have any idea if that's meant to mean anything, do you?' I ask.

He opens his mouth to reply when a heavy bout of retching interrupts us. Gabe looks momentarily apologetic before he stands and moves towards the door.

'You have to open it. Soon,' he says. 'You don't want to miss it.' He looks at me for a second longer, then leaves. Through the wall I hear Fi's groans and whines in protest as he attempts to help her, but I don't go and offer any assistance, not today.

Gabe is right about the envelope. I do have to open it. Although I reason to myself – with good justification – that there's no need to hurry. Whatever happened must have taken place after I'd registered, and I wasn't planning on going to the Annex unwashed. I grab a folded towel from the wardrobe and head to the bathroom.

Our bathroom smells of cheap citrus cleaner and mould. The tiles are chipped and cracked, and all the grouting has become black dirt over the years. But it's a bathroom. It works. I prop up the envelope behind the sink where the green image blurs in the foggy mirror. I stare at it, waiting for something – anything – to happen. But it's just paper. What is written on the inside is what matters.

After a few more minutes staring, and some lazy brushing of my teeth, I wedge myself into a corner of the shower and brace as the water spurts in random angles from the rusted head. It flashes hot for just a minute before turning so cold it could be spluttering out chunks of ice. Bent doubled, I hastily scrub my hair. The soap's so cheap that it barely lathers or smells but stings significantly as it trickles off my hair and into my eyes, but it does the job. Besides, it's all we have.

Outside the shower is, if possible, even colder. I furiously try to dry myself with the thinnest towel, sliding the water over my skin. Maybe when I find a job and we have some money I'll treat us to some new towels. I chide myself. What a stupid thought to be having, now of all times. As if towels are really a priority in our current circumstances. A few minutes of vigorous rubbing and my body is hardly dry, but, for the most part, it's not dripping.

Without prompting or reason, my wet hands reach for the envelope. A fast rhythm pulses in my chest and extends all the way down to the pit of my stomach, churning up the emptiness with a nauseating swiftness. The harder it beats, the stronger I struggle to ignore it. There is no card or note laying wait for me inside; I know this already. That is not the way amendment envelopes are. Just one thin sheet of paper which will unfold into a perfect four-pointed star.

I slide my fingers underneath the upper flap and release the first frictionless seal. The water quickly warps the paper and causes it to stick at the edges. I separate the lower seal with a little more force, tearing through one of the seams, before folding out the edges and opening the envelope flat. I hold the single piece of paper on my hand, its bent edges tilting towards the sky. Just three words are written, scrawled across the centre, penned in my hand.

I lose count of the number of times I read the words over and over. I say them again and again, sometimes out loud, sometimes in my head, until the sounds themselves become nothing more than dissonant syllables of disconnect.

A lightness floods me, before being replaced by a sickening weight that buckles my knees. It was always going to be for her.

Chapter Eleven

I PEER THROUGH the bedroom door. Fi's sleeping is fitful, full of twitching legs and exasperated moaning. The alcohol must be wearing off, although I'm confident she'll find more.

Gabe is no longer in the living room or – a quick check reveals – the apartment. He never leaves until he's seen Fi awake and conscious, so something must be on at the bar. Either that or he decided he didn't want to be here today. I can't blame him.

In the kitchen I pour myself another drink of water and try not to think about the heaviness in my chest. If I think about it I'm not sure I'll find a way out. Birthdays were always an event in our family – parties, cakes and presents – when we could afford them, and often when we couldn't. My mother's infectious laugh would fill the house as she showered us with attention and made us feel like we were the most important thing in the universe. Somehow, I thought Gabe would remember that. Especially today. Especially this one. But then there's no real reason why he would, just like there's no reason he should feel the need to stay and help me figure out the envelope. Having Gabe around all the time makes it hard to remember that we're the ones obligated to him, not the other way around, assuming of course that Fi still has a job after whatever she pulled last night.

Ripples have formed on the surface of my water. They reflect and build into peaks which splash up the inside of the glass. I try to steady my hand, but the trembling only quickens. The more I try, the faster it becomes. Soon it's not just my hand that's trembling. My legs, my lungs; my whole body is slipping out of my control.

Within seconds, all the emotions I had managed to suppress since seeing my envelope come rushing to the surface. Wheezy and rapid gulps of air are forced in and out of my lungs. My legs shake with such ferocity that I feel the muscles spasm in my thighs. Tears pour down my cheeks and collect in salty pools between my lips, but I make no move to wipe them away. The water in my hand sploshes higher and higher, spilling over the edge of the glass onto my bare feet. I try again to steady myself, or at least place the glass down, but I have lost control. With a loud smash, my hand is empty, my feet drenched and the floor showered with fragments of coloured glass and puddles of water.

I sink onto the cold linoleum flooring, gasping. Shards of glass stab at me as I rock back and forth, cradling my knees and choking on my own breaths. I shiver and cough and splutter. Blood from my legs seeps through my towel and swells into perfect circles. I can't feel it. I can't feel anything other than an overwhelming sense of loss. I sit there on the floor until the sobs become stifled whimpers and my throbbing head is dry and aching. How long that takes I do not know.

After a time, my feet start tingling from pins and needles, and I force myself to stand. My head is throbbing, pulsing behind my eyeballs and right around my skull. I blink a few times to try to straighten my thoughts and then slowly take in the scene around me. The place is a mess. An embarrassment. Thick scum lines the sink, and with all the broken bits of glass, empty cans and cigarette butts, it looks like a place even squatters would turn their nose up at – hardly a family kitchen. I thought I was keeping on top of things. Clearly that is not the case. Still rubbing my temples, I hunt down a dustpan to sweep up the shattered glass. I can't tell what mess is mine and what's Fi's.

My chest jolts as the front door clicks open and then shut again.

'Em?' Gabe calls.

I pinch at the rounds of my cheeks and rub away any stray tears before Gabe appears, his arms full of groceries.

'I hope you don't mind,' he says in a neutral tone. 'I just got a few bits. You've got nothing in at all.'

His eyes rest on mine. I cut in before he starts saying something pitying. The last thing I want from Gabe is more pity.

'You didn't have to,' I say.

'It's not much.'

'Well you didn't have to.'

My insides twist, and we both wait through an awkward pause for one another to speak again. A hot flush of red flashes in my cheeks.

'I should put this stuff away,' Gabe says finally and moves to unpack.

I mutter apologetically as he struggles to find a clean surface to unload before he begins to stuff boxes of cereal and grains into random empty cupboards.

'I should go get dressed,' I say, suddenly realising my current towel-clad state.

'Okay,' Gabe responds. 'I'll get on with this.'

I get dressed as fast as I can, not wanting to leave Gabe responsible for the chaos of our kitchen for too long. When I return he still has a fair way to go. He doesn't ask me to help though. Instead he looks me straight in the eye.

'So, what did it say?' he asks.

I take in a lungful of air, before saying the words out loud.

'Pick up Fi.'

'That's all?'

'That's all.'

'Does it say from where? Or when?'

'No, just *Pick up Fi*. I could have been a little less cryptic.'

'You wouldn't have been cryptic,' he says. 'You just have to pick up Fi. Sounds straightforward enough.'

With the food away, he begins to tidy, picking up stray drink cans and cigarette butts that she's left on the floor. At one point, he picks up a shard of the broken glass still glistening wet with blood from my thigh. He says nothing as he throws it straight into the bin.

'You don't have to do this,' I say.

'I want to help.'

He stacks the crockery and cutlery in the sink and runs them under the tap while I grab a damp tea-towel and start to dry, dragging knives through my closed covered fist and leaving long smeared smudge marks on chipped tableware.

I pick up a plate, turning it around and around in my hand. It's a repetitive action, one that lets me momentarily drift away in my thoughts. Then, without warning, my stomach corkscrews. It tightens with each rotation of the plate, slowly at first, then faster and faster, spinning then spiralling and coiling my insides. As my gut is seized by a paralysing realisation I drop the plate back into the sink and catch myself against the countertop, banging my knees against the cupboard as I manage to keep myself upright.

'Em, what's wrong?'

My lungs constrict beneath my ribs as I fight for air.

'Are you okay?' Gabe says. 'Em, you need to sit down.'

'I can't, it can't mean that. I can't do it,' I say.

I flick away his hand, but he persists.

'What can't you do?' he says.

'Any of it, I can't do it, the envelope, this place, what it says. I don't drive, how can I pick her up? I can't get to her. She's going to need my help, and I won't be able to get there. I can't stop this. I can't stop this.'

'Em, it's fine.'

'No, no, it's not. I'm going to fail. I'm going to fail, again.'

He peels my hands from the counter and clasps them.

'You are not going to fail,' he says. 'You did not send yourself something cryptic and you will not fail.'

He holds my gaze so fixedly and intently that sweat starts to seep over the surface of my hand. I don't think anyone's ever looked at me for that long before.

'Gabe —'

'No buts.'

'Gabe, I don't drive.'

'So?'

'So, how can I pick her up?'

'I'll pick her up.'

'It doesn't say you.'

'It doesn't not say me.'

'Gabe —'

'It's fine. I'll be with you. We'll do it together. We can do this.' He holds my gaze for barely a second longer before he lets go of my hands and returns to the dishes as if his words have solved everything.

'You have to work,' I say.

'I've taken the day off,' he replies.

I stop, surprised. 'You have?'

'I was going to offer to take you to the Annex anyway,' he says. 'If that's okay?'

The tension that has constricted my stomach is joined by the faintest fluttering. 'Thank you,' I manage to say.

'I wanted to,' he says.

While Gabe starts on breakfast, I leave to rouse Fi. It takes a minute before I can persuade myself to step into her room. She is in a deeper sleep now. One I'd love to leave her in. But I know she'll get up at some point. Then she'll go somewhere. Somewhere which I must pick her up from. Finally, I take the plunge. Taking the longest strides I can, I force my way through the mounds of rubbish and pull back the curtains, flooding her room with light and illuminating the true extent of the grime in which she is sprawled.

'Fi.' I make my way to her bed. 'You need to get up. Gabe's made breakfast.'

She grunts, twisting between the sheets to avoid the light.

'Fi, did you hear me?'

'I'm sleeping,' she groans.

The room aroma is a putrid stale blend of alcohol, cigarettes and vomit.

'Fi?' Ignoring the piles of clothes that require tidying, I snatch the bedcover away. Her body snaps momentarily upwards before she slumps back down, covering her head and muttering.

'Get up,' I say.

She gropes blindly for the pillow, but I get it first. Her scowling mouth and scrunched eyelids are exposed for just a second before she rolls over and buries her head in the mattress.

'Fi, I need to talk to you.'

'Later.' She squashes her face deeper into the mattress and puts her hands over her ears.

'I need to go out, and I need to talk to you first, so I'm not leaving this room until you get up.' I tug at her top. 'Finola!'

'Fine,' she snaps. 'Just let me have five more minutes.'

'This is important.'

'So's my sleep.'

'Fi!' I bring down the pillow and whack her across the head.

'For fuck's sake, Em, just fuck off!'

'Fi!'

'Five minutes!'

'If you're not up in five minutes, I'm getting a bucket.' I throw the cover back on the bed and slam the door, leaving the light fitting to wobble in my wake.

Gabe has made breakfast for three, and with Fi's left in the oven, the two of us eat ours together. It's bland. It's hardly his fault – there's not exactly an exotic spice rack of choice in our kitchen, or anywhere in the Kingdom. A momentary distraction infiltrates my thoughts as I consider trying to grow some herbs. Sorrel, rosemary — they're meant to be pretty hardy. Probably not hardy enough to survive this family though, I decide. That ends that.

I chew slowly, each mouthful like sawdust clogging in my

gullet as I struggle to swallow. I want to leave it, but Gabe is insistent.

"They take a lot of blood," he reminds me. "You really don't want to faint. Not today."

We are still eating when Fi appears, dragging her feet across the carpet. Last night's eye makeup is a good inch lower than where it started although she has managed to dress herself, even if her choice of clothing is somewhat eclectic. Around her wrist she wears her silver bracelet. I draw my eyes away from it before they start to water.

Fi collapses onto the sofa with a groan. Without waiting for her to speak I retrieve her breakfast from the oven, then swing her legs around and move to sit down next to her, planting the warm plate on her lap. She sighs, nudging at the edge of the food with her fingers.

'Fi, if you go out today I need you to ring me, okay? I don't care where you are. Whatever you're doing, if you need picking up you must wait for me and Gabe to come and get you. You must wait for us. Do you get that, Fi?'

She grunts, now pushing her eggs around her plate with her fork.

'Fi?'

'What?'

'Did you get that?'

'What?'

'You need to ring me.'

'Yes,' she snaps, putting her untouched plate on the floor. 'I'll ring you.'

'When?'

'I don't know, whenever you tell me.' She lies back on the sofa, closing her eyes.

'This is important. I need you to promise.'

'Fine.'

'I mean it.'

'Fine, I promise.' Her head lolls back, drool bubbling in the corner of her mouth. She is an amalgamation of everything hopeless, an exact combination of infantile and infirm.

She wasn't always like this, I remind myself. And it's not her fault. I wish I didn't need reminding of that last bit as often as I do. Amendments can take their toll on people even when they get it right. When they don't... well she got off lightly compared to others.

I take Fi's plate and put her food back in the oven; she always gets hungry when the sickness wears off. Gabe is gazing at her, his eyes off in some distant place – probably a place where Fi actually acknowledges him. There's a stab of jealously in my gut as I leave the two of them alone.

My bed is unmade, and yesterday's clothes are slung in a pile on the floor. After the swiftest of tidies – and a quick double-check of the envelope – I retrieve a book from the shelf. It's highly unlikely Fi will decide to read something, and even if she does, an eighteenth-century poetry anthology would rarely be her first choice.

I cast a last look at the envelope and its incommodious green hue before sliding it inside the book and returning it to the brickwork of reams and bindings. I could take it with me, but it's unlikely I'll forget what it says, particularly not with the burning that has begun to sear its way through my hand. From another of the books – a children's book – I take the remainder of my mourner's money. I count out the dwindling notes before tucking them into my pocket; I'll offer some to Gabe for the food and fuel.

I am almost done in my bedroom, when my eyes fall on my chest of drawers. I walk over, open the top drawer and retrieve my thickest pair of gloves and socks. There's no reason for it that I can fathom — today is no colder than the rest of the week has been — but I've a niggling feeling that I'll need them somehow. It's probably just a residual coldness from this morning's shower.

As we go to leave, Fi appears in the bathroom doorway, her apparently washed face now smeared in mascara stains. Thankfully, at least, a toothbrush hangs from the corner of her mouth.

'You promise you'll ring me?' I say.

'Yes. I promise,' she replies. A crease appears in her forehead, her mind visibly in the transitory place between thought and speech.

She's in there, the old Fi. I can see her battling the demons, struggling to form some kind of link in her purgatorial existence, but it's still too hard. I get that, more now than I can let her know.

She spins around, disappearing back into the bathroom, and then calls out, through a mouthful of toothpaste, 'Where are you going anyway?'

The words strike me like a bat to the stomach. I look up to the ceiling lights and wrestle away the rising tears. Gabe squeezes my hand tightly.

'Just to run some errands,' he says. My hand stays in his until the empty lift arrives.

Chapter Twelve

DESPITE THE EMPTY roads, the car journey is slow. Weather warnings have been repeated for days, and Gabe is driving with particular caution. Anyway, we have nothing to rush for – the Administration shuts down between 1 and 2 pm. We've missed the morning ceremony so we may as well take our time and absorb the derelict views. Buildings with boarded windows and graffitied walls are the norm here. A few people amble through their everyday lives, cocooned in as many layers of clothing as possible. I know we must be getting close when glass starts appearing in the windows. When the river comes into view I push myself up against the window. Even with all that is going on, I'm desperate to see that first glint of gold, glimmering off the spire. When I do see it, it does not disappoint.

The Annex has an opulence that exceeds even the richer sections; it's only made of stone and metal, but somehow it looks so much more. The thick girders and heavy lead glass have been pillaged and pilfered from a time and place when the world plundered the planet's resources without a second thought. It's different now. If it can't be mined in the Kingdom we can't have it. Not unless you're willing to go scavenging outside the city boundaries, and not many people are.

A cluster of marchers are gathered outside the Annex. For now, their placards are at their feet, but I'm sure they'll start waving about their fliers and chasing down cars soon enough. I don't get it. I don't get how anyone could be opposed to something which makes life inherently better. To be opposed to that seems along the same lines as self-flagellation. I may not know what happened to Fi last time, but I know for certain I'm not going to let it happen again. Come hell or high water, I will pick her up.

Gabe drives below the main building into the strip-lit basement and parks. Immediately I take my phone from my bag, clutch it in my hand and wait. My toes rub nervously together in my thin-soled boots. And it's only 1:20 pm. I sense a long day ahead. Gabe keeps the engine running. The tiny grates that blast hot air provide some deterrent to the silence that grows acutely conspicuous. I pick at the skin around my nails and forage my thoughts for topics of conversation, but none come to hand. In the end, I decide it's easier not to talk. Gabe decides differently.

'I've used both of mine. You probably know that,' he says, showing me his palm. The silver ridges of well-healed scars are just visible among the worn crevices of hard working hands.

I did know he'd used both because I overheard him talking to Fi about it before. As today doesn't feel like the type of day for hiding things, I just come straight out and ask.

'What colour were they?' I say. As the words leave my mouth, a sensation surges somewhere in the back of my head, telling me I already know the answer. It's possible that I overheard that part as well.

'One was black,' he says.

'Do you think about what happened?' I say, rubbing my legs, my hands now pink from the heater.

'I used to,' he says. 'All the time. Wondering what I'd done, who I'd done it to. I'd think about stuff too much, convince myself that … well, you know.' He shakes his head apologetically. 'Not any more, though, not when I can help it. It's too easy to get sucked into. Besides,' he adds. 'Most people don't believe in the whole colour superstition anyway.'

I understand what he means about getting sucked into the thoughts. Already I find my mind trapped in a future that hasn't even happened and focusing on a past that may never exist.

We whittle away the rest of the time talking about the registration, mainly the ceremony and the absurdity of maintaining out-dated traditions when most people are either too young or too ignorant to have any real understanding of the true significance. When people first discovered retrocausality could be harnessed, they needed some way to make the link between the envelopes and the amenders. DNA proved the perfect solution. The silvering skin was a side effect, but now it's used to keep track. The marks on the hand mean you know in an instant. We like to think there's no stigma attached to using amendments, but there is. We all know there is.

Gabe tells tales of fainting and fighting and fleeing at his own ceremony.

'You know, you were able to choose where you got scarred

before. Not that long ago,' he said.

'That can't be true.'

'It is. I saw it once. An old man, scars straight down his cheeks.'

'He got scarred on his face?'

'Nope.'

It takes a moment to sink in. 'That's horrible! Do I even want to know how you know that?'

'Probably not. But I do own a bar remember.'

Gabe grins. The dimples in his cheeks make me turn away, blushing. I divert my attention to my own scar, so new, yet already the tell-tale signs of silver are weaving their way through my skin. When we were young Fi and I used to draw lines on our hands, pretending that we had amended. This looks like one of those. Unreal. An imposter. Gabe carries on with more stories. I'm not sure I believe him about the scarring, but it offers a good distraction.

'If that's true, though,' I say, still studying my hand, 'more people would do it. Hide the scars, I mean.'

He shrugs. 'I guess that's why the Administration doesn't announce it. Maybe not many people know, or maybe it's illegal now, who knows?'

'Surely it would be in the rules if it was illegal?'

'I suppose.'

I think about it for another minute. 'They were probably painted on, or something?' I say.

Gabe shakes his head. 'You know an amendment scar when you see one.'

I can't disagree with that. I'm not convinced, but the stories are amusing and I'm appreciative of the effort he's making. A few times I feel my lips twitch or my eyes squint, teetering on the edge of a half-smile, but it never quite manages to form. I want to let it, I really do, but today's not the day to start smiling, not yet anyway.

'Do you think I have to go?' I say, staring at the single misplaced line on my palm. 'I mean, I must have done it last time. I must have registered then.'

'I don't know,' Gabe says. 'Ask someone up there, I guess.'

Just before two, I gather my things. Other people are leaving their cars and forming a queue by an elevator.

'I'll wait here for you,' Gabe says. He turns on the radio.

Randomly dispersed plainclothes guards loiter around the basement, hands in their pockets. They would be less conspicuous in their uniforms. Most of the people registering look on with a respectful disdain; it's not a job they would ever do, not this time around at least. They would rather risk the mines or the factories. Unfortunately for the Guards, they still carry the burden of the past; when the old world began to fall apart and the Cabinet needed some muscle to make certain elements of the population see sense. People still don't like to be associated with that. Not directly

The elevator is wrought iron, with a folding door and metal handle worn smooth over the years. Its rusted and weathered mechanisms are exposed, and from the mutters emerging in the queue, more than a few are dubious of its ability.

'It'll be fine,' I say to a girl beside me.

She's unconvinced and looks close to tears. Her bottom lip is trembling and her eyes keep flicking upwards. She reminds me of a frog. I half expect a foot-long tongue to spring from her mouth and snatch up a fly from the cobwebs in the corner. She hardly looks old enough to register, but then she can't be any younger than me, not even by a day. I consider telling her that I've made it up here once, and that if I have we all have, but I don't. I stay quiet.

As the last in the lift, I pull the doors closed. The chains clank and wind around the metal cogs, yanking us upwards. I lose my balance and bump into the boy next to me, who grunts, unimpressed. The faces in the elevator range from trepidation to sheer terror and only one person is smiling. His lips are as crooked as the teeth he reveals and one side of his nose twitches in a vermin-like manner. He looks like he wants to amend, like he's looking forward to receiving a black envelope. For all I can tell, he may already have one.

I feel a nudge to my left and realise we've stopped. I open the door and let the others elbow past, spilling their way into the Foyer. I can wait. I steal a glance at my phone.

Murmurs of apprehension and anticipation flood the room. It's a gaggle of voices, each as indistinct as the next one. Every snippet of conversation I catch is mundane and unimportant. Mostly, they confirm the emotions transparent on their faces, varying from hysteria to terror and euphoria. I wonder what happened twenty-one years and nine months ago – give or take –

to make today so popular. I don't know how many people I expected, but it definitely wasn't this many.

A few guards are standing idly around up here, too, but I can see no one that I can ask about my envelope. Things resembling queues start materializing in snakes around the wall. I slip into one of the coils and wait.

The girl behind me offers a timid smile. It's the same girl from the lift, froggy girl. I deliberately start rummaging in my bag for my papers as if I haven't noticed her, but from the corner of my eye I see her look of disappointment. A pang of guilt tries to coerce me into sparking up a conversation, but I've never been that good at small talk, even on the best of days.

We grind forward achingly slowly, a quarter step at a time, while the monotonous drone of dull conversation numbs my will to keep going. I think about stepping out of the line, marching to the front and finding an administrator, showing them my palm and explaining that I shouldn't be waiting here in this banal queue with these people. I even contemplate storming out altogether – after all, what difference can it make? I've clearly done it before anyway. We all have. What's even scarier is none of us know how many times.

I scrutinise my phone instead: the screen, the volume, the battery, the seal, the light, every feature I can possibly find that might somehow disrupt Fi's call. I've received no calls yet. Nor have I two minutes later when I next check, or a further five minutes after that. I think about turning my phone off and on again, just to check it's working, but merely the thought causes a sudden panic that the split second the phone is off might be the exact moment Fi decides to ring. I leave the phone on, though my heart-rate still takes a minute to go back down. The froggy girl behind me is now smiling as she chats away to someone else who looks like a far better conversationalist than I would have been.

It takes nearly forty minutes for me to reach the front. Behind the warped glass partition, an administrator taps her nails impatiently. I move my lips and try to form a question, but the queue behind me has me doubting that this is the right place to ask. There's a surge of heat around my cheeks as I desperately try to figure out what to do. The administrator raises her eyebrows expectantly, but the words and nerves continue to waver on the tip of my tongue, I open my mouth one last time, when she tuts loudly. Swallowing down the churning in my stomach I give my name and show her my documentation.

The whole time I'm waiting, my heart is drumming in expectation. I assume it must say something on the screen in front of her, she must know about my amendment, but if she does, she's doing a damn good job of hiding it. She processes the information efficiently, occasionally flicking out her tongue and running it along her unfaltering false smile. How fingers can do anything with such obscenely long nails I have no idea, but at least she manages to wear slightly less makeup than the one at the next window.

'All done,' she says. 'Now, if you can just place any electronic devices through the partition —'

'Electronic devices?'

'That's right, electronic devices: phones, computers, musical devices – anything that runs on a cellular or electronic source,' she says. Her lips are fixed in an upwards spiral at each end. 'Just through the partition,' she repeats.

A hammering starts in my chest. It moves from just below my breastbone until my whole body is pulsating. I tighten my grip around the phone and move my hands towards my chest.

'If you would just slide them through the partition,' she says again.

'I'm sorry,' I say. 'I, I —' My pulse is racing so hard I can't even hear myself think. I breathe out a heavy puff of air, count to ten in my head, then speak as slowly and calmly as I can. 'Would I be able to keep my phone on me, silently of course?' I say, even managing to add a slight smile at the end.

Her tongue flicks out again at remarkable speed. 'I'm afraid that won't be possible. All electronic devices are prohibited beyond the Foyer.'

'I understand that. It's just I —'

'No electronic devices are allowed in the ceremony. There are no exceptions.' Her head tilts to the side, although her smile and flicking tongue manage to stay perfectly horizontal.

'Could I give it to somebody then? They can hold onto it for me. I'll leave the ceremony if it rings. It's just —'

'I'm sorry,' she says, her forced smile now so high it has squashed her eyes into two tiny slits. 'But you will have to hand your phone in or find another place for it.'

'Please, if you would —'

'No cellular electronics are permitted beyond the Foyer.'

My back molars grind deeper into each other. Both of my hands are balled into white knuckled fists that tremble as I fight to keep them clamped tightly to my side. My tongue smacks against the roof of my mouth as I speak.

'Then can I speak to someone? Please?' I say.

'Speak to someone?' She cocks her head. 'Who would you like to speak to?'

'Somebody else. Somebody who will listen, perhaps.'

She flinches at the insult but remains professionally composed.

I however am not. 'Or someone with some actual authority,' I push.

'If you could be a little more specific —'

'A little more specific?' A bitter smile creeps across my face. 'Of course. Sorry. Yes, more specific. I need to speak to someone, specifically, who can tell me how I'm supposed to deal with this.' I slam my hand against the glass pane.

A shock wave of pain shoots through my arm and down my spine but it's worth it just to see the fake smile falter.

'Just one moment,' she says, once her lips have curled firmly back upwards.

I am taken to a broom-cupboard of a room by a stern-looking older administrator. No amount of pleading helps. I give embittered descriptions of my horrific life history and spin tales of the possible catastrophic events that will await should they refuse me, but none of it makes any difference.

'It was black,' I lie as a last-ditch attempt, but the decision is final – I must register and attend the ceremony, without my phone. However unique my situation is to me, they have seen it before. Rules are rules. I have to stick to them.

As the administrator's eyes and lips creep upwards in a sneer, I turn away.

'I'm ever so sorry we couldn't be of more help,' she says.

'Bitch,' I reply, almost under my breath.

Gabe gets out of the car when he sees me coming.

'What happened? Why are you the only one coming out?'

'Oh, I haven't registered. I haven't even signed in.' I snort, waving my phone by way of explanation.

'Shit,' he says. 'I'm so sorry. I should have remembered that.'

'It's not your fault. I should have thought.'

'It's not really a priority today, though, is it?'

'Not really.'

A piece of hair falls in front of my eyes, and Gabe moves as if to correct it. His hand hovers awkwardly by my ear while I swiftly replace it. His cheeks are a good shade redder when he speaks.

'What do you want me to do if she rings?' he says.

'What do you mean?'

'Well, do you want me to pick her up or wait for you?'

'Wait,' I say straight away before reconsidering and changing my mind. 'No, on second thought, don't wait. You go get her. It didn't say who had to pick her up.'

'You sure?'

'No, but I'm not going to get any surer.'

'Fair enough.'

As he smiles, I lean forward and kiss him on the cheek. My lips press against his stubble and sink into the hollow beneath his skin. The corners of my lips brush against his. I jolt back in realisation.

'God, I'm … oh God.'

'It's fine.'

'I'm so —'

'You should get back.'

'Definitely. I should. Thank you, thank you, for everything, for… you know what I mean.'

My cheeks are burning, my mouth arid and humiliation at an all-time high. I step backwards and stumble on a loose concrete slab.

'Em?'

'No, I mean it. I'm so grateful, you're so good, I mean you've been so good, to me, to us, to Fi, I mean.'

'It's no problem, any of it. If she doesn't ring, I'll see you here when you finish. If she does, I'll be back at home with Fi.'

'Well, thank you,' I say, stretching out my arm for a handshake before snapping it back to my side and turning swiftly on the balls of my feet.

'Em,' he says.

I spin around. 'Yes?'

'Do you want to give me the phone?'

In the Foyer I re-join the depleted queue. The smug smile is still plastered on the administrator's face, and she doesn't ask for my name before taking my documentation. Her face looks like it might crack when I say I have no electronic devices.

She gives me some papers and I pass through a door to the side of the Annex and into a long hallway. A series of doors confronts me. I hover in front of the first, but for no real reason dismiss it and move to the fifth door instead. The light above the door turns green the moment I reach for the handle. It swings open with barely a touch.

The room is cold and stark with only some non-descript furniture and a couple of plastic, vacuum-formed chairs to fill the space. The air is heavy with cleaning fluids and medical smells, and everything, from the doors to the walls, is mundane gunmetal grey. I don't feel like sitting so kick at a chair with my shoe and leave it jutting out at a strange angle. I continue to stand as I skim read the forms I have been given, before scribbling my name at all the appropriate places. I don't need to read the rules. Not today.

A low bulb is flickering by a door. I go over to it and try tapping it with my fingers to make it stop. When that doesn't work I try a more forceful rapping at the glass with my knuckles, but neither method makes any difference and I quickly grow bored. As I give up, an administrator appears in one of the doorways and motions for me to sit.

Her hand runs over her bulging belly as she waddles across the room and lowers herself carefully into a chair. Without looking up, she takes several vials and a tourniquet from a battered filing cabinet and begins to slip the leather around my arm.

She falters at my palm, thin lines forming between her eyebrows. Her eyes flicker between my face and my hand. My heart quickens as I realise she could know something, something from before. Maybe they have a list identifying us, maybe she knew who I was before the door even swung open. I want to ask her, but in a blink the lines are gone, her lips are relaxed and the strap is pulled tightly as the vial begins to fill with blood.

Her eyes continue to dart back and forth as the vials are filled. This look I recognise. I've seen it enough. Sympathy.

'You're done,' she says when the third one is full, but I don't move. Blood is swilling without direction inside my head, and images flutter loosely out of focus as a heaving thrumming beats behind my eyes. I wait for it to pass.

'I thought there'd be more,' I say, trying to shake my head clear as she tidies away a starkly empty area, including my thin pile of signed papers. 'I thought I had to give more blood.'

Her brow furrows. 'Last time. You would have had more last time.'

'But I don't need that now?' I say. She shakes her head and hands me two small orange tablets and a glass of water. The pity that drips from her face makes me cringe. I avoid her eyes.

'It's to replace the iron,' she says.

I swallow the tablets, without the water. I'm aware of her eyes, still fixed on me as she runs her hand across the fabric of her dress. She's barely older than Fi and she's lucky to have a job here, out of view, away from the risks of the centres. Administrators are not known to have children. Apparently, it affects their loyalty to the cause. It's all hearsay, but that doesn't mean it's not true. I've never actually spoken to one outside the realms of their job, and even then, only at school when they came into drill the us on the Rules of Amending from the *Book of Amendments*. When I look up, I catch her eye. The moment elongates.

I should ask her, I think, ask her what she knows about the colours, about how the envelopes reach us. Ask her about me, if there's somebody out there that knows what happened and what I did, what Fi did. Her eyes are locked on me. She's waiting for me to ask.

Instead – and despite the hundreds of questions that burn in my chest – I lower my eyes and stay silent because I suspect that just in that second, she may tell me, and I'm not sure I want to know.

A ringing starts, blaring from a speaker below the light, and kicks the moment away.

'You need to go through now,' she says, motioning to one of the doors.

My vision blurs again as I stand. I lean forward to balance myself. It passes quickly. Steadily, I walk towards the door.

'Emelia?' she says as my hand moves for the door handle.

'Yes.'

'I do hope it works out for you this time.'

'Thank you,' I say. 'So do I.'

She fell onto my lap and into my heart, my father would say, as he swept my mother up in his arms and carried her like they were newlyweds. Even when they fought, they made up with these passionate declarations of love and overzealous gestures. No wonder it broke her – she never saw it coming; none of us did. I knew I would think of them both when I came here.

I spin around, turning in a circle away from the memories and absorbing the air that surrounds me. It's unfeasibly pure: no muggy stench, no smog, no thick grey clouds that cling to your lungs and suffocate your skin. I close my eyes and imagine the breeze; this could be mountain air it's so sweet. Not that I've ever experienced mountain air that I know of.

House martins flutter among the rafters in the ceiling. It is a room conceived for greatness, though the main magnificence is in the delicacy: the refinement of the marble mosaic floor, the subtle warmth of deep wood, the breath-taking purity of unsullied light. Anyone could fall in love here.

I take one of the few spare seats near the front, as I don't want to get caught in some sudden kerfuffle when I try to leave. With that thought in mind, I shift again so I'm even closer to the exit.

My vision is still spinning. I close my eyes and cradle my head in my hands in an attempt to shield myself from the unfeasible brightness. It soon becomes apparent that layers of lead couldn't stop this light, so I use the time instead to observe my surroundings.

Some people look decidedly better than others. A pair of twins in sack-like dresses are busy comforting each other. Their faces are streaked in tears, but they have no scars on their hands that I can see, so it can't be that bad.

The froggy girl from before is sitting at the back, so close to her new friend that their shoulders are touching. The poor girl shuffles uncomfortably — she has little room to move away.

A hush filters through the room and I twist my neck around to see the cause. An imposing figure makes her way for to the front, almost Cabinet-esque in the way she holds authority in the room. She's not part of the Cabinet though, I can tell that straight away. Embroidered on her collar is the likeness of Margaret of Cortona, Saint of Second Chances — not to mention insanity and penitent women. A small, sadistic chuckle escapes my lips. I wonder if the Administration know just how good a fit their chosen deity is for some of us.

By the time the administrator has taken her place on the stage, the only sounds are the chirping of the martins and the creaking of the benches as people lean in for a better view. From this close, her face is a patchwork. Leather jowls wobble as she limps up to the podium, her paper-thin skin crinkled like linen and covered in a batik of liver spots that disappear down her neck.

I tune out almost instantly by staring at the creases in my hands: the life line, heart line and head line. Natural wrinkles, embed on my skin for as long as I can remember. I trace lines as they curve below my fingers and around my thumb, then I rub my finger back and forth over the single swollen incision. The administrator's lips have started to quiver furiously. Someone told me once that administrators get a third amendment, to compensate for the risks of the Marchers and the sacrifice they make, but I don't believe it. I've seen what happens if you don't follow the rules – no second chances and no third amendments.

'The *what ifs* ate away at man,' she says, with overly dramatic melancholy.

What if? The most constructive and destructive words you can place together. I've seen how *what ifs* can eat away at you. I've watched as it works its way from just a tiny thought in the back of a restless mind to an all-consuming ailment that grasps and grapples at your cells, crippling every fibre of your body, eroding your senses and taking your life with it. I've got more than enough *what ifs* to break me already. What if I mess this up? What if next time it's black? What if I just don't try? What if I make things worse? It's sentences like that that make you wonder if the Marchers have a point.

The attentive congregation continues to nod to the melodramatic trembling of the administrator's voice and the emphatic thrusts of her arms. The whole thing is a charade. Maybe I was just as captivated as them the first time around, but I'd like to believe I'm not that naive.

She calls out a series of numbers with digits that would seem to suggest birth-times and then states the corresponding name. An ashen boy rises and climbs to the front, his whole body trembling from his loosely tied trainers to his outstretched hands. He looks straight at her though. I respect that.

'Zero-zero-zero-four. Peter Andrew Abbot,' she repeats. 'I hereby seal your right to amend; gifted by science, granted by your Cabinet and protected by all hands of the Administration. The divine right of all who reside within the Kingdom. Absolute from this day until the day of your last departure.'

From the front I see clearly how, with a whip of her wrist, the tapered knife falls and slices through the boy's skin. His eyes bug comically from their sockets until they sink back in the relief of his dismissal. The release of tension is palpable. By the time he has submerged his hand and is making his way back to his seat, he saunters with a definite smirk on his face.

I concede to Gabe's thinking that it is barbaric and unnecessary, and I don't bother watching anymore after the second person. I pick at the skin beside my nail until a hangnail appears, which I pick at with even more ferocity until it's red and glowing. Then I move on to another finger.

The administrator reads the numbers unnecessarily slowly, enunciating every last syllable to the personal torture of each waiting member of her audience. The line is unchanging, theatrical and superfluous. 'I hereby seal your right to amend...' she repeats to the eager, the apathetic and the appalled, of which I may or may not be the only one. I'm sure this could all be done when they take our blood, but where's the drama in that? But that's the Administration's way I suppose. They may be scientists but they love a bit of drama. Not that the Cabinet don't either. My thoughts flicker back to that night Fi and I secretly watching the marchers being executed, and the way Nicholas Hall, head of the Cabinet, presided over the bodies. Drama queens the lot of them.

About half a dozen people in, I start to pay more attention. I'm a morning baby – Fi and I both are. Our mother always used to tell this story about how the stars were made from the fragments of the sun. She would say how all the stars were out the night I was born, so many that she could barely even tell if it was night or day.

It may well have been the words themselves that caused my re-emergence from my thoughts, but either way, I'm listening as the administrator calls my name. With a lightheaded sense of déjà vu, I pull myself to my feet. A hundred pairs of eyes follow me as I climb the steps, keeping my hands close to my body and my eyes straight ahead. I offer my palms to the administrator, who, unlike the others today, does not flinch at the sight of my hand. She has probably been warned. She raises the knife with the same grace and deference she did for those who went before, holding it just inches above my still-spinning head.

'Emelia Evelyn Aaron. I hereby seal your right to amend; gifted by science, granted by your Cabinet and protected by all hands of the Administration. The divine right of all who reside within the Kingdom. Absolute until the day of your last departure.' The knife comes down, slicing my skin and join the still fresh scar of my amendment.

Frantic whispering echoes around the eaves and even the birds join in, squawking as they charge around the pillars. My insides squirm. It was a tiny omission but there is no escaping it. They all heard.

I stare at the ground, trying to appear impervious to the buzzing of their remarks: Maybe it was a mistake. Maybe she can't amend. Maybe, maybe, maybe. I try to block them out, but they crescendo so rapidly that soon the house martins are nothing more than muffled minims of a music box against an orchestra of a hundred bursting lungs. The air is stifling, sticking to my throat as I struggle to keep my eyes ahead.

With my head down I weave through the splatters of puddles that others have created and plunge my hand into the font. A thick red thread now bisects my hand. After flicking off the water, I scurry back to my seat, biting down on my tongue and clenching my fists against the wound and the whispers.

The murmurs die down as the next name is called and a solid-set girl rises, but I can still feel the eyes, boring into me from around the room. I will the time away while the numbers continue to progress at the same lamentable pace, my mind all but disconnected from the event.

My thoughts flit erratically through the multitude of possible scenarios that led me to this point, only for each one to mutate and dissolve before I can grasp it. I envisage what Fi is doing and what Fi did; what did happen and what will happen. I think about the colours, the texture, the shape of the paper, the perfectly creased seams. I recall the single line, scrawled so definitively in my handwriting, a line I have no recollection of writing. I scour every crevice of my memory for something, a spark or tiny glint that might allow me a glimpse – however slight – of what happened before. It is more than enough distraction from the dwindling hushed remarks that occasionally still drift to my ears. I try not to think about Gabe though. It doesn't seem appropriate.

I am adrift in my thoughts when the congregation emits a collective gasp and I look up just as a girl's head smacks the floorboards with a sickening crack. Her eyes close and a droplet of blood trickles down her forehead. Her unmarked hand dangles off the edge of the stage. The chief administrator looks on with passive disdain.

Within seconds I am jostled and elbowed from the side as a green-eyed boy pushes past me and scrambles to her aid. Kneeling beside her, he looks embarrassed as he gropes with her loose-fitting dress. The administrators watch on, lips pinned in suppressed smirks, a few flagrantly stepping sideways for optimal view. I see a motion between two on the edge of the stage, a touching of hands, a passing of something small, like a note, like a bet.

I leap to my feet, blazing with rage, blocking out the whispers and blinding me from the gawks of onlookers. Green eyes smile as I stumble up the steps and stoop down to help. We hook ourselves under the girl's arms and haul her down to the pews. Her head lolls, and her chin bashes against her chest. The administrators could have managed this in a more dignified manner, but that's clearly not their aim. Entertainment currently seems their primary focus. A low jab for an intelligent bunch of humans. Together we drag the girl into the pew, where out cold and slumped forward, she remains wondrously unaware of her infamy.

The boy – was it Douglas? – nods his thanks and scurries to the back of the hall, leaving me the remaining seat at the front. It is not until I finally lean back into the seat that I hear them. And this time they don't bother with whispers.

Did you see her hand? It was definitely silver. Did you see how many there were? Did you see them?

I sink into the pew, wishing I could camouflage myself against the wood. No time has been wasted scuttling the precious juicy titbits, so even those who didn't see will have been told quickly enough. Obviously enjoying the scene themselves, the administrators make no attempt to stifle the movements of the people behind me as they blatantly try to glimpse the scars themselves. Laughter, snorts and belittling sniggers surround me. The sniggering gets to me. It snags on my insides, tugging infuriatingly at my gut. It is not until the slumped girl stirs and smiles that I realise belittlement requires my submission. Fi would never let people make her feel like this.

With a long intake of breath, I straighten my back. For the rest of the ceremony, I remain bolt upright, occasionally turning, smiling and raising my eyebrows at whomever I catch staring or resting my hand against my chin, placing my palm in clear view of all those who take to the stage. The whispers quickly change to a certain disquiet and deliberate avoidance of me.

The pace of the ceremony is decidedly quicker now. Despite her efforts, the lead administrator never regains the same level of awed silence she had previously commanded, and without it, the ceremony becomes somewhat perfunctory. Her only moment of drama happens when two names are called at the same time. At this point, another administrator joins her on stage, and they speak and slice the pair in unison.

I head for the door the moment the ceremony is over, though I needn't have worried about being caught in a stampede. A void develops around me, as if my amendment may be contagious. With a familiar flush, I slow my pace and lengthen my stride for a few steps before remembering the reasons for their avoidance: the envelope. One final backwards glance shows Douglas – if that was his name – kneeling by the revived girl. He is stroking the cut on her forehead. She gazes at him starry-eyed. I'm not sure if I envy them or pity them.

I'm the only passenger in the elevator. As it draws to a halt, its creaking cogs grind the doors apart, allowing the unnatural basement light to flood in. I close my eyes, but I don't step out.

All the time daydreaming in the ceremony and there was one thought I refused to let manifest; refused to even consider. But now I am here there is no escaping it. I open my eyes and see Gabe's car is still in the basement. An impossible weight restrains me, driving a hole through my chest. It was never going to be that easy.

He's nodding his head to the music that blares from the radio and thumps through the dented car doors. A group of guards shoot suspicious scowls at the back of his head. Gabe's not the only person waiting, and he hardly looks like a marcher. Still, they look like they're doing their job. I scurry past them and climb into the car.

'Anything?' I say unnecessarily.

He shakes his head. 'I rang the house, but there was no answer.'

My stomach sours. Fi's gone out, so at some point she'll need to get picked up. It's going to happen. Whatever it is, it's begun.

'Do you want to go home? I'll wait with you there,' Gabe offers.

I'm not sure if I nod, shrug or shake my head, but I know I don't manage words and this time even Gabe can't find something to fill the void; he starts the engine and pulls out of the basement. I lift my phone from the dashboard and commence my vigil.

The cold has emptied the air as well as the roads. It's a

smogless vacuum through which everything is clear. Every building is defined, every boarded-up window and smoke-stained brick individual and distinct. The metalwork of each crane and factory chimney juts out into the skyline in crystal-clear form, and every mountain is a picture of sublimity.

My eyes flick between the mountains, my phone and Gabe as he stares steadfastly at the road. I swing my head towards the window and the scenery, look down at the screen and twist towards him in a perpetual oscillation; swing, down, twist; swing, down, twist. Finally, I forget the view and fixate on my phone until my eyes blur.

The hot air blasts from the heaters. It thickens the air with a muggy, musty texture that sticks to my windpipe as I swallow.

'You okay?' Gabe asks.

'I'll be fine,' I say, though my mouth is dry and my head is throbbing. 'I just need a drink.'

'I know a place that's pretty close.'

I half-nod, half-shrug as I close my eyes.

Chapter Thirteen

THE PLACE IS not that close, but I don't have the energy to think about that. For all we know Fi could want picking up from the middle of the mountains. It doesn't make any difference to me now. Either I'll be able to pick her up, or I won't. We drive through half a dozen checkpoints before turning onto a narrow country lane and into the shingled car park of a small pub. I feel like I should be more surprised – I never realised that places like this still existed – but somehow it's like I expected it. The green, the river; none of it is a surprise.

Gabe leaves me outside while he goes inside to order drinks. I make my way over to an empty bench. The small stones dig into the soles of my shoes, and the melting snow creeps up to my ankles. Bare branches of willows droop into the fast-flowing stream, and a couple strolls over to the river where they throw the remnants of their lunch to expectant fowl, laughing at the birds' extended necks and gawking beaks, with their arms wrapped tightly around each other's waists. I sit down and study my phone.

Gabe appears with two steaming china mugs.

'Sweet milk. You probably need the sugar,' he says.

'Thanks.'

He hands me one mug and blows the steam off the top of the other which weaves upwards, emerging in a cloud between us.

I stir the drink. It is as thick as custard and smells equally as sweet. I gulp down the first mouthful and yelp as it scalds the roof of my mouth.

'You might want to wait a minute,' Gabe says.

My phone is between us on the table, and neither of us seem able to draw our eyes away. The couple who were laughing at the ducks and geese are now rambling away up a crooked path towards some old outbuildings, and the only sounds come from the gurgling river as it sloshes over the rocks and my own continually thumping chest, which is occasionally drowned out by the trundle of a vehicle on the shingled road.

A waitress appears and absentmindedly moves the phone out

the way to place down some sandwiches. I snatch it from her hand, scowling in disdain, before shaking my head and smiling apologetically.

'I thought you might need to eat,' Gabe says.

From the way I'm glaring at the waitress as she scuttles away, I suspect he's right. My mouth is salivating at the smell, but it makes my stomach turn. I smile gratefully and pick at the bread.

'Did you study physics at school?' Gabe asks, still looking out at the couple.

'You mean retrocausality? Of course I did.'

'And the other stuff too. Gravity, forces, that kind of thing?'

'A bit. Doesn't everyone?'

'No, it was banned when I was at school.'

'Banned? Why?'

Gabe chews on a crust and takes a slurp of his drink. 'There's one law, Newton's third —'

'For every action, there is an equal and opposite reaction,' I recite, flashing up memories of riotous science laboratories and elbow padded teachers.

'That's the one.' Gabe smiles. 'It says if you push on a table, the table pushes back at you the other way.' His biceps thicken as he leans down on the splintering wood and raises his torso up above the table. 'Every force has a reaction, just as big, but acting on something else in the opposite direction.'

'Why was it banned?'

'Because people weren't convinced it was limited to forces.'

We pick up our mugs and start blowing the steam from our milk simultaneously.

When you're young, you try to get your head around it. Like a game of Othello, you try to predict all the possible outcomes from your one seemingly insignificant action. Once, on the rooftop, Fi spent all morning drawing out a map to show how her correct decision making would ultimately end in fame, fortune and the devotion of an extremely handsome man who was also head of the Cabinet. Thus her status in life would be raised to one of extreme affluence and power and limitless chocolate. I was also involved in the plan, mainly to transport said chocolate to wherever it was needed.

It quickly became apparent to me that mapping your life in this way is utterly impossible. Trying to predict a life dictated and driven by the actions and whims of others is as sensible as throwing a grain of sand into the ocean and expecting it to wash up at your feet a year later on the other side of the world. Some people still believe it's possible though. People who still believe their decisions and actions hold a deeper significance in the universe, and that every permutation and variation of these actions must be considered and ruminated on with exacting fastidiousness. Living like that in the old world would have be difficult enough, but in the Kingdom, where amendments are involved, it is nothing short of torturous. For these people, life becomes an impossibility, a minefield of unceasing terrors which they must face every day.

When I have finished picking at the softest parts of the bread, I discard the rest into the river. Instantly, the crusts cause a frenzy. Tiny ducklings struggle to weave their way back to their mother; they dip and dive, dodging the giant beaks of geese and kicking furiously against the current which drags them backwards into a flurry of webbed feet. Each route proves more treacherous than the last. They tirelessly paddle from one hissing goose to another in search of a mother, who swims in hopeless desperate circles away from them. Wings flap and beat against their feathered chests.

I'm rooted to the spot. Paralysed. My heart pounds. Every way the ducklings turn, they're faced with impending catastrophe. I don't want to watch, but I'm unable to draw my eyes away from the chaos I've brought upon them. At that moment, my phones starts to ring.

The tone is shriller than I remember, more urgent. Unfamiliar numbers flash up angrily on the screen. Still, it has to be her. On a first attempt, my thumb clumsily slides over the dials, but I answer it quickly enough. Trembling, I lift it to my ear.

'Em,' she yells with a volume that almost negates the need for a phone. 'Em, I need you to come and pick me up. Em? Em, are you there? For fuck's sake, Em?'

'Where are you?' I say, expelling the words in a trembling rush. My eyes are fixed on Gabe's as he clearly strains to hear what she says.

'I'm at the bar,' she says. 'And Gabe's not here to take me home, so he must still be with you.'

The bar. Of course she's at the bar. With Gabe away she was bound to try her luck. We could've gone straight there. The bar is fine though; we can reach her there.

'Em? You still there?'

'Okay. We won't be long. Don't go anywhere.'

'Like where?'

'I mean it, Fi. Promise. We won't be long. Twenty minutes. Half an hour at most. Okay?'

'I'll be here,' she says, and with that she ends the call.

'She's at your place,' I say to Gabe, the shaking in my voice accompanied by a thumping which emanates from beneath my rib cage.

'Let's go pick up Fi then,' he says, then stands and offers me his triple-scored hand.

The phone stays clutched tightly in my palm as we drive. Whatever painkillers were in the font water are wearing thin. It starts as just a mild tingling, but pretty soon my whole hand is throbbing and itching furiously.

'Can we go a little faster? I say, tapping my finger on the edge of the door, trying to ignore my hand.

'If we crash or get stopped then we'll never get there,' he says.

'Who's going to stop us?'

Priority is rarely given to road safety even when the weather's good. If someone's careless enough to have an accident, they'll pay for it, with their amendment or somebody else's. Gabe doesn't reply, so I make my impatience more than apparent through my avid fingernail drumming, which quickens inversely to his speed.

I've been to the bar plenty of times. When Fi got the job, I'd take a bus there and arrive an hour before she was due to start on shift. I'd sit on a stool, talking to Gabe, wiping down tables that were already clean and taking drinks to customers who could easily get up and get their own. Fi always gave me a look when she got in and found me there and not at home, but what could she say? She wasn't the one cooped up on nurse duty all day. As our mother got worse, I could leave her less and less often and Fi's shifts got longer and longer; now I can't even remember the last time I was there.

Still, I know the route well enough, and I know that we still have a ten-minute drive when a light on the dash catches my eyes and stops my fingers tapping.

'God, no. Not now.'

I hear the words, but I'm not sure if they're mine or his, and it doesn't really matter.

'No, no, no, no,' Gabe yells, banging his fist against the dashboard as the red light flickers on and off absentmindedly.

'There's a station,' he says, but not to me. 'We can get there. It's fine, there's a station. It'll be fine.'

There's no confidence, though, not in his voice, which catches and trembles noticeably in his throat, or in his knuckles that continue to rap the plastic screening of the blinking light.

'I can walk,' I say. 'I'll go through the houses. We'll wait for you. I can do it.'

'You can't walk in this. It'll take too long. Don't worry, we'll be fine, we'll be fine.'

'Gabe, I can.'

'No, you can't. Even if you didn't freeze, you don't know this area. Anyway, it'll have a reserve, every car has a reserve.'

A large vein has popped on his forehead, pulsating between the crinkled lines of skin.

'Why are we slowing down?' I say.

'It's fine. I just need to go a little slower to get us there, that's all.'

With a shrill hiss, I suck in air between my teeth and scowl back at the glaring light. I fiddle with my phone, open and shut the glove compartment, twiddle and twist the dials on the dashboard.

'Em, that isn't helping.'

'What do you expect me to do?'

'Sit still, for one.'

The engine sounds become hoarse and shallow, and the car coughs as it struggles to move forward on the fumes. I continue to play with anything within my reach while I chew on the inside of my cheek with a silent glower. The car jerks and hops more and more before finally the engine cuts out.

It's funny, how the mind reacts when there really is nothing left, when all the power you were given has been siphoned off. The Dorothys and Alices, they tumbled and spun, flew, fell, plummeted and plunged into whatever sensational land fate had in store for them. Me, I just sucked in my cheeks and waited. Again.

Chapter Fourteen

WHEN I WOKE the morning that Fi received her amendment, she had already emptied every pill bottle in the house. She had thrown away every sharp object and long cable and had binned or hidden every inanimate object with even the perceived hint of menace. Yet deep down she knew it wouldn't be enough. An amendment was never going to be enough, a cotton bandage on a ruptured spleen. Amendments change actions, not hearts, not beliefs, not the long-standing desires and wishes we hold to and cling to without reason. Everyone knows amendments can't change those. They just try not to believe it.

So Fi did everything in her power, hung on with every scrap of strength she had left. She begged and bargained and promised with words of kindness and love, then guilt and blame and shame and responsibility; we both did. And it worked for a little bit. But no one can hold on indefinitely. The mind, the body, the heart, they are the same system, and when one of them lets go, it's only ever a matter of time before the others follow. When our mother walked out the door, Fi headed to her room and retrieved a bottle of vodka. I wouldn't have wanted to face what came next sober either.

Gabe's knuckles are translucent as he turns the key in the ignition. A heavy knocking hammers against my rib cage. He turns the key once and gets nothing but a mocking clicking in return. He tries again and then again, a third time. With the fourth turn, a harsh hacking splutters from the engine, jolting the bonnet and lurching us forward, but then it stops again.

The screen of my phone is black. I have no idea how many minutes it's been since Fi called. We told her to wait, but patience is not a family virtue. Time drains away beneath my cold feet as I redial the number and wait for it to ring. When it finally does, all I get is the familiar mis-pitched and extended tone of a busy line.

'Just keep trying,' Gabe says, without turning to me.

With the phone pushed to my ear, I pull air in through my nose and push it out of my lungs in short blows, my eyes scrunched as I focus on the ringing and away from the pain.

An ulcer has formed on the inside of my cheek where my teeth have ground against the soft flesh and a stomping throb which started beneath my temples has now spread across my skull, radiating pressure behind my eyes. But these are only physical pains. They're easy enough to cope with. I wish all pains were of this genre.

Gabe takes his hands off the steering wheel and wipes them on his jeans. It's his turn to close his eyes. He expels his breath in a long hiss and mutters repetitive sounds. Then he turns the key again. It starts as the same spluttering, the same hoarse choking and coughing, but this time it extends to a low rumble, and then more still – a growling from beneath the bonnet. He glances briefly at me before the car starts rolling again. Neither of us dare smile, and I don't stop chewing my cheeks.

The car's spluttering lessens slightly as it moves forward, gradually picking up pace, and after less than a minute the station's in sight, just the other side of the junction. I sigh and bury my head in my hands. My pulse has begun to steady and my muscles twitch with relief. We're so close now. There's no chance we won't make it. I remove my hands from my head and gaze outwards. On a sideways horizon something small starts growing, rapidly. I study it for a moment before I realise.

'Stop!' I scream. 'Gabe, stop!'

The truck hurtles towards us, articulated and rusted. Its heavy wheels plough through the snow as it blasts its horn.

'Gabe!'

I try to grab the wheel, but he pushes me back. The horn is so loud now it shakes my eardrums. As I lunge for the steering wheel again, he yanks it away. The tires of the truck screech as we swerve. I grasp his hand and look to the heavens.

The whites of the driver's eyes flash towards me. It's only for a millisecond and I use every moment of it on prayer, begging to an unknown deity. My whole world slows into that split second; the hammering of my heart, the pulsing of my blood. I can hear it all, feel it all and through it all I pray. I've often wondered how many would still pray if they had nothing to pray for and how many pray because all other options are out.

Whether our prayers are selfish or not doesn't matter; they are heard. I look back and see the steam rising from the heat of the tires, in long curved tracks. The smell of burnt rubber, friction and tarmac, fills my nose. The driver pulls away, hand on the horn, his fuming, ashen face fading into the distance, his white eyes seared clearly into my memory.

We freewheel into the station and I slump into my seat, my ribs close to cracking from the battering they just received. It is though there are multiple hearts in my chest, all drumming, all competing for my attention.

'Are you okay?' Gabe says. He reaches over and places a hand on mine.

I flick it away. 'You nearly killed us,' I spit.

'No, I knew —'

'Knew? Knew what? That you could have killed us?'

'We wouldn't have been able to restart her, not again.'

'He nearly hit us, Gabe! You nearly killed us!'

'I wouldn't let anything happen to you, I promise. Em? You know that, right? I wouldn't have let anything happen.'

I can't look at him. I turn away from him, my body still shaking to my core. I have drawn blood inside my mouth. I can taste it.

An old man with a hunchback limps towards us, his body bent forward and tilted to one side as though he should be carrying a cane. He presses a hand against his back, as if pushing himself forward, but still needs to stop after every few steps. Gabe climbs out of the car and walks towards him.

I used to think of life as a spider's web, infinite slender fibres intricately intertwined and bound together in so many places with fragile and beautiful links. While a slight tug, a twitch, somewhere along the line may indicate a reward for your unrelenting tenacity, it could equally represent an imminent danger. You would have to follow the thread to find out. The thing is, no matter how complicated the centre of the web may look, it is the epitome of order and control. If one strand breaks, it still maintains its structure, still holds, still catches flies and warns you of oncoming threats; you might feast, you might have to flee, but at least a web can be repaired. Life can't be repaired like that, not in the same way.

Gabe and the man are both staring at me, both pairs of lips pursed. The old man scratches at his nose, and Gabe's fingers twitch at his side. The men look away again when they see me watching and then talk for a minute or so more before Gabe strides back to the car. The old man wobbles into the station, stopping every few seconds to balance himself on whatever object is within his reach.

'How much money do you have on you?' Gabe says.

The station is dry, has been for weeks apparently. I feel the beads of sweat start collecting along my spine again, my fingers trembling around the tightly grasped phone. Gabe picks my hands off my lap and clasps them in his.

'It's fine. He's got some in a bike out back. He's siphoning it off now.'

'How long?'

'Not long.'

'Not long's not an answer.'

'Five minutes, Em,' he says, but he chews his bottom lip and avoids my eyes.

I hand him the last of the mourner's money and continue to try Fi's phone, but it's still the same tone. She has no one she could possibly talk to for this long; she didn't even ring me from this number. I try the bar phone, but there's no answer there. Still I keep trying; the ringing is a distraction from the swarms inside my gut.

The old man's movements are arthritically slow, weathered and worn, the erosion of his creaking joints visible under the translucent skin that covers him. He reappears, hobbling slower than is believable. I want to leap from the car and grab the rusted canister from him. Gabe tries to help, but the man shuns the offer; it's probably the first customer he's had in a month. The wait is agonising. The old man is breathless every few steps and constantly bends over to rest on his knees. Even when he's at the car, he continues to struggle, awkwardly wrapping his brittle fingers around the petrol canister. Gabe pokes his head inside the door and raises his eyebrows apologetically.

'He'll just be a minute, then we'll get going. She'll still be there.' He glances to my hand. 'Have you had any luck with the phone?'

I shake my head and motion to the old man. 'Does he know how important this is? Have you told him?'

'He knows it's important.'

'Have you told him? You need to tell him. I'll show him my hand if that will hurry him up.'

'It won't,' Gabe says.

That's when I see it. Wheezing for breath, the old man leans against the window of the car, his crumpled pink hands pushed up against the glass. Crumpled, yes, pink, yes, scarred, no. There are no lines, not even the headline; he has not even registered. There are no flecks of silver, no simple bisections, nothing but old crinkled skin. A shudder runs right down to the base of my spine. He is a true marcher, or at least he looks that way.

The old man lifts the canister to the car, but Gabe's eyes don't leave mine.

'It's fine,' he whispers.

My body starts to shake. I slide my hands between my thighs and hold them there, firmly clenched.

'It's fine,' Gabe repeats.

'All done.' The man's voice rasps from outside.

Plastering a smile onto his face, Gabe draws himself upright and, with his right hand, hands the man all the money we have. He thanks the man profusely and turns to leave.

Gabe's face turns pale. The man clings to his hand in a vice-like grip, green and purple veins swelling across his sinewy fist, but he isn't looking at Gabe; he's looking at me. He smacks his tongue against his rotting yellow teeth and shakes his head with unblinking eyes. Clenched down between my thighs, my hand throbs and burns. It's not just the palm this time but my fingers, my wrist; soon the whole of my left arm is on fire. My eyes water as the pain becomes agonising, and it takes every bit of willpower not to scream out and leap from the seat. But I don't. I don't move it, and I don't break the old man's gaze. He smiles, as if impressed, and nodding, releases Gabe's hand.

'Good luck,' he says to me.

Gabe climbs into the car, still thanking the old cripple.

The tires squeal against the wet road as we head towards the bar. Any earlier concerns Gabe had about speeding have apparently gone.

Chapter Fifteen

GABE'S BAR IS in Section Six — the same one we live in — but right on the other side. Where we live is run-down, but compared to here it's a palace. This is probably the last place our mother would have wanted Fi working — even I've heard about some of the dodgy dealings that supposedly take place around here — but she wasn't in a position to say much. Besides, I suspect there's very little truth to it, although Fi is not so convinced. One night, before everything with my mother reached its climax, Fi came home saying she'd met a man who offered to buy her amendments off her. She laughed it off, said he was drunk, but I could tell from the way she spoke, and the fact that she had woken me to tell me, that she was spooked. I don't see how it could work though. Amendments work on your DNA and there's no way you could sell that to someone. Not that I know off.

As the high-rises multiply and the smell of smoke grows thicker, the snow thins. Most of it is piled on the edges of the road in browning heaps or settled on the rooftops of stationary cars. Once again, my heart begins to race and as we turn the last corner, my breath is held.

Fi is barely a matchstick high, standing beside a mound of slush which has been pushed up against the walls of the bar. Even from here I know it's her; no one else would be out bare legged in this. Her dark hair is scraped up behind her as she gazes into oblivion and waits for us. She waited.

Gabe is grinning as my head flops down in relief. Every moment of the day replays in my mind, from the envelope to the ceremony to the last ten minutes where our life was so narrowly spared. We made it, the phone, the fuel, none of it could stop us. I made it, I didn't fail. Even my hand has stopped hurting. I close my eyes and let my body dissolve into the seat.

'Fuck.'

My eyes ping open, and I bolt upright at the horn. It blasts loud and prolonged as Gabe slams the heel of his hand down on the steering wheel. Fi has gone.

'She's gotten into that blue car,' Gabe says, the horn still blaring.

'She can't,' I say. 'She can't.'

'It's fine. We'll get her.'

He hammers on the horn again and again, accelerating past the bar and a drunk who is relieving himself against the wall. The other car, battered and bumperless, pulls away down a lane with Fi inside. With the horn still going, we gain on it, little by little, until we are bumper to missing bumper.

I sometimes get the urge, when it's really clear, to test déjà vu. I get a sudden impulse to tell the person next to me what's going to happen or what they're going to say. I sometimes get a driving compulsion to recite their lines to them as if they are part of my own personal play or just whisper them quietly so they can't decide if it was all just in their mind. I never have, of course; people don't do things like that.

Perhaps it's too much like tempting fate, after all, if you say it and it doesn't happen, how does that make you look? Like some lunatic who spurts out random rubbish. That's a good enough reason to keep quiet for the most part. You don't want to get a reputation for something like that. Not here. Other times, though, I keep my mouth shut for a different reason. I swallow back what I want to say, not because I don't want to appear odd, but because I want to hold onto it. I want to hold onto that knowledge of something beyond the boundaries of acceptable understanding, to know there is more than we ever let ourselves believe.

What I have now is not déjà vu; this is something else, something somewhere between a memory and a dream, like the recurring reverie from a previous night's sleep that wants to creep its way back into tonight's dreams and flood me with visions and alternate realities and all-too-real nightmares that I don't want there. In this moment I see Fi writhing in agony, her body purpled with bruises, her eyes vacant. I see her mouth moving soundlessly as she tries to make sense of the pain in her body. I see it and don't see it. I hear nothing, yet my whole body clenches at the wails. I lean over and slam my fist down on the horn.

A face appears, hair splayed against the glass and sticking across her face as she presses her nose up against the back windscreen of the other car. With a yawn which stretches her jaw and scrunches her tiny features, she squishes her eyes into crumpled lines. She reminds me of a wood mouse and an image of a little girl, this little girl – curled up asleep on her side, a blanket pulled in tightly around her as she clutches at a soft toy, whimpering in her dreams – jumps into my mind. I shake my head, and she's gone.

Fi's face appears through the glass, crinkled in common confusion and drink. I thump at the horn again and again until eventually her expression clears. Then she disappears from view altogether. My heart skips alternate pulses until the bumperless car slows to a stop.

I scramble out the door, slapping over the puddled paving slabs and through the stagnant filled gutters. Grappling at the door handle, I yank it open.

'Get out!' I scream. 'Get out. Get out.'

'Em?' she says.

'Get out! Get out!' I tug at her clothes and pull at the strap secured tightly across her chest. 'Get out, get out, get out!' I scream, but she doesn't move.

I collapse onto my knees, ignoring the snow that soaks through my jeans and the gusts of wind that sear my neck in ice. I ignore the pairs of eyes that bear down on me and the quiet questioning of a confused young girl.

'You were meant to wait,' I sob. 'You were meant to wait.'

'Em, I don't —'

'You were meant to wait.'

Two hands appear on my shoulders and guide me upwards and into his chest. The more I tremble against the cold and against the tears, the closer he pulls me in, guarding me against the world and the wind.

'Get out of the car, Fi,' Gabe says.

She rustles in her seat as if to move and then thinks better of it. 'I'm fine here,' she says, the consonants leaning over one another as her words slur.

'I'm not asking.'

In the silence of her contemplation, I hear Gabe's heart drumming against a background of incessant sniffing. I keep my eyes closed and for a second let myself imagine it's just the two of us, curled up somewhere together, alone. His pulse seems to quicken at my thoughts, and I draw myself away, though his hand remains wrapped around my waist. I wipe my tears, dragging the back of my hand carelessly across my face.

‘We need to go,’ I say, reaching across and unfastening her belt. I cough and splutter as I try to clear the phlegm from my throat. ‘Please,’ I add.

Fi turns to the man beside her, the source of the sniffing. His workman’s overall is unzipped and pulled down to his waist, exposing a white vest beneath. He sniffs again and wipes his nose on the back of his hand. A pattern of flowers intricately loops its way up his forearm from his wrist, curving under and around his biceps and disappearing beneath the white of the top to reappear at the base of his neck. All the flowers are the same shape, the same colour and the same design; they are all poppies.

With another sniff, he taps a cigarette from a crumpled packet and leaves it drooping between his lips before lighting it with a match.

‘Do what you like,’ he says. ‘No screw is worth this much hassle.’ He takes a long drag. No one speaks. He blows the smoke into the tattered roofing, watching as it billows and swells, coiling in loops and whorls around his head. The girl appears over his headrest, and he brushes her down without so much as a look.

‘Are you staying or going?’ he says with another sniff, wipe and drag. ‘Tick-tock, tick-tock.’

‘She’s going,’ I say, pulling at Fi’s hand.

‘Em, what are you —’

‘Just get out of the car, Fi,’ Gabe says.

Without warning, Fi leans over to the driver’s seat and kisses the man on his smoke-filled mouth. I turn to Gabe, unsure where else to look, and a second later she clambers out of the car and onto the pavement.

‘See you again soon?’ she slurs.

‘I hope so,’ he says. She shuts the door and blows him a kiss.

Chapter Sixteen

GABE SEES US into the flat before he has to leave. A problem at the bar apparently, though I never saw him take a call.

Fi stumbles over to the cabinet, pulling out empty bottle after empty bottle before she slams the door shut, rattling the glassware inside. After a minute of pondering silence, she does the same thing all over again, this time pulling out even more.

'There's nothing in there,' I say.

'I need to go out. I need some money.'

'We don't have any.'

She picks up my bag and starts rifling through it, throwing keys and receipts and finally my empty wallet on the ground.

'I know you've got some, you've got all her money. Don't think I don't know that.'

'There's none left, Fi. We needed it.'

'For what?'

'Food, bills, keeping a roof over us.' Paying a decrepit old marcher over the odds for fuel so I could save your backside.

She stomps around the living room, overturning the contents of every cupboard and drawer, before she starts on the kitchen.

'Fi, there's no drink and there's no money.'

'Then I'm going to a bar.'

'Where, Fi? Where are you going to go? You're banned from all the bars in the section.'

'I'll go to Gabe's.'

'How? Are you going to walk there in this state? You'll be arrested. Anyway, Gabe's working tonight. He won't serve you, not until you start paying. Or, perhaps, I dunno, working?'

'Well, you two seemed very chummy. I could take you, too.'

I ignore her.

'Fine then. I'll go somewhere else,' she huffs.

'Like I said, how are you going to get there?'

She glares at me and stamps around loudly for a few more minutes before dramatically storming off to her bedroom and slamming the door. I shudder. The flat is freezing and the slight scent of this morning's breakfast still hangs in the air. My stomach growls angrily at it.

Half-heartedly, I amble around, picking up her mess. My eyelids are like lead weights, and my body moves mechanically, without any real direction. I'm sure I should feel something: happy, elated, mad even, at her ungrateful ignorance, but I have no more room left for emotions today. I'm not sure which is more exhausted, my mind or my body, not that it makes a difference.

Fi's asleep when I check on her, curled up and shivering uncontrollably. I take the blanket from my room and lay it over her. It helps a little, but even though it's cold, I suspect the shivering is more an effect of the drink. By now my legs can hardly move. I'm so tired and consider slipping in beside her. My hand lifts at the blanket, but for some reason I change my mind. I leave her door ajar and choose to crawl into my mother's bed instead. I've no idea why; I've barely ventured in here since that day, yet tonight it feels less lonely than I would have thought.

It's well past noon when I drag myself out of bed. An undeniable glow of afternoon sun forces its way through the curtains and highlights the motes of dust that hang in the air. I lay flat on my back and study the bare walls. Now, in the daylight, the room feels far more full of ghosts than it did in the dark. I quickly gather my things and check in on Fi. She's tossing and turning; the blanket has been kicked off and is strewn over the floor. From her groans, I know it won't be too long before she's up.

I shower and dress and then finish tidying the living room. My hands are poised to beat out the cushions when Fi stalks into the living room and slumps onto the sofa. Glaring, but without words, she picks up a picture, and for a minute I think she's going to throw it, but she doesn't. She doesn't put it down though either.

'Do you want some food?' I say.

No reply.

'Fi are you hungry? Do you want something to eat?'

Nothing.

After an extended pause, more prompting gestures and further repetition of the question, I take her silence as a sign of her hunger. I hand her a glass of water and two accompanying painkillers — from a stash that I keep hidden in one of my books — and then wander into the kitchen and start cracking eggs into a bowl. The heat of the blue flame warms my hands briefly, before I tip the eggs into the pan and jump back in surprise as they sizzle and spit.

When I come back in, she's dressed in slouchy bottoms and two tops with hoods and zips, layered over a little slip. The photo is still in her hand. She runs her fingers over the glass frame. She always picks the same one, the one of us all, a full family portrait. I leave her to her thoughts and return to the food.

'Do you want a hand?' she asks a minute later from the doorway. The photo is gone from her hand, and her face is missing its regular glower.

'You could toast some bread,' I suggest.

She steps into the kitchen. 'Look, I'm sorry,' she says as she tries to locate the correct cupboard for bread. 'Last night, I was a bitch.'

'What's new?' I say curtly.

Fi laughs sadly and places the thin white bread under the grill. She picks her nails and stares at the glowing red filament as she waits for the toast to colour. Somehow, she manages to pile more and more little grains of guilt onto my sand dune with every pathetic attempt to catch my eye.

'It's fine,' I say eventually.

'It's not —'

'Really, Fi. It's fine. It's not like I'm perfect.'

She snorts and arches her eyebrows as she hands me the plate. I flush angrily.

'I'm not. I can be a bitch, too,' I say defiantly.

'When?'

'When I'm hungry,' I say snatching my plate from her with a faux angry look on my face.

'I'd forgotten that. You're right; you can be a bitch.'

We laugh a little; not for long though – it doesn't feel right.

When she's finished eating, she uses her finger to wipe the plate in even streaks. It's a horrid habit, but I don't say anything. She senses me watching, replaces the cutlery and pushes the plate to the centre of the table, before she changes her mind, pulls it back and stands up.

'I'll tidy up,' I say, as she clears my plate.

'It's fine. I can do it.'

'I don't —'

'I'm not an invalid, Em,' she snaps.

I follow her as she dumps the plates into the sink and then

collects the pan from the stove and drops that in, too. Then before even turning on the taps, she returns to the living room and collapses onto the sofa. Perhaps she assumes the dishes will clean themselves once they're in the sink. Sighing, I roll up my sleeves.

'Don't do that now,' she calls as I start running the water.

'It'll just take a minute.'

'Please, Em, come here, I'll do that later.'

'It needs doing.'

'Right this minute?'

There's a tone to her voice. I don't want to push it, and I guess it doesn't matter if I do it now or later, so I turn off the taps and head back into the living room.

This room never gets any light. The view is blocked by another grey high-rise buttressed up as close as humanly possible. Whereas it used to feel cosy and snug, now it feels claustrophobic. I perch on the edge of the sofa, tucking my knees up to my chest before readjusting to a comfier position with my feet underneath me.

Fi fiddles with a strand of her hair like a reprimanded child. Her lips twitch like she's searching for words.

'Em —' she starts.

'It's fine —' I begin to cut her off, but her glare stops me.

'I don't mean to do it,' she says. 'You know that, don't you? I don't mean it.'

'I know.'

'Do you really?'

'Fi —'

'Every day I go to bed thinking this is it, this is the last time I'm going to act like this. Every day I tell myself that. I tell myself that was the last drink, the last cigarette, the last everything. Every day, Em. It's just.... It's just as soon as I wake up, as soon as I remember...' She thumbs the scars on her hand. 'I miss her, Em. I miss her so much.'

'So do I.'

'I know, but it's not the same for you. You didn't —'

I bite my lips to quash the spark of resentment I feel and try to lock eyes.

'I know it's not the same,' I say. 'But I miss her, too. And I miss you.'

She bows her head and tucks her hands into the frayed sleeves of her jumper.

'I know how much you gave up, Fi. I get that.'

'It's so hard, Em, just getting through a day sometimes, it's so hard.'

'I know that.'

'It hurts. All the time. I'm so lonely, it hurts, Em.'

'I'm always here. Always.' I move forward and stroke her hair, but she only sinks farther away. I clasp her chin and lift her face towards me. 'I am always here, Fi. Always.' Her face is streaked and the whites of her eyes turn pink as tears tumble down her cheeks. I pull her in close and lay her head on my lap. 'I'm always here.'

I hope I sound sincere. It's not the first time we've had this conversation – or a similar one at least. She used to make promises all the time, and she meant them all, I'm sure of it. She doesn't bother now. I suppose that's kind, in a way.

I continue to stroke her hair as she sleeps resting on my lap. Her breathing provides a steady, strumming lullaby that my eyes find impossible to resist, and only when my toes have turned too cold to feel do I finally decide to move. I slowly manoeuvre my body out from under her, before propping her head up with a cushion and tucking a blanket around her feet.

In a desire to do something more, I wade through the debris of her room and collect the rubbish and empty glasses. I consider washing her clothes, or at least hanging up the relatively clean pieces, but I can't find the energy. The best I manage is to push them to the sides and arrange them into slightly more ordered piles on the floor. It must be hard for anyone to have a fresh start when waking up in a room that reeks of decay, death and cheap booze, but it needs us both to tackle it properly, tomorrow perhaps, if she doesn't find something to drink before then.

I manage to clear a path across the room and open the window. I dodge the heavy curtain as it flies out with the first gust of air and reveals a small stuffed animal rammed down the back of the radiator collecting dust. I pull it out, stretch its limbs and shake off the cobwebs before throwing it onto her unmade bed. I'll strip the sheets tomorrow, too.

In a last-ditch attempt to cover the stench, I light a candle that's on her dressing table. The honeysuckle smoke weaves upwards in circling plumes, and I doubt it will help much, but anything is better than nothing.

I continue to potter around the flat, picking up rubbish here and there, sweeping the most ill-affected corners of the most visible places. When the other rooms are halfway presentable, I head back to the kitchen to clean up. I'm running the plates under the cold kitchen tap when I hear her stirring.

'Em?'

'I'm just in here.'

'How long have I been asleep?'

'You needed it.'

'You tidied?'

'Not really.'

She appears in the doorway, bleary eyed and twisting her hair into a knot as she yawns. 'I said I'd do that.'

'It's fine, I'm nearly done.'

'Let me dry.'

She clatters about, rummaging through drawers until she finds a tea towel and begins polishing the mountain of glasses I've already washed. I didn't even know we had so many. Some of them are more obviously liberated from Gabe's bar, more likely than not with the contents still in them.

'How you feeling?'

'Better,' she says.

'Good.'

Her lips slip into the smallest of smiles that vanishes into the ether as she starts to dry. Her technique is poor, particularly for a barmaid. She whips the tatty cloth around chipped rims and cracking stems, not checking for smears or streaks before she jams them back into cupboards. Soon, she takes them straight from the sink still covered in suds and dripping onto the floor. She flicks some stray bubbles at me, her mouth twitching at the corners as the bubbles trickle into my ears or down my neck.

'Thanks,' I say dryly.

'No problem,' she says, flicking more.

I try to block her, but she reaches around me and scoops up a handful and sprays them into the air with a puff of breath. From some forgotten part of her, a whispered giggle escapes.

'Great. Really helpful.' I pick the bubbles out of my hair, tossing a few back at her slyly, before shovelling up a fistful of my own. They slop around in my hand, and I spin around and catch her by her shoulder, smearing them across her cheeks and pinning her to the cupboards as she writhes and squeals.

'Em!' she squeals.

Soon we're wrestling for the sink. Water splashes over the floor as we fight each other, screaming and laughing. Our sodden socks skid and slide on the ground as we wriggle and howl, squirming in and out from one another's holds. Winded and breathless, we grapple for a good grip on each other, dodging the other's cheap shots while desperately seeking our own. I'm on my knees, eyes streaming, blinded by soap and doubled over by a stitch in my side as she lunges for me again.

'Truce! Truce,' I say panting and waving my hands in a vague attempt to block the incoming onslaught. She hovers her cupped hand of wilting suds above me.

'Truce! I said truce!'

Her smirk grows wider as the lather dribbles from her hand. Narrowing her eyes she raises her arm, ready to throw.

'I said truce!'

With a final grin she throws her head back and slaps the foam back into the sink.

'Wimp,' she says. With a soft smile, she extends a hand down to me. 'Truce.'

I fall back on the cupboard doors, still cramped from the laughter that continues to ripple through my body. I close my eyes with a sigh and reach my hands up for her.

I snap my fist closed and my eyes open, but it's too late; I know it's too late.

I scramble to my feet. 'Fi, it's fine, I promise, it's fine.'

My pulse races and I try to take her hand, but she backs away from me, shrinking into the corner, wide eyed and shaking her head. I wait for the screaming, the accusations and demands, but they don't come.

'Fi, please.'

Wordlessly, she slides to the ground and wraps her arms around her knees. 'Not now, not now, not already,' she whispers.

'Fi, it's okay, it's okay, I promise.'

She chews at her bottom lip and stares into space behind me as she rocks just a few controlled times on the soaking floor. I kneel down next to her, lift her head and wipe away the tears.

'It's okay,' I say. 'It's all okay.'

When she looks at me, her expression is stone cold. 'Why didn't you tell me? You should've told me. I should've known. I should've known!' She flicks away my hand and straightens herself up against the door. 'Were you even going to tell me at all?'

'Of course.'

'When?'

I look down at my knees, my blue trousers drenched black with water. I pick at the fabric and avoid her glare. I don't need to look up to know it's still there.

'When, Em? When were you going to tell me?'

'I don't know,' I admit quietly.

She grabs my hand and draws her fingers along the lines. I bite my tongue to stop from wincing, but I can't help clenching my jaw; she just pushes harder.

'Can I see it?' she asks, still running her fingertips along the line.

'Later,' I say.

She chews her lip. In the pause, the uncomfortable silence, all I can hear is my own jack-hammering chest.

'You should've told me,' she whispers eventually.

'I know.'

Without warning, my head flies to the side. I gasp, stung by the force and surprise of her slap. In a flash of anger, I move to retaliate, but my hand never strikes her. Instead, it drops to my side, defeated.

We sit on the floor in silence; one of my hands cushions the stinging skin of my cheek, the other is firmly in Fi's grip. She doesn't apologise for the slap. A couple of times I go to move, but she tightens her grip and re-examines the scar. Fifteen minutes must have gone by when she springs to her feet.

'I need to see it,' she says, clambering upright.

'Fi —'

'I need to see it, Emelia. Now.'

It's been awhile since I've seen Fi standing up straight, as opposed to slouched on some sofa or hunched over a rapidly draining glass, and now that she does, she's a good three inches taller than me and looking down with an unwavering glower.

'Now, Em,'

'Fi, I —'

'Don't give me any bullshit about not knowing where it is. I will go through every book on that shelf if you make me, starting with the most tedious.'

She follows me to my room, hanging back and lingering in the doorway as I head to the bookshelf. She waits there, digging her toes into the carpet and repositioning her feet uncomfortably as though she's found herself uninvited in a place she desperately doesn't want to be. I don't bother with a façade of searching. I pluck the book straight from the shelf and slip the envelope into my hand.

Its colour hits me again – the emerald green only seems to have intensified since I last saw it. The untidy letters of my scrawl are still there, linked in their slanted loops across the page, and my knees wobble from the enormous weight of such a light object as I walk in considered steps to the bed. Nothing about it has changed since yesterday and yet everything else in my world must have.

The mattress sinks as Fi slinks down beside me. I only now notice the fumes from her last drink and cigarette still clinging to her breath and unwashed hair. They catch in my throat as I pass her the paper. My pulse tears away as I watch her eyes scan the paper.

'Oh God,' she says. Her skin turns sallow, her lips dry and grey in front of me. 'Oh God, Em, no. This can't be right. It can't be. There must be more. Why doesn't it say more?' She flips the paper over in her hand, scouring the creases and folds for the slightest sign of anything more; her breath quickens and shallows as her eyes flit erratically across the blank sides. She turns to me, the amendment left hanging limply between her fingers. 'What did I do?' she says.

I take her hand – our rapid pulses squeezed together between clammy palms – and brush the loop of hair from across her face.

'Fi, you didn't do anything, I'm sure of it.'

'You can't know that.'

'I do.' I say.

She shakes her head again, brushing me aside.

'You did nothing wrong, Fi. I promise you, I can feel it.'

'Then…' she pauses. 'Oh, God.' With a small gasp she covers her mouth; in the absence of words, the only sound comes from the paper as it falls to the ground, weaving on a breeze that I can't feel. 'What did he do?' she says. 'I thought I knew him. I thought… What did he do to me?'

Her eyes beg me for answers, but I can't give her any. The hair prickles along my spine and the cold breeze finds my neck, sending shivers across my skin as the scent from Fi's candle drifts into the room. What she's thinking would make sense. It would all make sense, but then maybe there are other explanations too.

I want to comfort her, offer reassurance, denial, solace, anything to fill the silence, but the lump in my throat won't let the words past. I gingerly brush my hands against her knee, but she recoils at my touch, then springs to her feet and rushes from the bedroom. The bathroom door slams shut moments before the retching starts.

I pick up the envelope and refold it along its pleats, sliding it back inside the book and onto the shelf. There's no need to hide it from Fi now, but I guess that's not why I'm doing it. For a while I stand in the cold and stare at the shelf. The numbness in my chest seeps down to my legs, and I stumble absentmindedly into the kitchen and pour two glasses of water. As my footsteps reach the bathroom door, the bolt clunks loudly into place. I sink down the wall and onto the carpet and wait, resting my head against the wooden door and letting the cold swallow me whole.

I wake in my own bed with vague memories of weakly gripping arms bringing me here. My jeans and jumper are folded neatly on a chair, the pockets emptied and contents placed next to a glass of water on the table. Through a break in the curtains, a sliver of sunlight severs the floor between the bed and bookcase and stirs me further from my sleep. I have slept straight through the afternoon and the night. As I roll over, a blinding pain shoots from my palm up my arm and buzzes into the back of my skull until I squeeze my eyes shut and bite down on my lip. Eventually I drive it away. With a jittering stomach, I check my hand; at least there are still just two lines there today.

When Fi first amended, she was in agony; blinding headaches, gut wrenching cramps, the works. Those pains faded eventually, but they were just replaced by a different type. She had already discovered the remedy for those though. For me it's different. All of my muscles ache, but it's just a dull throbbing until I try to move and a sharp burning races down my limbs. What's stranger though is what's going on in my head. I feel like it's in two places at once. Every time my mind wants to go in one direction it feels like it is being yanked into another. My emotions are just as bad. With tentative movements, I reach out for the glass and sip the water slowly, ameliorating the dry, furry taste that coats my tongue. Gently, I force my legs to stretch and then bend, loosening the joints until they eventually stop blinding me every time I flex. It will take some time for my body to adjust. I know that.

I finish the water by the bed, but it barely even starts to quench my thirst. In the kitchen, I pour one tall glass of juice, cold from the fridge and then another, only to be hit with a crippling headache which flashes through my skull and instantaneously vanishes. I have clearly not drunk cold drinks much recently, unsurprising really as I can hardly recall the last warm day.

Remembering that I now need to take iron tablets, I head to the bathroom where I ransack the cabinets, ignoring the best before date stamped on the bottle when I find some. The cap doesn't fit properly, and the tablets have speckled with age and humidity, but they're all I have. Next to the sink, a flimsy dress is drying on the radiator. It rises and falls, oscillating on the breeze of the warm air. I try to push it down, but it keeps floating back up. In the end, I take it off and dump it on the floor by the bath.

In a moment of extravagance, I decide to treat myself and turn on the water heater; we've got no money to pay the electricity bill as it is, so the extra expense hardly matters. The chances are that I'm going to be assigned work if I don't find something soon anyway. As my only experience is as my mother's carer, I dread to think where they'll place me. Probably the type of place you don't ever visit unless you have to and pray you won't end up in yourself. The same kind of place I considered sending our mother to. It's a shame Gabe can't hire me too, but he's got to stick to the rules as much as everyone else. More I suppose, now that all his amendments have gone. I'm not sure I'd make that great a barmaid anyway.

I soak in the bath and pick away at the flaking blood on my palm before finally submerging it. The first line is healing quickly, thin flecks of silver now well formed on the surface – the other line is still puffy and sore. I plunge my hand, and the scars, back into the water and out of sight, turning the tap with my toes to fill the water even higher.

The soap is as useless as always, but I let the suds sting my eyes and my hands before wiping them away; it gives me something else to focus on, and by the time I climb out, the water is cold and grey and my fingers are wrinkled and white. I smell clean at least. My head spins as I sit on the bath mat and try to shiver myself dry under the shroud of a thinning towel. I'm just dozing off when she raps at the door.

'Em, are you okay in there? Em, it's Fi.'

Maybe the clarification of her name is for her benefit. I'm not convinced it was necessary for me; still, her knuckles knock again, no louder, just a little longer.

'Em?'

I roll onto my knees, push myself up and unbolt the door.

'I'm fine,' I say, my eyes still half shut. 'I just dozed off.'

I squeeze myself between her and the doorframe. I know she's watching me, waiting to say something to me, but shivering and naked isn't how I want to start a conversation.

'I've made some tea,' she says when I reach my bedroom door.

'I need to get dressed,' I reply. Once inside my room, I lie on the bed before taking my time to pick out some clothes.

We sit on the sofa together. Fi ignores her tea and stares intently at my hand. I ignore her staring and sip intently at my tea. The room has warmed slightly, having her sitting so close radiating heat. I flick off my slippers and curl my feet up underneath me.

'I thought it wasn't real,' she says eventually. 'When I woke up this morning, I thought maybe I'd imagined it. Dreamt it or something.'

There's a silence while she waits for my response, but I can't think of anything to say that doesn't sound trite or callous.

'I'm sorry,' she says, after a while.

'You didn't make me do it.'

'I might have.'

'You wouldn't have.'

I pick at my nails. Outside, there is yelling, a man's voice followed by a woman's.

'I didn't know you knew him. That man from the other night,' I say.

She offers the same nonchalant shrug I've grown tired of seeing, and I respond with the same exasperated sigh I'm tired of producing. Outside the yelling comes to an abrupt stop.

'Just a bit,' she says. 'He's taken me for a drink a few times.'

'And brought you home? I guess you wouldn't remember that.' I bite my lip; it's the type of comment I'd usually say, only I'm not used to her being able to hear and remember them.

'I'm going to stop, Em. I mean it. I've let you down, I know that.'

'Fi, don't —'

'No. I'm mean it. And I'm going to work.'

'At the bar?'

'I'll be fine.'

I pick up my tea, trying to disguise my look of scepticism. The bag floats in the stewed brown brew, which is just about warm enough to still drink. Fi furrows her brow, pushing her thumbs into her temples and rubbing her forehead.

'Headache?'

'Uh huh.'

'Do you want some more painkillers?' I say.

'No. It's probably best I make myself suffer.'

'That's ridiculous.'

Her lips curl together in a vain attempt at a smile. 'I'll be better after a cold shower.' She stands up and takes the mug from my hand. 'Then maybe we could do something today, just us?' She looks pleadingly at me.

'That'd be nice,' I say, ignoring the scepticism still swilling around my stomach.

Her smile curves slightly more upwards, but not enough to reach her eyes.

While Fi is in the shower, I sit on the sofa and absentmindedly pick the fluff from my jumper. There are things I should think about, like how we can even afford our next meal, but my thoughts flit so sporadically that as soon as a new one enters my mind, the last one is long forgotten. I'm in the midst of some pointless contemplation when the doorbell rings. I stand to answer it, but it's barely a second before the key turns in the lock and the wooden door scuffs against the carpet.

I momentarily consider the fact that I have no idea when or where Gabe actually got his key. It's not like I mind him coming and going, but you'd think it was something you might mention to the people that pay the rent. Still, my indignation quickly subsides when I remember that for a fair while now I think that might have been him.

Gabe hangs his coat over the back of a chair. He is holding a bottle of champagne, which feels strangely out of place.

'She's up?' he says, motioning to the sound of running water in the bathroom.

I nod.

'That's good. I brought this.' He nods towards the bottle. 'I know you probably don't feel like celebrating, just, well, it's for your birthday and everything.'

'Thank you,' I say. I reach out to accept it but hesitate and withdraw my hand. 'It's probably not a good idea to have it in the house, with Fi I mean. She's says she's going to stop.'

Gabe's cheeks colour. 'Sorry, I didn't think,' he says. 'It's stupid. I should have thought.'

'It's a lovely gesture —'

'Really, it's just from the bar, it's silly, just —'

I reach out my hand. 'I'll put it where she won't find it,' I say, but he keeps it by his side.

'It's probably best if I just leave it at the bar, then if you ever come round —'

'That sounds best.'

We fall into an awkward silence. I follow his lead and sit back down on the sofa, rebuking myself when I start picking invisible fluff.

'How is she?' he says after a pause.

'Okay, considering.'

'And you?'

'I'll be fine.' I look away as he scans my face for tell-tale signs.

'You will be,' he says, staring straight at me.

It's strange to think he's probably already lived two full lives of his choice. Perhaps one where Fi and I played no part at all. It's stranger still to think I could have lived a whole extra life myself. I don't think I have, though, not like Gabe. The lines on his brow are so deeply weathered he could have spent one lifetime forming them, and another lifetime creating the sweeping crinkles and dug out dimples that appear when he smiles. I want to smooth them away, run my hand against his skin and rub away the creases, see what he was like before whatever worry or pain it was that found him. The room is so quiet I can hear him breathing, I can hear us both breathing.

Gabe jumps from the seat as the bathroom door creaks open. Still dripping wet, Fi's hair falls over her shoulder blades in curved tendrils, while the towel she wears reaches just an inch below decency; her silver bracelet covers nearly as much flesh as the towel. Her face is glowing, and though it's possibly caused from the brazen cold of the shower, I think it has more to do with the smile the stretches across her face at the sight of Gabe. It's certainly more heartfelt than the half-hearted efforts she's given me this morning.

'I didn't expect to see you this morning.'

'I just thought I'd see how you were doing. Both of you,' he adds with a glance in my direction.

'And you brought me a present I see,' Fi says eyeing the bottle before shaking her head and laughing. 'Probably not the best idea.'

Gabe blushes. 'Sorry, I know. It was for Em. I didn't think. She tells me you've stopped.'

'Must be nearly thirty-six hours now. And it's amazing how much cleaning you can do when you need a distraction.' She laughs again, but there's tension around her eyes and her mouth; she squeezes her temples with her thumbs. 'So, buying Em presents, should I be jealous?'

Gabe blushes and we both avoid eye contact uncomfortably.

'I'm joking,' she says. 'God, look at you two. Right, I need clothes.' She struts over to her bedroom and then turns back over one shoulder. She purses her lips and smiles. It's the type of smile I recognise, with glittering eyes and perfect teeth; the type that means she wants something. 'Gabe, could I just borrow you for a minute?' she says.

Gabe shoots a quick look to me. Fi's towel drops a little lower.

'It's important,' she says.

Chapter Seventeen

I GRAB MY coat and keys and slam the door behind me. Without wanting to, I think of them, I can't stop thinking about them. I can't think of anything else. I imagine the things they might be saying to each other, doing to each other. I coerce images from my thoughts that then twist and swim uncontrollably around my mind. My whole body is shaking, and a churning, nauseating, curdling feeling bubbles through my insides as I stand and wait for the elevator. I rush in and hammer the 'close door' button.

The doors shut around me at their own pace, and I close my eyes, trying to shut out images I don't want to see. A face, like a memory, appears out of nowhere in my head. A pattern of flowers curves up around his neck, ending at the start of his closely shaved hairline. The image rotates; his teeth are bared. In pain? In a snarl? I can't tell. As the view on the face pans out, I barely glimpse his eyes before the bell of the elevator steals the picture from my mind. I shudder at the lingering sense of déjà vu and the coldness of the grey eyes. At least it momentarily distracted me from what may or may not be going on upstairs.

Outside, it is only slightly milder than the last time I stepped outside. As soon as I open the lobby door, the wind whips the backs of my legs, and my gloveless hands rapidly sting from the biting air. I hurriedly shove them into my coat pockets. Then, against my better judgment, I look up. Gabe is standing at her window. I stop, paralysed, my vision entirely locked onto him. I know he sees me, but he doesn't move until a slight hand appears on his shoulder, at which point he draws the curtains. I think I may actually vomit.

I've no idea where I'm walking to; I have no money and no cards, so I can't leave the section. Still, it's better than in the house. The air smells dank and sodden, and yesterday's fresh snow is already melting and turning the ground to mush.

Is there really any point to these emotions, in this day and age? Fight or flight, I understand that, of course I do; we need fear to survive. Lust, it falls into place with the need and desire to procreate, it makes sense. But love and jealousy, when all they do is consume every thought, perverting them and sensationalizing them with our own distorted logic. What are their purposes? Worse still is that I render these feelings with absolutely no justification. Gabe has never done anything to indicate feelings for me, besides occasionally supplying groceries and providing an undoubted hand with rent money. But those gestures are for Fi, not me. It's bizarre. You would think that if I know these feelings are irrational, I should be able to switch them off. And yet for some reason my chest is on fire with an illogical raging heat. At least it's keeping me warm – that is, until I stop and feel the heat drawn away from every vessel and ventricle within me.

The door is metal, sandblasted and scratched; it distorts my reflection, snubbing out the details of my features and tarnishing the colours of my already dull clothing. I don't think I was always this dull, but it's all I remember ever being. Fi was the colourful one, in clothes as well as personality. I could never keep up, so I guess I just stopped trying. I stay there, staring at my image on the door, hoping for something, a flicker, a spark, a full bolt of lightning to strike my reflection out. But it stares back, a soulless blur.

I came home from school one day to find my mother huddled on the steps outside the flat, the contents of her handbag thrown on the floor: cards, lipstick, her keys, everything scattered around her feet. It was years ago now, but I remember it as if it were yesterday. I watched as she sat there, fists clenched and body twitching, muttering to herself. Her eyes flickered as she saw me, but she stayed rooted to the spot. For a while that was how we stayed. Then I walked over and picked the keys up off the ground. She slapped them out my hand.

'Don't touch them!' she snapped.

'There's nothing wrong with them, Mum. They're just your keys.'

'They're too shiny,' she said. 'It's unnatural. It's unnatural.'

I lifted her to her feet, and she continued to mutter her mantra. As she leaned herself against my white school blouse, a deep circle spread, soaking into the cotton; her hand was red and dripping where she had scraped away at the skin on her palm. Inside, I washed away the blood and bandaged it as best I could before putting her to bed. It had healed back to silver within the week. I binned the school shirt then and there. I knew I wouldn't be wearing it anymore.

'You think you'll find it there?'

'Pardon?'

'Whatever it is you're looking for. Think you'll find it there?'

The snow must have absorbed the sounds of the man's footsteps, as the sudden conversation renders me disorientated. His face cracks open in a smile, full of scrawny crooked teeth, which he taps his tongue against as he shakes his head in amusement.

'Don't worry,' he laughs. 'I'm not one of them.' He lifts his hand to show me the two scars across his wrinkled left palm.

I nod.

'So, what is it?' he says.

'Sorry?'

'What is it you're looking for? You're not going in. You'd have done that by now.'

'I'm not looking for anything.' I try to sound deliberately uninterested. It doesn't deter him.

'Really? Then you're one of the few.' He smiles and pulls the ear flaps of his hat down to his chin and around his face. 'Got a flat up there, see.' He nods vaguely behind me. 'You're not the first I've seen standing here, not by many.'

'Is that right.' I respond without a question mark.

'Aye, it is. And I figure they're all looking for the same thing. Feel they've missed out, you see. Feel they didn't get what they deserve. All those folks that stand here, staring at these doors. I figure maybe they think they'll be appreciated next time. That's what they had me thinking anyways.'

'Is that why you're here?' I say. 'So you can go back and be appreciated?'

The old man grins an almost toothless smile.

'Perhaps, I ain't figured that out. Maybe I just like to appear all wise and knowledged like. Offer you young 'uns my pearls.'

'And what would they be?'

'I'll let you know when I figure them out. 'Spect it'll take a man like me a lot more than two amendments to do that though.' The glint in his eyes changes to a look of concern. 'Don't stay out in this. You shouldn't be standing here listening to the ramblings of an old man, not if you don't have to.' He tips his hat, smiles and leaves.

When I look back, my reflection is even more distorted than before.

Outside the flat, I consider knocking on the front door, but I can't work out which is worse, interrupting them or letting them carry on. I give myself a quick internal motivational pep talk, then swing open the door as loudly as possible to announce my return. The entrance is somewhat anticlimactic; Fi is on her own.

'Where did you go?' she asks.

'Just for a walk.'

'In this?'

'I guess I'm used to it.'

She taps the sofa next to her, beckoning me over.

'I've got some things to do,' I lie.

'Please. Just for a minute.'

I shuffle over and perch myself on the edge of the sofa. The seat tilts forward, and I adjust the cushion behind me in a vain attempt to plump it out.

'So,' she says. 'What things do you have to do?'

'Just a few errands.'

'Like?'

'Finding a job I suppose.'

'Any luck?'

'Not yet.'

Her eyes are finding it difficult to keep contact, and she fidgets around, tucking her feet underneath her and shifting towards me. She has a look about her, but I can't tell if it's excitement, guilt or something else altogether.

'Well, I was talking to Gabe,' Fi says, tapping her fingertips against her knees and breaking the silence. 'And, well, we were thinking, it would be tight, but maybe, if you wanted, you could go back.'

'Go back?'

'To school.' She grabs my hands and squeezes them so hard she pushes the knuckles together. An unfeasible grin plastered across her face.

'Fi, I'm twenty-one. How can I go back to school?'

'Not in this section, I know you can't go back here, but you can definitely do it. Gabe looked into it.'

'Gabe looked into it?'

'I think he thought about it one day maybe, I don't know. But it's possible. That's what you wanted, isn't it? To go back to school? You're smart Em. You could get a real job, not just as a carer. You could be a doctor or a teacher or whatever you want.'

'Fi —'

'There are plenty of shifts at the bar, so I —'

'Fi —'

'The new term won't start until the spring, so I can save a bit by —'

'Fi!' I flick her hands off mine and push her back.

Her expression falls. 'I thought you'd be happy. This is what you wanted,' she says, her smile replaced by a look of confusion.

'Fi, it's only been —'

'Listen, I know —'

'No, you don't,'

'Em, please —'

'Listen to yourself. You've been sober two days, not even that, and now you're telling me to go back to school, sign on as an apprentice, you'll take care of everything.'

'I —'

'What?' I say. 'You think it's going to be that easy, not drinking, that you'll just stop. And work in a bar? Are you deluded?'

'I —'

'And what do I do when you start drinking again? Drop out of school again, try to find work when I'm even older and with even less experience? Or just keep hoping that maybe you can pay your way with Gabe a little longer.'

'Em,' she whispers, but she doesn't finish. She looks up at the ceiling.

I can see the water building in the corners of her eyes. My stomach coils. I've gone too far, I know I have. A rush of guilt floods through me and I reach out to take her hand, but she brushes me away.

'Fi —' I try to speak, but the guilt has turned my mouth to chalk.

'It's fine.'

'Please —'

'Honestly, it's fine. You only said what you thought.'

'I didn't mean it.'

'You did, you're right. I know what you think —'

'No, I don't. I don't think that,' I say.

The tears are trickling down her cheek.

'I know what I did was wrong,' she says. 'The way I left you to deal with everything. Even before.... I should have been there, helped you with her. I was a coward and you needed me.'

'But I didn't,' I say. 'That's the whole point. You think I did, but I didn't. I never needed you, Fi. We never needed you.'

The words sweep out over my lips and into the air before I can stop them. They strike her like a knife and she flinches away from me.

'I didn't mean it like that.' My adrenaline soars as I desperately try to pull the words back into my mouth. 'Of course I needed you. *We* needed you.'

'No, you didn't.'

'Fi, please —'

'I had one job,' she says, her lips trembling.

'That wasn't your job,' I say.

'Yes, it was.' The tears pour down her face and snot dribbles out beneath her nostrils. Her chin trembles more and more as she attempts to stifle the sobs. 'I just had to fix it, if she... I just had to...'

'Fi, you couldn't have known —'

'It didn't matter that you didn't need me, either of you —'

'You had to work,' I say lamely.

'You don't believe that,' she says. All her words are released between ragged breaths.

I reach out to her again, but she flicks me away.

'This is not your fault,' I say. 'None of it.'

'I could have —'

'No, Fi. There's nothing you could've done. This was her choice.' Fi tries to interrupt, but I shake my head at her. 'She knew the rules. She knew you couldn't go back twice. She made the choice. The rest... Well the rest was on her too.' Her eyes dart back to the ceiling. 'She was our mother. She should have been the one looking after us. You have got to stop blaming yourself.'

'I —'

'This is not your fault, do you understand me? This is not your fault, none of it.'

With her eyes still fixed upwards, she breathes in uneven shudders, shallow and noisy.

'You need to stop blaming yourself.'

'Your amendment —'

'Was *my* choice, just like yours was yours and hers was hers. We made our own choices. And we are fine, you and me. You hear me? It's all in the past. Everything that happened then, it doesn't matter. We are fine. We are going to be fine.' I lift her chin up and wipe away some of the mascara-stained tears. 'Now, I'm going to make us a drink,' I say. 'And you need to clean yourself up.'

My hands are shaking as I pour the water from the kettle. The tea bags balloon up and float to the top before lazily sinking back down, and it takes a second before I realise I'm waiting, waiting to hear the door open. That's what happens after every conversation we have: we fight, we cry, we try to make up, we fail, Fi leaves and gets drunk. That's the cycle I'm comfortable with, that's what I'm expecting. But the door doesn't open.

Binning the tea bags, I carry the mugs back into the living room. Fi is standing by the bookshelf, the same family photograph in one of her hands. It's one of the few we have of the four of us; our mother developed a proclivity for matches one month, almost all of which landed on photos with our father in them. I managed to save this one though. In Fi's other hand is a red velvet pouch.

She puts the photo down and tries to take the mug, but with only one hand free, she can't manage. Instead I put it down on the shelf and twist it so the handle is facing her.

'What's that?' I say.

Fi looks at her hand as if surprised to find something squashed within her fist.

'Oh, it's for you, for your birthday. I'm sorry I forgot to give it to you the other day. I–I–I'm sorry.'

Warmth spreads through my insides. It's accompanied by twisting guilt in my gut. Once again, I assumed the worst of her.

Butterflies flit in my stomach as I take the pouch from her and fumble with the tightly knotted strings. I have such difficulty it's as though my fingers are numb or in heavy gloves. When I finally manage to loosen the strings, I tip the contents onto my palm. A small gasp escapes my lips.

'It's beautiful.'

We both stare at the object in my hand, which reflects the colours of the room in mesmerizing spectrums. I take it between my fingertips and twist it around to see the charm, in which I catch sight of myself: a perfect virtual image caught in the mirror of a silver envelope.

'It's almost the same as mine,' she whispers. The way her voice goes up at the end makes it sound like it's a question. 'Do you like it? I'm sorry that it's late.'

'It's perfect,' I say, not taking my eyes off it. 'I can't believe you found me one.'

'Of course I did. It was your twenty-first.'

We hug. I can't remember the last time we did that, not like this, not a good hug. I hold her, my hand still clinging to the cold metal and her chest shuddering as she tries not to cry.

Chapter Eighteen

WE SCRAPE together a few coins from around the flat and use them to pay for a late lunch together – another menial event with disproportionate significance for us. We don't leave the section, just buy some fresh rolls and wander around, kicking the snow and devouring the bread before our fingers and the pastries harden in the cold. Our conversation is inconsequential, but that in itself is progress.

Afterwards, Fi falls asleep. She started to doze on the sofa, and I woke her to move her to her bed. She'd been struggling since we got back to the house; the conversation was flagging, and I watched as her eye movements become more erratic, while she sat on her hands to try to disguise the shaking. More than once, her eyes strayed across to the empty drinks cabinet.

I pick a well-read book from my shelf, flop down in the living room, open to a random page and start reading. I can hear Fi's nightmares from here, the whining and groaning. I barely manage a chapter of the book before the noises grow too loud to ignore.

She's soaked in sweat; the white bed sheets are translucent with it. Her skin is pallid and coated in beads, and strands of damp hair stick to her neck and face. She twists and writhes between the sheets, her face contorted in spasms of pain. As I watch, my pulse rises. I've seen a scene identical to this before. It's etched in me. It's not something I'm ever likely to forget.

I rush over to Fi, flip her body around and scour her skin for evidence of a new scar. I start with her hands, inspecting every inch, then lift her top and skirt, turning her limbs over between my hands. Every second I search, my pulse is getting faster. When I find nothing, I pull out her drawers, turning over the contents for evidence, for an envelope. My heart is beating so far up my throat it's making it's difficult to breath. Then I remember, my mother never received her second envelope either. That's the thing about breaking rules. You just don't know what will happen. The pounding inside my chest reverberates through every rib as I tear the clothes from her drawers and the books from her shelves. All the time I'm praying Fi will hear the noise and wake up and tell me to stop. Even when two arms clamp around mine and hold me tight I don't stop reaching out and kicking the debris on the floor.

'It's just the drink, Em,' he says. 'She's fine, it's just the drink. She just needs to sweat it out.'

'No. This is how she was. This is the same.' I pant. My head is swaying and the room is slipping out beneath my feet.

'It's just the drink.'

'No, she's done it, I know she has. She's broken a rule.' I struggle against his grip, but he doesn't move, his resolve unwavering.

'Em, it's just the drink.' Gabe twists me around, trapping my arms between us and pinning me to the spot. 'I promise you. It's just the drink.'

He turns me back to look at Fi. Her skin is still blanched and cadaverous, but her breathing is more even and her movements have diminished to just twitches and spasms.

'She's fine. She'll be fine,' he repeats.

'She's —'

'She's fine.'

Slowly reason returns.

'I need some air,' I say.

We sit on the steps outside the apartment. My body is still conflicted with the desire for space and the need to stay close to Fi, and now that I've calmed down a little, I realise how ridiculous my panic was. It was my amendment. My envelope. The only person who can't make that amendment again is me. Fi is fine, I tell myself repeatedly. Fi will be fine.

Gabe sits beside me. He has on the same top as this morning, and a thick layer of stubble casts a dark shadow across his face. We sit at first in silence, through which I try to remove the dirt from underneath my fingernails.

'She was like that you know. Our mother. When, she did it. That was what it was like.'

'I know,' Gabe says.

'I thought that was it, you know. When she came back like that, I thought we'd lose her right there and then. But then she clung on and I thought, maybe. Maybe she'll come back to us. Maybe there was a reason the amendment didn't work. Maybe, somehow we'll find a way through. But she clung on just so that she could…' The words get sucked in by the silence.

There's a long pause before anyone speaks again.

'Em. I'm sorry,' he says.

'For what?'

'For the other day. The car. The fuel. The truck. You could have lost everything. It was stupid.'

'You made the right call.'

'It was reckless.'

'It's fine. You made the right call. Forget about it. I have.' It was true; my mind had been far too busy to think back. The event at the fuel station was like an act from a long, forgotten film. In my mind, the whole day is best not thought about again.

'But I knew we had to drive somewhere. I fucked up,' Gabe says, apparently unable to shake the guilt.

'You didn't fuck up. She's here. Things are better this time.'

That's when I stop. Without warning I am there, where I promised myself I would never be. Without any indication, I have become one of those people who has to believe that whatever pain or stress or hurt there is now, it was worth it. I am one of those people who must believe this is better than what came before. I am the same as everyone else. The realisation is like a knife.

'That looks good,' Gabe says, glancing at my wrist.

I refocus my attention. 'Thank you, it's beautiful, isn't it?'

'I'm glad you like it.' He looks at me quickly before averting his gaze. 'She's fine, you know. Fi'll be fine.'

'I couldn't have gotten her without you,' I say. 'I owe you everything.'

Gabe's feeble attempt at a smile makes my chest ache, and my hand rises to his stubbled jaw. A nervous tingling spreads from the touch and fizzes down through the rest of me. Still, I don't move my hand and neither does he.

I struggle to form words, my throat suddenly parched and scratching. My voice comes out hoarse. 'You have nothing to feel guilty for,' I whisper.

But he doesn't respond. Instead, he leans in so close I can taste his breath. The elevator lift announces its arrival, but the sound is peripheral. Neither of us hear it, neither of us move. He leans in closer still until I'm sure my breathing has stopped. I close my eyes, chest pounding. I can feel the heat radiating from my skin; I can feel his skin, just millimetres away, and that's when I feel the blow against my ribs.

My head spins as my body tumbles downwards, step by step. Each time I land with a sickening crack and a blinding pain. When I finally stop falling, I'm not sure if I can move. Every cell screams in agony. I try to yell out, but just breathing turns my vision white from pain. I look on as Gabe flies down the stairs towards me, but he is too slow. Red flowers flash in front of my eyes before everything goes black.

When I come round, I am lying on a carpet, our carpet. My head is swimming, and the taste of blood fills my mouth. I force my eyes to open and gasp in gulps of dusty carpet air, spluttering as it invades my lungs. The pain is indiscriminate, at first I think my wrists are bound before I look down and see them free. They are probably just broken.

Gabe lies across the doorway. He's been dragged in. His face is marked in ugly bands of carpet burn, and thickening blood from a cut above his eyebrow conceals the greyness of his skin. I try to crawl towards him. Pain shoots up through my arms to my spine, burning my insides. I hold my breath, trying to block out the pain as I inch my way forward, yet I've barely moved a metre when something strikes the back of my knees.

'He's fine, a couple of scratches, nothing a big boy like that won't recover from. Just needs a bit of sleep, that's all.'

I recognise the voice, but my head is too fuzzy to place it.

'Your sister on the other hand...'

Fi! I twist my body around. Involuntary screams flee from my lungs as I try to raise my body off the floor. It's as though every bone inside me is bleeding. Fi is on the sofa, bruised and gagged, though from the swelling around her lips, the gag seems unnecessary. Her left eye has risen to a purple welt from which a clear liquid oozes and seeps down to her chin.

I try to drag myself towards her, but she shakes her head hurriedly. A new pain pierces my side, and I hollowly gasp for air. Lifting my shirt, I see the purple-black bruising emerging from beneath my ribs. I cover them back up and suck in air in a long hiss.

'It'll pass. Maybe,' he says. He sniffs loudly and then wipes his nose on the knuckles of his clenched fist. Sniff and wipe. Sniff and wipe. He sits on the arm of the sofa, repeating the sniff-wipe motion until he leans in over Fi.

She shudders as he extends a finger, stroking down her mutilated face with his decorated hands. The petals of the flowers are deformed, misshapen and discoloured; one of his eyes has swollen shut, but the other is tombstone grey. The déjà vu strikes again. A girl in a bed. A smell of burning flesh. I don't know where these feelings have come from, but I know why he's here.

'She was quite attractive before, you know,' he says yanking a handful of Fi's hair and forcing her to bite down on her gag. 'Thought I might even get myself a little bit.'

Fi struggles against his grip. The more she fights, the more he laughs. It doesn't stop her though.

'This one's got some tenacity. I like that. It took a lot to make her squeal. Wanna see?'

Fi raises her arm and covers her face. Silently, she quails in agony as she takes the impacts again and again. The metal bar swings through the air, striking her stomach and thighs. I watch, screaming helplessly, trying to drown out the sound of her bones splintering.

'See?' he says. 'Told you she was tough.'

Tears stream down Fi's cheeks, and her teeth draw blood against her lip. Another ricochet of the bar causes her to let out a muffled howl.

'Ahh, now I'm disappointed, I thought you were gonna take way more than that.' With a sniff and a wipe, he straightens up before slithering over and crouching down on the floor next to me. His lips are cracked and flaking with dead skin, his breath stinks of bile and booze and his nostrils dribble with a colourless syrup that withdraws back upwards with each noisy sniff.

I close my eyes and hold my breath, trying to shut out the image of Fi's terrified face.

'Now you weren't so lucky on the gene front, were you? Sister landed all those good genes, didn't she? I mean look at you. Your hair is the colour of shit to start with. You know that? It's like your whole head is just covered in shit.' He grabs a fistful of my hair and fondles it between his grubby fingers and then pulls it to his nose and sniffs again, this time deeply. 'Seriously, I'd just cut it off if I were you. Cut the whole lot off.' The idea forms as a black glint in his eyes. The corners of his mouths twist upward. 'Aye, I think that's a good idea.' He drops my hair and sneers. 'Don't go anywhere, will you?'

Then, just for good measure, he kicks me in the stomach.

I scramble across the carpet, my jaw clenched, while pain and tears blur my vision. Every muscle is on fire as I clamber towards Gabe. His breathing is shallow, and his face is swollen and bloated. Blood pulses from the cut on his forehead. He's alive; that's all I have time to check. I turn to Fi and claw along the ground. A searing pain shoots down every cell along my spine; our tiny living room now seems infinitely vast.

Fi tries to speak, but the cloth in her mouth restricts her. She leans out, but I'm still feet away when I try to reach her outstretched hand. I just want to touch her, feel her warmth, but a paralysing pain seizes my chest. The tips of our fingers are inches apart when the boot stamps down on my hand.

'No, no, no, you have to stay over there.' He kicks me backwards, spitting his words and spraying me in flecks of alcohol-drenched spittle.

I blink, trying to correct my spinning vision. It finally focuses on the handle of our bread knife protruding from his pocket. A terrifying sense of calm emanates from his body as he lights a cigarette, takes one long drag, then removes it from between his lips and stubs it out on my arm. I see the three silver lines marked along his palm. He's not going to be the one to amend this.

'God, look at you, hair the colour of shit and a face to match. I'd be doing you a favour. They do it to puppies you know. And kittens. Drown the ugly ones. No one wants an ugly dog. It's just an extra mouth to feed' He takes the knife from his pocket and grabs a clump of hair.

The blade is blunt, and the serrated edge rips, tearing my hair from my scalp with a pain so acute the root of every strand burns. My skin seethes in agony, minute and yet crippling. Don't scream, I keep telling myself, it's only hair, it's only hair. The tufts drift to the ground and scatter around my knees.

'See, you look better already,' he goads.

My eyes lock on Fi's as an anchor, and I watch her tears fall one by one.

Fi always used to squirm when she had her hair cut or washed or braided or brushed, though she was definitely worst when it was braided. Our mother would stand there, comb in hand, digging the pointed end into her scalp and marking out small sections to entwine.

'Sit still, Finola, it only hurts because you're moving,' she'd say.

'I'm only moving because it hurts!'

Twenty minutes to create, five minutes to destroy. As soon as she was out the door, Fi would pull at the plaits and shake her head until they all fell out. I never minded as much when mine was braided. It was only hair.

It is only hair. I remind myself again and again. It is only hair.

He doesn't speak through the rest of the styling, and I am far calmer than I would ever have given myself credit for; my mind is strangely detached from the whole situation. Hair litters the floor where I kneel, Fi's hysterical sobs begin to diminish and Gabe's chest rises and falls in small irregular movements. When the cut is finished, the man chucks the knife to the ground, stumbles over to the bookcase and starts to pick up the photographs.

'She dead?' he asks, lifting a photo of my mother.

I nod.

'Thought so, hadn't seen her in a while.' He places it back on the shelf. 'Went a bit nuts, right? Killed herself?' He picks up a few more, but he quickly grows bored and takes a seat in the beaten armchair, one wooden photo frame still in his hand. He rests his hands on his knees and stares at the picture. It's one of the two of us, Fi and me, and I can't be older than three; I'm pushing an empty toy pushchair while Fi holds my hand. As I watch, I see the sheen cover his eyes.

'I'll go back,' I say quietly. 'Let me get them help, and I'll go back and change it. Whatever happened I can change it. I still have one, I can still do that.'

In a snap, his face changes back.

'Whatever happened?' He lunges across the room and sweeps the photos off the shelf where they clatter to the ground. One by one, he starts hurling them at me, faster and faster until the air is thick with glass and wood.

My body is too weak to dodge. I lie flat against the floor, trying to protect my already shattered rib cage as the frames smash, covering me in shards of broken glass.

'You know what happened,' he hisses. 'You were the one who got the envelope. But you wouldn't save my little girl, would you? No, you took your slutty, drunken whore of a sister and let me watch my daughter die.' His face is purple, his eyes bulge from their sockets and drool foams in the corner of his mouth.

I try to cover myself as he dives towards me.

'You know what happened. And I watched her die. Do you know how long it can take someone to die like that? The pain they go through? The pain she went through, my tiny little girl?' He looks like an animal, a rabid dog or crazed bear. He digs his nails against his skull as he rocks backwards and forwards to kick me. 'I watched her choking, coughing up blood and gunk and black shit like you couldn't imagine. My perfect, perfect little girl.' When his legs tire, he tries to light a cigarette, but his hands aren't steady enough. I wait for another blow, but for now he's stopped.

Silence comes in the absence of his rant. Fi's not crying anymore; she's not sobbing or whimpering. She's not even moving. Her eyes are closed as she hugs her knees in a foetal position on the sofa. She's slipping away. Adrenaline courses even faster in my veins. I need to speak, I need her to hear how much I love her, how much I need her to stay with me now. But I can't say anything. Through the pain and the fear, the words won't come out.

'Thirty minutes too late, that's when they turned up, thirty minutes.'

He's back, hovering above me with movements too fast to follow. He fiddles with the lighter, wipes his nose as he sniffs and rocks back and forth, again and again. 'I sat with her body, watched her drift away. And then they blamed me. They said it was my fault.' He punctuates his breaths with words. 'Wrong road, no belt, no lights, ignoring warnings. All that fucking stupid bullshit they have to say because we both know it was never my fault.' He locks his eyes on me. 'It was never my fault.' In one almighty wrench, he pulls me up by the neck of my top. The smell of his liquor-fuelled saliva burns my throat and watering eyes. 'You knew. You could have changed it, saved her. But no, you just took your fucking drunk-arse sister and let my little girl die. Don't tell me you'll go back. You can't go back. Neither of us can.'

As I try to wriggle out his grip, he pushes me to the floor, towards Fi. I reach up and grab her hand; it's wet and cold and stained red. I can't see where the blood has come from. I can't tell how bad it is.

'Fi. Fi.' I scramble to my knees and shake her by her limbs. She doesn't move. 'Please. Please, Fi.'

Turning around, I clamber across the carpet and grapple at his feet. 'Please. Let me help her. Fi can amend it for you,' I say. 'She still has one left, she didn't use hers then, hers was something different. Please. Let me get her help. Then she'll do it. I promise you.'

On the other side of the room, still curled in a ball, Gabe groans. The man glances at him dismissively. Slowly he pulls another cigarette out of the packet and leaves it dangling between his lips, his rocking slowing as he considers my idea.

'They won't let her,' he says, shaking his head and sniffing. 'Not like that.'

'They will at the hospital. I'll go with her, tell them she was in an accident. They'll let us do that. If it's just an accident I'm sure they will. If we can get her to the hospital, they'll let her do that.'

He manages to light the cigarette and draws the smoke deep down into his lungs. I watch him process my words.

'How do I know she'll change it?'

'She will, I know she will. But she can't if you let her die. Please call an ambulance. I promise you, she'll amend this.'

He exhales heavily, blowing the smoke into Fi's face.

'I need to be sure she'll go back,' he says.

'You can be, I promise.'

He smiles. 'I need to be really sure.'

A few strands of hair still dangle from the jagged knife edge as he picks it up from the ground; his intentions causing the air around us to freeze. I push myself onto my knees and scuttle backwards as fast as I can, the agony in my wrists turning my vision white.

'What are you so worried about? In a few hours none of this will have ever happened.'

'No, you can't. You can't.'

'Just relax, you won't remember a thing.'

'You can't. You can't.'

'Oh, but I can.'

He's right, I realise. There's absolutely nothing to stop him from killing me and if that's what it takes for Fi to amend then I should let him. After all, what does it matter if I die now? It won't be forever. I won't even know. I close my eyes and try to accept my fate. I try to let the calm of inevitability wash over me, but I can't. My mind won't let me, not yet, not without a fight. The adrenaline rushes through me, soaking my cells, until the pounding of my pulse drowns out everything else.

I grab a cushion, the only thing I can reach and launch it at him with all the strength my broken body can muster. The pathetic throw lands inches from where I am sprawled.

'A cushion?' He laughs.

I scan around, with arms flailing, but nothing else is within grabbing distance, so instead I force my body up and lunge for his ankles. I catch him by surprise and momentarily unbalance him, but he rights himself in barely a second. He sneers in delight.

'Tick, tock, tick, tock. You're wasting time. I can play this all day, but your sister, well, I'm not sure how long she's got.'

Beads of sweat stream down Fi's eyelids. Her skin is glossy, marbled with blossoming bruises.

Shards of glass are all over the floor – broken pieces from the photo frames. They snag in the carpet, but I manage to pick up a largish piece and swing wildly at his legs. He knocks it out of my hand in one kick. The cut in my mouth has reopened, and the tang of blood is stronger than ever. I search around for something I can throw, anything, but nothing is left.

'Any other ideas?' He sneers. 'You know there's only one way out of this.'

He's right, the only way out of this alive is if I die. I'm just wasting time. If Fi doesn't survive this, then none of us will. My sight is blind with tears as I bury my head in my knees.

They say when you're about to die, truly at the end, when you have accepted that you have no other option, no way out and the futility of uncertainty has been removed, you become perfectly at peace. I saw it in my mother. Her breathing had steadied and her lips managed to curl at the corners in a smile as she summoned us with a whisper. She lifted her head off the bed so she could see our faces, then stroked our hair, and told us how beautiful we were and how lucky she was to have had two such wonderful princesses. Then she whispered something into Fi's ear and pulled me down and kissed the top of my head.

'Look after each other,' she said.

I lift my head and struggle to my feet. I feel every crack in every bone, yet somehow even the pain is passive now. This must be the end. Time extends around me, a thin piece of elastic pulled from both ends and bent around as if joined in one infinite loop. I take one last look at everything. I look at the blunt knife in the man's hand, the patches of sweat on his white top and the twisted poppies, bruised and bleeding sewn into his skin, a photograph of my mother, her eyes closed as she nuzzles us children, my darling sister, so perfect with her hair fallen across her face as if she were just asleep. I stare at the blood stains on the carpet where Gabe had been lying.

I muster just enough strength to roll out of the way as Andjrez crumples to the ground.

Chapter Nineteen

THERE ARE TEARS, then telephone calls, then strangers. I know I'm involved, but somehow I'm just a member of the audience, a spectator, watching these things happening around me, happening to me. There are lights and questions and uniforms and more uniforms. Questions I can't recall and replies I can't remember all take place within the periphery of my consciousness. Sympathies, accusations, condolences. I remember the condolences, but not what they were for. Were they for my loss? Please don't say I lost them. Please don't tell me that.

The needle in my arm makes my eyes heavy, but I don't want to let them close. I need to find them, Fi and Gabe. I need to see them, hear them. I can't have lost them, not now. I can't. I plead desperately in my head, begging myself to stay awake, but it's as if someone is pulling down on my eyelids with invisible threads.

When I wake, I'm crouched in a corner on a cold tile floor. The strip lighting buzzes, reflecting on the metal frames of the bed. There's a horrible noise, a cry, a wail. At first it seems to come from the walls, then from the whole room, and it just keeps getting louder. I try to cover my ears, try to block it out, but it just gets louder and louder, reverberating in the brickwork. It's coming from inside the room; other people hear it, too.

I hear their footsteps running down the hallway. Two nurses rush in, but they're not stopping the sound. They're just looking at me, talking to me. They're not stopping the sound. Maybe they want to get me away from it. That must be what they're saying. I try to get up, try to get away from it, but they're not helping me, they're holding me here, trapping me in this room with this tortured screeching. I struggle against them, desperate to escape, and watch as a needle slides into my arm. Somehow it seems to be working – the sound seems to be fading. Soon, I can barely hear it.

The next time I open my eyes, I'm in a bed, and it takes a few moments to adjust to the darkness. The sheets are cold and coarse, and a fan is dancing with its shadow on the ceiling, always one step out of sync. Watching it makes me dizzy, so I quickly stop. Everything smells of metal, and shards of light splinter through the slits in the blinds; it's not night-time beyond this room, yet I am definitely in bed. I want to find evidence of time, how long I've been here, where here is. I try to sit up, but my limbs are unresponsive. I manage only to move my eyes. A figure is lying in a bed next to me, unnaturally still. I think I see the sheet rise and fall, but then nothing, not for minutes. No arms twitching or legs stretching. Brown hair droops over the sheet, similar to mine, just a little darker, a little richer. I feel the sheets soften and warm as they dampen around my thighs, but I close my eyes again; wetness is a discomfort I can endure.

Something moves around me, a pattern of light flickers beyond the closed lids of my eyes. People, they are moving. Are they talking? I can hear nothing, not even my own breaths or heartbeat. It's as though I've been removed and placed into a perfect vacuum. True silence, I discover, is far more menacing than noise. I hold my breath and wait for it to end. Eventually I hear something. Heavy footsteps rattle the bed as a man walks over to me. Even with my eyes closed, I can tell it's a man – a woman wouldn't walk so gauchely. He attaches something around my wrist. Cold and metallic, it feels wet against my skin. Then he is gone.

Voices wake me and I'm disappointed; I'd been dreaming. The light was muted, soft but natural, and the whole sky was a vertical sea of grey, cloaked in cloud and cold. Gabe and I sat on a bench together with a bottle of champagne, smiling and giggling. He takes the bracelet from my hand and fixes the clasp carefully around my wrist. Then he kisses me. Even in sleep my stomach is light, excited. The image was so clear and vivid it could be a memory, but now I'm awake I feel it slipping away, one illusion at a time, in the way only dreams can do.

The words are delivered in forcibly hushed tones so as not to disturb anyone, so as not to disturb me. They are familiar in their timbre if not content, the conversation just audible above the whirring of the fan.

'How can you stand to watch this?' he says.

'I can't stand it anymore than you.'

'Then why won't you change this? Look at her, that's your

sister for Christ's sake.'

'You think I don't know that?' she spits the words; her teeth sound gritted.

'I can't understand how you can leave her like this.'

'Why don't you understand? It will make it worse. It always makes it worse.' Silence falls before they both sigh in frustration; this is not the first time they've had this conversation.

'The girl, Fi, what about the girl?' he pleads.

'I feel bad, I do, but I'm not responsible for that.' Another silence follows. 'Gabe, what happened, you and —'

'That has nothing to do with this. You could make all this right.'

'What happened —'

'What happened was a mistake, Fi, we both know that now. You said —'

'I said nothing. You assumed. That is not my fault. You should have thought of that before.'

'Fi —'

'Grow some fucking balls, Gabe.'

The footsteps march out of the room and away down the corridor outside, taking her voice with them.

Gabe lingers. I feel his warmth, his stare, but I'm tired. I sink back into my imagination, praying for the same dream again. More voices echo around, but they're just noises. Tones with no intonation. It's like I'm trapped behind some hazy screen which occasionally clears to allow me teasing glimpses of the outside world. They're arguing again, and they're louder this time. They don't think I can hear them. They're right. I return to my dream, the same thirty second loop. Gabe and I and the view.

'I need you to understand,' the voice is saying. The tone lilts as she speaks, so light a breeze could pick it up and whisk it away from me. 'I know Gabe doesn't understand, but I know you will. You do, don't you? You get that this is right. This is right, right for both of us. I promise. I promise.'

I'm not sure how long she stays there, perhaps a few minutes, perhaps all day; I have no measure of time. She places her hand on the top of my head and removes it quickly. A draft tickles my neck and prickles the hairs, chilling right along my collarbone and down my back. I can taste the honeysuckle on my dry lips. How does she always smell of honeysuckle? Her footsteps tread away from me, and I'm glad. I'm starting to prefer being alone, where there's nothing to distract me from my dream.

'I love you,' she whispers.

When I wake up this time, it's different. In the quiet I'm suddenly aware of my body and that the dampness has gone. When was that? Last night, this morning? Perhaps it dried over time. How long would that take, drying, lying like this? Surely more than just a few hours? Perhaps somebody dried me, but I'd remember that, wouldn't I?

My thoughts are interrupted as a hand weaves its fingers between my own. It's warm but worn – I know this hand. I know if from reality, but more so, I know it from my dream. It's not until my lungs start to tremble from lack of air that I remember to breathe.

The voice starts to speak several times. I can hear the smacking of the lips, the swallowing of a dry mouth and the deep half breaths that dissolve in the air before the words form.

'We need you back now, Em.' He sighs. His voice is exhausted but each word is carefully contemplated. I become acutely aware of his touch, his hand's slight dampness, the warm pulsing beneath his skin. I squeeze my eyes closed even tighter. My heart knocks against my ribcage.

'I don't know what Fi's told you,' he says. 'I don't even know if you've heard what I've told you. I just wanted you to know that he's gone now. He's far away. He can't hurt you or Fi or anyone else. Not anymore. So you can come back now.' His hand grips mine firmly. 'Okay? You can come back now.'

He pauses like he's expecting an answer, a contribution to the conversation. I want to open my eyes, confess to feigning sleep; he won't sit there forever, and I don't want him to leave, not just yet. My chest starts thumping, drumming so loudly he's bound to hear it. I could roll over and groan, stretch a little to pretend I'm just waking up. He's only going to realise I'm awake soon enough if I don't. It seems like a good idea and it's the only idea I've got, so I lean towards the side and try to roll my body over.

Nothing happens. I try again. I push down harder on the solid mattress but stay cemented to the spot. I try something small, wiggling my toes, my fingers. Still nothing. The panic rises inside me. I can feel and hear my own breath, ragged and gasping. The pulsing in my ears thumps harder. I can't open my eyes either; it's like they're superglued shut. I test every limb, every muscle, every fibre, but none of them respond. I'm paralysed. Soon, the paralysis reaches my lungs, and I can't take in any air. I'm going to suffocate like this, I realise. After everything I did to survive, this is how I'm going to die.

'Nurse!' Gabe is shouting. 'I need a nurse!' He doesn't let go of my hand; his grip tightens painfully as he keeps shouting. 'Nurse! We need a nurse!'

New hands join him on me, hands which hold me down and push my ambushed body towards the bed. Gabe's grip is crushing my fingers, and voices I can't decipher seem to be hollering instructions. I draw strength from every cell in my body, every atom of my will. I force my eyes to open. It's slight, the most minuscule of movements, but they're open and I can see. I see his face, the grey creases around his eyes, the fear in his eyes. I see the other faces, their mammoth mouths and waggling tongues, and once again, I watch as another needle disappears into my skin.

One morning my parents took Fi and I to a park. It was the type of place normally reserved for the elite — Cabinet families, high-ranking guards, etcetera — but they had opened it for the day to some of the factory workers and their families. We wandered around laughing, smelling the flowers and pointing in astonishment at the butterflies and insects. Before we left my father gave a quick check that no one was watching, then reached down and picked us a handful of violets and lavender. When we got back home, I placed mine between my two heaviest books, two children's encyclopaedias, to press them. They stayed there for years and I probably only looked at them a few times, but I couldn't bring myself to throw them away. Straight after my father left, I came home to find the books gone. 'You need to grow up, stop holding on to silly little children's toys,' my mother had said. She had left all the other story books on the shelf.

Three voices discuss my prognosis.

'It's all psychological, a depressive catatonic state.'

'How long will it last?'

'I can't say.'

'How do we stop it?'

'There's nothing we can do but wait.'

'Take all the time you need,' Fi says quietly. 'I'm not going to leave you again. I promise.'

'She doesn't need time,' Gabe responds.

When the doctor leaves, they both stay. They don't talk though and only one hand is holding mine. The fingers entwine with mine, the same way they do in my dreams. I know that world isn't real, but it's a far more tempting place to stay.

Chapter Twenty

WHEN I FINALLY open my eyes, it's without ceremony. I gasp as if I've been submerged in water and blink rapidly as my eyes try to adjust to the lack of light. I turn my head and stretch out the muscles which have seized and cramped along my neck. In an attempt to rub out the tighter knots, I find my arms in as feeble a state as, I soon realise, every other muscle I own. Laboriously, I arch my back and bend my knees, pulling at the tissues and flexing all my joints, as they creak and click from neglect. My throat is dry, caked and cracked from lack of use, and a bitter, bile-tasting chalk coats my tongue. I try to form a word, nothing in particular, but a slight croak is the best I can manage. I need some water.

A standard lamp stands in the corner of the room. It emits a dim, hazy glow with almost everything beyond its perimeter visible only as shadows. On my bedside table is the only receptacle in the room I can see: a small vase containing a long since wilted bunch of flowers, which droop downwards and flatten onto the polished surface. Hopefully the flowers are responsible for the pungent, rotting smell emanating from somewhere near. I smack my mouth loudly. No sink, no jug, no bottle of water is waiting conveniently within arm's reach. If I want my drink, I'll have to look outside this room for it.

I lift myself onto my elbows and hold steady for just a second before a blazing pain shoots through my torso, piercing my lungs. Winded, I drop back down, hacking violently and begging for air. It is excruciating and immobilising. I lock my jaw, lean forward and manage to find some comfort by compressing my rib cage against my stomach, though each slight movement still fires spasms straight down every nerve ending. With my muscles clenched, I wait for the pain to pass, puffing out air from my lungs in short sharp bursts. In time, the pain fades to a dull ache that continues to persist in sporadic degrees of severity, but is bearable enough for me to try to stand. With a deep breath, I swing my legs over the edge of the bed.

An IV drip is attached to my arm. I've watched a few pre-discovery films, end of the world type scenarios, where the protagonist wakes to find themselves attached to one of these. I always thought it stupid when they pulled them straight out of their arms without so much as a second thought, though now it seems like the most obvious action. I wince as my fingers grip the needle and tug at the skin, though the removal itself is nothing more painful than a swift sting. The last few actions have amplified my need for water.

The floor is freezing, and my toes recoil in shock as I place them on the ground. It takes a moment before I attempt again. I fix my jaw in preparation of more pain, then I stand. It's by all means a small success, but I'm too thirsty to congratulate myself. As I lift one foot from the ground, my body wobbles and my arms flap hopelessly around. By wiggling about precariously, I manage to salvage my balance and turn it into my first step and then my second, not stopping between. With a final lurch, my hands smack against the grainy surface of woodchip wall paper. I am halfway to the door and panting profusely. Driven by intensifying aridity, I brace myself and, with my body pressed up against the wall, edge along the skirting board, shuffling a semi-step at a time until my toe stubs on the wooden frame of the door. The metal door handle creaks as I twist it open.

A humming, a continuous buzz comes from the fluorescent lighting which reflects in the perfectly polished floor of the corridor. The corridor itself stretches farther than my readjusting eyes can focus. I scan my surroundings. Disused machines are scattered along the passage collecting dust; they are archaic, covered with plastic liners and trailing cables with frayed leads and exposed wirings. I've never visited a hospital before, but I suppose it's what I'd envisioned: empty and pointless. We were shown a film once, about what it's like to live without amendments. People crowded around a narrow little bed and sobbed at the various tubes and equipment that whirred and bleeped and flashed around a person's head as they lay propped up on oversized pillows with eyes closed. We were meant to see all the negatives, all the pain and anguish that was there before amendments. I remember wondering how anyone could have so many people that would want to watch them sleep.

I stumble down the corridor, resting my weight on banisters when they are available and leaning against the walls between steps when they are not. There are no staff, no duty nurses or doctors, at least not that I can see, not even a janitor to redistribute the thick dust that has clumped along the skirting board. The need for hydration propels me forward. Lights in the other rooms are off. I peer through one set of slatted blinds as I regain my breath after a few exhausting steps. The room is empty. A street light shines in through a bare window and casts a shadow on the bed, the unoccupied chair and, for a reason I have no need to fathom, a guitar. But there is no sink, no jug or filled glass.

I reach the nurses' station, where a computer monitor flickers only with a little red light and swivel chairs are strewn carelessly across the spearmint floors. Various empty files are open and paper is littered across the desk, but I only offer it all a fleeting glance. Behind them a door opens onto a small room, a kitchen.

A gurgling comes from below the sink as I turn the taps. I don't bother with a glass but instead plunge my lips straight under the stream. Water spews out over my mouth, over the bowl and onto my bare feet. I gulp in mixtures of air and water faster and faster until my haste gets the better of me. I stop, coughing up the water that has filled my lungs. My thirst is still only partially quenched. I wipe my chin and dripping nose before bending back down for more.

'You should slow down. You could drown. I've seen it happen, you know.'

Turning around, I see the figure, perched on the cupboards, looking down at me over her knees.

'You're Emelia Evelyn Aaron, aren't you?' she says, hopping down and thrusting out a hand for me to shake. 'I'm Perri, well, it's Peregrine, but why would someone name you after a bird? That's just stupid. It could be worse though. I could be called pigeon or woodpecker or house martin, imagine being called house martin, or hawk I suppose. So people call me Perri, unless they're cross with me. But I don't listen when people are cross with me or when they call me Peregrine. It's a stupid name.'

The woman saying all this is old enough to be my mother. She twiddles a frizzy spiral of her greying blond hair around her index finger and swivels her hips in quarter turns, swinging her shoulders. Her words seem in endless supply.

'You're awake then? I didn't think you were ever going to wake up. You looked far too happy sleeping. I liked watching you sleep. I like sleeping, too. Once, I slept for a whole week. I didn't even eat or drink or go for a wee for a whole week, I just lay in my bed dreaming. I like dreaming, don't you? Then they made me get up. Did they make you get up?'

Her verbose stream stops, and for a second I think she actually wants an answer, but before I have even considered the questions, she's started again.

'It's quiet down here, I much prefer it when it's quiet, don't you? I come down here because it's quiet. And because they have snacks. Not all the time though, just sometimes. Sometimes they hide them, biscuits, crisps, that kind of thing. They try and hide them, but I'm good at finding them, see?' From the worktop behind her, she pulls out a tube of cheese flavoured corn snacks. 'They hid these in the cupboard. They were so easy to find, hardly a challenge at all. I'm good at finding things. Do you want one?'

She holds the tube out to me, wafting the artificial cheesy smell just under my nose. My stomach growls as she waves the tube expectantly.

'It's okay,' she says. 'I won't tell anyone.' She tips some onto my hand and then watches carefully to make sure I'm actually eating them.

They're soggy and the cheesy coating fizzes unnaturally on my tongue, but they slip down my throat easily enough.

'We should go now.' She places the tube back on the counter, exposing her palm. The three silver lines are still visible despite the hundreds of other scars that plaster her skin. They bisect at every angle. Some of the wounds are fresh and crusted and browning, while others have puckered the flesh into ugly pink knots as they've healed over time.

'It's rude to stare,' she snaps with a glare before instantly flicking to a wide and wild-eyed gummy smile. She grabs my hand. The skin on her knuckles is white with coarse dry cracks that redden as she tightens her grip.

She drags me out of the room, picking up the pace as she pulls me farther and farther down the corridor. At first, I'm not sure my legs will hold, but the more she yanks at me the more strength they seem to find. We push through one set of double doors and then another. Soon we are sprinting. She lets go, splaying her arms out at the side and spinning in circles as her bare feet screech against the white flooring, the stains of her tattered nightgown glowing in the lights.

Unable to resist, I join her. The air sweeps the cells of my skin clean as we whip up the dust which corkscrews up around our feet. I turn faster and faster, the walls and door and corridor blurring into a mint-green smear. A chill runs across my scalp as I shriek in euphoria, hours of silence spilling from my lungs. I spin and squeal, my arms out wide as a windmill, until my knees give in and I skid to a halt, slamming my body against a double door, doubled over breathless and laughing.

When I look up, Perri is glowering, her teeth bared at me and her fists balled at her side.

'Why did you have to do that? You ruined it, you ruined it all.'

'Sorry, I didn't mean —'

She cuts me off as she clamps her hands around her ears, shakes her head and starts singing a tuneless arrangement of la la sounds that are amplified on the plaster walls and down the corridor.

'Please, I'm sorry, I didn't mean to ruin anything.'

My words only make her sing louder and shake her head faster. As the sleeves of her nightdress slip up her arm, I see that the marks were not restricted to palms; grotesque scabs and welts in perfect parallel lines cover the skin from her wrist to her elbow on her left arm. Her right one, by compassion, is blemished only by liver spots and moles.

I step forward, my hand outstretched, but she backs away into the wall.

'Please,' I say.

'Thief!' she screeches.

I jump back as she screams at me, gnashing her teeth. 'Thief! I know you stole them, you bitch. Give me them back! Give them back!' She lunges at me, pulling my nightgown and clawing at the skin.

I try to back away, but she digs her nails in. I kick at her shins and her hands fly back up to her ears, the singing starts again.

'Please, I'm sorry, I haven't stolen anything, I promise, I —'

Two nurses push me out of the way and force her hands away from her scalp and behind her back.

'She stole from me, she stole them! It was her, I know it was her!' Perri screams, as they lift her up and start down the corridor, scraping her feet on the tiles.

'It's all right, Mrs Finch,' they repeat in hushed tones. 'Everything's all right.'

As they pass me, she reaches out a clawed hand and swipes,

just missing my cheek.

'You're ugly,' she says. 'You're an ugly thief.'

One of the nurses turns to me and motions down the corridor.

'Best get back to your own bed. You don't want to be down this end, Miss Aaron, not until you have to be.'

They don't offer me a second glance as they slide a needle into Perri's arm and start to drag her over to a heavy set of white doors at the end of the corridor. Droplets of yellow liquid trail behind them, and by the time they enter the code to the door lock, she has stopped struggling. The doors open and a barrage of screams cut through from the other side.

'Free Unity!' one voice screams above the others. 'I'm here to free Unity!' The nurses take Perri and slip away into the hidden ward. The resonating voices from beyond are once again silent.

On the way back, I find a glass in the kitchen which I fill, drink and refill. Remembering the files from earlier, I look back on the desk, but they are gone. I look around. The chairs are tidy and pushed underneath the tables and a few pens are lined up underneath the monitor, which no longer blinks. I swallow my drink and refill the glass for a third time, feeling a weight return to my eyes.

My door has no lock, and Perri's comment about watching me sleep makes me see shadows in every flicker of light and every creak in the corridor. Several times they jolt me out of my near sleep state and set my pulse racing. I must drop off at some point, though, as I feel the sunlight warming my face in an attempt to rouse me. I try to block it out, first with my hand, then a pillow, yet somehow the light still manages to filter through. I groan loudly. Last night's walkabout is evident in the multitude of aches that hound my limbs, and I desperately require more sleep. I try rolling over but it's no good; I know I won't drop back off while it's this bright. Half-conscious – and with my only intention being blocking out the light – I slip out of bed, leaving the heavy wool blanket in place. When I reach the window, I fumble for a way to close the blinds without opening my eyes, but in the end, I give in and face the inevitable glare of white light with extreme squinting.

The sky is crisp and clear, with no sign of the foreboding clouds that had dominated the horizon before the attack. I scan the area around to get some bearings. The roads are lined with green, and pocket-sized patches of garden are also far more vibrant than I had expected. Yellows, pinks, there's a whole symphony of colour. It begs the question: How long have I been asleep? How long does it take for snow to melt and a flower to grow? One week, two?

Wide awake, I prop myself against the window. Ten minutes have easily passed before I spy another person. A small child, nursing her arm, is carried out of the building by her father. Soon after, a bickering couple with exaggerated hand gestures marches in, only for the woman to reappear and leave in a car moments later, making space for the sleek grey car that slips into its place.

I wait for a person to climb out of the driver's seat. After a few minutes and no sign of movement, I decide they're probably waiting for someone and deliberate heading back to bed. At that second, the car door opens and a large metal contraption appears. A moment later, it springs open wide into a wheelchair. An actual wheelchair. I gawp at it in surprise. Next, a man's torso appears. He leans out the door and stretches towards the chair. The wheels slip away from his grip several times before he finally manages to heave himself out of the car and into the awaiting seat. The few people around stare in amazement, but after mentally chastising them I realise I'm doing the same thing, just from a less obvious view. Once securely in the chair, he slams the door and wheels himself into the building, but not before he looks up and sees me. My pulse rockets.

With a mighty clang, Fi swings open the door of the room and forces herself into my sanctuary. I glance back out the window, but the man is gone. I'm surprisingly deflated, not that Fi gives me time to dwell. Her arms are around my aching chest before I've drawn breath, and she sobs silently into the cheap cotton of my nightgown while squeezing me tighter and tighter.

'I knew you'd be okay,' she says. 'I knew you would, I knew you would.'

She smells musty, organic, human, especially in comparison to the stringent smell of antiseptic and cleaning fluids that fill the air. I soak up her honeysuckle scent, catching a faint whiff of alcohol on her shirt. Still, I breathe it all in, wrapping my arms around her and consuming her warmth. It's been months, if not years, since she held me like this. Strongly, supportively. Like someone I could rely on – like a sister.

At first, I try to battle my body's urge to tremble and sob but it's futile. The tears are contagious. Each time I think I'm in control they swell again, filling my lungs and shaking my whole body. I try inhaling slowly, then quickly, then barely at all – nothing seems to stem the flow. The tears run down my face and into her shirt faster than I can wipe them away, and pretty soon I stop trying.

Eventually, we pull away from each other. Fi's eyes move slowly as she scans my face, while wiping the stray tears that continue to escape and retreat down my cheeks. She frowns briefly, sucking in air through her nose before she changes her expression into a tightly pursed smile that puckers the skin above her lips.

'You look good,' she says.

We stare at each blankly before her face cracks into a smile and mine has no choice but to follow. Laughter erupts which causes my neglected muscles to contract too fast. I feel a stabbing below my ribs, but I don't stop. Fi throws back her head, her mouth wide, teeth on show and her eyes crumpled into two flat lines as I massage my side against the stitch. She wipes another tear from my face and holds her hand there, pinching her lips together again as the laughter dies away.

'I knew you'd be okay,' she whispers, wiping her own face with the back of her hand and then clasping my hands, so our silver chains form a mirror image. 'Things are going to be better now, I promise, Em. What you said, about it not being easy, you were right, but it's okay. I'm okay now. We're okay.'

She lets go of me, tucks a fallen strand of hair behind her ear and runs her tongue over her painted lips. Her cheeks are coloured too and her nails varnished. She looks beautiful. She was always beautiful, but this is different. The creases are still there but they're deeper because she's smiling rather than frowning, and her expression is clear, without the hazy fog of drink. Her eyes flicker back up to my head. I reach up to stroke my scalp, but she grabs my hand.

'There's someone who wants to see you.' She grins. 'Is that okay? Are you up to visitors?'

'Do I look up to visitors?'

'You look perfect. Well rested.' She jumps to her feet. 'He's waiting outside. I'll just go get him.' She moves toward the door then dashes back and restrains me in a short, but particularly constrictive, hug before heading back out the door.

Sweat starts forming on my palms while she's gone. I lick my thumb and rub the skin under my eyes, trying to reduce the signs of my crying. Unnecessarily I pinch my cheeks. I blush at the thought of seeing Gabe; the extra redness will probably make me look like a clown. I attempt to brush out the crumples in the nightgown – though they are too well embedded – and sniff quickly under my armpits. I'm in need of soap. I'm sure I reek of sweat, if not worse; the only reason I don't notice it is because I've been confined with my odour for so long that I can no longer smell it.

Running my hand across my hair, my stomach seizes. I had forgotten. I had forgotten about the attack and about the knife, about my hair. My fingers pick at the tufts that sprout out in random directions and uneven lengths, so brittle and coarse it could be straw, and the temperature in the room drops by what feels like a hundred degrees. My ribs constrict around my lungs. Perri was right; I am ugly and I don't want Gabe to see me like this, but the thought of not seeing him sends physical pain through me. When the door opens, I look up at the ceiling and hastily brush my face before any more tears can slip out.

Fi holds the door open somewhat ceremoniously as the creaking black tyres turn into the doorway. After a split-second realisation, nausea kicks me hard in the stomach. Gabe had no amendments left. He saved us with no amendments left, and this is what happened. This is why he wanted Fi to go back, not because of me, but because of him. Gabe is crippled, and my amendment put him there.

I painfully swallow back the tears and prepare myself, but the face that greets me is smiling. His square jaw is brushed with a well-maintained stubble and his eyes a luminous grey blue that remind me of a brewing storm.

'Em, this is Luke.'

Chapter Twenty-one

HE WHEELS IN. The collar of his pastel shirt is turned upwards at the back, the cotton stretched tight around his arms. He pushes himself forward with one hand. 'It's great to finally meet you, Emelia,' he says and pulls me down and kisses me on each cheek in turn.

Fi's look is of giddy excitement, possibly caused by the headiness of his aftershave which has now fused to my top. The sigh of relief I expel at Gabe not being crippled falls accidentally on the nape of Luke's neck, and I feel his body respond beneath me. Quickly, I push myself away, blushing at my actions. If Fi noticed anything odd, she certainly doesn't look like it. She gazes adoringly at Luke.

'Luke's been amazing,' she says. 'I met him here. He comes to visit people, people in the other ward. Don't you, Luke? And well, we just hit it off.' Fi flushes as she speaks and moves closer so she can rest her hand on his shoulders, like a dated couple's portrait. They stare at me expectantly. Her face begins to fall as I struggle to react.

'Oh. I'm so pleased for you,' I say, not sure why I'm having to force myself to smile.

'It's not like that,' Fi says. 'We just have…' She searches for the word.

'A connection,' Luke finishes for her.

'A connection.' Fi attempts to ruffle his closely shaven head, like a strange pet.

'Well, whatever it is you have, you look good,' I say to Fi again, this time more convincingly.

Not that she's listening to me anymore; she's adjusting something on the back of Luke's chair.

'Finola's been remarkable through the whole ordeal,' Luke says, filling the silence. 'Your sister really is incredible.'

'Luke saved me,' she says, her head reappearing. 'After the attack, I had no one. I don't know what would have happened if he hadn't found me here.' Her bracelet is dangling over her wrist and onto his shoulder.

'You would have been fine,' Luke says. He reaches up and kisses the ends of her fingers.

'What about Gabe?' I interrupt. 'Surely you had Gabe?'

My question is met with silence.

'What about Gabe?' I repeat.

The pair of them exchange a look. It's the type of look parents frequently use, foolishly assuming their children are unable to read them. Children can read their parents, just like I can read my sister. Her face is loaded with fear. Whatever the news is, she doesn't want to tell me. A lead weight falls like a hammer in my gut.

'No,' I say. 'He was fine. I know he was. He saved us. He saved us, and he was here. I know he was here. He spoke to me. I know he did.'

'Em —'

Pain shoots down my side as I try to move.

'Em, listen —'

I push her away.

'He's fine. Tell me. He's fine. He's got to be. He's got to be okay.'

'Please, Em, you need to calm down.'

I try to stand. I wrestle first with the bed sheets and then with air. The more I struggle, the more the oxygen slips out of reach. I desperately try to stay steady as my vision spins around the room. I am hyperventilating, or worse, suffocating. Finally, as my vision goes almost completely, I wobble and fall back onto the bed. Even the pain across my ribs doesn't compare to the agony I feel inside. Fi crouches next to me.

'Em.'

Pathetically, I attempt to swipe her away. I don't even have enough energy to cry.

'Em, he's fine. He's fine,' she whispers.

My head is throbbing too much to register what she says. She repeats it. This time it starts to sink in.

'He's fine?' I say.

'I promise. I would never lie to you, you know that.' There's a small sad smile on her lips as she nods.

'He's fine?'

'He's fine. In fact,' she glances at her watch, 'he'll probably be here any minute. He comes every morning.'

'He does?'

'He does.'

'Then why? You, you…'

But I can't finish my response. Maybe I just misread her. The air in here has grown too hot and humid, and I sense the dizziness starting again. Every part of me is so utterly exhausted. I sink onto the bed and roll over into the mattress, closing my eyes as Fi runs her hands over my hair and kisses the top of my head like our mother used to.

Finally, my pulse slows and the breathlessness is almost alleviated. I'm almost asleep when a gust of air causes my sheets to lift up and fly off the bed. I jump up, momentarily forgetting the agony the action will leave me in.

'Sorry,' says Luke. He's over by the window, leaning out. 'I was just letting in some air.'

Glaring, I snatch back the sheet and cover up my legs. Though I've never been the best at aesthetic maintenance, the hair on my legs is embarrassing, even for me. That is a minor cause of the mortification; the bed is covered in an abhorrent array of stains.

'I spoke to the nurse,' Fi says, brushing over my obvious embarrassment flawlessly by flattening out the blanket. 'You'll be fine to leave in a couple of days, if you want to.'

'If I want to?'

'You know. If you wanted to stay here for a while, that would be okay, too.'

'Stay here?' I study her expression, trying to decipher what she means by that. Then it twigs. 'You mean on the other ward?'

'Em —'

'You think I should be on the other ward. Is that it?'

'I just want —'

'You think I'm crazy. You think I'm like her!'

'Em, it was just a suggestion.' Her voice rises above mine, and her eyes flash with an anger that makes my blood boil. 'It was just if you felt you needed time,' she snipes.

'Well, she doesn't.' Gabe stands in the doorway with his eyes fixed solely on me. 'She doesn't need more time. And she certainly doesn't need the other ward.' In his hand is a bunch of flowers, the same type as those wilted in the vase beside me.

My body floods with relief.

'So there's no point putting these in the vase then,' he says as he walks over. He brushes my cheek with his hand and whispers as though I'm still asleep. 'I've been waiting for you to wake up,' he says. Deep dimples are pushed in the sides of his cheeks.

He's healed well. There's a new pinkish scar by his temple and a slight crook to his nose, but you wouldn't notice, not unless you knew. I fight every instinct I have to reach out and touch him.

A cough from the corner of the room strips us of our moment.

'I wish I could stay and chat, but I have to go,' Luke says, his wheels creaking along the floor.

'Okay,' Gabe replies without taking his eyes off me. The way his lips move makes my insides giddy.

'Em, Luke has to go now,' Fi says.

'It's fine,' Luke replies. 'I know Em and Gabe have an awful lot to catch up on, don't you, Gabriel?'

Gabe bristles and his fist tightens around the stem of the flowers. He turns to Luke, who is now just a few inches from the bed. 'Yes, we do,' Gabe agrees. 'We have a lot to catch up on.' He spins around on the bed to face Fi. 'Aren't you opening up today?'

'I've got plenty of time.'

'I'd prefer it if you weren't late,' he replies.

I flick my eyes between the two of them. The air has adopted a stiffening tension, and right now I can't read Fi at all; her hostility is intimidating. I'm caught between not wanting to breathe yet being even more terrified of what will happen if one of us doesn't.

'Thank you for visiting, Luke,' I say, breaking the silence. 'I'm sure I'll see you again soon.'

Fi and Gabe break their glare and look at me with attempted normality. I ignore their glances and look only at Luke.

'I'm sure you will see me very soon,' he says. He thrusts his hand towards me.

I reach out before I realise he doesn't want to shake hands, that's not what he's doing. He's stretching out his hand so I can see his palm, and the second I do my whole body turns to ice. It has only one line. One thin silver scar, perfectly etched across the headline of his palm. Luke is *unamended*. A man in a wheelchair, *unamended*. He turns his hand movement into a strange wave-type salute, accompanied by a nod, and for a simple gesture, there's something bizarrely intimate about the moment. So much so that I find myself blushing.

'It was a pleasure meeting you, Emelia. Until the next time.'

He offers no remarks to Gabe but allows Fi to push his chair to the door where she bends down for a mutual kissing of cheeks.

'I'll see you tonight then, Finola,' he states. Then he's gone.

Fi watches him down the hall before she comes back into the room. I speak before the tension has a chance to return.

'I'll get my things, if you know where they are?' I say.

Gabe and Fi exchange another look.

Fi drops down next to me, her hand on my knee and my stomach plummets.

'The doctors want to keep you here for a couple of days,' she says.

'I don't need to be here. I want to go home.'

'Em, it was touch and go for a while there.'

'But I'm fine now.'

'Just for a few days, that's all. You need to rest.' She's using this unnaturally calm voice which isn't Fi at all.

It only makes me more determined. 'I need to go home. I can rest at home.' I spit my words, testing her patience to the limit.

'Em, just stop behaving like —'

'Like what? What am I behaving like?

'Em —'

'I want to go home. Gabe says I can, and I reckon the doctors do, too. So just get me my things, and I'll be on my way.'

Fi glares at Gabe. Her eyes narrow, and his dimples sharply disappear.

'Fi, I want to go home. Today.'

She sighs and rolls up her sleeves. My jaw hangs open at the sight.

From her hands to her elbows is covered in tight and twisted knots of skin. In some places they are pink and flesh coloured, but other patches are a blistering red, raw and rigid. It is like someone has set fire to her skin. Cooked it even. The word cooked sticks in my mind and a bitter smell of burning flesh catches in my throat. Her hands are the worst. The knots cover her nails and knuckles. I don't see how she can move them; if it is possible it must be agony. What's more I don't understand how I didn't see them before.

'I've got to work now, Em,' Fi says. 'Em? Em, are you listening?' Her words act like a pinch. I draw my eyes away from her arms.

'I, I…' My eyes fall immediately back to her hands, but once again I start at the sight; this time, all I find is a set of perfectly manicured nails. I blink a few times more, then rub my eyes completely, but the image stays the same. There are no burn marks. Not anymore.

'Tomorrow, then?' she says.

'Sorry, what was that?'

She sighs again. 'I'll see if we can get them to let you out tomorrow,' Fi says. It takes a second, but the reality of her words set in.

'Let me out? You're saying I have to be *let out?*'

'You know what I mean. Look, I've got to go to work. I don't have time to argue this.'

'I'll go with Gabe,' I say.

'That's not a good idea.'

'Why not?' Gabe interrupts. His dimples are firmly back in place though this time with a slight sneer. 'I'll take her home.'

'Em will need constant supervision,' Fi says as if I'm not in the room.

'That's fine, I can do that.'

'What about the bar?'

'We'll just keep to the same arrangements.'

'What about tonight? What if she needs help when you're working?'

'I'm fine.' I try to interrupt, but she's not interested. Neither of them are.

'Fi. Sorry, it's Finola now, isn't it?' Gabe starts again. 'The farthest I will go is down to the bar, one flight of stairs. Em will be fine at my place.'

'At yours...?' I try again.

'That is of course if she wants to go to yours,' Fi continues.

'You'd rather she went... where is it you live now? Oh, I'm sorry, I remember. You're not allowed to say. How inconvenient.'

'Stop it!' I scream the words, but the sudden outburst takes even me by surprise.

Fi turns to me. Her face has softened, but Gabe continues to glare at her with unwavering resolve.

'Why can't I just go home?' I say.

A nurse comes to the door. Fi promptly moves to close it before the nurse can come inside the room and then takes a seat next to me on the bed. Her frown lines are back in their old places again.

'They took the flat,' she says. 'I'm sorry, I just couldn't find the money. I tried. I promise I tried.'

I see Gabe bite down on his lip, but he stays quiet. Fi hasn't had the money for weeks, and I've suspected all along that Gabe was paying the rent, but perhaps in her state she didn't realise. No doubt when she sobered up she refused the charity.

For some reason I'm relieved. I'm not sure what I'd been expecting them to say, but losing the flat has seemed inevitable for a long time and I had expected something worse.

'We managed to get your things, books and clothes and everything. They're at Gabe's now.'

'And what about you? Where are you living? Why aren't you allowed to say?'

'Gabe's being overly dramatic,' she assures me, fiddling with her bracelet and then mine. 'I'm still working at the bar. I'm just staying with friends. I'm doing some other work now and some courses, too.'

'With Luke?'

'Partly, yes. But like I said, I'm still at the bar, so I can see you every day, just as much as I used to.'

I'm not sure what memories Fi has of us before, but this visit has well exceeded our generally weekly conversations.

'Are you okay?' Gabe says after a while.

'I'm fine,' I say.

I am. I'm glad even. I think back to the last time I was at the flat, the smell of blood, my face forced into the carpet, Gabe and Fi bleeding out hopelessly in front of me. I try to conjure happy memories, too. I don't succeed.

'It's a good thing,' I say, and at last they both manage to summon a smile, however sad and pathetic.

Fi hugs me before she leaves for the bar. I cast one more quick glance down to her hands, but as I suspected there is nothing there in the way of scars or burns. I think back to the IV line in my arm. It's more than likely that there was more than just IV fluids in there and wonder if that was perhaps the cause for the funny vision. Either way, it is clearly over now.

Gabe follows Fi out of the room to allow me to dress. I can hear them continue their conversation but it is in whispers, no doubt for my benefit. My skinny jeans are now anything but and hang baggily off my hips so I have to hitch them up after a few steps; hopefully I'll have something that fits better at home. Lifting off the nightshirt reveals scarily visible ribs, several of which jut out peculiarly or curve around in unnatural angles, but they don't hurt much at the minute. And neither, I realise, does my hand. Both scars are now completely healed and solid silver, though at least there are only two. It still begs the question: how long was I asleep?

Gabe knocks on the door.

'Are you ready to go? I think I've just about managed to clear it with the nurse.' He laughs at my slipping trousers and starts to unbuckle his belt. 'I think you need it more than me.' He starts to pass it to me and then hesitates. His forehead crumples into worry lines. He looks so young.

'There's something I want to tell you — I need to tell you — before we go.'

From the look on his face I assume it's not going to be good news. I perch on the edge of the bed, the well-worn mattress sagging beneath even my weight. Gabe begins to pace, the belt folded into his hands. He attempts to talk with several false starts before coming to a halt about six inches from where I am sitting, where he continues to huff and puff while wringing his hands. I don't think I've ever seen him look so nervous. When he does finally start talking, it is mid-sentence.

'— and I don't want you to think it's just because of what happened or that I feel sorry for you or something. Because it's not. Not at all.' His voice has the lightest quiver to it. He looks to the ceiling and clears his throat.

A tingling has started in my gut, and I can't decide if it's nerves or something else. Gabe avoids my eyes time and time again before eventually reaching out and taking my hand.

'I can't do it,' he says. 'I can't face the thought of another car journey or meal or even walking down this corridor without you knowing.' There's desperation in his voice. 'If I had one left, you know I'd use it, don't you? You know I wish I could, don't you? I'd do anything to keep you safe, Em.'

'I know,' I say, trying to reassure him, but it doesn't work.

'If I could take it away —'

I put my fingers against his lips to stop him. Tears swell and then fall from his eyes. Without thinking, I catch one with my lips. Then another, then another. I kiss his face, his scarred temple, the crooked bridge of his nose, his furrowed brow. Again and again I kiss him, moving my lips down until they're against his. Our tears mingle under the fluorescent glare of the strip lighting and we kiss. It doesn't feel like a first kiss; In fact, I'm certain that it's not.

Chapter Twenty-two

GABE TAKES MY hand and leads me out through the automatic door of the main entrance. Outside, he wraps an arm around me, though it's really not that cold, as we walk to the car.

In the car a female voice emerges with a crackle from the radio. It's a timeless genre, bluesy, sultry; the tune is familiar and though I can't remember the lyrics I hum along anyway, my head leaning on Gabe's shoulder. When the song ends, he turns the radio off. He hasn't spoken since we left the hospital, and his body is uncomfortably stiff. Nervously, I lift myself up into the seat. His eyes are focused forward, his knee bobbing up and down as he taps his shoe in the bottom of the foot well.

'What is it?' I say.

'What?'

'Whatever it is you don't want to tell me.'

'There isn't anything.'

He's a bad liar. I arch my eyebrows accusingly.

'Nothing important,' he says.

I squeeze his hand. 'I don't want any lies, not now, please. I need to know you're being honest with me.'

'Really, it's nothing.'

'Then you can tell me, can't you?'

He looks at me for the first time and sighs reluctantly. 'Fi and I have had a few...issues.'

'I could see that. Don't worry, you'll work things out.'

'It's not that simple.'

'Trust me, she just wants the drama.'

'Em —'

Gabe tries to continue but something else has caught my attention. Outside, the sun is high. A breeze pushes the clouds rapidly across the sky and drives the blossoms off the trees in a cascading storm of petals. How long has it been spring? How long have I been asleep?

'Em. I need to tell you —'

'How long was I asleep?' I say.

'What do you mean?' Gabe looks confused.

'In the hospital. How long was I there?'

'You mean Fi didn't tell you?'

'No.'

He sucks in air through his nose and takes one hand off the steering wheel to flex his wrist and mutters something under his breath.

'Gabe?' I push. This time he responds.

'Just over a month,' he says.

'A month?'

'Give or take.'

My stomach is hollow. 'How many weeks?' I ask as my throat dries and cracks.

Gabe fidgets nervously.

'Gabe, tell me. How long?'

'Five. Well, six weeks five days. Forty-seven days.'

I don't know how to respond. That's not a month and he knows it. Forty-seven days of life gone. Just like that. And nothing but a half fuzzy dream to remember them by.

'At least I didn't miss the spring,' I say eventually. Gabe flicks on the indicators and swerves the car into the curb. He leans over, takes my hand and kisses me.

'You are incredible,' he says and kisses me again. 'You know that? You're incredible.'

I don't feel incredible. I feel lost, confused and like the whole world was moving and I was trapped on a treadmill unable to get off. A lump forms in my throat. Worst of all – worse than the missing time – is that life has been better that way, better without me. Despite their arguments, even Gabe can't deny the transformation in Fi, and it's only now that I have her back I realise I thought she was lost forever.

'How long has Fi been back at work?'

'A week or two.'

'And she's better?'

Gabe doesn't reply, but his knuckles are tight on the wheel as the car starts moving again.

'Em, I need to —'

'And is she better?'

'She doesn't drink now, if that's what you mean.'

'Gabe?'

We turn off the main road, where the high-rises block out the sun and the trees are now sporadically placed with thinner branches and duller blooms. I hadn't realised we were so close. The car pulls up outside the back of the bar, adjacent to rubbish bins and empty crates. He switches the engine off.

'I don't want to do this now. Not now. Let's just get you inside. I'll explain when we're upstairs,' he says. 'I promise.'

Reluctantly I climb out of the car and follow him up to his flat.

Just a few of the pieces of furniture are from my flat, but they are enough to turn Gabe's small place into disarray. My bookshelf and a badly scratched table are shoved into the corners, while his own sofa and chairs sit at awkward angles to make room. Bright patches of unfaded carpet glare impudently up from the floor while families of dust bunnies have colonised the skirting boards. He clearly hasn't moved anything in a long time. I've been here before, nights before my mother got too bad to leave. A few parties, nothing big. It was always filled with people at Fi's invitation. From what I saw, Gabe was always passive to the whole event. I used to think he looked bored; now I realise maybe he just felt out of place. He shows me around the rest of the flat and informs me that my clothes have been pre-emptively hung in his wardrobe in his room, where I will sleep; his own displaced belongings are strewn haphazardly in the spare room, where the bed is hidden under boxes and clothes. My stomach twists guiltily.

'You don't have to sleep in there,' I say.

'Good,' Gabe replies.

I blush. I hadn't meant that, but I have no intention of taking it back either. In his room, a crumpled sheet is pulled over the bed. Books litter the floor in piles; some of them are mine, others I don't recognise. There's a warm, musky odour, the smell of cigarette smoke embedded in the floorboards from the bar below. I flop on the bed and beckon him to join me.

'So,' I say. 'Tell me about Luke.'

'Luke?'

'He's part of the problem between you and Fi, right?'

Gabe sighs and rubs the skin on his forehead. His thumbs try to push out the frown lines that have deepened since the hospital. His jaw clenches and unclenches.

'Em, there are a lot of things we need to talk about.'

'And is Luke one of them?'

Gabe sucks on his bottom lip. 'He is. Luke is a marcher,' he says.

He pauses like he's waiting for me to react, but I don't. I'd figured that much out for myself already. Why else would a man with only one scar be in a wheelchair? People aren't born like that, not now. It would have to be an accident, and he couldn't have been much older than Fi or Gabe, thirty, perhaps. I ponder the thought for a second.

'I wondered. I thought that maybe something had happened before he registered. Or maybe it was something that couldn't be changed.'

'If only,' Gabe says.

'He wanted me to know,' I say. 'He showed me his hand when he left.'

'I know. He likes people to know.'

I think back to the way he hoisted himself out the car in the car park and the way he pulled me for a hug when he greeted me.

'I thought they were all meant to be crazy,' I say.

Gabe grunts.

'And what's he got to do with Fi? With you?'

Gabe's jaw is locked. His teeth grind together as he strains for a response.

I offer another question to help. 'So that's the problem between you two?' I say. 'That Fi is friends with a marcher?'

Gabe's eyes flash angrily. 'That she's friends with a marcher? Em, he's the reason you're still here. He's the reason you had to spend nearly two months in a hospital bed.'

'What do you —' It clicks before I finish the sentence and wallops me like the steel bar to the stomach.

'Em.' Gabe reaches out, but I shake him away. 'Em, please.'

'She wouldn't do it,' I whisper. 'She wouldn't amend for me.' Then I remember something else, something worse. 'The little girl? Did they find her? Did they? Was she, was she...'

Gabe's expression says it all. He hangs his head, and I choke on the tears that rise up in my throat. An image flashes up in my mind of the small girl. I push it down before it can take hold. Fi didn't amend. She wouldn't amend. She could have gone back, changed it. I couldn't have, but she could. She could have told herself not to get into the car that day, not to go to the bar. She could have warned us about the man attacking us at the house. She could have saved the life of an innocent child. But she didn't. She let a girl die. She let a man come into our house, tear the hair from my head and try to kill us all. And when he didn't succeed, she left me in a hospital bed soaked in my own urine for nearly two months. Fi is a marcher.

If I had any food in my stomach, I'm positive I'd be sick, but somehow, I manage not to wretch. A memory of a conversation stirs in my mind – Gabe begging Fi to go back, her telling him to grow some balls.

'I heard you,' I say. 'I heard you with her.'

'I tried, Em, I promise I tried.'

I look up at Gabe, my eyes stinging, my vision blurred. The muscles of my torso feel like they've been re-ripped and stitched together a dozen times in the past five minutes.

'What if I hadn't woken up?' I whisper.

'I'd have found a way, I promise. She wouldn't lose you, not forever. I promise, I'd have found a way.'

He runs his fingers through my hair. It feels comforting until I remember the straggled ends he's touching. Hastily I brush him away.

'Are you okay?' he says. 'What can I do?'

He doesn't expect an answer and my chest aches even more with the added sight of his despair. What can he do? Neither of us can do anything to make this right. Nothing we can do can bring that little girl back. I cannot amend my amendment. Gabe has no amendments left. I lift myself up to my feet and catch my reflection in the cabinet mirror.

'You could do one thing,' I say.

'Anything.' Gabe smiles without dimples.

'You could get me a razor,' I say.

Then he grins, and for the first time since the hospital, I feel a lightness inside.

'I can do one better than that,' he says.

In the bathroom, he pulls out a pair of clippers. 'What grade?' he asks.

I laugh in spite of the pain. It's not all short. Some scraggly loose ends reach my jaw line, but in general my hair is little over an inch long. It all has to go. Right now it looks like a castoff doll, savaged by an overeager owner who naively believes that their beloved doll's hair will grow back after they hack at it with the kitchen scissors. It is not a look which I carry well. There's a soft buzz and vibration as Gabe places the clippers against my skull. I don't move or flinch, instead I stand and watch as my image changes. With every piece that falls, Gabe kisses another part of my head.

He doesn't stop kissing me when the hair is done. Instead, he starts moving his mouth farther down my neck, across my shoulders and along my back. He kisses my lips, softly at first, as though he's afraid he might break me, but I kiss back more firmly and he responds. Taking my hand, he leads me from the bathroom and back to his bedroom.

'Em, I need to tell you something,' he says, stopping a little way short of the bed, but I silence him with a finger to the lips. I begin to unbutton his shirt. The house is empty, but he still kicks the bedroom door shut.

The condensation pools and slips down the windows in tiny estuaries and provides miniscule glimpses of the fading sun outside. The room smells of me and him and sweat and kissing. Gabe pulls the blanket over us and my head melts into his collarbone, rising and falling periodically with each of his breaths. He smells sweet, comforting.

'Do you still think you love me?' I say.

'More than ever.'

'Promise?'

'Promise.' He kisses my shaved head, his lips warm and wet against my skin. We lie silently.

'What are you thinking?' I ask after a while.

He doesn't respond.

'Gabe?' I say. He rolls over and smiles.

'Nothing really. That I can't believe it took me so long to do this, I guess. Why, what are you thinking?'

I hesitate before I reply.

'I was thinking about Luke,' I confess.

Gabe sighs and pulls me over to face him. 'Please, Em, don't. Don't think about him. Don't let him anywhere near your thoughts.'

'It's just, he seemed normal, that's all.' I think back to the moment before he left and the look that felt as though he were seeing right into me.

'He's an intelligent guy,' Gabe says. 'He's seen a lot, he's done a lot. He can be fun.'

'But…'

'That doesn't make him a good guy.' Gabe inhales, still searching for the correct phrasing. 'Besides, there's something else. But you'll think I'm being weird.'

'Try me.'

Gabe sighs again. 'It'll sound ridiculous, but the moment I saw him, it was like I'd met him before.'

'Maybe you had?'

Gabe shakes his head. 'Maybe. But, I don't think so. If I had, it wouldn't have been any place good. And anyway, it wasn't like that. It felt like…'

'Like what?'

'Like, I knew him before. Before I used my amendment.'

It takes me a moment to gather my thoughts. The image of me and Gabe in the snow returns to my mind, as does the vision of the little girl and Fi's blistered and burned arms. I know you're not supposed to remember anything that's happened before, but I can't shake the feeling that all of those things are somehow connected.

'Do you think that's possible?' I say. 'To remember like that?'

'I don't know.' He shrugs. 'Anyway, that's not the reason I don't trust him.' His voice is refocused as he diverts the conversation away from his past lives. I oblige and listen. 'It's the way he says things. The way he can make you think things. Do things. What kind of person, a stranger, can convince someone to leave their sister dying? How can someone have that much power? That scares me. And Fi's not a weak person. So, if he can make her do that, what else can he do?'

'To her?'

'To both of you.'

I kiss him and smile. 'You're quite overprotective you know.'

'I've got a lot to protect,' he says, but he doesn't smile. 'You've not met him properly yet. He's calculating and manipulative, but he's smart and funny and charming and everything he says is laced with so many meanings I don't think he even knows them all. He will say exactly what you want to hear or what you think you need to hear. You saw his palm.' It wasn't a question. 'I never want you to be alone with him.'

'Then you had better never leave me alone,' I say.

He rolls on top of me, kissing down my arm before breaking away. 'If only I didn't have to go to work,' he says.

Gabe promises it's his last evening shift and bombards me with apologies until I push him out the door. With the smell of his sweat still soaked into the pillow, I curl back up on the bed, and for the first time in over five weeks, I sleep dreamlessly, and when he crawls back into bed smelling of smoke and whiskey, I stir only very slightly. I am still half asleep when he leaves again for the morning shift. Apparently seven weeks in bed just wasn't enough.

When I finally wake up, I find my muscles have adopted a new kind of stiffness, accompanied by a groaning dull ache that has burned its way right into the sockets of my joints. I had wanted to get myself sorted today. Maybe go out for a walk. As it is, leaving the flat seems highly unlikely. Instead, I decide to tidy.

I start in the living room, beating the sofa with my hands and dislodging dust which rises in plumes only to settle back where it started, even more visible than before. A thin vacuum cleaner, also coated in dust, leans against a wall in the empty pantry. Gabe used to make such an effort to keep our little flat tidy for us and make sure we had food, yet grime has built solid on parts of his floor and the fridge appears to have not seen fresh food for months. Later, I'll do some shopping, but then I remind myself I have no money.

I drag the vacuum into the hallway and turn it on. Lines like the tracks of neatly mowed grass form, two shades lighter than the carpet had been before. It's amazingly satisfying work. Systematically, I work my way around the hall and living room, moving smaller objects, mainly books and cups, from off the floor and out of the way. When my muscles start to ache, I push through; they won't get stronger from doing nothing, I tell me myself. That said, I quickly concede defeat when I try to push the heavy sofa, instead cleaning just the visible area around it. I reason that no one will look under there anyway.

Once I'm satisfied with the state of the living room, I head to the bathroom. I sweep up the stray ends of my hair which fell to the ground and swill around the toilet bowl with a bottle of bleach from the kitchen. I can't find any glass cleaner, so after wiping the sink, I decide to tackle the rest of it another day and attack the bedroom instead.

Having been displaced from the wardrobe, Gabe's clothes are scattered in various random piles, from the floor to the unused desk and any spare surface area in between. Several of my own garments spill over from the drawers in which they have been carelessly stuffed, a clear mark of Fi. A little rearrangement should easily make room for everything. I open the different chests, pulling out their various contents until everything is empty and the bed is barely visible under the mounds of fabric. The room smells of laundry, though not entirely fresh. It is a random array of my clothes, mainly winter wear, a few items for the spring, a few of my mother's knits, but almost all of them are castoffs – Fi's hand-me-downs. In fact, in the heap I only manage to identify half a dozen that I can specifically remember choosing myself and some I could swear having never seen before, suspecting Fi has only passed them on to me in the move.

I pick out a cardigan, one I know for certain is mine. Every evening for weeks, my mother, cross-legged like a school child and huddled close to the radiator, would cast on, picking and unpicking and swearing under her breath when she missed a stitch or miscounted a line. I remember the way she would reward herself with a sip of her cheap home brew, while our father watched with far-eyed, misleading contentment. She made one for Fi, too, a lilac jumper with yellow flower buttons, though Fi never wore it. I know mine never looked particularly good on me either, but as far as I was concerned, nothing ever did with my gangly legs and scrawny arms, and I knew it made my mother happy to see me wearing it. That was enough, even if I was never sure if the look of pride she showed when she saw me in it was for me or her knitting. Either way, I'm glad to find it here.

I put it back on the bed and begin to refold everything as small as possible before placing the items back in the cupboards. When I've finished, I've managed to make a whole drawer free for Gabe's things, not that he has that much: a couple of pairs of jeans and a few T-shirts, with a handful more in the laundry basket.

I straighten the bed sheets, throw the evidence of last night's intimacy into the wastepaper basket by the door and survey my newly cleaned abode. For a moment, I worry that Gabe will think I've overstepped the mark, but I brush the thought aside. He loves me. Warmth spreads through me, and I repeat the thought. He loves me.

I sit on the bed and glance at the clock. It is past three, and my stomach growls as if to confirm this. I haven't eaten yet today, and there's no food in the flat. I could go and ask Gabe for money, but I'd rather not – I'd like to at least appear independent. My eyes hover over the small wooden bedside table. It is three drawers high, and the surface is stained with circular watermarks, the perfect place to shove spare change. It's not like I need a lot. I loop my fingers through the cold brass rings. Then I hesitate. If there was something he didn't want me to find, he wouldn't leave it in the bedroom, would he?

I convince myself easily, after which I tug at the drawer, but it sticks, the wood is stiff, bowed; it hasn't been opened in some time. I tug again, this time with force, half expecting a flurry of moths to fly out as the drawer springs open, but it is full, over full. Something jams, and it only opens an inch. I feel inside the drawer, trying to dislodge whatever is jamming it and, wiggling my fingers, I find the culprit – a thick wodge of papers. I twist and jiggle them, poking them down the best I can. Nothing wants to give.

It could be anything: old birthday cards and cherished childhood photos, probably a stack of old bills. I don't really care. All that currently matters is my escalating need to open this drawer. Grimacing, I manage to squeeze my hand over the top of the papers and push them down. Hard. There's a sudden release, and my pulse leaps with excitement as I push down even harder. The rip slashes through me as I hear the paper tear.

Effortlessly, the drawer slides open and the consequences of my determination lie out in the open, torn. On top is a large white paper – a receipt from a shop with a name I don't recognise for something expensive. I cast it to the side and stare at the rest. Guilt swells as I flick through the photos; two of Gabe with what I can only assume is his father and one of a woman – his mother I suspect – with her hair pinned in intricate waves sweeping down the side of her face. She is trying to smile but looks terrified. The photo shows her shoulders covered in delicate lace, her wedding day perhaps. Fortunately, the tear in this one is small, just the corner, unlike the other objects in my hand.

Chapter Twenty-three

BOTH ENVELOPES are badly torn. I vainly hope that perhaps they are just envelopes, but the thought is quickly extinguished. Who would send a black and green envelope nowadays? The paper is faded and now torn and has a much more substantial weight than either mine or Fi's. I place them back on the table and step back. My chest is pounding deafeningly, but I'm not surprised; after all, deep down I know this is what I was looking for. Now I've found them, I should put them back. I don't have to look inside. If I'm that desperate, I could always ask him to show me. I pick them back up, half resolved to put them away, but instead slide my fingers between the torn seam of the black paper.

The key turns in the front door with such a tiny click that I thank God I heard it. My pulse races as I stuff the envelopes and papers back in the drawer – disregarding any thought of strategic replacement – and try to push it closed; it doesn't want to budge. The clicking of heels has moved forward into the kitchen, accompanied by Fi's voice calling my name, and there's a dull thud as she places something on the counter. Her steps get closer, just feet from the door. I turn sideways and force all my weight onto the drawer. With one final heave, it clicks into place, less than a second before the door glides open.

'Em? What are you doing? Didn't you hear me calling?'

I try to position myself naturally on the bed.

'Sorry I must have been miles away.'

She looks dubious as I shuffle around, wiping my clammy hands on the backs of my thighs.

'Can I sit down?' she says but doesn't wait for an answer and sets herself at the farthest point from me, creating a dip in the mattress.

I reposition. Fi scans the room nervously as if looking for something and then plays with a stray strand of hair, picking at the split ends. The insensitivity makes me seethe.

'I'm sorry about the house,' she says eventually.

'It wasn't your fault.'

'Still.' There's another silence with a tangible awkwardness that creates an unexplainable bristling sensation.

'Have you spoken to Gabe?' she asks.

'About what?'

'You know.'

'No, I really don't.'

'Don't be awkward, Em.' Fi looks down at her hands and pulls at her fingertips uncomfortably.

Unsure of how much she would have wanted him to tell me and what she thinks I may or may not know, I feel my insides tug with divided loyalties.

'Did he tell you about me, about what happened?' she asks.

'Not really, just bits and pieces. How long I was gone, that kind of thing. Oh, and that you decided you didn't want to waste an amendment on me. Not that I needed him to point that one out, but you know. It's understandable.'

'That's not fair.'

'No, honestly, I get it, why go back? A six-week coma, it's just a bump on the head really.'

'Em —'

'Sorry, catatonic state, wasn't it?' My voice sounds unrecognizably bitter, but I can't stop the words from spilling out. 'And I always was the ugly sister anyway, so the haircut's probably an improvement.' I can see it's hurting her, and I don't even mean to keep talking, but it feels good, venting like this, as if I'm not really the person saying the words. 'I bet you're gutted you didn't get that mourner's money for me, too. How much was that you were counting on? I'm not married and don't have any children, so it probably wouldn't have been that useful. Have you got any more relatives you can help die?'

I crossed the mark. I felt it as I said it. I wait for a snarling response, an equally hurtful dig, but she's silent. She studies me, and for a second her eyes are so dark I barely recognise them. Then, without speaking, she stands up and walks out. I bury my head in the pillow, pounding the bed with my fists.

Pain accompanies a thud like a punch on my back, and when I turn around Fi is standing in the doorway, her eyes warmer, fruit in her hand.

'You're always such a bitch when you don't eat,' she says.

I pick up the orange lying on the sheet beside me and stare at it. My head is still hot with tears. We have always been the same,

Fi and me, inflicting pain and then demanding forgiveness. We long for and despise the other's integrity, morality and selfishness and have proven time and time again that whenever we are together we are less than the sum of our parts. But we are sisters, isn't that how it's supposed to be?

My body trembles at the current olive branch, and I grasp it before it falls out of reach.

'I'm so sorry,' I say. 'I don't blame you.'

'I know how it must look —'

'Let me finish. Whatever the reason was, you were right. You were right to wait.'

She sits down and kicks off her shoes, curling her feet underneath her.

'I know it sounds stupid, Em, but I knew. I knew you'd be fine. I can't explain it. You just looked so happy lying there, so peaceful, like that was where you wanted to be. I knew you'd come back when you were ready.' She squeezes my hand with such tenderness it causes more tears to roll down my cheek. She brushes them away. 'I'm so glad you're here,' she says. 'Even if you are a bitch when you're hungry.'

She takes the orange from my hand and digs in her nail. A sticky spray fountains from the incision and fills the air with a citrus scent. Extracting a single segment, she moves over to the bin and peels the rest directly into it, throwing me segments and grunting with laughter when I fail to catch them; my muscles are not quite ready for acrobatics. A piece of peel lands on the floor nearby, and she picks it up and drops it in the bin. She freezes; her smile snaps out of place as she looks at me. Disgust, confusion? I can't place the look at all.

'You're fucking him,' she says. It wasn't a question. 'Wow, that didn't take long.'

My mouth turns dry as Fi lets out a low drawn-out breath which edges on a whistle. Her glare doesn't falter. Her eyes are narrowed and nostrils flaring. My stomach churns as I rack my mind for a response, but I don't know what she expects me to say. For some reason, I thought she'd be pleased. I'd been thinking about it all morning, how I'd tell her, assuming we got past the fact she hadn't amended. I'd imagined how she'd hug me and laugh and say how happy she was for us both. How we'd both be crying, but they would be good tears, tears that signified the end of a terrible past. The tears trickling down my cheeks now seem to be signifying the end of something different; I'm just not sure what.

'We've both wanted this for a long time,' is all I manage to say.

'Really?' Her eyebrows rise impossibly high on her forehead, finally lowering into a face-pinching scowl. 'I mean, the fact that you've wanted it, that's always been pretty obvious. Pathetically obvious actually. But him?'

I try to blink away the tears as they slip down my face and chew down on the inside of my cheeks hard enough to draw blood, but it doesn't stop her words or the tears or the constricting tightness that binds my chest.

'How long exactly has he wanted this?' Fi continues. 'Really, I'd love to know. How long has he wanted this? Years? Months? Hours? 'Cause it sure as hell didn't feel like he wanted you when you were in the hospital and he was busy fucking me.'

It feels as though something hard and heavy has struck me. I try to hold it in, try not to let her see. She has to be lying. Gabe wouldn't do that. Not to me. He just wouldn't. I want to scream at her that she's lying. Grab her hair and force her to take it all back. Deep down I know though; Fi's a lot of things – manipulative, self-obsessed, selfish – but she's not a liar.

Her lips are curled in a snarl, her eyes all ice as she enjoys my pain. 'Really? He didn't tell you? That does surprise me. I guess that's one of the bits and pieces he's forgotten to mention. Must have slipped his mind.'

I pick up her shoe and hurl it at her. She laughs as it rebounds off the door and lands at her feet.

She says some more things before she leaves, more insults, I think, more details. I can't be sure. I can't even hear anymore. The floor somersaults out from beneath me, and I don't even remember whether I kicked her out or she just left. It doesn't matter. I sit on a newly cleaned floor, barely propping up my head on the bed and watch as a strip of sunlight makes its way across the room, crying until my skin becomes taut from tears. I don't cover my eyes when the light falls onto me and makes me squint nor do I move to be back under its warmth when it has passed over me. The colours fade – the carpet from cream to brown, the curtains from blue to black. The clock in the kitchen still ticks away, occasionally chiming, and I try counting the hours, but the sounds get blurred before they reach me, and more than once I confuse the chiming with the growl of my stomach. The few segments of orange have long since been used up.

It's as if I'm back in the hospital bed, my mind having no influence on my body and entirely unable to make my limbs move. I try to slip back into the dream, the one where Gabe and I are sitting on the bench and kissing in the snow, only now Fi's face steals in and takes the place of mine. And it doesn't stop; he starts kissing her neck, undoing her buttons and stripping her clothes, constantly saying her name. Fi, Fi, Fi. Em, Em.

'Em?'

My eyes are shaken open. I flinch at the sight of him in front of me and push my back up against the bed.

'What are you doing on the floor?' He laughs and offers a hand to pull me up.

I don't accept it. I try to form words, but they never reach my vocal cords. I try again, trembling.

'Did you sleep with her?' I say.

The words are barely a whisper, but he hears them. All the colour drains from his face, and his skin transforms to a dirty white. I don't need to hear an answer.

'Em…' His eyes move around and he stutters, tripping over his tongue whilst his brain searches for words to make things right. I'm surprised I can't hear the cogs grinding.

'When I was in the hospital, Gabe, did you sleep with Fi?' I say. 'It's a simple *yes* or *no* answer.'

Gabe is hunched over towards me, half his normal height, his tongue still an apparent obstacle as he struggles to speak.

'I tried to tell you. Em, you've got to understand,' he says.

I try to stand and push myself up from the ground. I want to seem strong and not let him see I can barely move, barely breathe. He hasn't even tried to deny it. My stomach heaves, and I can't look at him. He tries to help me up, but I shove him away.

'Em, please listen. I need you to listen, I need you to understand, I need you —'

'To understand?' I shout. I don't want to shout. I lower my volume. 'Explain it to me then,' I hiss. My nails are digging into my palm, whether to stop me from lashing out at him or tearing into my own skin I can't be sure. 'Make me understand.'

He reaches for my hand, but it swings up and slaps him squarely across his face. His expression changes; he almost looks afraid as he grabs me by the wrists. I squirm and wriggle as I try to break free, but his grip doesn't lessen.

'Let go of me!'

'You need to calm down first.'

I spit in his face. I've never done anything like that before, but I can't bear his hands on me, not now I know. My skin crawls at the thought.

'Let go of me,' I snarl.

'No,' he says simply.

I hiss and spit and kick, more animal than human as I try to squirm out of his hands. How has so much changed since this morning? This morning just the thought of his hands on me flooded me with heat and anticipation and excitement that was so consuming it made me dizzy. Now his touch makes me feel sick.

I catch sight of a face in the mirror contorted in a twisted snarl, my body writhing, my nails ready as knives against anything standing in their way. Hands hold back my flailing arms, a voice begs me to stop, to listen. I see it all. I see my mother.

I freeze, paralysed by the image for a moment before I collapse onto the bed sobbing. Am I her, already, after only one? Perhaps it was inevitable, genetic. Maybe even one amendment was too much for me to handle. It's not impossible. I sink deep into the sheets, still wailing and gasping for air. At least I had the dream, I think. At least I had that perfect dream so many times. If only I could close my eyes again and believe it was all real. Is that what my mother thought, too? At least, at least.

The grip on my arm has relaxed but it's not gone. Gabe looks at me with suspicion, unfair and accusatory. Doubt flickers across his eyes before he speaks.

'Five minutes, please. Give me five minutes. Then if you want to leave I will help find you somewhere else to stay. But please, can I try and explain?' He takes my unresponsiveness as agreement.

Gabe lets go of my arm and swings his legs over the edge of the bed. He's not looking at me, and I think about how I could run now. Maybe I could use the lamp by the bed to knock him out. The thought is fleeting, I don't mean it, I need him. What else have I got? What else can I do except listen? Still, I retreat farther back, far enough to give myself fair warning should he decide to grab me again.

His hands rest on his knees, and I don't need to see his face to see that he's crying; his shoulders shudder every time he breathes.

'I'm waiting,' I say coldly.

He turns to face me, his eyes bloodshot, his skin still sallow and insipid. Pity flashes through me but is short-lived.

'So,' I say again. 'Make me understand.'

He inhales deeply. 'I have never lied to you. Ever.'

'You just failed to tell me things,' I say. 'Like sleeping with my sister. No wonder you said things were difficult between you two. What happened? Did she dump you for Luke, and you thought you'd take the second-best option? You could've probably done better, you know.'

'It's not like that. Please, Em, let me speak. I'm trying to make you understand.'

I bite my tongue. When he carries on, he doesn't look at me; instead he picks up a half-filled glass of water which sits on the bedside table and runs his fingers around the edge.

'When you weren't there, Em, when we thought we'd lost you, Fi couldn't amend straight away; they wouldn't let her, not until she was well, and she was pretty bad. You weren't the only one who got hurt. He beat her badly. Really badly. You never had to see that.'

He pauses as if I'm meant to say something. I don't.

'We were both broken, Em. We had no one; we were just comforting each other, that's all it was.'

'Comforting each other with sex?'

'Yes. It sounds ridiculous, but that's really all it was. Em, you and I, we weren't even a thing then. You'd never so much as looked at me before the thing on the steps.'

'That's not true.'

'When? When did you do anything that I could construe as more than friendship?'

I don't offer a reply.

'Years, Em,' he says. 'Years I've been waiting for you to notice me. How often did I come around and pretend to be waiting for Fi just so I could spend an hour talking to you? How many of Fi's ridiculous parties did I let her have on the off chance you'd come along? And when you finally did notice me. When I finally knew you felt the same…' His voice trails off into a whisper. 'I thought you were gone. I thought I'd lost you, and I couldn't bear it. I'm so sorry, Em. I'm so, so sorry. I just wanted to block out the pain. I never thought Fi would leave you there. I thought once she was better, once they'd let her, I was sure she would go back. I was sure she would.'

'But she didn't.'

'No, she didn't.'

I can hear my breathing, feel my pulse against my eardrums. Does this make it better or worse? What kind of person does something because they think someone else will take it away from them? What if it never happens? Can you really blame them then? What if Fi had gone back? Then none of this would be an issue. My head is swimming with all the *what ifs*, unable to stay fixed on one line of thought before veering cataclysmically into another. And in my head, all thoughts end in images of them together.

'But you must have wanted to,' I say eventually.

Finally he looks at me. 'I don't know. That's not an excuse, I know that. But if I could take it back, if I could take it all back —'

'But you can't.'

'No, I can't.'

I shake his hand away when he places it on my arm – it still has the imprints from where he held me earlier.

He tries again, running his fingers over the marks muttering, 'I'm sorry, I'm sorry, I'm so, so sorry.' His lips replace his fingers, kissing up my arm, my neck, my mouth.

I draw away. 'I can't. I'm sorry,' I say, standing.

'Please, please don't say you're sorry. You have nothing to be sorry for. Em, please believe me, you never have anything to be sorry for.' He pauses. 'I meant what I said in the hospital. I do love you. You know that, right?'

'I know.'

He smiles with relief, like those little words have just solved everything.

'Please, please tell me what to do,' he begs.

'There's nothing you can do,' I say, then pause and correct my last statement. 'You can find me a bag and some money.'

I watch his heart break in front of me and feel the same blistering tear in every fibre of my being.

Chapter Twenty-four

THE ONE CONSTANT has been the pain. Half the time it's the muscles in my chest – the ones directly around my heart – that feel as though they're being stripped and torn from my body one myocyte at a time. The rest of the time, it's my head that aches from the constant crying. Sometimes it's an acute pain, a thumping between my eyes or a throbbing behind my forehead; sometimes it's like my whole skull is being crushed by an unseen force. Most of the time, it's as though the skin has been pulled tight and stretched around my temples. Bright lights hurt, loud sounds hurt, coughing, eating, swallowing, breathing, they all hurt. At least it's constant; that's the only way I know I'm still here.

The door stays shut to that room – the room where we, and, I soon learned, they were together – as does the door to the outside, as well as the windows and curtains. Everything has stayed shut for weeks. Some days I manage conversation, although the topic is consistent and painful. Reluctantly, Gabe gives me the details I beg for, then attempts to comfort me after they are delivered and I fall back into despair. When, where, what was said. I don't believe he has held anything back, and that at least is some source of comfort. I'm sure he loves me the best he can, but I'm not sure whether that is why I stayed or if I'm just here because I have nowhere else to go. It's most likely a bit of both.

I don't sleep at night. I've reached the point where just the thought of closing my eyes and falling asleep makes my heart race and my body break out in a cold sweat. I'm so terrified of what I will see in my dreams that I lie under the blanket, eyes wide, shaking and soaking. And that's before the nightmares start. For the past week, Gabe has slept in the room with me. Not in the bed, but in a chair. I've found it easier having him there when I wake up. Unless of course the nightmare is about them, but that's infrequent – I have a steady rotation of terrors to work my way through.

Fi knows I'm here, but I haven't seen her. Her name is taboo, made even more so by my unwillingness to say it. Sometimes her laughter drifts up through the floorboards from the bar below, and I cover my head with a pillow to shut it out. I've heard her footsteps, too, walking up the staircase, stopping outside the front door. She never knocks though, never asks to come in. It's wrong. I know it's no more her fault than it is his, but for now if I can only choose one, then I choose the one that brings me the least pain to look at, the one that only betrayed me once, but some days even that is too much to bear.

We've had moments of respite, of reconciliation, of romance almost. Moments when Gabe and I have held each other close enough to echo one another's breathing and have allowed ourselves a second of hope. But these moments are fragile and held in place by the most delicate of lines, which inevitably snap and plummet me back deeper into the seemingly bottomless chasm.

One day last week, I received a letter from the hospital informing me of my eligibility for disability allowance. It didn't cite what the disability was. Still, it's money; I would be a fool to turn it down. On the other hand it means the Cabinet are probably keeping tabs on me; on all of us.

"Maybe we can figure a way for you to work at the bar," Gabe suggested.

"Do I work on your shift or hers?" I said.

He didn't suggest it again.

And now I'm waiting for him to come home. That's all I really do. Wait for him to leave and then wait for him to return; those are the two turns of my hourglass. The time between is lost in sleep. I've considered leaving the house and I'm sure that I could, but I haven't, not yet.

Today he is late. I tried ringing the phone in the bar but hung up when I realised that Fi might answer. I tried his mobile, too, but the same concern stopped me short there as well.

When the door opens, I'm in the living room, lying on the sofa, running my tongue over my furry, yellow-tasting teeth. The seat is too soft and misshapen; my constant presence on it has stretched the springs beyond their elastic limit so they offer no support and poke out uncomfortably into my skin. I have bruises from where I lay like this yesterday and the day before. Still I lie here staring at the door, torturing myself. What if I'd registered earlier? What if I'd told Gabe to refuel? What if he'd just stayed with her? What if he's with her now?

When my father first left, I was terrified to go to sleep. I convinced myself that somewhere, wherever he was, he was going to amend, and if I went to sleep I wouldn't wake up again. It wasn't as irrational a thought as it might sound. He still had one of his amendments left when he deserted us, and he and my mother were both over twenty-one when Fi and I born. If he regretted having us that much it would have been an easy enough solution to the problem. I never discussed this fear with Fi, but she must have thought it too. Why wouldn't she? Anyway, I've started having the same thoughts again recently; that somebody will come along and amend me out of existence. Maybe it would be a good thing, I decide. Today has not been the best of days.

Gabe closes the door with an unusual slam. Normally he is careful not to wake me, especially when the previous night was as bad as last night, so it's probably accidental. Either that or the sound has gotten to me; silence does that, nibbles away at the senses until half are dull and useless and the other half are so acute that even a whisper is deafening. I roll over and squash my face into the back of the sofa.

He kneels down beside me, stroking my shoulder gently, although he knows I'm awake. He smells strange, not his usually smoky, dirty smell, but cleaner, more floral. He smells of a woman. I swivel around fiercely, as if hoping to catch him off guard, but I have to laugh at my own stupidity. What am I hoping to catch him doing here?

He is wearing a smile so beguiling and sweet I almost soften, but then I see the bedroom door behind him and remember who else had been there and what happened there and my emotions freeze.

He kisses my forehead. 'How's your day been?' he says.

I grunt a response.

'Have you eaten anything?' he adds.

I just scowl. He always asks, I rarely reply and next he'll offer to make me something to eat. My mother used to refuse food for days, starve herself until her cheeks dented inwards and her teeth were covered in a yellow, gunky glaze. Occasionally we'd resort to spoon feeding her; sometimes she would accept it, and other times she'd spit the food back at us or let it dribble down her chin and onto her clothes. She didn't understand what she was doing.

Gabe forces me into a sitting position against the arm of the sofa, and when I'm upright, he produces a bunch of flowers. The unwrapped loose stems show white patches where the thorns have been stripped.

'Em,' he says. 'I'm not going anywhere, you know that, right?'

I don't say anything. I'm transported back to all the times I've heard that: my father, my mother, Fi. Words don't mean anything in the end; they just make it easier to recollect all the promises that have been broken. The fewer words I hear the better.

'I know you think it's just words,' he says, handing me a glass of water. 'But it's not. Em, I spend every second trying to work out what to do with you. I know I can't make up for what I've done. I know that. But I don't know how to make you realise that I'm not ever going to leave you.' He hangs his head. His voice trembles uncertainly. 'Unless…unless that's what you want. Maybe you want me to leave you, Em. Maybe you're just not strong enough to say it.' He takes in a large gulp of air. 'I've spoken to Fi about it, and she agrees. Maybe you'd be better somewhere else, somewhere where people can look after you better than I can.'

A chill unfolds along my bare arms and spreads up the back my neck. I know what those words mean: where people can look after you. I said them often enough, although I never had the guts to see them through. I can feel my muscles tightening as the panic creeps its way up through my body.

'Please,' Gabe says, wiping the tears away. 'Tell me what to do. Tell me what I'm supposed to do.'

I want to speak, but the words fail to leave my mouth. All that comes out is a rasping wheezing sound as I struggle to fill my lungs. Gabe takes me in his arms and cradles me, holding me tightly and rocking me while I shiver away the fictitious cold. It may be spring outside, but I feel like I have been trapped in winter for an eternity, it has been cold for so long. My fingers are so numb they could be frostbitten.

'Don't leave me,' I whisper.

He pulls me in even closer. 'Never,' he says. 'Never.'

'I'm sorry. I'm sorry.'

'You have nothing to apologise for, Em. Nothing.'

Gabe suggests a walk, but I'm not convinced.

'Please,' he says. 'Just a short one.'

I close my eyes to mull the decision over. I've probably missed half the spring, but console myself with the fact that I can always stay asleep until the next one. My mother slept through two after her failed amendment. It was the following year when she woke that things took an even worse turn. It's that thought about my mother that strips the remaining heat from my veins and jerks me into reality; the similarities are starting to mount up. I respond with an overemphatic nod.

'Great,' Gabe says, the smile just a little shy of dimples. 'I'll just put these in something.'

He kisses me on the forehead before heading to the kitchen and rifling through a cupboard for a vase. In the end, he makes do with a jug that belongs in the bar and starts cutting down the stems while I go and get clean. I'm not entirely sure when the last time I bathed properly was.

Using my fingers, I draw a picture in the condensation of the bathroom mirror: a circular face, two long lines for hair and a semicircle of a smile. It's only there for a second before the water pools and runs and the smile drips down the fogged glass in perfect droplets. I wipe the image away with my towel, steam from the shower having already made it damp.

Gabe moved my clothes into the spare room after I tore them all from his wardrobe and cupboards one afternoon when he was at work. I ruined a lot, a lot that weren't originally mine; I poured bleach over some, took scissors to some others. Gabe didn't say anything though; he just tidied them away without a word. I've not been into his room since.

I try to convince myself that it doesn't matter what I wear, it's just a walk, but I know that it isn't true. It's not an issue of forgiveness. I forgave him weeks ago, and the pain he inflicts on himself far outweighs anything I can bestow with mere tantrums and hysteria. But forgiveness doesn't always weave a path back to love, and the problem is, I don't have a clue what does.

I rummage through the piles of clothes that lie around the floor, most of which are musty and drab. After turning the mounds over a few times, I find a long dress that I don't recognise. It's probably years old, but fashion's never been a concern. When I try it on, it's too loose and too long, essentially a long blue bin bag. Water gurgles through the pipes, and with Gabe securely away in the shower, I pick up the dress and head to the kitchen, grabbing up my handbag and a random red lipstick from the side table and not bothering to wrap the towel back around me.

Pulling open the drawer, I flinch. A bread knife lies on its side, its serrated edge gleaming. I hastily grab the scissors and slam the drawer shut, leaning on the work surface to catch my breath and blink away the breathlessness before it takes too strong a hold. I take the scissors firmly in my hand. The fabric frays as I hack at it, but there's nothing I can do about that now, so I just cut a little of the length and pray there's still enough material left to be considered decent by the end of the night. I chop about eight inches off the bottom, but I suspect it's not enough. I take another three inches off and slip it over my head. With no mirror in my room, I realise I will have to use Gabe's. I clutch the leftover material and my bag, and I hold my breath as I step through the door.

The room looks no different than the last time I was in here, a bit tidier perhaps, but it's probably the absence of my belongings. I stare at the bed sheet, full of creases and still crumpled in a poor attempt at being made, and take shallow breaths of Gabe-scented air. Unwanted images start creeping their way to the surface. I force myself to turn away from the bed and examine the dress in the mirror, my eyes steering clear of anything above my shoulders.

The hem is haphazard, but it somehow suits the floatiness of the material. In a moment of unusual artistic inspiration, I fashion a belt out of the narrow cut off strip and cinch in the dress at the waist. I tie the belt in a bow but quickly change it to a scruffy knot. Bows and crewcuts don't go together that well.

The curtains are still open, and although outside is already dark, much of the blackness is speckled with the flickering yellow light of the sodium street lamps. In the dullness of the window's reflection, I allow my eyes to wander up above my neck and over my face. The longer I look, the less I recognise, and it's not just the hair. My collarbones are clearly visible, and my shoulders extend unnaturally far. Even my wrists look smaller. Do I look better, I wonder?

I find an old mascara in the bottom of my makeup bag, the plastic casing coated in dust and powder. It's gloopy and clogged together, but it does the job. I smear on some lipstick too, but it's garish. I try to rub it off, smearing marks around my mouth. By the time I've scrubbed it off, my lips are red-raw and even more discernible than with the lipstick. A large part of me wants to crawl back onto the sofa and curl up. Only images of my mother doing the exact same thing help to steady my resolve.

I add a little more mascara in hope of distracting from my lips and then shove it in my bag, abandoning the lipstick on the side. The mascara lands with a jingle. I reach inside, and my skin glances against something cold; curling my fingers around the chain, I pull out the bracelet. The overwhelming sense of loss bleeds through me. I can barely remember what Fi said when she gave it to me, the memory now so clouded by the dream that I wove around each link of silver. The sentiment turns to anger as images of them re-emerge, and I wrap my fist around the chain and hurl it into the room, deliberately not looking where it lands. Then I head back, pick up the unwanted lipstick and chuck it into my bag, just so it doesn't feel quite so light and empty.

When I walk into the living room, Gabe is already dressed and waiting. His clothes are sticking to his skin – damp from the shower – and wearing a shirt has transformed him. He looks older. He has more lines on his forehead, darker skin beneath his eyes. Even a few flecks of grey. Maybe it's just the first time I've looked at him in a while. I'm sure we've both aged over the past few weeks; he, infuriatingly, looks even better for it.

'May I?' he says. He links his arm through mine.

I stay rigid as he kisses me briefly on the lips before leading me out the door and down the stairs.

'We're not driving,' he says as I head to the car.

'We're not? Where are we going?' I feel an unnerving sense of unfamiliarity.

'For a walk, like I said. It's not far.'

He slips his arm around my waist and leads me across the road to an apartment block. One third of the windows are boarded up, another third broken and of those remaining most are blacked out so thickly that only the smallest slivers of light escape. Gabe retrieves a key from his pocket and unlocks the door.

'Just wait and see,' Gabe says, reading my expression.

The lobby is old and the elevator antiquated — almost identical to the one at our old apartment. An image flashes in front of me, accompanied by a rush of cold. The flowers on the neck, the sniffing nose, the dead glass eyes of a pretty girl I never even saw. I shudder them away and climb inside the lift. Gabe stands behind me, still holding me firmly, and presses the top floor. If anything, the elevator appears to make him even more tense than me. My weight increases as it accelerates up, before wobbling to a stop, and the doors open onto a narrow stairwell. I step out into the dark.

Faint red lights create elongated shadows and a dense smell of wet paper and moulding paintwork clogs the air of the space we move into.

'There's a little bit of a walk I'm afraid,' Gabe says.

Cobwebs brush against my skin and my breathing gets noisier with every step. Gabe bounds up the stairs. I struggle to avoid low-hanging light fixtures and misplaced cables. He suggests I lean against the rail, but it bows with only a fraction of my weight on it, so I make do without. Loose threads from my fraying hem weave around my knees and between the cobwebs, and despite the flimsiness of the material, I'm convinced I will overheat and faint. The thought brings back something else; another non-memory I can't possess. I have walked somewhere like this with Gabe before, I am certain of it, but I don't think it was stairs we climbed before. My feet tread heavily as if sinking into mud and I look back, searching for some kind of clue among the spiders. Then Gabe calls my name and I shake myself out of the moment.

By the time I reach the top of the fourth and final staircase, my back is coated in sweat, my thighs are burning and I am desperate for any form of light.

'Are you okay?' Gabe asks. 'I should of realised. I thought it would be fine.'

'For you maybe,' I puff. 'What are you? Some kind of mountain goat?'

The tiniest of dimples appears, causing a ripple of warmth to spread across me.

'Maybe.' He wraps his arms around me and places another kiss on my lips which, for the first time, I begin to reciprocate, only for him to pull away. 'I need to show you something,' he says.

He pushes the metal bar of the fire door, holding it open for me to step through, and then without warning, he darts in front of me and slips around a corner.

'Wait there,' he calls from a place I can't see.

'What? What do you mean?'

'Just wait there. Just for a second.'

The fire door slams shut and I jump back. There's a slight chill in the air, though any kind of breeze is broken by the wall behind me. Aromas of tar and toil drift up from the road below, but they're scant; diluted by our height. The sounds too are muted; cars, people, far off whirrs of machines. Impatiently I wait. Two minutes later, there's still no sign of Gabe.

'What are you doing?' I call out.

A reply comes from the distance. 'Just one more minute.'

I tap my foot noisily against the ground and sigh obviously. It's another two minutes before he speaks again.

'Okay. You can come round now,' he says, finally reappearing to guide me around the corner. 'But watch where you step.'

As I turn the corner, my heart leaps. The ground, and every spare surface, is covered in hundreds of lit candles, glittering and dancing against the backdrop of the night. They flicker on upturned wooden crates, plastic chairs – they're even staggered on a disused bird feeder. The rays of light reflect around me, gathering in bright clusters of gold and white. And it's not just candles. Tiny green fairy-lights are tied to the metal rail that lines the perimeter of the rooftop, their colour even more vivid than the flames.

'Gabe…' I don't find any other words to follow.

'Do you like it?'

'How did you…? Why did you…?' I circle on the spot, trying to take in the scene. An evening mist has settled around the street lamps below us, blurring their light into a fuzzy orange hue while unlit lanes stand out like black veins running through the illuminated section. Thousands upon thousands of tiny lights, in dense, bright clusters, diminish into a few fireflies as they reach closer and closer towards the skies. Gabe slips his arm around me and draws me close. I feel a twisting in my stomach. It's not from him. I don't know what it's from.

I stare at the blackness of the mountains. 'When Fi and I were young, we'd talk about running away to the mountains, living on berries and making friends with forest animals.' I blush at the memory. 'Can you imagine living this close and never visiting a mountain?'

'I'll take you.'

'And get us lost forever.'

'It's where I grew up,' he says.

I look at him, taken aback. Gabe is not what I'd envisaged as mountain folk.

'I didn't know that.'

'My father worked on the mountains. His father before that.'

‘How did you end up down here then? With the bar?’

Gabe’s hand brushes against my side. ‘That’s a story for later,’ he says. ‘Let’s eat now.’

A woollen blanket is draped across the concrete floor. There’s proper fresh bread, cheese and meats, and saliva pours from beneath my tongue as my stomach growls. Gabe leans down and takes a bottle from the ground, tearing off the wrapping around the cork. ‘Shall we?’

He twists the neck, and we watch as the popped cork rockets upwards and is lost to the stars. Then Gabe fills the glasses, and I kneel down on the blanket, curling my legs underneath me.

‘To new beginnings?’ he says hopefully and clinks the drinks.

I know what reply he wants, but I don’t want to make promises I can’t keep, and the saliva in my mouth is replaced with a dry coarseness. I choose to divert the question instead.

‘Where did you get all this food from?’ I say.

‘Here and there. I have contacts.’

‘It seems like a waste. Surely we should save some?’ A shadow of disappointment creeps its way onto Gabe’s brow. I work quickly to deflect it.

‘I mean, if we can’t eat it all.’ Then, with my brain still whirring I ask, ‘What did your dad do in the mountains?’

Gabe answers as he sets out plates. ‘He counted the trees,’ he says.

‘Really?’

‘Pretty much. He got contracts, mainly from the Cabinet. Orders to grow things. Fell things. That type of stuff.’

‘And your mother?’

‘Mothered.’

‘Where are they now?’ I can’t believe I have to ask. He knows everything about me, yet I can barely form the skeleton of his life.

He sits and takes a piece of bread, dunking it in a thick sauce before passing it to me. A sweet, nutty taste runs to my taste buds, and I pick up another piece which I devour just as quickly. After a minute, I become aware of Gabe watching me. His face is unreadable – no dimples but at least no lines either.

‘So, your parents. Where are they now?’ I ask again.

‘I’ve heard a few rumours.’

‘But you don’t know?’

‘I don’t.’

I don’t hide my surprise. Somehow I’d imagined Gabe came

from the type of family that did everything together: country walks, father-son building projects, those sorts of things.

'What happened?' I ask.

'Lots.'

'Such as?'

Gabe shrugs, sighs and opens his mouth as if to speak, but he doesn't respond. He is sitting on the other side of the rug, and I suddenly wish he were much closer.

'I was angry, really angry for a while,' he says. 'But I guess I got over it. Well, I tried to at least.'

'What did your second envelope say?' I ask.

'Not my first?'

'Just your second,' I insist.

Gabe chews a mouthful slowly, looking at the ground before reaching over and taking my hand. When he looks up, his eyes shine in the light.

'Be better,' he says quietly.

'Be better?'

'*Be better.*' I feel the prickly heat affecting my vision, and my voice quivers when I try to speak.

'Have you been?' I say.

'I thought I had. I had been. Until…' He stops and stares straight into my eyes, holding them there without blinking until he drops his head and looks away.

I want to reach out my hand to comfort him but it won't move, and when it finally does, Gabe flicks it away absentmindedly as he reaches for his glass and downs the contents.

'I know how badly I fucked up, Em. I wouldn't blame you if you left. Maybe it's payback for last time.'

'Do you believe that?'

'Maybe.' He refills the glasses – mine is still half full – then switches his tone and tries to laugh, but it sticks in his throat and comes out as a strained chortle. 'Is this first date conversation?' he says.

I don't reply. For the first time, I'm too busy trying to see him. The real him, rather than the perfect Gabe of my imagination. He's had so much loss I never knew about. I wonder how I could have been so self-absorbed. Be better. I think of how he was after my mother died, after I lost Fi. To be better when it's going well, that's one thing, but when it's not – that's a whole handful of different.

'You are better.' I take his glass and replace it with my hands. 'It was one mistake. One mistake in how many years? You are better.'

He looks at me, but he can't hold my gaze. Either he doesn't believe me, or he doesn't believe that I do. Somehow I do.

'It was a mistake,' I say. 'Right?'

'Of course.'

'Will it happen again?'

'God, no, never, I promise. If I could —'

'I know. I know you would.'

He moves next to me, and his hands cup my face as he kisses me. 'I love you,' he says, kissing my cheeks and my forehead. 'I love you so, so much. I will be better, I promise I will be better.'

He leans away to give me space, but I pull him back, kissing him again. For the first time in weeks, I don't want space.

Chapter Twenty-five

GABE HOLDS ME afterwards, still naked, sweat gluing our bodies together. His breath tastes of mine and mine of his, and the warmth of his fingertips causes a tingly sensation to run across my skin. Almost all the candles have gone out, and the air is filled with the scent of burnt wicks, while the wax leaves thick white trails as it dribbles down the glass holders. I watch the droplets swell and fall, then swell and fall again. Its mesmerising effect sends me quickly into a dreamless doze.

When we stir, I ask Gabe questions about his childhood. He answers briefly, perfunctory, so I tell him memories of rooftop picnics and pressed flowers.

'Don't we have to go soon?' I say, rolling over to face him. The stars have all but faded, and the heavy rumble of trucks rattles up from the road below.

Gabe burrows his head in my neck. 'Not unless you want to go.'

'No, I'm good.'

The blanket is wrapped tightly around us, and I continue to let him nuzzle me, his soft lips buzzing against my skin. His words come out muffled now, lost in my shoulder.

'Are you content?' I ask.

He continues to nuzzle, nibbling my ears, his knees tucked in behind mine. 'Now? Yes, very.'

I think about his answer while my head sinks into his shoulder. We lie together, whispering, cuddling, occasionally giggling and watching the first rays of sun sneak up and over the jagged mountain skyline.

For a few minutes, the warmth makes our eyes close, and when I open mine again, the light has flooded our rooftop. I kiss his stubbly chin and stretch out, reaching around for my dress, which I slip on over my head, the smell of city smoke and candle wax mingling in the air. It smells like a new day.

We eat dessert for breakfast, while birds fly from their roosts, their silhouettes gliding against the orange of the sun, their songs drifting above us.

'Can I ask you something?' he says as we collect the plates and fold up the blanket.

'Of course.'

'Fi.'

I stiffen.

'Speak to her,' he says.

'We don't have anything to say. Besides, she knows where I am.'

'You can't do that. You can't forgive me and not her.'

'Gabe —'

'No, hear me out. Not a day goes by that I don't miss my family. Don't wonder what they're doing.'

'But you hadn't done anything wrong.'

Gabe presses his lips together. 'I was young. So are you. All I'm saying is if in thirty years' time you use your last amendment to fix this, then what was the point? Why not just fix it now? Wasted amendments aren't the ones that don't work out; they're the ones you didn't need an envelope to fix in the first place.'

I fiddle with the cutlery and blow out the candles that still have wicks to burn, watching the grey smoke spiral up.

'Em?'

'What would I say?' I turn to him. 'I understand why she, why you…. I just can't face her, not yet.'

'Soon?'

'We'll see.'

He takes my hand from around a candlestick and kisses my fingers one by one.

'When you're ready. Just don't leave it too late.' He hands me my phone. 'I can clear this up.'

Under his vigilant gaze, I relent. On my phone I write a dozen messages, only to delete them again; each one seems too contrived or laced in arrogance, too soppy or too detached. In the end, I press send in the black of the stairwell where my cowardice at Fi's response is overruled by my fear of tripping in the dark. When I'm sure it has sent, I shove the phone back in my bag and fumble around for the banister.

'You're amazing, you know,' Gabe says.

Fi replies before we are back at the flat, offering to meet for dinner tonight, and my skin breaks out in a chill. It wasn't meant to be that soon; she was meant to want some time to think about it.

But then, she's had weeks, months I suppose, to figure out what to say.

Gabe squeezes my hand.

'Be better,' he says.

'That's yours, not mine.'

'I'm lending it to you. Consider it a freebie.'

Fi suggests a restaurant in the Central. Knowing I wouldn't know where it is or how to get there, she's given me the bus links, too. Gabe's phone buzzes soon after mine, and I know it's her.

'She's just asking if I can cover her shift, that's all,' he says as he kisses my head and opens the front door to the flat.

I know he's telling the truth, but that doesn't help settle the jealousy swirling in my stomach.

Back in my room, I rummage through my piles of clothes. All my things are the same, all grey or navy or dull, muted colours in sensible styles – practical and presentable. I was always the presentable child, never the pretty one or the beautiful one, or even the quirky one; just the presentable one. Adults would gush over Fi, asking her to perform twirls in her frilly floral dresses while I got a polite, sympathetic smile. 'You look very smart, don't you?' The older I got, the less it mattered. I had the brains, not that I ever got to use them, but I had them. They were what mattered most, that's what I told myself.

I haven't touched the disability allowance, and three envelopes are stacked up on the hall table. I could give some to Gabe, for rent, but he's not going to ask and I'm not going to offer, not yet, so I grab them from the table, still wearing the dress from last night with the hem unravelling around my thighs.

'I'm going out,' I say, leaning through the alcove to where Gabe stands in the kitchen.

'Do you need a ride anywhere?'

'No, I'm not going far.'

He reaches over and kisses my forehead, then my nose, then my chin and at last my lips.

'I love you,' he says.

I think it back even if I don't say it.

Being outside – and alone – feels good. There's a warm breeze, despite the greyish tint to the clouds, and the air smells like rain is on the way. Just stretching out my legs is a relief, and for a moment I feel like I could walk anywhere, to the mountains even, though after a few minutes, my thighs start to ache and I reconsider the sentiment. Each section has a small array of shops, generally housed in old shopping malls. They have a good selection of things, but if you want anything specific — latest designer clothes, certain materials, car parts — you'd need to go to the Central and see if you can order it to be made. Even if I had the money, new clothes would not be my first priority so I don't even consider going farther afield. A local mall will do just fine.

What you can get depends on what the season is, and what the factories have been making. In the days before the discovery they used to fly all different types of vegetables and meats in from every corner of the globe. It seems ridiculous now; all the radiation that food must have flown through to get us. I glance up at the sky wondering how it must've looked all those years ago, littered with the giant tin-can airplanes, and shudder at thought.

By the time I arrive the sun has begun to break through the clouds creating dappled patches of light on the ground in front of me. I make no attempt to hurry as I saunter up the concrete steps into the mall. Inside warm air and aromas of leather polish rise to meet me.

Evidence of the old-world clings to the walls. Posters advertising exotic fruits hang in tatters above doorways. Billboard images of men draped across benches in their underwear stretch along the glass railings of a rusted escalator. In some malls the escalators work, but mostly they're viewed as a waste of electricity. Besides, the majority of the stalls are downstairs. That's where I immediately head.

It's not quite 9 am and the place is half empty. It's likely that most people are already at work. My parents always left by eight for the factory, and factory workers have notoriously nicer hours than miners. I wonder what the hours of a career might be. If the patients are anything like my mother twenty-four hour supervision will be a must. That's assuming I get myself sorted again. If not I may find myself on the other side of the white door.

I am still musing my future when one of the hawkers attempts to cajole me over to buy one of his hand knives.

'All handmade,' he tells me. 'Made each one m'self.'

I scurry past as fast as I can.

It's not long before I'm cursing my choice of clothes. Even with a full head of hair, I liked to have a crowd to hide behind, but the new cut and revealing dress make me stand out like a sore thumb. I continue to stroll past the rows of shops as casually as possible, but my heart is drumming ridiculously. It's not my imagination. People are staring, I'm certain. Either that or I'm paranoid; maybe that's what comes from being crammed up in a little flat for weeks.

After a few more minutes wandering I find a second-hand shop that smells like mothballs and cheap deodorant and where the sales assistant is happy to keep her nose in her book and away from me. Finally, I start to browse.

Piece by piece, I scrutinise through a decade of garments. Clothes are tightly packed together and hanging haphazardly on rails that weave around the walls. More are stuffed into boxes that are packed to bursting and shoved in the corners. A cloud of dust flurries up with every disturbance I make, mottling the air in front of me. A more morbid person than me would probably wonder where half these clothes are from, but I quash that thought and continue my perusal.

After a minute or two I pull free a dress from one of the boxes. Black, a slashed neck, with a slight trim the thickness and colour of a scar along the hem. I hold it up and stretch it across my body; it looks like it will fit. But then, it's black. Black and presentable. Black and practical. It is not what I'm after. Instead, I reach in again and pull out a short red lace number, something I would never have considered wearing before. I don't even bother checking if it will fit. It's what I'm after. It will do.

The dress is cheap, although it still makes a sizable dent in my disability cheques. I'm about to leave when I catch sight of a pendant hanging over a wire stand. The silver is tarnished to near black, but the shape is still perfect, a single flawless snowflake. It glints ever so slightly as it swings. The false-memory of Gabe and I on a mountain side floats into my thoughts before it is broken by the wail of a child, somewhere out in the mall. I retrieve a few more notes from my bag and hand them to the cashier. She looks me up and down and then at my hand. Amendments don't stop judgments.

When I return, Gabe is in the flat, listening to music and reading in his room. I like just watching him. His head nods steadily to the beat until he notices me, and then he places the book on the bed and pats the sheet next to him, beckoning me over. I go to take a step, but my body tightens – being in here on my own was one thing, but I can't sit on that bed, not yet. Not before I have to face Fi. Gabe doesn't persist; he rises and comes out into the hallway, shutting the door behind him.

'Did you get anything nice?' he asks.

'It's okay.'

'What time are you meeting?'

'Seven.'

'You better start washing your hair, then. It'll take ages to dry.'

I glower for a second before my lips twitch. He's right to make light of it.

'Are you going to be okay getting the bus?'

'I'll be fine.'

'I know, but I can drive you if you'd rather.'

'Don't be silly. You open up.' I lean in and kiss him. 'I've got to have a shower,' I say, slipping the blue dress off over my head.

Gabe hesitates for a second before reaching around and unclipping my bra. In a sweeping motion, he lifts me up and carries me into the bathroom.

When I am dried and dressed, I examine the finished product. The dress is a good fit, slightly baggy across the thighs – a combination of where I used to hold my weight and the elastic having been stretched too far – but not bad overall. Gabe fixes the clasp of the necklace, his warm breath on my ear and neck, the snowflake landing gently on my breast bone.

'We have to go,' he says.

I cling to his shirt; he smells unusually clean.

Chapter Twenty-six

THE SEATS OF the bus are covered in a wiry material that scratches at the back of my legs and causes my dress to ride uncomfortably up the back of my knees. I try adjusting it, but it springs back up every time we brake or change direction. I tug the neckline up and pull down on the sleeves. An awful lot more flesh is on show than when I left the flat. At least it feels that way. The bus smells of over-brewed tea and petrol fumes which cling to my nostrils. A pair of youths are sitting at the front, throwing something at each other, the stuffing from inside the seat, I think. A little way into the journey, they turn their attention to me. Cowering behind the backs of their seats, they giggle as bits of foam begin to fly towards me. I refuse to acknowledge them and eventually they grow bored and turn their attention to an elderly woman across from them, who offers far more entertainment with her flustered scolding.

It's a fairly lengthy journey at this speed, so I try to pass the time by cleaning the pendent. It digs into my skin and leaves black stains on my thumb, but by the time I have to change buses, it has at least a little glimmer to it – it would match my bracelet beautifully. As the bus slows for the fourth time, I get up and wobble precariously down the aisle. The children, poised to flick the fluff at me as I exit the bus, stop suddenly when they see the guard wandering up the street in an attempt at a casual patrol.

This is the stop Fi gave me. I glance around, thinking I must have gotten it wrong. Only one restaurant is in sight, and Fi would never choose a place like this. Not in a million years. I'm on the verge of backing out and jumping on the next bus back to Gabe's when I catch sight of her through the glass.

It takes another second to confirm it's definitely Fi. She has changed so much. A churning returns to my stomach, knotting everything together. This type of place does not want people like me, like us, in there and the last thing I want is trouble. From across the street I watch as a waiter waltzes over to Fi. My nerves rocket and I hold my breath, expecting to see her turfed out any second. The waiter leans over and flicks his hand. A second later Fi's head sweeps back in a laugh. Another thirty seconds pass before the waiter turns away from the table. He too is laughing.

With a deep breath, I ready myself to head inside. A small slope leads up to the glass doorway. The walls are also glass, and perfectly polished, not a bug, scratch or fingerprint in sight. It looks like there's enough glass here to replace all the windows in our tower block. The tiles outside are swept clean, and buckets of plants hang from an awning. One in particular catches my eye; lavender. The smell drifts into the air around me as I wipe my hands nervously on the front of my thighs. I'm still not convinced I should actually go inside when a gust of air wraps itself around my ankles and persuades me up the ramp.

The smell of lavender is replaced by alluring aromas of citrus and steak. On a quick assessment of the place I decided that they could easily fit in twice the number of tables and probably require half as many staff. A man, dressed entirely in black, bounds over to me before the door has had time to close.

'Can I help?' he says.

'I'm meeting my sister here.'

'Name?'

'She's just —' I point to where she's sitting against the window.

'Of course. The table in the corner.' He gesticulates to the corner, in case I can suddenly no longer see it.

The tables are covered with a magnitude of plush coloured cloths and far more cutlery and glasses than I could hope to use in just one sitting. Plates are stacked on more plates then more plates, finally topped with an intricately folded napkin. My dress barely reaches my knees, and apparently the fashion has changed to full length; at least that's what's being worn by the group of girls laughing loudly at the table across the way. I stare at the back of Fi's head before finally finding the courage to speak.

'Hi,' I say.

She turns to face me. The undeniable anguish on Fi's face is replaced by a wide grin.

'You came?'

She places her glass on the table, stands up and hugs me. It's a strong hug, overly forceful, and my body tenses as I wait for her to let go. She's sitting at an unnecessarily large table. I go to pull out the chair nearest to me – a huge velour monstrosity – but the waiter gets there before me.

'No, sit over here.' She indicates the place set across from her, leaning her arms across the table. I start to move the chair, but a waiter is there first again. When I finally sit down, Fi clasps my hands.

'You look well,' she says, her gaze wandering across my face and down my body. Anywhere to avoid eye contact.

'So do you,' I say. And I, in contrast, mean it.

Her skin looks clear, the creases have gone from her forehead, her cheeks and clothes are filled. My jaw clenches at the sight of her hair hanging loose in dark waves around her shoulders. I want to reach up and stroke it, to remember what it feels like, but instead I clench my hand in a fist under the table. Fi seems to be abiding by the fashion in a floor length blue gown. Her bracelet jangles around her wrist, bright and sparkling and causes her glass to ring when the chain strikes against it.

A waiter appears with a jug and fills the glasses before placing menus in our hands. The water's lemon scented and far too cold. I put it down to warm up and leaf through the menu.

With every item I read, my heart rate increases. I can't pronounce half the dishes let alone hazard a guess at what food they actually contain. Half our mourner's money would be gone on one starter.

'Fi, I can't afford to eat here,' I say in a hushed tone so I'm not overheard. 'Is there anywhere else we can go that's a little cheaper?'

'Don't worry, I'll pay.'

'Have you looked at the prices?'

'I've been doing a few other jobs,' she says.

'Really, like what?' Short of dealing or prostitution, I'm not sure what would bring her this kind of income.

'Oh, it's nothing. I'm surprised Gabe didn't tell you.'

My molars grind together, which I try to disguise with a smile.

'No. No, he didn't.'

'That's why he lets me do the evening shifts. So I can do other things during the day. Besides, I think it's better to stay on this side of town tonight.'

I'm about to ask why when she reaches her hands over the table, and I'm not quick enough to move mine away.

'I'm glad you managed to sort things out with him, Em. Really I am. And I'm truly sorry for what I said; it shouldn't have come out like that. I was upset. I just thought you should know about us. Gabe and me.'

'I understand,' I say, leaning back into the chair and taking my hands with me. 'It must be hard knowing someone only slept with you because he thought you could amend it. I would have been upset, too.'

It was a low jab and I should feel guilty, but there's something satisfying about seeing the flicker that crosses her face, even though it's gone in an instant. Instead, she offers her most compassionate smile, perfect teeth and fluttering eyelashes.

'I just want what's best for you, Em,' she says. 'If you think that is with Gabe, well, who am I to judge *him*?'

There's too much emphasis on that last word, and I continue to wear down the enamel on my teeth as we stare at each other, locked in a stalemate. My phone beeps in my pocket, Gabe no doubt, but I don't get it. I won't be the one to look away first. Fi starts tapping her fingers against her glass of water while I sip mine, despite it being so cold it makes my teeth ache.

Our glaring match is interrupted by a noise from across the restaurant. The indistinct conversations crescendo, and several tables simultaneously start to laugh as a collective buzz tickles the air. Craning my neck, I try to see around Fi, but she's already on her feet and gushing excitedly.

'Oh, I'm so glad he made it. Emelia, pull that chair out, will you? Tuck it in behind you, make some room.'

Emelia? And without a hint of animosity.

The laughter fades and the rubber squeaks as it runs against the polished flooring towards us.

'Finola.'

Luke's arms extend towards Fi as she bends down and kisses one cheek, then another and then back to the first. I'm half expecting a quick curtsy, but thankfully she stops.

'I hope you don't mind me interrupting. I won't stay for long. I just wanted to give my best to your sister.'

Dressed in heavily pocketed shorts and a T-shirt, he certainly isn't abiding by the dress code either. As I hadn't, Fi pushes her chair out of the way, then takes a seat one across, and fills his glass with water. Luke's eyes, however, haven't moved, and the undivided attention causes my stomach to coil peculiarly.

'I know how difficult it can be,' he says. 'Going from your old life to now. Believe me, I know. And I wanted to let you know

I'm always here if you want to talk.'

A man from another table is waving furiously. Luke offers him a polite nod of recognition and turns back to me.

'I'm sure you have plenty of people to talk to, but I wanted you to know, the offer is always there.'

My mouth is dry. I take a sip of water and mutter something that's barely even audible to me. He mirrors my movements and reaches for his own glass. I shift my gaze awkwardly to the menu, but I don't read it.

'Well, I'll leave you to enjoy your dinner,' he says. 'I'm sure you've got a lot to catch up on.'

He places his hands on the edge of his wheels, but then he changes his mind.

'I almost forgot.' He reaches down the side of his chair next to his leg, and his hand returns with a crumpled brown paper bag.

'This is for you,' he says, handing me the packet. 'Apple cider vinegar, for your hair. It's meant to help it grow faster apparently.'

The small bag weighs heavy. I pull out a glass bottle of ochre liquid.

'I'm not sure if you're supposed to rub it in or drink it. You might want to check that first.'

His smile causes another internal sensation, this time slightly lower. I unscrew the lid and waft the bottle under my nose. I jar my head back quickly.

'Probably best not to drink it then?' Luke says, laughing.

Flustered, I tighten the lid and place the bottle down by my bag.

'Thank you,' I say. 'It's very kind of you.'

'My pleasure. Although if I'm honest, I'm kind of hoping it doesn't work. I think this look suits you.'

I run my hand over my shaven head and squeeze the base of my neck.

'Thanks, but I'm not so sure.'

'Trust me, you look incredible.'

The room has grown inconceivably warm. The lining of the dress sticks to my back and clings to my thighs. A ceiling fan whirs slowly above me, but the air has stopped moving. I begin to pick at my nails before correcting myself and instead gulp down another glass of water.

'Right, I should leave you two to it,' Luke says, turning to Fi. 'You need to order some food.'

'Why don't you stay for a drink?' Fi says, placing her hand over his. 'After all, you're the reason we got the table.'

A queue is now gathering outside, and although plenty of tables are still empty, more have filled, including one occupied by two ladies both in dresses above the knees. For some reason they look familiar, as I realise, do quite a few of the faces sitting at the tables.

'Is that…' My eyes fall on a man with dark, slicked back hair.

'Alistair Hall,' Luke tells me. 'Cousin to the *great* man. Though the two do look remarkably similar.'

'They do,' I say.

I stare a fraction longer. It may not be the head of the Cabinet, but he's still an impressively imposing figure and not someone I ever thought would be sitting in the same restaurant as. When Fi clears her throat with a cough I realise I've been staring too long, although it's not just me. Luke's gaze if just as fixated. His eyes hold an expression I can't quite read.

'It's a lovely place,' I say, feeling the need to break the tension and casting my eyes over the ghastly velveteen chairs and miles of glass.

Luke laughs, his attention back on our table. 'It's ridiculously pretentious,' he says. 'But they do phenomenal food.'

'Luke's friends with the owner,' Fi adds.

'Well, more like firm acquaintances than friends,' he says. 'But he was happy to sort out a table. And don't worry about the bill, that's all sorted.'

'Really I don't want to —'

'It's sorted,' he repeats.

Our table falls into a sudden thick silence as Fi and Luke stare expectantly at me. Being here with Fi is bad enough, and I was clearly not as ready for forgiveness as I thought, but adding Luke to the mix – does that make it better or worse? Either way, it's clear I'm not getting out of it. I tug at the hem of my dress.

'Please stay for a drink with us,' I say to Luke. 'As a thank you.'

'Are you sure?'

'Positive.'

It's not like I have a choice. Still, when Luke mouths another thank you silently at me, something twists in my insides and releases an unexpected army of butterflies.

Luke orders a bottle of wine from the waiter, who returns

promptly and fills our glasses less than a third of the way.

We clink with forced smiles and eye contact, the second of which prompts the same unexpected sensation as before.

The wine is sharp and fizzy, and one sip leads easily to the next and several more. Without meaning to, I slip into a momentary daydream of snowy mountain peaks. Luke catches my eyes, and I feel a blush heat my cheeks. Then my phone buzzes again, and I push my bag under my seat.

Fi's glass stays full, and I am impressed. When the waiter comes to take our order, Luke's and my glasses are already empty. Fi orders several dishes without my consultation, and I'm about to object when I realise I'm relieved; I had no idea what I should choose. When Luke makes motions to move, Fi pipes up again.

'Stay for one more glass,' she insists. 'Just until our food is here.'

'I really shouldn't. I've got the car outside.'

'Well, I'm not drinking, and Em can't have a bottle to herself. That would just be rude.' She tops up his glass before he can respond and then proceeds to overfill mine.

'And I want to propose a toast,' she says, raising her untouched glass with one hand and reaching across to squeeze my arm with her other.

'To the people we love and the people who love us.'

'To people,' Luke adds, holding my gaze and curling his lips ever so slightly as he knocks my glass with his.

Conversation is skittish. It skims over any topics of depth before they can lead to heated debates. The mood is gracefully, and expertly, engineered by Luke's diplomatic diversions, which several times prevent light-hearted disputes from escalating into something more. Odd moments occur between the two of them, subtle gestures, such as Fi biting her manicured nails in response to one of his digressions or the silencing split-second glances he casts her more than once. But then he offers me glances of my own, too, glances which evoke a multitude of responses from the kaleidoscope of butterflies far too rapidly multiplying between my intestines and my liver. He smiles profusely, but almost always tight-lipped, subtle and secretive. And almost always directed at me. He offers half smiles with a flash of his eyebrow when Fi refuses to be side-tracked, a tilted head and suppressed grin when he catches me yawning, a smile that narrows his eyes when he catches me watching him. I don't want to be pulled into it and

Gabe's words about him echo around in my head, but something about him causes the most physical responses in me. I half-heartedly begin to wonder if Gabe's reason for wanting to keep us separate is decidedly less than altruistic.

Fi is midway through a rant on the condition in homes and some bill that the Administration is hoping to pass, when her phone starts ringing. She looks from Luke to me before foraging around in her bag for it and does a noticeable double take when she sees the name of the caller. She shows the screen to Luke, who shrugs and turns his attention back to me, attempting to reignite an earlier conversation about architecture, though he barely listens to my answers and repeats the same questions almost immediately after.

Fi stands, excusing herself, and absentmindedly stumbles outside, where both Luke and I continue to watch her through the glass. Her hands wave rapidly as she tries to keep the phone pinned to her ear with her shoulder, and she reminds me of a conductor, trying to control a runaway orchestra, angrily swiping her hand through the air in a strict two-two beat. But her forehead is furrowed and whoever the orchestra is, it clearly is not following her lead.

'Do you know who she's talking to?' I ask Luke.

'Just some people from work.' He shrugs. 'It's wrong of them to call her now.'

'From the bar?' I say, but I already know the answer. Gabe wouldn't disturb us. He wouldn't ring her. I remember the message from earlier that I still haven't read.

'No, Finola's been doing a bit of work with me recently, more volunteering than a job, I suppose.'

'Really? She didn't say. What is it you do?'

Luke runs his hand through his hair and then takes a sip of the wine, draining the rest of the glass. When he finds there's no more, he takes Fi's untouched flute.

'It's kind of hard to explain. I guess you could call it public affairs, support work. We help people who are having difficulty adjusting.'

'To what?'

'Their amendments.'

I unintentionally raise my eyebrows. Fi helping someone cope with an amendment seems more than a little unlikely to me, unless the therapy involves an endless supply of alcohol and random men. Luke reads my scepticism.

'You must have noticed the change in her,' he says. 'Every day she's improving.'

'Oh, I'm not denying she's changed.'

'And now she's helping others do the same. She really is remarkable.'

'Who's remarkable?'

Fi's hands appear on his shoulders.

'I was just telling your sister what a phenomenal transition you've made.'

'Well, it has its downsides.'

She turns to me, and I know what she's about to say. My stomach steels itself.

'I'm so sorry, Em, I've got to go —'

'Seriously? We haven't even eaten.'

'I didn't think they'd call me. They know I usually work nights.'

'What is it you've got to do? Surely people can't need your help at this time?'

Fi's nostrils flare as she casts a look to Luke, but if he notices, he doesn't show it. He drains the rest of Fi's glass, and she turns back to me. Fi emits a strained laugh accompanied by a high smile which overstretches her top lip.

'Oh, it's nothing really, it's not far,' she says. 'It might not even take that long.'

She looks to Luke again; this time his snub is more obvious. Her smile dissolves.

'Let's see if they'll wrap the food up for us,' I say. 'I'll head with you and we can eat it on the way to your work.'

'This isn't the type of place that will wrap up your food for you, Em.'

'With the prices here, they should give it to you in a bin bag if that's what you ask for.'

Someone clears his throat behind me, and a quick glance up has me wanting to bury my head in the linen. A wicker basket is placed in front of us with warm bread that ripples the air above it. It's followed by a spread that makes last night's picnic look and smell like bird food. The salivation ensues. Fi glances at it sadly.

'I wish I could stay,' she says softly. 'I really do. But I don't have a choice. I'm so sorry.' She turns her gaze to Luke. 'You can stay with her, can't you? Please?'

Her voice tightens and quivers in a way that would make it difficult for anyone to say no to. I know I never did. Luke looks at his watch and then at me. Then he smiles.

'It's far better than any other offer I've had tonight, if you don't mind the company?'

'Really, don't feel that you have to babysit me.'

'I don't. Not at all.' He flashes another grin. 'But I will have to make a quick phone call, if that's okay?'

'Are you sure?'

'I'll be one minute. Please start without me.' He smiles at me again as he leaves, ignoring Fi's furtive glances.

Fi reaches across the table and grasps my hands.

'Next week?' she says. 'I promise, next week. Is that okay?'

'It's fine. Fi, honestly, don't bother.'

She squeezes my clenched hand and crouches down to my seated level.

'Please, Em, let's give this another go, we'll talk properly, I promise.'

'Fi —'

'Please. I've missed you.'

'Why?' I say, slipping my hand out from under hers and leaning back into the chair.

'What?'

'Why? Why have you missed me?'

'Em, you're my sister.'

'So? Look at you, look at how much better you are now. You're better without me.'

'That's not true.'

'All those months I tried to help you. It did nothing.'

'That's not true.'

'Yes, it is. You're better off without me.'

'Em —'

'You're better off without me.'

She reaches for my hand again, but I flick her away.

'You don't mean that. Please stop saying it.' A tear slips down her cheek.

I'm not trying to be hurtful this time. I'm really not. But the truth seems undeniable.

'Fi,' I say softly. 'I'm not being cruel, and I'm not trying to hurt you. I'm just saying it like it is. You are better off without me. And I'm better without you.'

‘You don’t mean that,’ she whispers, and more tears run freely down her face.

‘Yes, yes, I do. You deserve to be better. And I want to be better. I want to be better.’

In a flash her expression hardens. She stands, straightens her dress and wipes her face. ‘I guess that explains it all,’ she says, then arches her heels, swivels and walks away. My heart feels ready to crack, but I don’t call her back.

She waits by the glass door as a lady fetches her coat, and I know she’s staring at me; I can feel the glare. I know she’s crying, too, but I don’t look up, not until she’s outside and her back is facing me.

Luke hangs up the phone and opens his arms, and Fi kneels on the ground in front of him. His lips move slowly by her ear. She hangs there for a few moments before she leaps to her feet, throws her arms up into the air and marches away. Without meaning to, I catch her eye. The look she gives me is one of pure venom. My heart pummels wildly against my ribs as I hastily look away. When I look back up, she is gone.

Chapter Twenty-seven

'SHE REALLY has missed you,' Luke says, now back at the table.

I stay silent, chewing on meat that doesn't require chewing.

'She talks about you constantly.'

'She misses the idea of me, that's all,' I say.

That's what I miss, the idea of her. I lost my Fi a long time ago, and that Fi I still miss. I missed her so much I screamed at the imposter who lay in her bed, wore her clothes, drowned in her honeysuckle perfume and downed vodka from the glasses my parents were given for their wedding. I screamed at her until the tears ruined my vision and my throat was raw for days after. My Fi, the sister I would do anything for, the one who would dance with me on a rooftop and make me laugh so much I thought my stomach would rupture – that Fi is nothing more than memory. Just like my mother, or happy days as a family, or the dream in the snow with Gabe. I've seen glimpses of the real Fi – moments when she would talk about the future or mention our mother without seething through her teeth with a bottle in her hand, but every time it was still just a shadow, a spectre, she wasn't complete. And this new Fi I've seen tonight, with the lovely dinner and the helpful volunteering and manicured nails, this Fi is nothing more than an illusion. And sooner or later, every great illusionist discovers that all their tricks have been revealed. Either that or something goes terribly wrong.

'Do you like the food?' Luke says, calling a waiter over with a flick of his hand.

'It's lovely,' I say. And it would be if it was hot. The sauces are now gelatinous around the drying meat.

'I'm sorry it's cold. You should have started.'

'Really. It's fine.' I cut another morsel and pierce it with my fork.

'I can order some more?'

'Really it's fine.'

'So,' Luke asks. 'What do you plan on doing now?'

'What do you mean?'

'Well, are you looking for work?'

'I just got my disability allowance.'

'Really, for what?'

I knew he'd ask that, and I knew I'd need to make up an answer. I scrape the sauce along the edge of my plate with the blunt end of my knife and find it's too difficult to construct something plausible.

'I don't know,' I admit.

'Really? How did you apply for it then?'

'I don't know.'

'And you're fine with that? With the Cabinet watching you like that?'

My throat emits a croaky half-laugh. 'I think that Cabinet have got more important things to do than watch me. You know, like running the country.'

'The Cabinet is watching everybody,' Luke says, plunging our conversation into silence.

The silence is broken by an ear-piercing screech as my knife grates against the china. I move a piece of vegetable around with my fork; my mouth feels too dry to swallow it.

'Sorry,' says Luke. 'I didn't mean to make you feel uncomfortable. Let's change the subject. You ask me something.' He leans back into his chair and places his hands on the table, palms up.

He's invited the obvious question, and to be fair, I do want to know, but that seems a little easy and I guess he's the type of person who likes you to think outside the box. I push the vegetable around my plate some more before putting my cutlery down entirely.

'You haven't been in your chair long.'

'No, I haven't, but that's not a question.'

'Why haven't you amended it?'

'Not, how did I do it?' He arches his eyebrow. 'How do you know I can amend it? It might be some disease that left me like this as a child. I might not be able to amend it.'

'But it wasn't, and you need to answer my question. Why haven't you amended it?'

'I'm sure you know the answer.'

'Because you don't believe in amending.'

'Correct.'

'But you haven't said why.'

His smile is surprisingly satisfied and it causes a reoccurrence of peculiar flutterings in my intestines.

'Okay, but then I get to ask you another question.'

'Fine.' I lean back into the chair which seems to have softened slightly.

Luke opens his mouth to speak when a waiter arrives with another bottle of wine. I study Luke's face, the deep setting of his eyes and the clean shave of his cheeks, when he takes the bottle and insists we can pour it ourselves.

'Entropy,' he says, filling my glass.

'Entropy?'

'Entropy, chaos.'

'That's not an answer,' I say shifting my position and picking up the drink.

'It is.'

'Well, not a good enough one.'

He tips back his head a little as he laughs. 'Okay, you're right.' He pushes his plate to the side of the table and takes several large sips of his wine before placing the glass down and leaning in on his elbows.

'Entropy increases. Chaos, disorder. Not just on Earth but in the universe. This isn't me, this is science.' He uses his hands to stress the point. 'We live in a universe where only chaos is constantly increasing. How long can something last like that in a state of constant degeneration?'

'And you think not amending will somehow change that?'

'I think amending is at the root of it. We look at retrocausality as though it is the answer to all our problems, but what could be more entropic? We have no consequences, no repercussions. We think only of the effects of the actions on ourselves. It frays the edges of our existence.'

'That seems a bit extreme.'

'Maybe, but it's my turn for a question.' He sits back and tilts his head, like he may see something different if he views me from another angle.

'Why did you forgive him?'

'Pardon?'

'Gabe. You must have forgiven him. Why?'

I run my hands over my head. At some point the waiter must have taken our plates away, so there's no cutlery left in front of me to distract me: instead I twist the thin stem of the glass. Ripples appear on the surface of the wine as I try to stop my hands from trembling.

'So,' he says quietly. 'Why did you? You haven't forgiven Fi, not yet, so why him?'

Luke curls his own hands around mine, removing them from the wine glass. He cocoons them safely, patiently waiting.

'I'm sorry,' he says. 'I shouldn't pry.'

'It's fine,' I say. 'You answered my question. I should answer yours.'

'You don't have to.'

'I want to.' As I start to speak, my phone beeps again. I pull my hands out from beneath his, remove the phone from my bag and switch it off without looking. Then I slug back the contents of my glass before refilling it and trying to speak again.

'Have you ever been really lonely?' I say.

'Everyone's been lonely at some point, I'm sure.'

'I'm not talking about a bad week, missing someone, pet just died, lonely. I'm talking about real loneliness.'

'Of course. I'm sure I must have been at some point.'

'If you had been, you'd know about it. Believe me. The thing is when you're really lonely, it's like divisions of time are meaningless. Hours, days, weeks, they don't matter; you have nothing to look forward to and nothing to think back on. You get so tired of your own voice rattling around inside your head that you just want to block it out. You sleep all the time you can because maybe, just maybe, tomorrow something might happen to make that loneliness stop. You become a void in your own existence.'

'And Gabe fills that?'

'Yes.'

'Couldn't anyone?'

'Who would want to?' That's an unfair comment to Gabe, and I know it's not true. I know not everyone could fill the space he does. Not everyone has such a longing desire to be better, to help me be better. But I don't want Luke to know that.

'I'm sure there would be plenty of people wanting to fill that void,' Luke says. 'If you gave them the chance.'

His hands are on top of mine again, and I'm unsure when he placed them there. He slides his fingers between mine.

'I would.' He leans in across the table, his lips just inches from my face, and cleans something from my cheeks. 'I would fill that emptiness.'

'You don't know me,' I say.

He smiles slightly and runs one finger down the side of my cheek. His touch runs like electricity through my skin.

'Believe me, I do,' he says. 'I knew you from the minute I first saw you, lying there asleep on the hospital bed, smiling like your dream was the only place you wanted to be. I knew you from that instant.'

I shake my head, but his hand is still there, cradling me, protecting me. No, protecting me is what Gabe would do. Luke's look is different, almost admiration. He doesn't think I'm weak. I think back to that moment on the mountain side. The one in my head that I know never happened.

'Tell me,' Luke says, as if reading my mind. 'Now that you've amended do you see things?'

'See things? Like what?'

'I don't know, you tell me?'

I hold his gaze as tightly as I can, but the image of Fi's burnt arms pushes its way to the forefront of my mind.

'You don't see things from before you amend, if that's what you mean,' I say. 'You must know that.'

'How would I?' he says and flips his hand palm upwards.

'You know what happens. You've spoken to people who've amended.'

'I have,' he says then leaves the rest of his sentence dangling in the silence. His eyes refuse to falter, but I'm not going to give in. I'm not going to give him want he wants. Heat builds through my palms and up to my cheeks.

'No,' I lie. 'I don't see things.'

Luke continues to study me and I'm certain he knows I'm lying. So much of me wants to walk away, go home and forget about him, but something is holding me here.

'You can feel this, too,' he says. 'This connection. I know you can.'

His words take me by surprise. I can't put a finger on what I'm feeling. Confused? Excited? He's right. There is something there. My pulse is racing. But is that a good thing? I swallow again, trying to eradicate the dryness of my mouth.

'And I wouldn't replace you at the first chance I got,' Luke says.

I whip my body back away from him, guilt rising through my gut from even thinking about betraying Gabe.

'It wasn't like that,' I snap. 'You only know her version.'

'And you only know his.'

'And what? You think he didn't tell me the truth?'

'I think he told you whatever truth would get you into bed.'

Invisible hackles protrude along my spine, and the warm heat I had previously felt is now red-hot and furious. I gulp down wine, but it does little to douse the flames. I move to pick up my bag, knowing I should leave now, before he can insult me or Gabe any more. But if I do, it's like they won, like I didn't want to hear the truth. Like I won't be able to handle the truth.

'Whatever story Fi has spun to make her seem like the victim, it will be a lie,' I hiss.

'Your sister doesn't lie.' Luke's expression stays placid. 'She's many things, but she's not a liar. You know that.'

I drain my glass, then top it up and ignore the fact that Luke's is also empty. My jaw clicks as my teeth grind together.

'So, what do you know that I don't then?' I say.

'I know that Finola had feelings for Gabe.'

'Years ago maybe,' I sneer.

'Do you think feelings like that ever go away?'

'You seem to think they can come on just as quick,' I spring back.

It silences him for a second. 'I believe in attraction,' he says slowly. 'And more than just physical and mental attraction. I believe that real attraction is something far deeper and more spiritual than we can understand.'

'That sounds like a cheap chat up line.' I laugh coldly, though Luke remains impassive to the insult.

He relaxes back into his chair. 'Forget what I think then. Tell me what you know.'

'About what?'

'About Gabe.'

My muscles tense. I know where he's going, but I'm not going to give him satisfaction. 'I know he grew up on the mountains. That he thinks his family is still there.'

'Anything else?' Luke waits for a reply.

'He's been there for us. Always,' I say after a pause.

'True, but I asked what you know about him. What you know about his history, his life.'

My mouth is bone dry, and my jaw is locked so rigidly, it's burning. I rack my brain, but I can't find anything further to add. I'm not telling him about Gabe's envelopes, even if that's what Luke wants. He seems pleased by my silence.

'The truth is that Finola had feelings for Gabe, and when she was at her most vulnerable, he abused them.'

'That's not true.'

'I can assure you it is. I was there, remember. What's more is he did exactly the same to you. Fortunately for Finola, she managed to see a way out. I just hope for your sake you can do the same.'

'You don't know Gabe,' I whisper, my voice trembling.

'What, you mean I don't know how he wants to *be better*?'

My insides knot around each other, and I begin to speak, but my words fade before they leave my lips. I expect Luke's expression to be of sneering satisfaction, but instead it's one of concern.

'I assume he used that on you as well? Don't worry, I'm sure you're not the only ones to have fallen for it. A line like that's never going to date.'

'You don't know him,' I say again, but my voice is weak and broken and lacks conviction.

'I'm not denying he's done his homework. He looked after you girls well. He's been there wherever you needed him. But look at where it's got him. A slave in the bar and the bedroom.'

Luke pauses for effect, and I want to slap him, but my hands don't move. His words are hitting far too close to the bone.

'You're right,' Luke continues. 'I don't know Gabe, not well. But I know men like him. Men with no friends and no family. Why is that?' He doesn't wait for an answer. 'There is only one reason why someone his age would have no one else in his life, and it's because he's got something to hide.'

I press my lips together and try to block out what he's saying, but I can feel it in my gut. Every word, everything Luke has said about Gabe, it's all true. Luke looks at me, his eyebrows slanted and his brow crinkled as he reaches for my hand.

'I'll back off,' he says. 'I promise I will end this conversation now if you can look me in the eye and tell me one thing that you know with absolute certainty about this man. Anything other than what he's told you.'

Luke's eyes don't falter as he waits for an answer. The wine churns in my stomach, and my skin prickles from the indescribable cold, which in a flash is replaced by a suffocating heat. I push myself up from the table, knocking the chair onto the marble floor where it lands with a clatter. Several pairs of eyes rotate towards me. A waiter rushes to stand the chair upright.

'Is there a bathroom I can use somewhere?' I say, my voice trembling as I blush.

'Just down there,' Luke says. 'Emelia, take as long as you need.'

I shove the chair back under the table and stagger to a door at the far side of the restaurant. A twisting feeling snowballs in the pit of my stomach. My lungs are clamped shut, unable to expand, unable to breath. The dizziness spirals upwards, and I'm not sure if I'm going to be sick or pass out; still, I lock myself in a cubical, slump to the floor and reach for the lid of the toilet.

Acid burns the back of my throat as mouthful after mouthful of wine and dinner reappear. The ammonia tainted air stings my eyes and hastens the deluge of tears. Each time I think it's over, there's another round. Another replay of Luke's words, another wrench in my gut, another realisation of Gabe's lies and manipulation. Bile-filled vomit clings to my teeth. Luke was right, I was used. My stomach has cramped from all the retching and my head pounds. I want to close my eyes and forget the night entirely. Unfortunately, I know that's not an option.

I unlock the door and wash my hands in the sink. Red bloodshot eyes, blotchy pink skin with patches of smudged makeup and a bristled head stare blankly back. I look like a new born rat, furless and grotesque; all I'm missing is the whiskers. I even seem to have mastered the pathetic squeak as a few weak sobs escape.

I splash my face with running water and wash away the remains of the makeup. My eyes are still ringed with the unmistakable redness of tears, but it's better. I open my bag and pull out the unwanted lipstick from last night. Last night, is that really when it was? I take off the lid and run the garish paint over my mouth; after all, I can't look any worse than I do now. I stare at my reflection. There's no point imagining it looks any different; this is what I have, this is what I am. And it's all I've got.

Luke is over at another table talking to an elderly couple, both of whom are trying desperately to disguise their age. The man's thin hair has been dyed unnaturally black, and the woman's hair, also delicately frail, has been rolled and piled to within an inch of its life above her scalp. Still, they seem happy, finishing each other's sentences, laughing in unison. From where I stand, I can see their legs linked together under the table.

When Luke sees me, he bids them a good evening and wheels back to our table, now emptied of everything except the last wine and water. Taking my seat, I reach for the water first.

'You don't have to stay,' Luke says. 'I can wait with you for a bus if you'd like.'

'We haven't finished the wine.'

'It's only wine. It doesn't matter.'

'But it's my turn to ask a question,' I say.

He doesn't reply. Instead he tilts his head by the smallest half degree and tops up our glasses without taking his eyes off me. I feel my stomach flip nervously as he hands me my glass.

'Ask away.'

We drink through that bottle and another, my glass filled far more frequently than his, but I'm not complaining. I ask where the money comes from, and how everybody knows him. He asks about boyfriends, my mother and the attack. Soon there is no need for Luke's questioning probes – my tongue is the loosest I've known it and by the end of the night I have divulged more than I would ever normally dream of. Some things are repetitions from last night with Gabe, many are far more truthful than I was able to express then. Through the course of the evening, I choke on my drink from laughter and make my lip bleed by biting down to stop myself from crying.

Chapter Twenty-eight

IT IS AS if he controls the air when he speaks; every syllable carries to the farthest corners of the room. A natural silence settles around him, and though I know other people are listening, I can't tear my eyes away to see, just in case I miss something. No wonder Fi is so mesmerised by him.

'So, what happened?' I say. 'How did you end up like this?'

Luke picks up the bottle and fills my glass. For once he leaves his empty.

'I got picked up at school,' he says, 'I was bright — not the cleverest maybe — but I learned fast. One of the factories offered me a job at sixteen and I took it. Figured it would be better than chancing my luck and ending up in one of the mines. I started at the factory at sixteen and I worked my way up. At twenty-three I was my parent's boss, can you imagine? Even got to meet the Cabinet once.'

I let out an impressed low whistle. He laughs.

'Yeah, they were doing a tour of the factories and places and I got asked to show them around.'

'Hall too?' I ask.

Luke lets out a derisive snort.

'The only time that man meets the normal people is when he's murdering them,' he says. A tangible silence begins to form in the air but he doesn't let it stick.

'Anyway, I had an interview for a new job. I'd gone as far as I was going to get at that factory and wanted a new challenge. To be honest I was pretty much a shoe-in. Still, I prepared all my questions and things that night, then went to bed at about ten. Next morning, I slept through my alarm. Like really slept through it. I didn't wake up until gone midday.'

He looks truly baffled as he says this, like he still can't understand how it happened.

'I'd slept for fifteen hours. I missed the interview completely. I've never slept that much before or since. You know, later I even accused some people at work of spiking my drinks. I just didn't see how it could have happened.'

'So what happened?'

'I was distraught. I rang the new place, but what were they going to do? They could hardly give a job to someone who can't even wake up for the interview. So, I got in my car to drive to the centre near me. All I could think about was going back and sorting it out. I have no idea why I drove. It would have been just as quick to walk. It wasn't raining. I had no need to get in the car. Nothing was on the road, no ice, no animals, no other drivers. I was wide awake. My car was in perfect condition, yet somehow in the tiny road between my flat and the centre, I ended up wrapped around a lamp post.'

I can see him in all his detail. I imagine how he looked when he slept so deeply he barely stirred to breathe and later, distraught and angry at his own foolishness. Then I see his body crushed between the metal of the car and the post. In my imagination, he is dressed as he is now, just with blood tarnishing his clothes and skin.

'I woke up three days later,' he says. 'No use of my legs but not a mark on my body, not anywhere, not a scratch. I was desperate to amend, of course I was, but I couldn't get to a centre. Anyway, they wouldn't let me in the state I was in, screaming and ranting. There was nothing I could do. I couldn't go anywhere. At first, I couldn't even sit up, couldn't feed myself, go to the toilet by myself. I didn't care about any of that, though; all that mattered was the accident itself. I became obsessed with the feeling that I shouldn't have crashed. There was no reason to it. I shouldn't have missed the alarm, and I shouldn't have crashed the car.'

Goose bumps have formed on my arms. I want to rub them warm but fear any sound might stop him. Instead, I just keep drinking. I slip my shoes off and curl my feet underneath me as he carries on with his story.

'I started looking into it, the number of accidents that happen on the way to centres, the number of people who don't get to amend. It was amazing. So many accidents, unexplained, unnecessary. Not just car crashes. People slipping on dry floors and breaking bones and not being able to reach the centre. Dog bites, gardening accidents, lifts breaking down and delaying people. Incidents with random strangers accosting people, freak weather, traffic jams on a quiet road.'

'You don't think it's coincidence?'

'I know it's not. There's too much for it to be coincidence. And the thing was, these people who didn't get to amend for whatever reason, they were fine. Better than fine. It might not make sense to you right now, but believe me, whatever it is, God, the universe, fate, it doesn't want us amending.'

'And so that's why you joined the Marchers.'

For the first time, he falters. Perhaps the rest of his speech had been rehearsed. If not rehearsed, then certainly re-used.

'The Marchers aren't what you think, not anymore.'

'So you don't plan attacks on annexes and centres? You don't kidnap and murder administrators?'

His eyes widen. 'God, no. There are some crazy fundamentalists out there, there always are, but that's not what I am. God, no, I'm not one of those. And don't forget,' he adds with a change of tone, 'The Marchers only started because they were needed.'

I hesitate, thinking of how to respond.

'If the Guards hadn't been so extreme when the Cabinet came to power, the Marchers would have never had to form in the first place,' Luke continues.

'Yes, but if the Guards and Cabinet hadn't been so extreme, then the Administration wouldn't have been properly formed and people would be abusing amendments left, right and centre.'

'You think they're not now?'

'You think they are?'

A thick crevice forms between Luke's eyebrows. Deciding I am not in a sober enough state for a heated discussion on historical politics, I redirect the conversation back to the topic of him.

'Then what do you do?'

'What do you mean?'

'You're an activist, right? That's what you mean when you say you help people.'

'No, I mean I help people.' He says it forcefully but not rudely. 'I don't push my ideas on anyone. I wouldn't do that. I help people. If they want, I help them with their decisions, but I always let them make their own choices.'

'Did you let Fi make her own?'

He places his hands on mine and cocks his head again.

'Your sister made the right choice.'

'That's not what I asked.'

'No, I know that. But I've already answered that question. I don't, and I can't make anyone make choices they don't believe are right. Your sister was no exception to that.'

'So she wanted to leave me like this, leave me with these memories. Leave me seeing all these things.'

'Seeing things?'

Luke's eyes narrow and my pulse steps up.

'About the attack,' I hastily add. 'Seeing things from the attack.'

He leans farther in; beneath the table my knees brush his. Obviously he doesn't feel it, but I don't move.

'Let me ask you something now. What would have been gained if Fi went back? If she stopped herself getting into the car or warned you of the attack or rang the police or even just got Gabe to put more fuel in the car. What would be gained?'

'You really need that answered?'

'Yes. Because from where I'm standing, things look better, much better than they did.'

'You have no idea what it was like before.'

'I know enough. I know how you spent your days surviving on mourner's money whilst Finola got drunk and high and every other combination of intoxication there is. I know Gabe let her drink herself silly regardless of how much it was hurting you both. I know you still lived in the same house as where you watched your mother die, tearing her skin from her face. And I know you thought you were in love with a man you struggled to have a conversation with and who manipulated every circumstance to suit his own agenda. And now…' He looks at me as if in awe, momentarily closing his eyes and exhaling quietly. 'Now, you're free.'

'Free?'

'Free. There is no one who needs you anymore. You have no binds, no constraints. You are the one who decides how your life turns out now. Finola learned that while you were asleep.'

'Asleep? I was in a coma.'

'What I mean is you can choose your own destiny, your own life. You are strong. All the challenges, they have made you so strong. If your sister had amended, then what? You'd always believe she was incapable of any form of independence. How many years would you have waited, mopping up her disasters or at least anticipating them? You would never have had a chance to be your own people, either of you.'

I reach for my glass, but it is empty; the bottle is, too. With my mouth still closed I run my tongue over my top teeth, refusing to look up and meet Luke's eye. Everything he's said is true. I would have followed behind her, cleaning up her mess and shelving my own ambitions. I don't even know what those ambitions are anymore. I glance around and find the restaurant has emptied. A few of the staff are polishing glasses behind the bar while another two are shuffling around re-laying the tables for tomorrow's service.

'We should leave,' I say.

Luke agrees. Together we head outside. The temperature has dropped significantly since I arrived and the air is filled with a blend of early blossoms and city smoke. I had always imagined the Central to be a hive of activity, even at night, but this evening the streets are eerily empty. I consider mentioning this to Luke, asking if it is always like this, but the quiet between us is a comfortable one and I don't want to change that. I don't offer to push the chair. I know he'd refuse; I saw the way he was in the car park. With the road deserted, we stand beneath a streetlamp. The air smells in need of rain, like the clouds are over filled but refusing to let up. It's not cold, but my body shivers involuntarily.

'Are you cold?' Luke asks.

'Not really.'

'Do you know how you are getting home? I mean, do the buses still run?'

'I don't know.' I realise I haven't thought that far ahead. I just assumed Fi would manage to get me home somehow.

'I would offer to drive you, but my track record in cars sober is bad enough. It's probably not worth it drunk. You could ask Gabe to come and get you.'

I don't warrant the remark with a response.

'Do you want to come back to my place then? I'll let Finola know where you are.'

'She won't forgive me yet, not the things I said to her.'

'Yes, she will. Remember, you're not the only one he fooled.'

'Thank you,' I say.

I get the distinct impression he doesn't want me walking behind him, but as he is leading the way, it's fairly difficult not to, particularly as the pavement is only just wide enough for the chair in places. After he takes several furtive glances back at me, I end up on the road beside him. The elevation of the pavement also helps compensate for the difference in height, and I feel only marginally taller. At times, I have an urge to reach out and hold his hand or lean down and rest my head on his shoulder. But it's just the wine, I try to tell myself.

Luke turns into a high rise. It's an old building, painted in a faded pinkish red. He backs into the tiny elevator first, leaving me to squeeze in behind. I move so I'm facing the doors and his head is level with, and quite possibly lost within, my backside. It's not the worst view he could have of me given how I looked earlier; still, I concentrate on not making any unnecessary movements.

The lift opens onto a long corridor which is badly lit and has only a few doors coming off either side. I've heard the older flats are often the largest, but it's tough to get into them. Usually they're kept aside for people with families or, I suppose, money.

Luke unlocks the door with a key and pushes it open for me to walk through.

Chapter Twenty-nine

I AM GREETED by a sense of homeliness that I wasn't expecting. The flat is large and open plan, with feminine touches of cushions and candles placed stylishly on sideboards and over the mantelpiece. Canvas artworks in all forms and mediums are strategically arranged on the walls. I don't need to be an art critic to recognise when things are expensive or old. Some of these look pre-discovery. The table in the dining room is large, but judging from the stacked books and papers, he's not one for entertaining. The kitchen supports this theory. The worktops are pristine with no sign of used crockery or food smells. Backless swivel stools sit under a breakfast bar and a fridge that, for its enormity of size, would not look out of place in a canteen, that is, if it were not covered in letters.

I wander over towards it, my eyes unsubtly scanning the notes. A few steps away I pause.

'It's fine,' Luke says. 'Read away.'

Whether written on scraps of old wrapping paper, scented notelets or old Christmas cards, each letter says the same things: *Thank you, I owe you so much. You have shown me the truth.* One is even written on music manuscript. Another draws my attention. *My head may not remember, but my heart always will.* The warmth of relief relaxes my muscles; he didn't lie, he does let people make their own choice. He's not a bad guy. The relief rouses another sensation in my gut. If Luke has told the truth about everything else, what does that mean about Gabe?

'How long has it been since your accident?' I say, distracting myself from my thoughts.

'A couple of years. Two now I guess.'

'Is that all?'

How can someone have made such a difference to so many people in such a short amount of time?

'Sometimes I can't even remember before, if I'm honest,' he says. 'That all feels like someone else's life. This is the first time I've ever really felt like the real me. I just wish my parents were here to see.'

'They're, they're...' I try to think of a different word to use. 'Gone?' Luke nods.

'About a month after my accident. They were both old. It wasn't a surprise. But I think seeing me like that, well, they wished they could have done something.' The memories appear in the contours of his face. I find myself wanting reach out, wanting to touch them.

'A lot of them I already knew from before.' Luke changes the mood in an instant. He picks off one or two notes from the fridge and hands them to me. 'This guy.' He gives me one on embossed headed paper. 'He got the job when I didn't show up.'

'What's he thanking you for?'

'Nothing he couldn't have worked out himself. It's the same with all of them. They all want to be told what to do, but society tells them what is best for society, not for a person.'

'Whereas you?'

'Tell them what they need to hear.'

It's almost exactly what Gabe said Luke did, but Gabe managed to make it sound negative. Hearing it from Luke's lips makes it sound so simple.

'What if what they want to hear isn't what's best for them?' I say.

'Why wouldn't it be? People don't have enough faith in themselves, in their abilities. If they think something is right for them, then it probably is. Why should they be dictated to and constrained by a society that doesn't even know who they are? Society wants what's best for society. Do you think the Cabinet would really let us amend if there wasn't something in it for them?'

'Like what?'

Luke doesn't answer. Instead he turns, reattaches the notes before he opens the fridge door and removes a bottle of wine. He doesn't ask if I want any before proceeding to pour two glasses and hand me one. If anything, it tastes even better than the wine we had in the restaurant, but I doubt the reliability of my senses after nearly two bottles.

I take the liberty of wandering around, glass in hand. Several doors open off the main living space, a bathroom, clean and empty, a bedroom with a few sets of clothes strewn randomly. The last door leads to an office. It's fairly empty, a large calendar on the wall with just a few numbers and letters written sporadically on different dates.

'Shall we sit down?' He ushers me away and closes the door behind me.

I walk over and take a seat on the sofa. Despite its homely appearance, it's surprisingly uncomfortable and has very little give in it. I adjust my position several times before finding one I can live with, with my legs tucked under a cushion.

Luke turns on some music and then lifts himself out of the chair and shuffles down next to me.

'I'm sorry about earlier.'

'Why? You didn't say anything that wasn't true.'

'But there's a time and a place to say things. That wasn't right.'

'I'm glad you did though. It made me think.'

'About?'

'Me. Gabe. Me mostly, I guess.' I cover my mouth in a vain attempt to stop a yawn escaping.

'Long day?'

I think back through the evening, this morning, back to last night. Last night, the smell of the melting candle wax, the rough fabric of the rug rubbing my knees. Gabe finding comfort in my body. Using my body. The thought makes me grimace, even if it hadn't felt like that at the time.

'It's been a long few months.' I correct myself. 'A long few years.'

'And now that they're over, what are you going to do?'

'How do you know they're over?'

'I know that they are if you want them to be. You've got nothing left to hold you back now.'

But what have I got to pull me forward? I have no education, no training, no money. Apprenticeships I was offered in school expired when I became a carer for my mother.

I fiddle with the stem of the glass. Condensation slides down from the frosted flute.

'You're intelligent, Emelia,' Luke continues to speak. 'You're smart and witty and kind, but you've spent too long worrying about what will make everyone else happy. You need to take a risk, any risk, just so you know you can. As soon as you've taken the first one, the others become easy.'

'And you still take risks, do you?' I pry.

‘Yes.’ He leans across the sofa and starts kissing me.

It half takes me by surprise, but at the same time I expected it. He’s forceful, passionate. His hand starts travelling up my thighs, but I don’t stop him. Instead, I encourage it. Unintentional soft moans escape as he pushes me onto my back and hitches up my dress.

He lifts his arms up, and I pull his T-shirt over his head before he leans lower, entangling our limbs. I tug at the hair at the back of his head as he kisses my neck, my chest, my stomach. I run my hands over his back as his smooth warm skin engulfs me. I feel every vertebra, every crevice, every taut muscle along his arms and up to the gentle mounds of his shoulders. I feel the dip along his spine and the slightest ridges of the thinnest scars.

I snatch my hands away from his body and leap from the sofa, stumbling on the underwear around my ankles. Two lines cut across his back, barely visible, if not for the way they glint with the tiniest flecks of silver. Luke has two silver scars on his back. Two silver amendments. My legs wobble, and I’m unsure whether to scream or run or cry or simply fall to the ground. I stand staring as though I’m waiting for a slap to jolt me out of this state.

‘Emelia?’ Luke reaches out, a look of concern on his face.

‘On your back, what are they?’

‘What are you talking about?’

‘The scars on your back, they’re silver.’

‘I don’t know what you’re on about.’ He sits upright and reaches for his chair.

I jump backwards. ‘You have two scars on your back. Two silver scars.’

‘You’re imagining things.’ He heaves himself into his chair.

‘Then show me.’

‘They’re from the crash, just scars, that’s all.’

‘Not a scratch, you said not a single scratch.’ I pick an object, a vase, and hold it in between my hands like a baseball bat.

‘Emelia, calm down, really, look.’ He slowly tilts his shoulder towards me, leaning in close. In a flash, he bats the vase from my grip. The china shatters around my feet.

‘Why did you have to do that, Emelia?’ His voice is a sinister hiss. ‘Why did you have to ruin things? We could have been so good together.’ He shakes his head, and when he speaks again his voice is gentle and soft. ‘Emelia, let me explain, please, sit down and let me explain.’

'Don't you come near me.'

'Please.'

'Everything you said, it's all a lie.'

'I haven't lied to you.'

'What about never amending? As far as I can tell, that's a pretty big fucking lie.'

'That's it, that's the only one.'

'The only one? Does Fi know? Does Finola know that everything you've said is absolute bullshit? All these people. People you helped. These people gave you their money, their trust.'

'These people are happier because of me. What does it matter if it's one lie?'

'It's all a lie.'

He starts towards me, one hand outstretched.

'Let me explain, please. You're special. I know you are. Don't ruin this now.'

I step back, not looking where I'm going; it's the wrong way, I know that, but I can't see a way around him and he's blocking the only way out. I stumble, tripping over my feet. My left hand breaks part of the fall, but my other elbow bangs hard against a wooden doorframe and throws the door backwards as my body tumbles through it. I lie sprawled on the floor, clutching my arm, still too terrified to take my eyes off him. I have no way to predict his next move. Luke's expression is fixed, as is his body; he makes no attempt to move towards me. It's like he's waiting, scared the worst is yet to come. I force myself onto my knees, but he's still frozen.

As I rise to my feet, I see it. The calendar. The plain wall calendar, 365 days showing with just a few marked with numbers and letters S3-M6-1, S7-L34-3. Similar combinations of letters and numbers, always on the second of each month. The dates of the attacks.

'You. You organise it all?'

He sneers, his top lip flicking, baring his teeth, his eyes narrowed to the slits of snakes as he rolls towards me.

I scramble to my feet, pulling myself up on the doorframe, but now he has completely blocked my way. I look around the room for something, anything to throw at him. I tug at a lamp on the desk, but it's fixed at the wall. I try harder; the stand quivers, but nothing more than that. I desperately search for anything I can use, but there is nothing, no one else here to save me. No Gabe waiting to resurrect from the floor, no collected and neglected kitchen knife. I use the only thing I've got. I launch my body at him. The momentum carries his chair back, but he grabs my arms and pins my body to his.

'Oh, that would be too easy,' he hisses.

He sniffs at my neck and hair, his sickly warm breath making me gag as he forces my face around and tries to kiss me. My neck tenses with all its strength as I fight him. My head snaps around, and I spit in his face by reflex. To my surprise, it distracts him. He loosens his grip to wipe his eyes; it's enough time. My elbow connects with his skull, the shock shooting up the nerves in my arm as the pain makes us gasp simultaneously. I strike again and again with my arm, it weakens after every impact. But I can't stop. Each crack reverberates up through my radial bone and rattles inside my skull. It isn't until I feel my elbow wet with blood that I stop.

I push myself off him. The music comes to the end of a track, but another one doesn't start. Sweat drips down my forehead; my mouth tastes chalky and dry, and my lungs seem to have shrivelled as I constantly strain to fill them with air. He is sitting in his chair, his legs hanging down perfectly straight, his arms drooped by his side, his head fallen forwardly limply at an angle. He can't be dead, I'm sure he can't be dead. I'm not that strong. His hair has fallen over his eyes; I can't see if he's breathing.

I step closer. Still, I cannot see or hear any signs of life. I reach out and take hold of his hand. He gives no resistance when I lift his arm, and I press two fingers against his wrist. I flinch when I feel something, but I lose it so quickly it could have just been my imagination. I can't find it again; I need to check somewhere stronger. I move forward, brushing his hair from his face and tilting his head back upright. As my fingers travel down his neck, his hand whips up and grabs me by the wrist. Forcing my body around, I feel the crack so strongly that for a moment I think it may be my own limb. Not until he howls with pain do I realise it's his. He glares at me, unable to speak as he pants in pain, clutching his arm to his chest. I bolt for the door, snatching my bag from the end of the sofa. When I glance back, he is still sitting hunched in his chair, whimpering.

'Emelia,' he coughs. 'I'm not letting you go, not now I've found you.' He looks up; his breaths are flecked with blood which trickles down his chin. 'I do hope Finola will be okay,' he says. Then he laughs.

I bang my fist repeatedly against the elevator button, the walls of my stomach constricting and convulsing. I squeeze myself in before the doors have even fully opened and panting and heaving try to force them shut, convinced that any moment Luke will come tearing down the corridor and stop me. I am still shaking when I reach outside; Luke's light is still on above me, a torso's silhouette staring out into the night.

I run until I can't see his window, then his building, and then I run faster than ever. My lungs burn with every wheezing breath, and my muscles consent only due to the adrenaline that has flooded them. Soon even that isn't enough. My legs crumble and I fall to the pavement. The air smells of smoke, thick and fresh and a large freight carrier rumbles past me, spraying tarmac and shingles onto my ankles and knees. The shrapnel stings, but not enough to distract from everything else, not enough to distract from what I have to do now. I try Fi's phone, but there is no answer, nor is there the second, third or eighteenth time. I have only one other person I can call, and he picks up before the second ring.

'Where are you?' he says before I can utter a word.

'I don't know.'

'Can you get home?'

'I don't know.'

Those are the only questions he asks.

I offer him some landmarks, and he suggests a fuel station to meet at. His instructions are pretty straight forward. 'Just keep walking down the road until you reach it. And stay away from all the houses and buildings. Just stick to the road.'

I hear an engine start before the line goes dead, but no doors slam; how long had he been waiting for me to call? My heart twists beneath my ribs, and I try not to think about anything other than putting one foot in front of another as I walk towards the station. It takes me just a few minutes to reach it; Gabe will not be here yet.

A small lamp hangs above a rusted metal sign indicating the toilets. The light is flickering from a poor supply of electricity and a vast surplus of moths. The cubicle is without a lock, the seat stained yellow and the bowl is clogged full of urine-soaked tissue, but I don't care. Slumping onto the plastic, I empty my swollen bladder. The flush clearly doesn't work; still I try it, only to receive a dry hollow splutter. It is only when I stand to leave that I realise my underwear has gone.

Water splutters out of the taps in random spurts, eventually producing a steady stream under which I scrub my hands before lowering myself into the sink to clean my arms and armpits. Taking pools of water in my hand, I throw them over my legs and the inside on my thighs, trying to wash it all away. I rub my arms dry the best I can against the dress, leaving my legs to chill as the water slowly evaporates into the air.

Crouched down against the outside wall of the station, I wait, my damp buttocks icing against the paving slabs while the first hint of a new day arrives with muted grey clouds and the whisper of a sunrise above the rooftops.

The headlights obscures Gabe's face as he stops the car in front of me. He opens his door and walks around to open mine for me. He doesn't speak, he doesn't try to kiss me, he already knows. He wraps a coat around me and guides me into my seat, fastening the belt around my shivering body.

The car is muggy and hot, and the hum of the engine only amplifies the silence between us as we drive back. When we reach the junction for our section, he keeps heading straight.

'You look tired,' I say.

'A long night.'

'I'm sorry.'

'You're only half the problem.' He flinches as he spits his words. When he looks at me, his eyes are softer. 'I didn't mean that. You're not a problem.'

'Where are we going?'

'Somewhere we can talk.'

'About what?'

He doesn't answer.

'About what, Gabe?'

'Let's just wait until we get there.'

I cross my legs away from him and stare out the window. The tower blocks become less frequent and smaller in height. Low rises start to appear too, just five or six stories high, small patches of green with dilapidated park equipment spaced in between them. We are heading towards the mountains.

I close my eyes and see it in the winter, the light disperses through every flake of snow as it crunches beneath my feet, but I've never been here before. Although part of me knows I have been.

In an attempt to fill the silence, I turn on the radio and search for music. I twist the dial, but every station is talk. Talk of the attacks, talk of the Marchers. I hadn't realised today's date, the third, and the thought of the calendar sends a tirade of chills down my spine. I don't need reminding of what they can do. All the same, the radio offers nothing else to listen to and anything is better than silence. I tune in to one station, where two voices are debating 'Prop Six' when Gabe pushes my hand out of the way and clicks the radio off altogether.

'Some quiet would be good,' he says.

Before long, we are twisting up the narrow roads that disappear on one side into deep ravines. Gabe occasionally shoots me glances, his thumb tapping in sporadic rhythmic bursts on the steering wheel, but he doesn't speak.

My heart starts to race; how well do I really know him? I've known him a long time and I've known him intimately, but that doesn't mean I *know him* know him. How easy is it for someone to spin you a web of lies? What if none of it's true, the things he said about his family and why he doesn't see them? Luke didn't lie about everything; what he said about Fi, about me being free, that was true. What if the things he said about Gabe were, too? What if Gabe's driving me up here with no intention of bringing me back?

I wind down the window. It's suddenly gotten too hot.

'Are you alright?' Gabe asks.

My head doesn't know whether to shake or nod, and the window gets jammed. No amount of pushing will make it budge. I undo my belt to put some weight behind it.

'Em, what are you doing? Em. Stop it, stop it!'

Gabe grabs my arm and pulls the steering wheel with him, but I don't let go. Gravel kicks up against the wheels and we swerve towards the steep wall of the mountains. I battle with the door lock, desperate for air, desperate to get out. Gabe pushes me against the seat, panting as he pins me back. The tires squeal as the car veers one way then the other, first towards the wall, then towards the ravine. It screeches to a halt, inches from the drop off. My unbuckled body flies forward towards the windscreen. Gabe's arm stretches out in front of me, catching my chest and pushing me back into the seat. My chin thumps against my collarbone, and then my head whips back onto the headrest. A solid crunch rattles through my head as my tooth pierces the side of my tongue. We've stopped. We're alive. We sit panting, his hand still against my breast bone, blood oozing out over my lips and dripping down my chin.

'Are you okay? Em? Are you okay? Oh, God, Em.'

I wipe my tongue on the back of my hand.

'I'm okay.'

'You're bleeding.'

'It's nothing. I bit my tongue, that's all.'

I run my finger over the side of my tongue, wincing when I touch the raw tear. But it's superficial.

'I'm fine,' I say.

Gabe's back stiffens, and he pulls back his hand.

'What the hell were you doing? Were you trying to kill us? Or just me?'

'No. No, I don't know. I don't know what I was doing. I'm sorry, I'm sorry, please, you've got to understand, I didn't know what I was doing. I'm sorry, I'm so sorry.' I clutch his hand, trying to pull him back over to my side, trying to kiss his cheek.

'Not here,' he says.

He restarts the engine and drives, occasionally shooting a jaw-clenched glare in my direction until he parks in a small lay-by a few miles farther on.

Chapter Thirty

GABE OPENS THE car boot and pulls out a paper bag.

'I thought you might want some other clothes to put on.'

In the bag are a pair of jeans, a black top and my boots. I wriggle around in the car seat to pull up my jeans under my dress without revealing my lack of underwear. I lift the dress over my head and turn around to see if Gabe is watching. I want him to be watching me. He's not. Instead, he has snapped a long branch off a tree which he now appears to be stripping. I slip on the top and ankle boots and climb out of the car.

There's a strong wind up this high. It stings my neck and makes the hairs along my arms prickle. Gabe has his back to me, and I consider wrapping my arms around him as I approach but quickly change my mind. Instead, I cough unsubtly to announce my arrival.

'Here you go,' he says, turning around and handing me the stick. 'It'll help you get up the track.'

'Where are we going?' I say.

But he doesn't reply; he's already heading into the trees. We make our way along the vague remnants of a path, indicated by a few well-trodden shrubs and broken branches. The trees are splattered with infantile leaves, making it look as though the wood has not yet decided whether to let itself grow or give up and return to a state of dry barren twigs. The broken kindling crunches beneath our boots as ants and insects scurry up the trunks of trees and away from our lumbering feet.

My body quickly begins to feel the strain of the climb. My leg muscles burn with each upward step, and my arm aches as I force my weight down it and through the walking stick. Sweat builds on my neck and head, meandering down my back and soaking into my top. I take a moment's respite, propping myself up against the peeling trunk of a birch tree.

'Not much farther,' Gabe calls down, but he doesn't come back down to help me.

I push myself off the trunk with a groan and muster enough

strength to stride up the rest of the way. The sooner I get there, the sooner I can rest, I hope.

The clearing is small and sheltered, lined on three sides with trees in bud and small shrubs that dance in the wind. The frail branches splinter the morning sunlight as they sway, embellishing the rippling grass into a flowing sea. Gabe is sitting on a bench staring out over the edge at the miles that stretch out in front.

'How far can you see?' I say.

'All nine sections,' he says, without looking at me. 'When it's clear.'

I pick at the splinters of the rasping wood of the bench, a set of initials are crudely cut into the back.

'You built this?' I say.

'A long time ago.'

I know he won't speak until he's ready, so I stand up and walk over to the edge. Everything is so small from here. Patches of light from the sections blur in the thick morning haze that hangs above them. The buildings are indistinct, just fuzzy outlines. It's strange. From this height, one tall tower block looks no more significant than another, one section no richer, one road no busier. They are all just bricks and light and smoke. Today, I notice, there is a lot of smoke. The mountain peaks fracture the skyline to the left, shouldered by the spirals of yet more smoke that weave up from the factories. My feet teeter on the edge; it's a long way down.

I wander to the end of the clearing and back, trying not to pace. Gabe's eyes never falter from the horizon unless they close for a second while he sighs. I must have walked the length of the clearing a dozen times before he finally speaks.

'It was love at first sight, you know,' he says. 'I didn't even believe in all that stuff, and then I met you and I knew. I know you don't see it, but there's something about you. Something that draws people in. I bet he saw it too.'

I don't reply and Gabe continues.

'You were it for me,' he says

'And now?' I say. 'Do you still think that? That I'm it for you?'

'Of course. Then, now, always.'

'But?'

'But what? But Luke?' He bristles at the name.

'I, I…' I can't finish the sentence; I'm not even sure what I intended to say. I swallow hard, the sting from my split tongue causing me to flinch.

Gabe gets to his feet when he sees me in pain. 'Can I see?'

'Honestly it's fine.'

'Em.'

I stand with my tongue out, in the middle of a clearing, halfway up a mountain.

'You might want to get it stitched.'

'Really?'

'Probably not, but then it might stop you from sleeping with other men.' It was said so factually, so resolutely, with no anger or bitterness, just hurt.

'Gabe, I —'

'I'm sorry. I shouldn't have said that. Forget it, it doesn't matter.'

'Gabe —'

'I'm sure he made you feel amazing about yourself. No, screw that, I'm sure he made you feel like shit. That's the way he works, right? He made you feel shit about yourself. Made me out to be the bad guy. Made it so the only way you could possibly feel better was to fuck him.'

'Why? Is that what you did with Fi?'

His eyes flash angrily. For a moment I think he's going to walk away and leave me there. I'm sure I see the thought cross his mind, too. Instead, he just hangs his head.

'No, maybe. I don't even know.'

I walk in front of him and sit back on the bench, but he doesn't join me. Instead, he walks over to the edge of the clearing, where he sits cross-legged and starts picking at the grass, chucking clumps out over the edge. Each strand is separated from the others as they whirl on the now infinitesimal breeze.

When I join him, his eyes are glazed. He looks barely out of his teens. He reaches into his pockets and hands me the contents, one black, one green.

'I don't need to see them,' I say.

'Yes, you do.'

'No, I don't.'

But he doesn't take them away.

'Not this one then,' I say.

I hand him back the black envelope. It is torn. My stomach lurches at the guilt, but he doesn't mention it. I realise now he was always going to show me; I only had to ask. The colour is enough though; I don't need to read the words. They can be no better or worse than my imagination. It can only be what it is: black. My hands are trembling as I unfold the leaves of emerald paper, the same way I've done a hundred times with my own. But I know it's not mine; the small black lettering is tilted to the left and detached; the writing is most definitely Gabe's.

Be better it says.

'You didn't say it was green,' I say.

'Would it have helped?'

'I don't know.'

I lay my head on his lap, and he rocks back and forth. When my eyes are covered in a veil of tears, he wipes them away, lifting my head up and kissing me. We kiss, just kisses, neither of us wanting any more than that. We feel no time constraints on this. Afterwards, we stare at the changing skyline, watching the clouds as they sweep and mingle and rush from our view. From time to time, I examine the folded envelopes, one black, one green, but I don't open them again. I know the writing was his; the words are the same as he always said. The sun has climbed high and a pair of buzzards circle on the thermals, their wings outstretched as they glide effortlessly.

'Gabe —' I start.

'You don't need to tell me.'

'I do.'

'No, you don't. Please don't.'

'I didn't though, we didn't, we nearly —'

He kisses me to stop me from speaking, but I pull myself away.

'Gabe, please.'

'Not now, not here.'

Reluctantly I back down, for now. Gabe adopts a new energy.

'How was Fi? Did you get to talk much before she left?' he asks.

'How did you know she had to leave?' I lift my head up, my back stiffening.

'She rang me.'

'She rang you? I thought you weren't talking.'

'We're not, we weren't. She said that she'd left you, that you'd fought. She sounded upset, but then there were a lot of upset people last night.'

I sit between his legs, my back in his chest, his arms wrapped around me.

'Why were people upset?'

'Politics.'

I blush at my own ignorance. Gabe knowing any more detail will be lost on me is a sign he knows me well. Politics has never been at the forefront of my interests; in the grand scheme I am nothing, my opinion counts for nothing. I hardly see that it would benefit me if I did pay it more attention.

'Did you know she has a new job?' I say.

'Fi? A new job?'

'She said you knew, that's why you were letting her do the evening shifts, so she could work in the day.'

'No, she said I should take the day shifts so I could look after you. What's she doing?'

'I don't know. I don't think it's good though.' The familiar unease that comes with talking about Fi has returned. 'Did she say where she had to go last night?'

'Nope, just that she'd had to leave and hoped you would forgive her.'

'She's going to need to be more specific if she says something like that.'

Gabe tuts at me with raised eyebrows.

'I know,' I say. 'Be better.'

I gaze out over Unity and the sections and imagine how different it all might look when the seasons change. I think of it in winter, covered in snow, perfectly untouched with light splintering through the bare trees. I imagine Gabe there, kissing me, handing me a gift. The dream. It was never a dream at all.

'My bracelet?'

'What about it?'

'Who bought it?' I spin around, my knees infringing on his lap. 'The one Fi got me, the one she gave me, who bought it?'

'Why, did she say something?'

My voice rises excitedly. 'You got it, didn't you? You got it and you planned on taking me up here to give it to me. But you let Fi pretend it was from her.'

'Did Fi tell you that?'

'Why did you do that? Why did you let her give it to me? It was from you.'

'Em, I never told Fi I wanted to take you here.'

'But you did buy me the bracelet?'

He studies my face. 'Yes.'

'And you planned on giving it to me up here?'

Gabe's skin is a full tone lighter. 'Em —'

'I saw. I saw you take me here. I don't know how, but I did.'

Gabe doesn't respond. Deep wrinkles have chiselled a chink between his eyebrows.

'Em —' he says again.

'Why did you let me think it was from her?' I say.

'Em, you need to —'

'Why?' I ask again. Gabe sighs. He moves his hand behind my ear, as if to push back a piece of hair that used to be there.

'It seemed like the right thing to do. I was trying —'

'To *be better*?' I shudder as a gust of air whistles through the trees and across my scalp. 'Of course you were.' I turn around and slump back into his arms. 'Did you tell me about the bracelet? When I was in the hospital?'

'I don't remember.'

'What about this place. Did you tell me about here?'

'No, I don't think so.'

'I can remember it though, this clearing, your initials.'

'I told you about here though, the other night on the roof,' he says. 'You probably remember it from that.'

'Maybe.' I sink back into the grass, unconvinced. I have seen the place a hundred times before and it was real, it really happened. 'I amended it,' I say. 'You took me here, you gave me the bracelet, you kissed me and told me how you had always loved me. I had to take it away. For her.'

Gabe's hand brushes my cheek. There's a tremble to his touch, but he tries his hardest not to show it.

'I had to give you up,' I say. 'For her.'

'If that's true, then you made the right choice,' he says.

'Did I?'

'We got it back, didn't we?'

But if Fi doesn't forgive me for the things I said last night, then how can I be better off than before I made the amendment? My envelope may not have been black, but one way or another my sister was lost to me then. Just like she is now.

'Do you ever wonder what it's like outside of here. In the rest of the world?' I ask.

'I try not to,' Gabe says. His tone indicates he wants to drop the subject but I don't, so I keep going anyway.

'What about the old days then? Do you ever consider what it was like here before we could amend?'

'Messy,' Gabe says as he fiddles with my ear in another attempt at distraction.

I try to brush him away as sensitively as possible. 'Why do you say that? Messy?'

'All the wars, the lives lost, country against country, countries against themselves, religions against religions. All the pointless deaths and accidents. Think how many lives have been saved.'

'But think of how many lives were lost *because* of amending. All the wars that it caused.'

'True, but they are over now. Think of all the years of peace we've had. That's not something you'll find outside the Kingdom. Not without amending.'

'But the Kingdom's not perfect is it? People still die. Administrators. Marchers. How many other people have been lost because of amending? How many are there like my mother, like Perri?'

'Perri?'

'She was in the hospital, someone on the other ward.'

Her scarred arms float forward in my arms. The way the nurses dragged her out. The scream of "free Unity" from the other side of the door.

'They're just the small picture,' Gabe continues. 'I don't mean it meanly, but she's insignificant; so is everyone like her.'

'How many people does it have to be before it starts becoming significant?'

'I don't know,' he admits.

Gabe kisses the back of my hand and twists me around so I am back curled up in his arms. The sun is fully exposed, the clouds burnt down to just a few thin wisps scattered in the clear sky. Gabe is still hurting; I can feel it in his hold, too firm, too rigid, but he's trying, trying to forgive me, trying to be better.

'Gabe, how did you know Luke was a marcher?' His grip tightens around me.

'I don't know; someone must have told me.'

'Like who?'

'Someone at the bar probably.'

'Why would they know?'

'I don't know. Does it matter? I've met a lot of his type before.

They become easy to spot.' There's an odd tension to his voice. He lets go of me. 'Do we really need to discuss him now?'

I try to sink back into him and pull his arms back around me, but they're stiff and tense.

'It's just…' I take a deep breath. 'He does the attacks. I know he does,' I say.

Gabe sighs heavily. 'Please don't think about him, Em. There's nothing we can do. If the Administration or the Cabinet wanted him, they could get him.'

'Really? You think that? You think they let them get away with it? Why?'

'I don't know. It's all about show. Every so often they execute some marchers and remind us mere mortals who's really in control. At some point they'll get him, when they're ready. And I'll be on the front row to watch.'

A small gust of wind causes the branches to sway and sends a group of mynah birds into the air. They settle on the grass just a few meters away from us, squawking. Their long yellow legs scratch and scrape against the ground.

'Gabe, there's something else about Luke,' I say.

Gabe doesn't speak.

'He has all three, Gabe. All three scars.'

Gabe frowns.

'What do you mean, scars?' he says slowly.

'Silver scars. Has two on his back.'

'How do you know?'

'I felt them; I mean, I saw them.'

'Which one, Em?"

'Both. I felt them on his back, and when I looked at them I saw they were silver.'

'And you're sure they're silver?'

'They were silver.'

'But actual silver? Amendment silver?'

'Gabe, I'm telling you, he has his registration on his hand, but the other two, they're on his back. They were amendments.'

Gabe shakes his head disbelievingly. 'You can't be certain —'

'He told me, he admitted it.'

'He told you he amended. He knows you know?'

I nod.

Gabe recoils. His hands tremble. The response has stunned me, scared me even. Everything I said up to now he has taken with a resolved sigh or shrug of his shoulders. I was expecting this to be the same.

'Gabe?'

'What did he tell you, what did he admit?'

'Everything. Amending, the attacks —'

'He admitted to the attacks?'

'Yes, no, I can't remember. There was a calendar on his office wall. It had numbers and letters written on it.'

'So?'

'They were all written on the second.'

Gabe is on his feet and pacing, pressing indentations into the already scrappy grass. I scramble to my feet.

'Did you see anything else?' he says 'Is there anything else you can remember, anything we can go to the Administration with? I need you to think, Em. Is there anything we can take to them?'

'Why? You said if the Administration wanted him, they would get him.'

'But maybe not before he gets to you.'

The air is left hanging in silence. I hold my breath and wait for the outcome, aware I have not yet realised or accepted the enormity of my situation.

'Why? What would he want with me? What can I do?' I whisper. 'You just said how every person is insignificant.'

Gabe grabs me by the shoulders. 'You could expose him, all his money, everything he's got, all the people he persuaded to give up their amendments.'

'Give them up? What do you mean?'

'Exactly that. He gets them to agree to send an amendment and then rip up their envelope without reading it.'

'Why? What's the point?'

'There is no point. It's a power trip.' He stands, leaning his weight against the bench and tapping his fingers against the wood, occasionally running his fingers over the initials.

'He definitely knows you know?'

I nod again, though Gabe doesn't look up to see; the question was more for him than me.

'Gabe, he's just a cripple in a wheelchair. How can he hurt me?'

He doesn't answer, and I realise I don't want to know.

'We should go back,' he says.

Gabe marches down without waiting for me to grab my stick. I follow after him, barely keeping my balance as I dodge and weave the low branches and fallen trunks. He looks back only to check if I am there. He doesn't offer any words of advice or support and only stops once when I yelp in pain as my jumper snags on something.

When we reach the car, Gabe stands in front of my door.

'Gabe, what's going to happen?'

He wraps his arms around me and pulls me in so close I feel his heart drumming.

'Nothing will happen to you. I shouldn't have scared you. Nothing will happen to you, I promise.'

From the moment we climb into the car, he doesn't let go of my hand.

Chapter Thirty-one

A LITTLE WAY into the drive back down the mountain, my phone starts buzzing. I don't recognise the number or even the section code. I show it to Gabe, but he's as ignorant as I am. For some reason, my hand shakes as I answer it.

The voice on the end is not familiar, nor are the terms she's trying to explain to me.

Administrative rebellion. Unquestionable offence. Unequivocal evidence.

'I'm sorry,' I say. 'I'm not quite catching you. Can you explain that to me again?'

The woman's deep sigh is amplified down the phone line.

'Finola Aaron, your sister?' she says with a voice dipped in the condescending syrupiness that can only come from an administrator.

'Yes, that's right, what about her?'

'She is at the Administrative Court. She has pleaded guilty of crimes against the Administration.'

'Crimes against the Administration?'

'Yes.'

'What does that mean?'

'It means you should come down to the court, Miss Aaron. Immediately.'

When I hang up the phone, I'm trembling too much to speak, but Gabe says it for me.

'Luke.'

When my mother died, I had to send documents to the court to absolve us of any charges that may have arisen from knowledge of her wrongful use of an amendment. It was the last thing I wanted to do, put in writing that we were not to blame. I felt like I was to blame. If your own daughter's aren't enough to live for what does that say? All in all it was a short process and the court cleared us from any wrongdoing. It was all done by post. I have never been to the court before. I couldn't even point to where it is on a map.

'It's okay,' Gabe says. 'I know where it is.' He is white.

The hills and trees retreat behind us as Gabe speeds back into Unity. We pass through a checkpoint, then another, but after travelling within the sections for only a few minutes I realise we are not heading towards the Central. We are heading towards the coast.

'It's there,' Gabe says, and points out a shadow on in the horizon. I strain my eyes to see; the burnt-red building is lost in the smog until it's upon us. The upper levels and protruding turrets disappear into the clouds which hover in the stagnant air above us, giving the impression of infinite and impossible height, while tiny windows, implausibly small if not redundant, plaster the sides. The perimeter is marked with a stone wall, topped with rusted and coiled barbed wire.

'It looks like a prison,' I say.

'It was.'

We park outside, wordlessly, before Gabe leads the way inside and into a narrow, empty hallway. Leaded paint and ammonia are thick in the air. Hung on the walls are images of the Saint Cortona in all her roles; Saint against temptations, Saint for the loss of parents. I never knew it was possible for a saint to hold so many titles, let alone so many pertinent ones. A dozen steps later and we push ourselves through another door.

Flecks of dust meander sluggishly to the ground as they glint in the apathetic light. The floor is covered in slate tiles scarred with parallel scratches at all angles; people have been dragged across these floors, dragged into this place. Administrators are seated at plastic desks with rounded edges and thin metal legs that screech and grind as they shuffle pieces of paper. Nothing looks comfortable, nothing looks aesthetically pleasing.

We appear to be the only people not dressed in a uniform. Fingers tap furiously at the screens in front of them; it's possible such rapid movements help ward off the unnatural coldness. The desks are void of personality, no cups or glasses or drinks or photo frames, and no brief exchanges of conversation with colleagues can be heard. All eyes are fixed downward, as if looking up will only cause them grief.

I head to the nearest desk. The woman's head is bowed, and though she doesn't acknowledge me, her lips clearly pinch at my arrival. Still, her eyelids, smeared with a careless smudge of blue eyeshadow, stay firmly pointing down until I cough, far more loudly than I had intended.

'My sister,' I say. 'Finola Aaron. I was told —'

"ID,' says the administrator, cutting me off.

I hand it over, as does Gabe.

'Section?'

'Six.'

She raises her eyebrows and continues tapping.

'Floor eight,' she says, handing back our ID cards. 'And you will need to leave all your belongings down here.'

I dump my bag on the table in front of her.

'At the cloak room,' she says, without looking up.

We hand in my bag, stuffed with Gabe's wallet, keys and phone in exchange for a black token and are then directed to an elevator. Standing outside is an armed guard. He apologises as he frisks us both, all the while Gabe refusing to let go of my hand.

'I'm sorry, sir,' the guard says. 'I must see your palms.'

'You're checking to see if they're scarred?'

'No, sir, I'm checking to see that they're empty.'

Reluctantly we let go, only to re-join as soon as we're given a satisfied nod.

The numbers above the elevator make their way from six to four then back up to six again. On the next run down it stops at the fifth floor, fourth floor and then the third floor, before once again heading back upwards. I smack my tongue against my teeth.

'Is there another way up?' I say. 'A stairwell we could take or something?'

I can tell the guard hears me, though he decides I don't warrant a reply. Gabe squeezes my hand.

A small bell eventually chimes the elevator's arrival and after a short pause the doors open. We are quick to step inside.

The guard reaches in after us to scan his card and then presses the floor number.

'You know where you're going?' he asks.

'I know,' Gabe says.

The doors closes and the elevator begins to move.

'Gabe, I said some awful things to her —'

'She'll forgive you.'

'What if she doesn't? What do I do?'

'Sometimes just saying sorry is enough.' I try to believe him.

The elevators open straight onto a desk of the same moulded plastic and an equally apathetic-looking administrator flanked by two guards. They were clearly expecting us.

'Cell D4,' she says nodding to one of the guards as we approach.

We are both frisked again before we are allowed entry, and we are warned or advised that guards are outside at all times 'should they be needed.' I take a deep breath and follow him.

The cells don't have doors, just simple concrete walls partitioning them. Many of them are empty, but the occupied ones are opposite each other; privacy is not an option. On the floor of each are two buckets, one of which is filled with water. The air is stale and ripe with the smell of urine and stagnated water. I cover my mouth with my sleeve and stifle a gag, but I'm unable to stop my eyes from running.

Fi is sitting cross-legged on the tile floor of her cell, talking to the man in the cell opposite. He is about sixty and sits with perfect posture. His face shows the tell-tale stubble of a normally impeccable man, but he seems in good spirits, smiling and talking with Fi. If the smell is affecting them, neither of them show it; from here, Fi looks as flawless as she was last night. If anything, the drab surroundings elevate her to a new level of beauty, although her all-black ensemble is decidedly less attractive than her normal choice of clothes.

When she sees us coming, she stands and steps to the edge of her cell. I can't see any viable reason as to why she doesn't step outside it, but that doesn't mean there isn't one.

I go to hug her, but her eyes dart down the corridor cautiously before granting me a brief and somewhat formal embrace. Her honeysuckle scent is lost beneath grimy aromas of soot and body odour, and her top feels damp.

'You didn't need to come here, either of you,' she says, shooting a glance at Gabe.

'What do you mean, we didn't need to come? What's going on, Fi? Why are you here?'

'It's fine, Em, honestly, it's all sorted.'

'They're letting you go? What do they think you did?'

The stubbly man scrapes his feet noisily along the tiles; I turn and glare to make him stop.

'Fi, what do they think you've done? What is this place?'

'It's nothing. Really, it's fine.'

'Fine? You're pissing in a bucket.'

'Em, you need to be quiet. People can hear.'

'Of course they can hear. You're in a fucking cell with no

doors.'

'It's complicated.'

'I'm intelligent.'

She looks down and picks at her nails; they're already bitten down to the quick. Without the pall of distance between us, it's evident the transformation from last night is far more than just clothes. A deep crease is dug between her eyebrows where her brow has been furrowed, the loose sallow skin beneath her eyes almost grey, and there's streaked bruising on the palms of her hands as if she had recently been caned. I step forward, but she flinches away from me. She's not keeping quiet because she thinks I won't understand; she's not telling me because she's afraid.

'Fi.'

I force my arms around her, and this time I don't let go. I feel her trembling, terrified. Against her body's objection, I hold her longer, tighter. I squeeze her between my arms until my muscles ache and then burn. Eventually she relents, and her muscles turn limp beneath my hold. She sinks into my shoulder and sobs.

'You can tell me. You can tell me,' I say.

Her body convulses with ragged breaths; she releases it all, barely able to hold her own weight. Heavy tears soak my top as I cling to her, trying to restrain her shuddering form. The man opposite tuts, as if offended by our demonstration.

When the sobbing stops, I wipe away her tears from beneath her bloodshot eyes. She stops me and tries to say something, but she is shaking too much.

'It's okay,' I tell her. 'It's okay.'

Shaking her head, she moves back away from me; I grab her hand to stop her.

'Fi, you can tell me. Please, it's okay.'

Her whole body trembles as she inhales once and then again. When she finally manages to locate the words, they are spoken without sentiment or emotion.

'They're going to kill me, Em,' she says.

I struggle to stay vertical, to comprehend what she just said.

'Who?' I say. 'Why? What do you mean? Luke? The Marchers?'

She looks shocked. 'No, they would never do that to me. The Administration. The Cabinet.'

'The Cabinet. Why would they want to kill you?' Then it hits me.

I feel the blood siphon away from my limbs and lungs. The floor falls away beneath my feet, and I start to slip down the wall. Gabe grabs me before I reach the tiles, but Fi stands rooted to the spot.

'You attacked a centre?' I whisper. 'You killed people?'

'It was meant to be empty. I thought it was empty. When I heard the screaming, I wanted it to stop. I wanted to get help, but I couldn't. I just ran.' She starts to dig her nails into the palm of her hand, repeatedly scratching lines while she shakes her head back and forth. 'They were waiting for me when I got home.'

'Home?'

'To yours. Gabe's. I didn't know where else to go. But they were already there. They were waiting. They knew it was me. The Guards, the Cabinet. Somehow they already knew.'

'But you didn't know people were in there? Can't you explain? Can't you just amend this?'

She scrapes her feet along the floor, and I feel the eyes of the man opposite boring into the back of my head. Farther down the corridor, someone coughs; it echoes around us, chilling the air and emphasising the silence suspended within her doorless cell.

'Fi, did you hear me? Why can't you amend? Won't they just let you amend it? Explain you didn't mean to kill them, explain it was an accident. They'll let you amend. Fi?'

Gabe's hands appear on my shoulders, as if he's worried I might lunge for her. Why would he think that?

'Fi, amend this. Tell them you will amend this.'

She mumbles something to her bare feet, still shaking her head as if to rid herself from some internal demon.

'Finola, amend this!' I struggle against Gabe's grip as I lunge for her. 'Finola, amend this, tell them you'll amend this. Tell them you'll put this right, tell them!'

She steps out of her cell, and a guard to the left starts to come forward. Gabe stops him with a shake of his head.

'I can't, Em.'

'You can. You can and you will. Put this right.'

'This is how it's meant to be.'

'What? With you dead and me alone? You can't do this.'

'You'll never be alone. You never have been.'

Gabe's grip loosens to a gentle squeeze.

'Please, Fi. Please. If not for me then for those people. They died, Fi.'

'Someone will amend for them.'

'And what if they don't, what if they don't have anyone to amend for them?'

'Then it was meant to be.'

I take advantage of Gabe's slackened grip and slap Fi squarely across the face. A red handprint blossoms across her skin. She bows her head and winces as she touches it and then massages the muscles of her jaw before turning back to me and taking my hands.

'There's too much chaos in the world, Em, and it's increasing all the time, all around us.'

'That's bullshit. They're not your words. They're the words of a pathetic, manipulative, twisted little cripple.'

'They may not be my words, but that doesn't mean they're not true.'

'Nothing he says is true. He's a fucking liar. He's got the scars, Fi, on his back. He's got them both. Ask Gabe. He knows I'm not lying. Tell her. Tell her!'

But she doesn't look at Gabe, and he doesn't speak.

'Tell her! Tell her this is all Luke. Tell her why he's doing all this. Because I've seen his scars. He's doing this to me. How do you think they knew where you'd be? This is Luke. Please, please believe me. Fi, go back, go back and amend this. Gabe, tell her.'

This time she looks at him.

'It's true,' he says. 'She's telling the truth.'

She offers him a sympathetic smile, as if he's only saying it to appease me, and then turns back to me.

'You know, you're so beautiful,' she says, stroking my hair. 'So beautiful, so strong. I wish you could see it. You're so strong.'

'Fi, listen to me. I'll explain, I'll tell them he's the one behind all this.'

'You're so lucky, you know, to have someone love you the way Gabe loves you. He'll always be there for you. You deserve that, and I'm sorry I ever made you doubt it.' She kisses my cheek before she turns to the guard. 'Thank you,' she says with a nod.

He appears at our side. Gabe pulls me backwards.

'Fi, Fi. Finola!' My heels scuff the floor. 'Finola! Finola, don't you do this. Don't you dare.'

'I love you,' she says and then steps back out of sight. People aren't dragged in here; they are dragged out.

My fists pound against Gabe's chest, and with each strike he pulls me closer. I push myself away.

'We'll tell them. We'll tell them about Luke. They'll see it wasn't Fi. They'll see it was him. We can do that, can't we?'

'We can try,' he says.

There is no bargaining, no negotiation. My pleas and begging turn into screams that reflect and echo on the concrete walls.

'We do not negotiate with terrorists or their families.'

'If you could use the proper forum for your information then perhaps in the future…'

'I'm afraid there is a protocol for these procedures that we must follow.'

I pick up a chair and throw it across the table at one of the administrators.

'Why don't you want him?' I scream. 'He's a fucking murderer. He's murdered them all.'

Soon, hands are around my arms in a crushing grip, pulling me away from the table. I cry out in pain.

'We'll go, we'll go,' Gabe tells them.

But they don't let go, they just grip tighter, dragging me away.

'Look, we're going,' Gabe says again.

When they don't listen for the third time, he raises his fist. One guard moves for him, but Gabe sidesteps, and the man topples comically forward. Another goes to strike him, but Gabe blocks the punch and the one that follows. For a second, I think Gabe's going to land his own blow, his eyes are bulging and knuckles ready, but instead he shakes his head and then raises his hands up, palm out, as if in defeat.

'Look, I know you don't want to deal with this. I know you don't. So we're going to go, okay?' The guards don't move. 'You get that right? I know you don't want to deal with this. I *know* you don't want to.'

Gabe's eyes lock momentarily on the man in front's. My heart leaps up to my mouth. Then the guard nods once. Gabe doesn't wait for any incidents; he marches me straight over to the door.

As we leave, one guard's gaze returns to us; he looks at Gabe and me, frowning slightly. He opens his mouth as if to speak, but it stays in a silent gawp as Gabe leads me through the door. We don't have time for sentimental afterthoughts.

In the car, I pound my fist against the dashboard until my

knuckles are raw. Even then I don't stop until the pain makes my beating futile.

'This is my fault,' I say eventually.

'No. This is Luke's fault.'

'How do we get him? How do we get him for this?'

'I don't know.'

I picture her, frothing at the mouth, limbs flailing and smacking against the cold metal bed. The dashboard cracks beneath my punch.

'Take me home,' I say.

We sit in the car outside the bar. It's three o'clock, two hours past opening time, and a few people are pacing up and down the street staring at their watches. They look like they could do with a drink.

'Let me go and tell them we're shut,' Gabe says.

'Shutting the bar won't help anything. Go. I'll be fine.'

Gabe takes my hand and kisses my red knuckles lightly. 'You don't have to,' he says, but his eyes don't meet mine. He knows what I'm about to do. 'If I could —'

'I don't know how I'm going to fix this.'

'You'll find a way.'

I bury my head against his shoulder

'I used to think I'd have a choice,' I say. 'You know, in how I used them. I thought I'd use them to make sure I got a really good job or a really good husband. Silly, right? Do you think anyone gets to choose how they use theirs?'

He kisses the top of my head. 'I think anyone who does is either extremely lucky or extremely lonely.'

'I love you,' I say.

'You, too, always.'

We get out of the car, the drizzle sticking to my skin and beading in my hair.

'Are you sure you don't want me to come with you?' Gabe asks for a final time.

I don't reply.

Our hug is shorter than I want, and I shiver when he pulls away. My eyes stay on him until he's greeted the punters and unlocked the door.

'I love you,' he mouths back at me as they file through the door.

I walk with little purpose. It doesn't matter what time I get there. Nothing can change today. Not yet. The road is splattered with puddles, and my shoes are quickly soaked through. My feet squish and rub uncomfortably against the thin fabric of cheap sodden socks. I stop to readjust them, but within a few seconds, they are blistering my ankles again; no fumbled repositioning offers any substantial amelioration of the pain or annoyance. At least it's not a long walk.

Visions of Fi, both real and imagined, hammer away at me. Each image is shunted out for another always more hideous and grotesque than the last. They quicken my pace and drive me through the constantly thickening rain. I turn the last corner and freeze. My body is consumed by a paralysing fear. My chest batters my insides with such force on my lungs, they feel bruised. I clench my fists, push my shoulders back and stride forward. With every step, my heart beats louder and faster, and my hands become damp, then sticky, then slippery with sweat. But I will not let him see that. I will not let him win.

Chapter Thirty-two

HE IS SITTING in his chair smiling, no, smirking. His mouth, his eyes, every part of him is smirking. Knots twist and squirm in the pit of my abdomen. How did he know I would be here? What a stupid question; after all, he's the reason that brought me here.

'Emelia.'

'How did you know I'd come to this one?'

'It's the closest to the bar, and Gabe is far too self-righteous to shut up shop and leave the alcoholic amenders with no place to go. Especially after last night's events. People are extremely predictable. Even you.'

He's blocking the entrance to the centre. I walk as confidently as I can around him, but the path is narrow and he grabs my arm.

'Do you think it will really make a difference?'

'I will make sure it does.'

'I have no doubt of that. And I am sure you will be successful. This time. But really, amending is just an action. You will have stopped nothing. Do you really believe you can change her beliefs so easily?'

'They're not her beliefs. They're yours.'

'You think your sister is that weak? Do you think she'll be grateful when she finds out? Because she won't. She won't thank you for this. Like I said, people are predictable.' I struggle to free my arm, but his grip pinches tight on my skin. 'I meant what I said before. You're one of the special ones. Emelia. I know it. And you'll know it too, soon enough.'

He lets go of my arm, and I bolt up the steps to the centre.

'I look forward to seeing you again, Emelia,' he calls.

I slam the door behind me.

Despite my racing pulse it takes less than a minute until Luke is pushed from my thoughts. My senses tingle nervously. There is something in the air, like a dense static charge that prickles across my tongue. The room is dim, with a low roof and small hallway covered in bright wallpaper decorated with flowers and animals. It is not the kind of decor I had imagined for an Administration building. I step farther in, wondering if this is the same centre I have been to before. Nothing seems particularly familiar, but then I wouldn't have stayed here for long. The corridor leads to small reception area, no seats, just a high wooden counter, behind which a woman stands or possibly sits on a high stool.

I walk over, and the administrator smiles, crinkling the loose skin under her eyes. Warmth is not something I've experienced from an administrator before, but that doesn't mean the last one wasn't pleasant too, I realise. Days must be empty for her, to see people constantly only for them to never appear; it doesn't seem possible and yet it must be. No wonder so many of them go mad. I think for a moment that her smile could be insanity, until I remember the date. I suspect many administrators smile on the third of the month.

What's your surname, lovey?'

'Aaron.'

She types it into her computer.

'This section?'

I nod.

'Finola or Emelia?'

'Emelia.' My name gets caught in my throat. 'Emelia.' I show her my ID card.

'All right, my dear, you can go through,' she says and tilts her head towards a door on the right.

I walk over and go to open it, but I stop.

'Sorry,' I say. 'But could you tell me what the colours mean. What green means.'

'Green, dear?'

'Yes. A green envelope.'

She looks at me sympathetically. 'Is that what it was last time?' she asks.

'I know black means something. I just wondered if green did. If you could tell me.'

She looks me up and down with a straight lipped mouth. 'They all mean something to somebody, deary,' she says.

I face the door, disappointed but not surprised. I place my hand on the door.

'You made the right choice, if it was green. You made the right choice, dear.'

When I turn around, her head is busied in something on her desk. I mumble a thank you and open the door.

The chairs in the room have intricate pillars carved into their wooden backs; they are old but softly padded. No doubt at one time these were the height of fashion. They should look completely out of place with the metal filing cabinets and plastic shelving that line the door, but somehow they fit in. They, along with a tattered patterned rug, add a certain patina to the room. The shelves are stacked, row after row, with open envelopes. The colours are clear, graduating through the spectrum. There must be thousands. How long will this many last, I wonder. A year? A week? And how many people's lives will they inadvertently ruin? So many pieces of paper, so many altered lives. Far too many to count. I brush my fingers along the sheets of paper, before turning my attention to the rest of the room.

The administrator has her back to me, her shoulders hunched; either she's leaning over something or she's exceedingly old. She turns to face me; it's a bit of both. Smiling, she walks towards me, the thin silver blade badly concealed in her hand before she dumps it on the table and pulls out a chair which she sinks into, inviting me to do the same. I stay standing.

I look at my palm; it already looks cluttered with the two silver scars. There'll be no hiding from the third one, or hiding it. I won't be able to lie to her, to Fi; I never can. Like we always say; we're lots of things, but we're not liars. The muscles in my stomach begin to loop and knot. Luke's words, about Fi not forgiving me for this, echo around in my head. I withdraw my hand, placing it against my chest.

'Does it have to be on my hand?' I say.

'Sorry?'

'The scar. Does it have to be on my hand?'

'It does.'

I pressed my lips together and inhale through my nose.

'It's just, my sister, if she found out. She wouldn't want me to have used my last, not on her.'

'You had a very lucky sister.'

'I have,' I say.

'Have?' The administrator questions.

I follow her line of sight as it moves down my body to my right hand and a drumming crescendos from somewhere inside my chest cavity. When I see it, a small gasp slips out between my lips. I don't remember picking it up, but it is there, hanging by my side, the corner of the envelope pinched between my fingers as it rests against my leg. And it is black.

I throw it away from me. It lands on the table, perfectly still, an epitome of calm. I allow myself a deep breath before I try again.

'Please,' I say, 'on my back, my leg, anywhere just so she can't see it.'

'I'm sorry, dear, but I can't do that. There are rules.'

'But it's not in the rules, is it? It's doesn't say in the book that they have to be on the hand, does it?'

'It may not say —'

'And besides, the rules are broken; I know they are.'

'Really?' The administrator adopts the tone of a primary school teacher. 'And how do you know that?' She leans in over the table, her breath fogging in a room that isn't cold.

'I–I.' I swallow hard. 'My friend, my boyfriend. He runs a bar. He says he's seen it. He has seen it. I've seen it, too. On a person's back.'

Ignoring my comment, she leans back down and taps the glass on her watch a few times before picking up the blade. In a long sweep, she runs her finger along the handle repeatedly, each time stopping where the metal reaches an edge, before her attention flickers back to me. She seems surprised to still find me there.

'Please.' I try for one last attempt. 'My sister. I'm a good person.'

'Then you have nothing to hide,' she says, putting that blade down firmly on the table. 'If you want to reconsider, wait a few days perh—'

'No, I can't do that.'

I bite down on my lips, trying desperately to ignore the niggling feeling that nibbles away at my insides. Her gaze has not faltered from me. What is it with administrators and their rules? Some must break them; I know they do. I just have to find something that will make them. Something they want. Then it hits me.

'I can stop it,' I blurt out.

'Stop what?' she says, her concentration focused back on her watch face and holding it up against her ear.

'The attack, last night. Please, this isn't just for me and my sister. Please let me do this, let me stop this.'

She lowers her hand, her liver spotted skin now a sickly pink complexion. Her eyes are narrow and piercing. I shudder.

'What do you know about the attacks?' she hisses.

'Please,' I whisper. 'She's a good person, my sister's a good person.'

Her nostrils flare and lips purse as she sucks in her cheeks and straightens her back.

'Please, help me.'

'If you —'

'I just want to make things better. Please. Let me help them. Let me help my sister.'

The administrator pushes herself away from the desk. She grabs the blade, clamps my shoulders and twists me around, and for a second I think she's going to hurl me out the door. Instead, she pulls down the back of my top, exposing my shoulders, where she slices through the skin in a single swift stroke. My body flinches as she holds the envelope against the wound.

'That's my part done,' says the administrator, handing me my envelope. 'Now you do yours.' The door slams shut behind her.

I collapse onto the desk, shaking. The envelope is motionless on the table. It is still perfect, no creases, no bloodstains, just perfectly black. A burning spreads over the top of my shoulder blade, and I reach behind to touch the mark. My fingers come back red. Even now I can't believe the Administrator actually did it.

I pick up the pen beside me where it wobbles in between my fingers. My bottom lip starts to wobble, too, but I steel myself with stern words. I'm not going to cry, not now. Not now I have a chance to change something.

My pain materialises in a thick scrawl along the paper. Heavy handed and carelessly scribbled, it is barely recognizable as my own hand, but it says what it needs to. I fold the edges, lick the seals and press them firmly shut before I write my name on the front. I turn the envelope over and scribble today's date, which seeps into the paper and disappears. I leave it and go.

I half expect to see Luke outside waiting for me, jeering, so I prepare myself to barge him out of the way. I consider doing him some real damage, pushing him out of his chair and leaving him there. It's not like it would matter; it would all be gone tomorrow anyway. But the path is empty, no Luke, no one at all.

For a while, I aimlessly wander the streets. I stare into empty flats through the broken windows, kick fragments of glass with my feet and knock the heads off the few flowers I find in bloom.

Nothing helps, nothing fills the hollowness or numbs the ache that stretches across my back. I should have an urge, an unquenchable desire to do something, rebel and indulge in the freedom of no consequences. But there will always be consequences weaving their way through the ether; I have learnt that. When pink colours tinge the edges of the clouds, I head back to the bar.

It smells of him: the stale tobacco, the strong, cheap whiskey. I fill my lungs, trying to absorb it all. I feel safe in here; I want to hold on to that. The bar runs along one of the long edges of the room, lined with mismatched stools; the paint flakes from the counter, exposing the various colours of its previous lives. A large mirror hangs on the wall behind the bar, obscured by an array of bottles; it has become speckled and dulled with time and offers only faded reflections now. I am grateful for this, as, I suspect, are many of the patrons.

Most of them are alone. They sit drinking away the dregs of their last life, half-smoked cigarettes smoulder precariously on the edges of their ashtrays. Most of them are men, mainly middle aged. They are all second amenders; I don't need to see the scars to know that. The ones who aren't alone still stare at their hands, hacking and wheezing whilst discussing how they'd do it so much better if they just got a third chance. One man with a whiskered chin winces as he plucks blindly and apparently unknowingly at the unsightly sprouts on his face while another tears at the corners of his beer mat, tapping his foot and nodding his head to a tune that only he can hear; his eyes are wet and fixed on the small flickering television hung in the corner.

I run my hand over the bristles of my shaven head. Even in here, I feel a draft. I wonder how long that will last. Taking a seat on one of the worn leather stools, I wait for Gabe. I'm sure he wouldn't mind if I helped myself to a drink, but it doesn't feel right. Instead, I pick at the shedding layers of paint on the bar, peeling bits back like dead skin. I don't manage to reach the wood though, just one more dead layer after another. Eventually, I stop adding further damage to the bar and try to pick my nails clean instead.

Gabe's propped up by his elbows at the far end of the bar listening to a woman. I watch as her eyes light up every time he offers her a smile or responds sympathetically to her ramblings. He is listening selflessly, an act I can barely recollect seeing elsewhere. She occasionally flicks her auburn hair flirtatiously, tapping or brushing his hand with her heavily ringed fingers or throwing back her head in a high-pitched giggle. From the slight sway, I'd guess she's been here for most of the day; still he tops up her glass with a white spirit, refusing to take any more money from her. She returns a heartfelt smile by way of gratitude though I suspect this is not a one off.

The Halfway House. Gabe didn't name it; it possibly named itself. I wonder what awaits these people away from here, away from Gabe. A family? I doubt it. An empty flat or one too full of memories to bear? Perhaps the material possessions just act as a reminder of how superficial and empty their lives have been.

I wonder if my mother would have hung on a little longer if she knew of a place like this, a place where she is not the only one who is alone. How long do they have left before they join the rest of them, unable to hold on to the torment of their imperfect reality? Nothing reminds them to go home or stop drinking. There are no ticking clocks in here.

Gabe catches sight of me and comes over.

'You okay?' he says.

'All done.'

He takes my hand and then looks back at me, his eyebrows angled in confusion.

'I didn't want her to know,' I say, pulling it away from him.

'They let you…?'

'They took a little convincing.'

He lifts himself up and leans over the bar to kiss me. I know people are staring, but I don't care; after all, it's his bar and it's not like it will ever really happen.

'Now what?' he asks.

'We wait.'

We try to find reasons to smile as we wile away the evening hours, pouring drinks that will be poured again and polishing glasses that tomorrow will be covered by yesterday's dust.

At ten, Gabe calls last orders. A few disgruntled patrons moan and grumble about their early turn out, but most of them know him well enough not to object. He leaves the last few glasses by the sink, and we head upstairs.

The television in his flat had always seemed so inconspicuously small; now it seems obtrusively large, jutting out into the living room with its smooth black surface reminiscent of a lake; you'll never know what monsters it holds until you plunge in. Gabe takes me by the hand to lead me into my small bedroom.

'Not tonight,' I say.

Tonight, I want to be in his bed.

I walk into the room and strip off my clothes; the top scrapes against my back. In the mirror I see the scar, ugly and red, but it is small and will fade; it will not be easy for anyone to see, myself included. Gabe gently kisses the skin around it, then up my neck and then my lips. I wrinkle my nose at the smell of smoke on his skin.

'I need a shower,' he says, with a gentle peck on the cheek.

With the water gushing through the pipes and steam billowing from under the bathroom door, I wander naked into the living room. Perhaps I switch it on to satisfy my curiosity, perhaps I just want to see her face again or perhaps some deeper part of me is doing it as a form of revenge for the hurt she caused. I think the main reason I switch it on is so I can deny it. Deny it ever happens, deny it is as cruel as I first thought, deny that she was there and killed those people.

When the screen flickers to life, a man's face is magnified. He is only identifiable as a man from the stubble. His face is contorted, grotesque and inhuman as he gargles the foam that spews from his mouth and down his nose. As his skin yellows, the engorged veins across his forehead darken from a greeny blue to a purpley black and his thrashing limbs clang against the metal frame. Then he stops. A few more bubbles swell and then burst under his nostrils. Two men appear with a sheet which they pull over the corpse, although it seems a little late to preserve the man's dignity. The image moves to Nicholas Hall who stands behind the bloated body. On his face is the same expression of apathy I recalled from all those years ago. There is no remorse, no single word of condolence. No emotion at all.

As the camera pans out, it shows a row of three more blankets loosely laid over mounds on metal beds. They are not people. Just people-sized mounds. An arm hangs loose below the central one, a silver bracelet around the wrist.

The screen flashes white as the image is sucked into a dead black screen; Gabe is standing behind me, remote in hand.

'It's never going to happen,' he says. 'Never.'

Silently we head to bed. I lie curled up in his arms, images of distorted faces rushing behind my eyes. I can't believe I will ever fall asleep, yet I do.

Part III

Chapter Thirty-three

I JOLT MYSELF awake. Whatever dream I was having has left my pulse racing. Soaked in perspiration I throw Gabe's arm off me. As I do the dream disintegrates in the flood of light, leaving only vague recollections of people's faces and strange foam, bubbling through bared teeth.

The sun has broken over the crests of the mountains, and birds dart across the skyline, dipping between the rooftops, lit by the backdrop of a rose-tinged sky. A chilly breeze prickles my skin and it takes me a second to recollect where I am. Quickly the evening returns; Gabe, the rooftop, the picnic. Did we set things right between us? In my gut I can feel that we did. Gabe stirs behind me, and his arm brushes over my shoulder. I wince loudly.

'You okay?' he says.

'Yeah, I must have just slept strangely.'

'Em.' His voice cracks slightly.

'What? What is it?'

He doesn't speak. Instead, he places his hand on my shoulder as if to comfort me. I can feel it trembling.

'Gabe what is it?'

I shuffle onto my knees and twist around in order to face him. That is when I see. A single envelope propped against an empty wine bottle.

'What the...'My eyes fall straight to my palm. I gasp in relief at my twice scarred palm.

'My hand,' I say. 'There's nothing on my hand. It's not for me.'

'Em, it's for you,' he says calmly.

I shake my head. 'It's not. It can't be. This isn't my house. It's no one's house.' I lift my palm to show him. 'My hand,' I repeat. 'There's nothing on my hand.'

'Em....'

'No. It's someone else's. Someone must live here. This isn't mine. It can't be mine.'

'Em, it's yours.'

He takes my hand and places it gentle between my shoulder blades. Every part of me is shaking now too.

'I need to see.'

He lifts a silver plated platter and I crane my neck to see warped reflection in the faded metal. It's so small, so fine, almost lost in the shadow of my head and spine; it could just be a scratch.

'How? How can it be there? It can't be. It's not right. I must have scratched it somehow in the night. It's just scratch, just a scratch.' But even in the cloudy reflection I can see the familiar flecks.

'It's there,' he says.

I stare at the black envelope. Slowly, my brain begins to move. I would send a black envelope for only two people, but I would only need to hide it from one of them. Fi is going to die. My sister is going to die.

'Do you want me to open it?' Gabe asks.

I shake my head.

'No,' I say. I need to do this. And now, before I lose my nerve. I have no control over my hands as I pick it up and slide my finger under the seal. The paper catches at the skin, but I barely acknowledge the stinging.

The scrawl is careless and rushed, barely recognizable, and yet distinct. The loops of Ts, the slant and twists on each of the letter Os: it is undeniably mine.

All my strength evaporates. I didn't need to read it, of course I didn't, not with the colour, but my eyes still can't get past the first word. Reconcile.

What was it someone said? The wasted amendments are the ones you never needed an envelope to fix. I can't remember where I heard it, but it plays on repeat in my head.

It's not just a single word that's written though. There's more. More than I can focus on, more than I can digest or interpret right now. Right now it's merely a riddle of words that morphs between the paper and my eyes, too many meanings to be construed, too many interpretations with dire consequences. How far in the future had I got before I realised I had to come back to tonight? There is no mention of Gabe. Does that mean he's not part of my future or just that he's not relevant in the amendment? Perhaps it doesn't mean anything at all. How much can I read into eight, no, seven, words?

I stare at my hands as if by some magic the scar will

materialise on the surface. It doesn't feel real, not without it there. I run my fingers over my back just to feel it hurt; I need the veracity of it.

'We should go,' Gabe says. The colour has returned to his cheeks, but his eyes are still black with worry. He strokes my head. 'It's fine. You'll fix this.'

'How do you know?'

'You wouldn't have sent it if you couldn't.'

I laugh to myself. I'm sure that's what he said the last time. Yet less than four months later, we're back here again.

I look at the writing, the paper warped only by my heavy hand. Did I send it because I thought I could change it or because I couldn't live with myself if I didn't?

'Em, no one is going to die,' Gabe says. 'I promise.'

Gabe gathers up the evidence of last night's feast while I reread the words over and over again.

I have never understood the one line rule and, have always been convinced it was created just to toy with us, test our reliance. Boundaries I understand, no numbers or dates, that makes sense, but fifty letters? How much more damage could you really do in seventy-five? A hundred even?

I compose, edit and scratch countless versions of the message before just clicking send. My toes curl inside my shoes; after all she might not want a reconciliation. It's not like she has a reason to be angry with me, but then it's not like she needs a reason. She's Fi.

'She'll reply,' Gabe says.

It takes three minutes according to the time stamp, although my body measures it as far longer; my heart has beaten enough for double that time and my throat swallowed enough for ten times, yet the elevator has only just delivered us outside. In her reply, she suggests a restaurant. The swallowing doesn't stop.

'Suggest somewhere else if you're not comfortable,' Gabe says. 'If it doesn't feel right then it probably isn't, so don't go. Invite her to ours instead.'

The word ours should have caused a flip in my stomach, but it's too cramped and knotted in there already. He is right though; my vision of plush sofas and people in fashionable clothes desiccates my already parched mouth. I send a message inviting her for dinner at ours. "I'll cook." I add on the end before quickly deleting it. I'm not sure if that would work in my favour. She replies that she'll be there at seven.

'That's the hardest part done,' Gabe tells me.

I straighten up, stretch out my spine and rub the top of my back. The searing pain seems to imply Gabe may not be right.

Gabe offers to drive me to the store to get some food, but it's a long time until seven and I need a way to fill the hours, so I walk instead. Most of the shopping here happens in old malls, where hawkers set up stalls selling everything from lacy dresses to handmade knives. I contemplate walking to one of them — the closest is only about fifteen minutes away — but I only want food, so head to a small convenience store. The prices are sky high and they hardly ever have what you want, but I'm past caring about money. I'll have a job soon enough.

A guard stands outside the store, picking up stones and throwing them at a small flock of birds. The birds flit about and continue to peck the moss from the gravel despite his constant barrage. I keep my head down as I pass him. One of his pebbles skims my calf before I reach the sanctuary of the pavement and the sliding doors of the shop. He doesn't bother to apologise. Sometimes they really don't help themselves.

Inside, I wander down the narrow aisles of drab packets and less than enticing tins with a less than inviting smell of settled dust. I pick up various cans just to drop them back down, their cheap paper labels slipping off and tearing on the ringed metal canisters. Nothing looks like a reconciliation meal here.

A deluge of smells from freshly baked breads and cakes wafts carelessly in the air around me. I know they are beyond my budget, but that doesn't stop the saliva building up beneath my tongue. For a moment, I reconsider her offer of a restaurant, but we would get no privacy there among the chattering of strangers and the clattering plates. I swallow the saliva and force myself away from the smell.

After much careful scrutiny, I select two potatoes, large and with minimal eyes, that will cook nicely in the oven. In a moment of weakness, I pick up a tin of sardines and then quickly swap it for cooked meat; the less specific the label, the cheaper the content. It is as I am standing at the till, pulling the money from my purse to pay, that it happens.

One minute I am staring at the note in my hand, trying to decipher the small number inked on the corner. The next moment the note has gone. A small silver pendant now dangles between my fingers. The surface is tarnished to near black but the shape is perfect. A snowflake. A dense air drifts down, drowning out the sounds of the shop as the pendant swings in slow motion. Back and forth, back and forth. The silver glints. A baby's cry echoes out from somewhere in the distance and a smell of old leather rises up in the air.

'Are you paying or what?'

In an instant, the pendant has gone. I blink again, trying to make sense of what I just saw, before hurriedly pushing the money into the cashier's hands. It is just the stress, I try to tell myself as I march through the streets back home. It is just the stress. Still, I touch the place on my breastbone, where I am certain I can feel the pendant fall.

I am two minutes away when Gabe calls to say he has opened the bar.

'Fi called,' he says and then leaves the statement hovering between the phones.

I hadn't thought about who would cover her shift, but three's a crowd seems more than apt for this situation.

'Okay,' I say.

I am outside the bar by the time he hangs up. For a moment, I am torn. I contemplate heading up to the flat, but I would do nothing there other than brood and try and find some form of fallacy within my second envelope and scar. I don't want to wander around aimlessly for the rest of the day, so that leaves only one option. I push open the door and let the smoke fumes engulf me.

Even in the daylight the bar is dim and the small, blacked out windows serve neither to circulate air or light. Already the place has customers. A red-headed lady holds an unlit cigarette between her fingers whilst tapping it against an ashtray, and a man picks at the peeling layers of paint on the bar while he waits for Gabe to serve him.

I walk through and sit at the far end of the counter, my fingers momentarily consider joining the man in the destruction of the bar top before I realise I may well have a stake in its longevity.

'He needs to repaint it,' says the man beside me. Thin whiskers of hair sprout from his chin and nose and ears, which combined with his unruly eyebrows and fluffy white hair give him a startling resemblance to a mad scientist. 'He can hardly whinge at us picking at it if he can't be bothered to paint it.'

Gabe places a glass of still swirling dark ale on a beer mat in front of the man.

'If you want me to paint it, I'd have to shut the bar for a few days. And then you'd have to find somewhere else to go.'

'He could always go and see his wife,' the red-headed woman butts in. 'That's if she's still there after tonight.'

'Aye, she will be. And I'm sure you'll be there soon enough to keep her company,' the old man snaps back.

The woman quickly returns to her drink, and the man mutters into his glass before turning his attention back to me.

'So Princess, you're Fi's sister, aren't you?'

'Em.'

'Aye, I remember. Em. Gabe's bit.'

'Leave her alone, Art.' Gabe places a fruit juice down in front of me.

'I'm just making friends, that's all. Aren't I, Princess?'

I shrug. 'He's fine.'

'Well, just let me know if he's not. I'm pretty sure he doesn't want to get barred from here as well as every other bar in the section, do you, Art?'

'Like I said, just making friends.' The man bows his heads and sips his drink.

Gabe smiles at me. 'You okay?' he mouths.

I nod.

He brushes against me as he removes an empty ashtray. 'I love you,' he whispers.

Gabe busies himself with other customers; the redhead already needs another drink and a guy in the corner is asleep with his head on the table. Gabe rouses the man only to watch him drop straight back off again.

'We don't see much of you here.' The protruding hairs quiver like tentacles under the man's nostrils as he breathes. 'Is today a special occasion?'

'No, nothing special,' I say running my finger around the edge of my glass.

'And there it is. The first lie. You looked away when you said that. That's a beginner's mistake. So, Princess, what's special about today?'

'Honestly, there's nothing,' I say, making sure I don't break eye contact.

'Ahh and now you're trying too hard.' He leans in as if telling me a secret, his voice a quiet hiss. 'I've seen them all, Princess, all the bullshitters you can imagine. They think they're good at it, but they're not, none of them. It's smeared all over their ugly faces. Just like you.' He picks up his drink and takes long drawn out sips; the foam sticks to the top of his lip like a comedy moustache. He places his hand on my arm, his wrinkled skin clammy and hot.

'Don't worry, I don't really care, whatever it is I was just making conversation, being polite. You know?'

I remove my arm and tug at the frayed hem of my dress, the loose threads dangling over my legs, tickling the back of my knees uncomfortably. There's no way I can move without looking rude, which for some reason I still seem to care about.

'Sorry, Princess,' he says, placing his hand back on his glass. 'Don't mean to make you uncomfortable. Not a good day for me, that's all, not a good day for lots of us.' This time he gulps back his drink, his eyes focusing beyond the room.

I pick an ice cube from my glass and crunch it noisily.

'They're going to pass it, you know, six years, that's how long you'll get, that's it.' He bites down on his bottom lip, his voicing trembling. 'Say they can't cope with the numbers, all them people. Oh, they've got enough room, believe me I've seen it, massive these places are. They've got the room. And there are plenty of them, sitting, shuffling papers, scratching their fucking arses all day. But no one wants to get their hands dirty. Oh, they could cope, they just don't care. So, six years, that's all they're going to get.'

'And then what?'

'Get yourself some money, love, and then you never need to find out.'

He drains his glass of all but the last foamed dregs, the white swirls slipping down his open gullet before he sets the empty vessel down on the bar.

'They're saying it's for the good of Unity. They're saying it's to help the rest, the ones who have a chance. But that ain't right, princess, that ain't right. You give 'em all a chance. That's what you do. Give 'em all a chance and pray. Tell me princess, how can a person be on your side if they're holding the noose?'

He picks up his glass and brings it to his lips, but then he hurls it at the mirror behind the bar. The glass shatters, raining on the bottles below as remnants of the dark ale run in tiny rivulets down the mirror, which itself remains unbroken.

The red-headed woman scowls and tuts, but the other customers seem decidedly unperturbed by the outburst. Gabe replaces Art's glass with a new full one before he begins to clear up the broken shards of glass that balance between the bottles.

I get off my stool and walk around the bar.

'I'll do that,' I say.

'It's fine, it won't take a minute.'

'Please, it'll give me something to do.'

One by one, I pick up the slippery fragments of glass and gather them in my hand. I feel Art's eyes boring into my skull and quicken my pace. When my hand is full, I close my fingers around the glass in a fist to carry it to the bin.

'Good job, Princess.'

Ignoring the flow of misogynistic remarks, I find a cloth and start to wipe off the mirror in small circular movements. Observing my work, I find that the small gleaming corner of the glass looks distinctly out of place in comparison, so I clean the rest. To begin with I only do the bits I can see and reach, but then I begin to move the bottles out of the way, pushing them to one end and piling them precariously on snippets of spare surface so I can clean the glass behind them. I ignore the comments about knowing a woman's place and you've missed a spot, love, and pull a barstool around from the other side, kneeling on it to clean the top. Then I start on the frame.

When I'm almost done, Gabe comes over and rests his chin on my shoulder. 'That looks great,' he says.

I wriggle out from under him and tuck the cloths into a half-open drawer, using the gained second to wipe any marks from beneath my eyes before offering him a closed-mouth, high-eye smile.

'I should get you down here more often.'

'I'd like that.'

'Good.' He smiles, the dimple half-moons along his cheek. 'Do you want to have a drink? You'll need to go up and get ready soon.'

'What's the time?'

'You've got a while yet.'

I twist his wrist to see the time and then pour myself a drink after selecting a nearly full bottle from the back row. Gabe doesn't say anything; he knows. I glance back at the mirror. The pattern is foliage, ivy. I think back to the writing on the envelope, take a sip of my drink and feel the vapours burn down the back of my throat.

He continues looking at me as he fetches a bottle and tops up the redhead's glass. Her ears are cocked towards me. I want to tell her that this is a private conversation, but she was here first. Besides, if she had anyone to tell this to she wouldn't be sitting here all evening, which is where I assume she's going to be.

At six, there's an influx of people, bridging the gap between leaving work and arriving home. I offer to help Gabe in the bar a little longer, but he insists I go and get changed.

'She's not coming until eight,' I say. 'She said she wanted to pick something up first. I can stay and help for a bit.'

'This is normal,' he tells me as he struggles to decipher between the orders being yelled at him from the length of the bar and the requests to turn up the television. It doesn't look normal.

Chapter Thirty-four

I LEAVE THE noise of the bar and take the steps two at a time up to the flat. It's chillier up here and the remnants of last night's dinner are piled high on the sides on the kitchen. As a half-hearted attempt at cleaning I shove a few things into the sink. Then I strip myself of the bedraggled dress and step into the shower. There's a minute's worth of hot water while I lather up my body before an icy rain splutters down, searing my skin. With suds slipping off my hair and down my body, I have no choice but to rinse myself under the freezing water as quickly as I can. Still half foamed, I leap out of the cubicle and rub my goose-bumped skin dry with a towel. My teeth continue to chatter well after I'm dry and dressed, and I'm still shivering when I put the food in to cook. The blast of hot air from the open door rises around me, and for a moment I consider putting my whole arms in just to warm them up. I can almost see myself doing it. I don't.

A moment, as it happens, is all it takes. I have barely sat down on the bed when the first yawn escapes. It's just one yawn but it's so long and so wide it makes my eyes water and it is immediately followed by another and then a third. Each one leaves my eyes and body heavier than the last. A sharp stinging emanates from my back which spreads upwards, tightening the muscles in my neck. I reach around to massage the ache but find my arms are stiff and unwilling to stretch that far. I don't push them. Instead I lie down, head on the pillow, and close my eyes.

I forgot how much amendments can take it out of you, especially when they're combined with a night sleeping on a rooftop under the stars. This time is different from the last too. I can't pinpoint why exactly, but there's a fuzziness to my thoughts, like they're somehow overlapping one another all the time. I'm thinking about the fuzziness of my thoughts and the peculiar moment with the snowflake pendant when I drift off to sleep. It's a deep sleep. A needed one.

I am woken by a noise. The sound occurs somewhere beyond my level of consciousness and it takes a minute for me to recognise it as a telephone ringing. In a groggy, half-dozing manner I sweep my hand around for the phone. I catch it between my fingers and don't even bother to open my eyes as I answer it. Gabe's voice rattles through from the other end.

'Em? Are you alright?'

'Uh-huh.' The word comes out as a yawn and I don't really register the questions.

'Where are you? Fi's been here waiting. It's nearly nine.'

'Fi?' There's a moment of blankness before my insides catapult upwards into my throat. 'I'm coming now,' I say, now fully awake, rummaging around my pockets for keys. 'How long has she been there?'

'A while,' he says.

I bolt down the stairs, without a second glance at myself in a mirror, or the food in the oven. There's a brief spell of cold, but I'm outside for less than a minute before I'm standing at the heavy steel door mouth open and bursting with apologies. I am rehearsing my exact words, ready to grovel and seek forgiveness when I push the door open then stop mid-step. For a millisecond it almost feels as if I have gone into the wrong bar.

I am met by a suspended, silent awe. There is no drunken leering, no friendly chatter, no clattering of glass as drinks come down, heavy-handed on the weak-legged tables.

Every particle is hanging suspended and motionless as if any movement could result in the collapse of this ethereal moment and cause the Earth as we know it to come crashing down about our heads. A slow shudder crawls across my cropped scalp. Only one person would manage to create an atmosphere like this. Luke is here. The simple thought of his name makes me inexplicably reel. I shake it off and let the door close behind me.

He has a substantial crowd; the redhead, Art, even the sleeping guy has left his table and is slapping Luke on the back with such force it knocks him part way out of his chair. Fi stands behind, watching on like some proud owner whose prize mutt has just won best in show at a crappy dog show. Just seeing him near her causes the blood to rush to my cheeks in a manner I can't ever recall before. *Reconcile*, I remind myself as I attempt to breathe down some of the colour from my cheeks. That's why she's here.

Gabe scurries around the bar. The room is filling even as I stand. He takes money, offers brief banter and refills glasses but still manages to look down at the ground every time Fi glances towards him; she seems to be revelling in making him uncomfortable. I am about to move towards them when something glitters on the ceiling that catches my attention. My chin tilts up in the direction of the light. My eyes squint.

Crystals drip from the two interlocking loops which dangle only inches above our heads. Gravity and light unite within the chandelier, creating the most exquisite light display which spreads out across the tables and seating below them. Velvet chairs and highly polish cutlery. This is not Gabe's taste. I go to move but hold myself back. Saliva bubbles up from beneath my tongue as nutty aromas of freshly baked bread waft from all directions. I close my eyes, letting my senses absorb it all.

'What happened?' Gabe asks me, suddenly at my side. 'Are you alright?'

Without warning I am disorientated, lost somewhere between the here and now and the light that was. Then in the blink of an eye, I am back. A burning urge to glance back up at the ceiling builds from my gut, but I fight the temptation back down. I don't need to look up to know it is gone. The aroma, too, is one of unwashed ashtrays and homebrew.

'I just fell asleep,' I say when I find my voice.

'I was worried she was going to leave.'

'I'm here now.'

'Are you sure you're alright?'

'I'm fine,' I take a step farther into the room and hiss, 'What's he doing here?'

'I've no idea.'

I'm staring at Luke when he turns his head and catches my eye. As much as I want to, I don't let it go. I'm not sure I can. He offers a perfect smile that squeezes his eyes ever so slightly at the corner and I feel my cheeks reddening again, though this time I'm not sure if the sensation is one of anger, or something altogether different.

Gabe squeezes my hand and whispers in my ear. 'Go talk to her. I'm here if you need me.'

My eyes linger on Luke for a millisecond longer before I twist around and place a small kiss on Gabe's cheek. I don't move right away though; it still takes two deep inhalations, several seconds of self-coercion and one final ushering gesticulation from Gabe for me to muster the courage it takes to stride those few steps over to my sister. I have barely started walking when I am upon her.

‘You came,’ I say, only then realising I wasn’t sure she would.

I am caught in the headlights of my older sister. Her skin glows in a way I can barely remember and her eyes sparkle as she smiles. It’s a timid smile, no confidence, certainly none of her old bravado, but it appears genuine.

‘I’m glad you asked me.’ She pauses. ‘I’ve been wanting to call. I just didn’t know if, if you...’ She lets the sentence trail off. ‘I would’ve liked to have taken you for dinner. Here doesn’t really seem…’

‘What?’ I ask, my tone far more provocative than I anticipated. ‘*What* doesn’t here seem?’

‘Nothing, it’s nothing,’ she says and bites down on her lower lip. Her eyes dart over to Gabe before coming back to me. She begins to pick at one of her nails but quickly stops.

‘I’ve cooked,’ I say, managing to soften my voice to one I feel is more productive of reconciliation. ‘Not much, but there’s some food upstairs. Enough for two.’

I glance unsubtly at Luke. Fi falters before plastering on a wide, tight-lipped smile and wrapping her arm around my shoulders, squeezing uncomfortably tightly.

‘Oh, I know. Luke wasn’t planning on staying,’ she says. ‘He just drove me here and wanted to come in and see you. And Gabe, too, of course,’ she adds, her hands still clamped to my shoulders. ‘Luke just likes meeting people really.’ Her throat resonates with a high-pitched giggle that sounds remarkably un-Fi like. Finally, she draws me in for a hug. ‘It’s so good to see you, Em, I’ve missed you. And we have so much to catch up on.’

I try to allow the hug to reach me put I can’t. Just feeling her arms on me is enough to make me think of her arms on him. Images of Fi’s arms wrapped around Gabe, while I lay forgotten on a hospital bed, rise in my mind. I take a step back and gently prise her fingers from my top and try to maintain some form of smile in the face of burgeoning bitterness.

Is reconciliation by order a reconciliation at all, I wonder. It hasn’t changed what has happened between us, it hasn’t changed either of our viewpoints or beliefs, nor has it changed how I feel. I must have thought it was possible though, otherwise I would never have sent the envelope. I remind myself of that fact several times in a very short space of time.

‘Perhaps we should get a drink,’ I say.

We walk over to the bar in silence and are only a few steps

away when Gabe and Fi exchange a brief nod. It's tiny; the same sort of nod you might exchange with a complete stranger on the street, or the man you see at a bus stop on a daily occurrence. Still my stomach twists and tightens. Before I can stop myself, I shoot my most dagger-eyed glare at my sister. Fortunately, her back is turned. Maybe here was not a good place to reconcile I concede, not with Gabe so close. Not with some many demons lurking.

'What can I get you ladies?' Gabe leans across the bars towards us as he asks, as if we were actual customers who are actually going to pay.

'Just a water for me,' Fi replies.

'Are you sure?' Gabe asks. 'I've got some nice wine in. Or fruit juices if you're not drinking?'

'Water's fine,' Fi insists.

'I'll have the same,' I say. Gabe quickly obliges.

With my drink in hand I follow Fi to where Luke is sitting with his crowd.

'I don't want the food to spoil,' I say when we're just out of earshot.

'Don't worry,' Fi says. 'We'll just me a minute. I know Luke has other places to be tonight too.'

The redheaded woman is reluctant to give up her prime position next to Luke and lingers around somewhat awkwardly until she is finally dismissed by a theatrical kiss on her hand. I half expect her to pull out a bottle of perfume and fall on her knees, but she leaves and concentrates on grabbing Gabe's attention away from the two men who have just stumbled in through the door. My pity for her mounts as she proceeds to empty the contents of her purse on the counter and begins to count the coins one by one.

Only Art is still sitting by Luke, with Fi and me hovering.

'Art,' Luke says, as the whiskered man knocks back another drink, this time in a smaller glass. 'We won't let them do this. Not to her, not to any of them. Not without a fight. What the Cabinet is doing is downright inhumane. It doesn't matter if you agree with amending or not. This is bigger than that.'

Art grunts indecipherably and staggers to his feet, tipping his head at the younger man. Still mumbling, he lumbers across the room, knocking people's glasses and stamping on their shoes before he takes a seat at one of the dark corner tables. He slumps down onto the table top, his shoulders shuddering. It's a private moment, or at least it should be, I think as I make myself look away. Fi on the other hand turns towards him, but Luke grabs her hand.

'No,' he says.

Fi freezes, arm rigid and for a second I think she's about give Luke a piece of her a piece of her mind, but his face remains impassive and unreadable. It's an entirely silent exchange, yet it chills the air around me so quickly that my fingers numb. A half-second later Fi shakes away the stiffness. Luke drops her hand to her side and smiles.

'So, didn't you bring me here to see someone?' he says.

The previous minute is all forgotten as Fi's eyes light up. She turns her attention to me and for a brief moment I think that I am the cause of this sudden change in demeanour. My assumptions are quickly dispelled.

'So Em, this is Luke, of course you've met before, but the hospital doesn't count. You weren't, well I mean, we weren't…' She stops and re-thinks her wording. 'Luke is —' there's another pause as she searches for the word, '— a good friend.' She squeezes his shoulder. 'And I can tell that you two will get on like I house on fire. I can just feel it.'

'I doubt that,' I mutter beneath my breath.

'What was that?'

'I said I'm sure you're right.' I push my cheeks up into a smile that surely Fi will tell is fake, but she reciprocates it in apparent earnestness.

'I've told Luke everything about you.'

'That's sound ominous.' My voice is deadpan, clearly sarcastic, but Fi doesn't even blink at it.

'Why don't I leave you two to get acquainted? I need to get myself another water.'

After one more grin she ambles to the bar, picking up empties and ashtrays on the way. I watch her go, willing her to find a reason to return. When I can no longer deny the inevitable, I turn back to Luke.

It's an impossible sensation to explain — something between a bubbling in the stomach, combined with nausea and it swells each time he looks directly at me. It's not just in my stomach though; my legs, my head, none of me seems immune to it.

'Why don't you take a seat,' Luke says, apparently unfazed by the silence with which I am barricading myself. He motions to Art's vacated chair. I move obligingly to take the seat, but change my mind.

'I'm fine standing,' I say. 'After all, I'm sure we won't be down here for too long.'

Luke cocks his head. Something akin to a smile twists on his lips.

'I'd probably stand too,' he says. 'If I could.'

Mortification surges through me. I open my mouth to apologise but he beats me to it.

'Don't worry,' Luke says with a grin. 'I'm winding you up. And I promise I won't stay long. Finola just needed a lift and asked if I'd come in and say, hi. I have no intention of gate-crashing your night.'

He is dressed in heavily pocketed shorts and a T-shirt which cuts low enough to see a fuzz of chest hair. I'm not sure where I am supposed to look. Every time my eyes wander too far down they land on the chair; up and they can't help but fall onto his. I find my gaze shifting uncontrollably while my toes twist in my shoes. With no other way to avert my attention I sip at my drink as my mouth dries at an unprecedented pace.

'I know how difficult it can be,' Luke says. 'Going from your old life to now. Believe me. I know. I wanted to let you know I'm always here if you want to talk.'

'My old life?'

'Before the attack. I know our circumstances are different, but trauma is trauma,' he says, indicating his chair. 'It changes you. Whether you want it too or not.

Deep lines taper from his pupils, reflecting the lights from the room. My insides ripple and I try to look away from them.

The smash of a glass from behind the bar breaks my concentration and like everyone else in the room my eyes whip around to see the cause. Whether Fi or Gabe dropped it I can't be sure; they are standing together and both look suitably abashed. Gabe curses as he picks up the shards of glass from the floor. At least I'm not the only one with jealousy issues. When I look back to Luke, he is searching for something. A moment later his line of sight is transferred back to me. His eyes darken as he traces my body up and down, studying me as though he might find an undeclared secret etched somewhere against my skin. It is not my face he is looking at, but every other part. My waist, my stomach, and obviously, my hands. Then my back begins to tingle. It's only slight but for some reason I am sure he can sense it.

'We really should go upstairs,' I say. 'I've left food cooking.'

'You should finish your drink first,' he says. 'You can spare another five minutes can't you?'

I press my lips together until they pinch.

'I guess so,' I say.

Surprised by my own lack of reluctance I sip slowly. I want to know what his next move will be. It's not just that though, it's my envelope too. Something's telling me I need this conversation and that Luke is part of whatever happened before. Behind the bar Fi has now begun to rinse out glasses. Get him gone, that's my first objective. After that it's just a matter of making Fi stay.

'So, Luke,' I say, finally sitting in the vacant chair. 'What do you do?'

'I guess you could call it support work.'

'So, volunteering?'

He leans back into his chair. I do the same, crossing my legs.

'In its essence, yes.'

'What does that mean?'

'I help people. People who having difficulty adjusting.'

'To what?'

He reaches for his glass which he swills around a little before putting it back untouched.

'I help people with their amendments,' he says.

I raise my eyebrows. 'Do people need help?'

'Sometimes, yes.'

'Then I'm sure they're lucky you're there.'

He sips his drink, covering his thin smile, his eyes still crinkled in amusement. It's a game, we can both tell. I'm not sure who is winning, but at least I don't think I've lost just yet.

He reaches down the side of his chair and pulls out a crumpled brown bag. 'Apple cider vinegar. For your hair. It's meant to help it grow faster apparently, though I'm not sure if you're supposed to rub it in or drink it. You might want to check that first.'

'I'm sure, I will,' I say. I take the packet and put in straight down beside me. Not wanting to stop the flow of banter I try to pick up where the last thread was lost.

'So these people you help, do they not find it hypocritical?'

'Hypocritical?'

'Well you say that you help them with their amendments, but how can you help them when you don't know what they've been through? When you don't even believe in it?'

'Does a doctor have to have broken a bone in order to be able to set a cast?' he says.

'Oh I see, you think of yourself as a doctor?'

'No. Not at all, I was just giving example. It's no different to me saying that pilots didn't have to build planes to fly them.'

'If you're going to compare yourself to a pilot I should let you know that didn't end well. High altitude nuclear fallout, remember? No one flies now.'

His smirk is undeniable and infuriatingly provocative.

'You're not going to give me an inch, are you?' he says.

'Probably not.'

He leans forward in the chair and his musky scent, like autumn oaks, clouds the air between us. 'Is there a reason? Something I have done?'

I scoff so loudly that the sleeping man jerks up from the table beside us.

Leaning back now, he offers a slow nod.

'Your sister is a grown woman.'

'You took advantage of her.'

'I'm fairly sure you're confusing me with another man in your life.' His chins tilts towards Gabe in the most miniscule of gestures. I don't follow it though. I don't bite. Instead, there's a moment of hard-edged silence. Luke breaks it.

'Look,' he says. 'I know I've got some ground to make up with you, for whatever reason, but believe me, I'm really not a bad guy. I don't believe in amending. Is that really the worst thing possible?'

I go to respond, but Luke isn't finished.

'Andjrez, that was his name, right? The man that attacked you? He believed in amendments. It didn't make him a good guy. There are good guys and bad guys on both sides of the fence.'

'I think if we worked on percentages you'd find one side is a little more biased than the other.'

'I think you'd be surprised.'

I reach for my glass of water only to find it empty. My lips are dry to the point of cracking and it's only now that we've both stopped speaking that I realise my heart is doing ten to the dozen. A flush of heat floods my cheeks. I've done my time here. I want out. I shift around to face the bar and signal Fi with a brief wave. When she sees me, I offer my most guilt inducing eyes. Within half-a-minute she is standing back with her hands on Luke shoulders.

'So, did you two get better acquainted?' she asks. 'Did Em tell you any deep dark secrets I should know about?'

'Oh I'm sure Emelia's got a hundred deep dark secrets she's keeping hidden from me,' Luke says. 'But don't worry. Give me time, I'm sure I'll find them all.'

There is a no tone of threat in his words. If anything, the inflection is one of humour and good nature. But my body reads beyond the inflections. A spasm of nerves wrenches in my gut. A moment later and the midpoint of my back starts to throb. Instinctively my hand moves to scratch it, but I freeze. All eyes are on me, rendering my whole body. Beads of sweat form on my palms and beneath my skin my pulse has begun to race. It's all psychosomatic, it has to be, but it doesn't feel that way. The blood pools around the scar, pulsing and burning into me, itching profusely, screaming of its whereabouts.

'Em, are you okay?' Fi asks. 'You're completely white.'

Her hand on my arm causes me to flinch. When our eyes meet I see hers are wide with worry.

'Sorry,' I say, shaking the feeling away. 'I'm, I'm —'

'Do you want to sit down?'

'I'll be fine.'

'Em, seriously. You don't look good at all.'

She moves to hold me but I back away.

'Em?' she says.

'You two should go upstairs,' Gabe says, appearing between us. He takes my hand from its rigid, mid-air position and squeezes it firmly in his own.

'You probably want to get off too, Luke,' he says. 'I've heard the Cabinet are planning on closing the roads into the Central later. I'd hate you to get caught up in all the riots.'

'Riots?' I ask.

Fi puts a condescending hand on my shoulder. 'Hopefully it won't come to that,' she says.

'It already has.' Luke looks up from his chair to the old flickering T.V. set. A banner sweeps across the bottom of the screen. Images of Molotov cocktails and centres flash up behind the words. From the table on the corner Art lets out a stomach curdling wail.

Chapter Thirty-five

EVERY VARIATION of scream and cry fill the air, from suppressed whimpers to gut wrenching howls. Glasses smash against the ground, while fists hammer against walls and tables and even one another.

'What is it? What's going on?' My eyes move between Fi and Gabe and even Luke in hope that someone will be able to shed light on the sudden pandemonium that has broken loose in the bar. Gabe is taken. Already he has one arm wrapped around the shoulders of a weeping patron while holding back another with his free hand. Luke, too is busy, his hands cradling a sobbing woman. Fi is on the ground, rummaging for her phone as it emits a shrill, high pitch siren into the chaos.

'Fi,' I try to move her bag out the way and force her to face me. 'What is it? What's going on?'

'It's too difficult explain right now, Em.'

'Try me,' I say. She ignores me and continues to fish for her phone. When she finds it I immediately snatch it from her hand.

'Finola, what the hell is going on?'

Her eyes fall solely on her phone which continues to ring. Using my thumb, I cut the line dead.

'Em!'

'Tell me what's going on.'

Still with her eyes fixed on her phone she momentarily grits her teeth before releasing them with a sigh.

'It's the Cabinet. They've made their decision. A bad decision. Prop Six is going ahead.'

'People like mum?' I say. She ignores me. 'Well if it's that bad a decision surely they'll rethink it?'

Fi snorts. 'Em, you don't understand. The Cabinet live in a different world. Passing this law was the last straw. Now there's no way out for people like us.'

'People like us?'

'You don't understand, Em.'

'Then try explaining it to me. That's what I'm asking you to do!'

Her phone starts to buzz in my hand, I shut it off before she realises it is ringing again.

'Look, all you need to know is that right now there are two lots of people in the Kingdom. Those sat in fancy restaurants, wearing the latest fashion and talking about the weather, and those who the Cabinet and the rich are screwing for everything they can. This law means that they can screw you till you're dead. Literally. Look, Em, I know tonight was meant to be about us, but I need to go and talk to Luke right now. I can't stay here. Is it okay if we do this some other time?'

Some other time. It takes a second to make sense of what she's saying.

'Fi, please.' There's desperation in my voice. She can hear it too, but it's not convincing her.

'Em, it's fine, we'll catch up tomorrow.'

'No, we won't. Fi, please, listen.'

'Em, you're being ridiculous.'

'I don't trust him. You're not safe with him.'

'Em —'

'Please, don't trust him. Don't go with him.'

She closes her eyes and inhales deeply. Her lashes flutter with the air.

'Em, Luke is good man. Look, I promise. I know I've messed up before. I know I've made mistakes before, but you have to trust me. Luke would never hurt me. He would never hurt any of us.'

She slips the phone from my hand and walks across to Luke. For a second all I can do is watch her go.

Using my elbows, I push my way through the various states of weeping customers and thrust myself towards Gabe. In my head the same string of words echoes round and round. *Make sure Fi stays with you*. Make sure she stays with you. Fucking amendment rules; would it have been too much to ask that they actually gave some instructions on how to do that.

'Gabe,' I slide between the pair of potential brawlers and positions myself next to Gabe. 'She's going to go. I know she is, I can feel it.'

'You have to stop her,' he says.

'I don't know how. I don't what I'm supposed to do.'

'Have you asked her not to go?'

I offer him my dirtiest look.

Gabe sighs, then grits his teeth and turns to the men beside him.

'One more word and the pair of you are barred. For life. Understand me? I am not in the mood. Not tonight.' Both of them nod sheepishly. We don't wait to hear what is said as he pulls me over to the side and back towards the bar. Once there he drops my hand and proceeds with a series of long, deep-rooted breathes. Each one makes my stomach roil.

'Let's think about this,' he says.

'We don't have time to think!'

My knees are jerking on the spot as I try to show Gabe's level of composure. Any second now she's going to walk out of the door and that will be it. The envelope will be wasted. My sister gone. When I look back over she is on her phone. A second later she hangs up then draws Luke's attention away for a conversation.

'She'll do whatever he tells her to,' Gabe says, more to himself than me. 'We've got to find some way to get rid of him.' He spins and clasps me by my shoulders. 'Show her, Em. It's your only option. You need her to stay. You need to show her.'

I don't need time to form a reply. My head shakes rapidly, but the words take longer to come.

'I can't. She'll leave. She'll see it as some kind of threat.'

'You don't know that.'

'I do. I do know that. That's why it's there in the first place. If she sees it she'll bolt. By the time she calms down, it'll be, it'll be…' I don't need to finish the sentence. We both know what I'm trying to say.

Across the room Fi stands behind Luke and begins to wheel him towards the door.

'Fi,' I lurch across the room towards her. 'You are not seriously going are you? You can't it's not safe out there.'

'I'm going home. I'll be fine. Don't worry. Luke will drive me. I'll be perfectly safe.'

'Please, stay here. You can both stay. Can't they Gabe?'

'Of course, I'll make up the spare room.'

Fi smiles. It's so compassionate I want to throw something at her.

'That's very sweet,' she says. 'But you've got enough going on to deal with.' She motions to the chaos in the room. I'll ring you tomorrow?' she says, and leans in for a kiss.

I am still stunned motionless when Luke takes my hand and

wishes me farewell.

I want to chase after her, I need to chase after her, but I can't. It's not that I don't want to, it's because it is happening again.

The whole thing is in slow motion. I squeeze my eyes closed in an attempt to push it down. For a second I hover there; the sounds, the sights, the worries of my world kept at bay by the thin film of my eyelids. Then, when I know I have taken as much time as I dare, I open my eyes again.

It is as though the world has become layers of transparent films, stacked one upon another. The world in which I stood in only moments ago has been pushed down into the pile. I can see Luke and Fi, now opening the door to leave and Gabe beside me, speaking directly at me. But his words have no sound. They are too far away, too far down the stack. I move my head, scanning the area, but the whole bar has gone, or moved away least.

Instead I am standing in a living room, while another me, dressed in red with a snowflake around her neck, sits only feet away.

'You're intelligent, Emelia,' Luke says, his hand encroaching on my knees. 'You're smart and witty and kind, but you've spent too long worrying about what will make everyone else happy. You need to take a risk, any risk, just so you know you can. As soon as you've taken the first one, the others become easy.' I see what's coming. The primal side of me tries to lash out and scream, but they don't know I'm there. Even if they did, the other me doesn't seem to care.

'And you still take risks, do you?' I watch myself say, unashamedly flirting.

'Yes.' Luke leans across the sofa and starts kissing me.

I want the image to stop, but I can't draw my eyes away. It can't be real, it wouldn't make sense to be real, and yet at the same time, I know that it is. Luke's hand is reaching up my thigh, but I don't try to stop him. I let him. I want him.

'Fi?' I cry out into the room. 'Fi?' I can't even see them now. Their stacked image is a blur against a thousand other frames. Noises seep through from some, music, shrieks, tears.

I turn back to the image I don't want to see, of Luke and I. I am stripping him of his T-shirt now, pulling it over his head as I run my hands across his body. I feel sick. My head is swimming and I'm certain that at any moment I'm going to pass out. That's when I see them, when both of the *me*s see them. Two thin, silver, undeniable scars on Luke's back.

'Fi!'

I slam myself back into reality.

'Em? Em what happened?' Gabe's hands are on me, but I don't have time to answer. Stumbling I push my way out from his arms and out of the door.

The spring air is a blast of cold that knocks me back half a pace. My head is still swirling, spinning and although my feet are moving it is more through their own volition than mine. In front of me, two figures are moving towards a car. They are the only two figures on the street, I don't need to see the wheelchair to know it is them. Willing some strength back into my legs I force myself towards them.

'Fi!' I shout again. The walking figure stops and turns. I pant as I race to catch her up. 'Fi wait.'

It is not until I am upon them that she speaks.

'Em? What are you doing? Go back inside.'

'You need to wait.'

'I said I'll ring you tomorrow?'

Beside her Luke has also stopped.

'Finola?' he says. This time his tone is far less humorous.

'You can't,' I say between my wheezing breaths. 'You can't go with him, you can't trust him.'

Fi's eyes narrow. She lowers her voice. 'Em, you're being ridiculous and you're making a scene.'

'You have to believe me, please. You have to. I am telling the truth.'

Luke places a hand on Fi's elbow.

'Remember how you first felt after the attack,' he says as if I am not there. 'She has been through a lot. She needs your compassion.' Then he speaks to me. 'Your sister will be perfectly safe in my hands,' he says.

'You're lying,' I spit. He doesn't so much as flinch.

'That's it, Em, we're going.' Fi twists around and opens the door to the car. 'I'll speak to you tomorrow.'

'No, no!' I attempt to wrestle the keys from her hand, but she snatches them back away from me.

'For Christ's sake, Em. What is wrong with you?' Her cheeks are scarlet and I know I'm only one second away from driving her away altogether, but I can't stop. Not until she knows.'

'He's a liar,' I say again. 'Luke is a liar.'

'Emelia —' Luke starts.

'Ask to see his back,' I snap. 'Go on. Ask to see his back.'

These words are enough to make Luke fall silent. His eyes flash up at me and I know with absolute certainty that I am right. That everything I have been seeing is real. Everything from the mountains to the snowflake, but especially the scars. Luke has amended. Fi shakes her head.

'Em, you're being ridiculous. I've got places to be.'

'Ask, to see, his back,' I say again.

'We need to go,' Luke says, breaking our gaze and wiping the sweat from his brow. 'Finola, get in the car.'

'Fi, you need to see his back. Ask him to see it. Ask him to show you.' My jaw is locked tight. My eyes are fixed on Luke's. Despite the tiny, cold droplets of perspiration pepper his forehead.

'Finola, you need to get in the car now. Do not make me wait.'

'Ask him, Fi,'

'Get in the car,'

'Ask him.'

'Car now!'

'Stop!' Fi's hand comes down on the roof of the car with a force that sends rats scampering from the nearby dustbins.

'Emelia, stop it. I don't know what this is. What you're trying to prove, but Luke has never lied to me. Never. He saved my life. Do you understand what that means? He saved my life.'

'And so did I,' I say. 'Or have you forgotten that? I used my first amendment for you.'

'I didn't ask you to do that.'

'You don't know that though, do you?' It's a low blow, but it's not one she can deny. I lift my hand to brush my cheek and am surprised by the wetness. I didn't even notice I was crying.

'Fi,' I say as gently as I can. 'I'm your sister. Have I ever lied to you?'

She shakes her head. There are tears in her eyes too, welling, glistening, but she holds them back better than I.

'Ask to see his back, Finola. Please. Then I'll go. If I'm wrong, I'll go. Please, for me. For mum.'

Fi's lower lip trembles. She takes in a short wobbling breath, then breathes it out as a sigh. It's a long sigh. Half a decade of tension built up and buried, then released in one unending stream.

'Luke,' she says softly.

Luke is over by the back of the car. Fi moves towards him in teetering, tentative steps.

'Can you?' she says.

He arches an eyebrow, rolling his eyes in the process.

'You can't be serious?'

'Like you said. She needs compassion. Just show her she's confused. Then we can go.'

All my organs from my lungs to my bladder are swilling around. For a second I think it's about to happen again, that slipping away.

'No,' I say to myself, concentrating all my efforts on Fi and the here and now. 'Not right now.'

Fi is standing less than two feet away from Luke. Her expression is apologetic, but nervous. Luke's is anything but. He takes a sharp breath in through his nose then leans forwards and lifts the back of his shirt halfway up his back.

'Is that what you wanted to see?' he says.

'At the top,' I say. 'Between the shoulder blades.'

He pulls down the bottom of his shirt with a sharp tug. His look of impassiveness replaced with something far less patient.

'No,' he says, shaking his head and looking solely at Fi. 'I'm through with this. Either you believe me and you come with me now. Or you don't. It's up to you.'

'Luke, I just —'

'No, you've already wasted enough time. You know what's going on tonight and yet you're standing here squabbling with your sister like some spoilt little brat. There are lives at stake here. Thousands of them. Tell me, Finola, do you even believe in what we're doing?' The words have the intended impact. Fi recoils as they strike.

'You know I do,' she says meekly.

'It doesn't look like that from where I'm sitting. You're hardly serving the cause, are you?'

Fi pales. Her eyes go from the ground to me, then back to the ground again.

'Get in the car now,' he says. 'Or that's it. We don't have time for second chances. You want those, go back to using your amendments like the rest of the vermin you surround yourself with.'

This time the words strike me too. I move to grab him, but Fi stops me. Not with her body, but with her eyes.

There is no hiding the tears anymore. They run down her

cheeks in long tributaries, branching out at her lips and cheeks before pooling on her chin and cascading to the ground. Her pristine nails are halfway to destruction as she rips them down to the quick.

'Are you coming, Finola?' Luke says. His voice, his expression, everything indicates the finality of the sentence. It grips around my chest like a vice.

For one last time Fi meets my eyes. Like her, my vision is blurred, distorted by the veil of tears that replenishes far quicker than they fall. I lift my hand. It's a miniscule movement, barely an inch from my hip, but I reach out to her. She sees and then she steps away.

'I'm sorry,' she says. 'We'll talk, when you're feeling better.'

She turns and faces Luke.

'We need to leave now,' she says. The air evaporates around me.

Chapter Thirty-six

FOR A SECOND I believe that it has happened again, that I have slipped away, but I know from the fact that all I can see is her and him that it can't be true. My senses have been trampled though; numbed and battered by a broken heart that pounds out; the only tangible evidence of my existence. It is over. I failed her.

The pair stand together, her hand back on his shoulder as if that's where it belongs. A wiry smile stretches across Luke's face as I struggle to keep myself standing. The game has ended and he has won. My sister will leave with him. Tomorrow — should the colour of the envelope ring true to its superstition — she will be gone.

'Emelia,' Fi says. Her voice is gentle, quiet. The way she would say my name when she was trying to rouse me from my sleep, or comfort me during a fight between my parents. I lift my head to meet her gaze. 'I'm sorry.'

With no time to think I lunge towards the pair. Some part of me — elbow, knee, I can't be sure — bulldozes Fi to the side.

'Em, this is ridiculous!' There's a thud and I know she's hit the ground but I don't bother to check she's alright. Right now there's only one thing on my mind.

In one sharp movement I sweep past Luke, pushing him down from behind and pinning his head down to his knees. I stretch the fabric down, exposing the flesh at the top of his spine. Two scars shine in all their silver glory.

'There!' I jab my finger into his skin. 'I told you. I told you he was lying.'

Behind me. Fi's gasp is expelled into the air.

'No, it can't be.'

'Now do you believe me? Everything he says is a lie. I let go of Luke's back, but I'm not concentrating. Instead my attention is focused on my reeling sister. Luke grabs me by the wrist and twists. The pain shoots all the way up to my spine.

'Why did you have to do that, Emelia?' he sneers. 'Why couldn't you just have let us go?'

'Your back?' Fi stammers. 'Em is right. You have the scars? I thought… I thought....'

'You thought I was mad?' I choke out. 'Please, Fi. He's a liar. He's dangerous.' Luke tightens his grip.

'Fi,' I pant. My vision blurs with tears once again, this time caused by the pain. Fi doesn't see me though. She doesn't see anything other than him.

'You said you never amended.' Her voice is reticent, barely audible. 'That none of us should ever amend.'

'And that's what I believe.'

'But you, you…'

'Things are complicated, Finola. You know that.'

'Fi!' I am gasping. My whole arm is on fire with a burning that has spread up my neck and down my spine now. I try kicking out but there's no where I can hit. It feels as though my wrist is going to snap in two. '*Fi*!'

Fi flinches at her name. Finally, her gaze draws down on me.

'Em!' She grabs Luke's arm to pull it off mine. 'Luke, what are you doing? Let her go? You're hurting her.'

'You need to listen to me, Finola,' he says.

'You need to let go of my sister.'

An expression of contemplation flashes across his face before his eyes fall on me with a sneer.

'It's not that simple,' he says. 'We need to talk about this, Finola. About her. You need to let me explain.'

'You lied.'

'For the good of the cause. I was protecting the cause, Finola, surely you can see that?'

'You lied.' And once again I am lost to them. All they can see is one another, all they can hear are each other's accusations. In their deliberation Luke's grasp on me slackens. I take the chance and yank my arm away. The force sends me tumbling back and into Fi. I right myself and grab her by the hand, but it's still not enough to break the spell between them.

'We need to leave now, Fi. We need to go.'

'Don't go like this Finola,' Luke says, ignoring me altogether. 'Don't leave like this.'

'Fi, we need to go.'

'Why lie?' Fi is still talking only to Luke. 'Why did you have to lie to everyone? To me?'

'You don't understand,' he says. 'Please, let me try to explain to you.' She edges towards him. He has a new aspect to his face, a pitiful woe and it's drawing her in, draining her of her anger. Mine on the other hand surges. Clamping my hands around her arms I pull her backwards towards me and the safety of the bar.

'We need to go, Fi. He's a fraud. You don't need him.'

His face hardens. 'I'd watch your words, Emelia,' he says.

I snort. I have plenty more words, plenty more truths and I want him to have them all.

'You're a conman,' I say, leaning forwards and spitting my words at him. 'You're a disgusting cheap crook who plays on people's insecurities and preys on the innocent. You don't deserve amendments and you sure as hell don't deserve my sister. You deserve to rot in a gutter. And soon, everyone will know that.'

Something undecipherable shadows his expression. For a second I think it is fear, but it's darker than that. Blacker and colder.

'Don't make threats, Emelia,' he says. 'Not unless you have the courage to see them through. I'd hate for something to happen to you or your sister.' A quiver jerks my knees as I stand but I hold my ground. He's all lies. I know that now.

'You're a fraud, and soon everyone will know.' I repeat the words through gritted teeth. 'Stay away from me and my sister.' With my knees still shaking I spin back around, grab Fi and frog march her through the door or the bar.

'Finola,' Luke calls into the darkness. 'Don't do this.'

As we stumble back in Fi is a dead weight in my arms, numbed to immobility and slippery with an icy sweat. Gabe ushers us to the table in the farthest corner of the bar, then disappears outside.

'He's gone,' he said, when he comes back in a moment later. We exchange a look which we both wish could offer more. Still, he holds my gaze, trying to understand all that has just happened, but I can't offer him any real answers. I don't even want to speak, not with Fi there. Not with her so raw. 'Just stay here while I get this place sorted. Don't either of you move.'

For nearly an hour Gabe works on emptying the bar of its sobbing clientele. It's delicate and difficult for him. I know he'd let them stay, listening to their tears and fears all night if it were possible, but Fi and I need him too and he knows that. So gently, with reassuring condolences, he guides them out one by one.

Now and again I feel Fi's body shudder beneath me as we huddle close. Occasionally, a surge of fresh tears swell and surface and she opens her mouth to speak, but each time she closes it again without a word. I want to comfort her. But Fi doesn't let people do that. I know that from experience. When the door is finally bolted, Gabe fills two glasses and places them down in front of us. I don't wait before downing mine in one.

'Luke has scars,' Fi says, suddenly finding her voice. 'He's amended. Everything he's said is a lie.'

She picks up her glass and swills around the drink inside it. I place my hand on her shoulder, but she shakes it off.

'I wish I could say I'm surprised,' Gabe says.

'I believed him. Everything he said. Everything the Marchers stood for. It made sense. I believed it.'

'He's good at what he does,' Gabe says pulling out a seat and sitting down. 'That's what makes him so dangerous.'

Fi looks at her fingers. 'Maybe,' she says.

Gabe and I exchange another look.

'Fi, he's a liar,' I say. 'He's a hypocrite and he's a psychopath.'

She mumbles into her hands, her quota of words for the night apparently exceeded.

'You take her upstairs,' Gabe says to me. 'I'll finish up here. I won't be long.'

I want him to come with me. I don't want the responsibility of Fi on my own, but I can't say that. She's my sister and it's my amendment that got us to here. I just need to make sure it wasn't all a waste.

Upstairs we grab a blanket and curl up in the living room to wait for Gabe. I switch on the television. Fi still isn't in the mood for talking and the silence is enough to drive anyone to drink.

'Good God,' I say at the scene.

Tens of centres across the sections have been burnt in response to the Cabinet's ruling. This is not the normal one or two centre attacks. Ashy smoke billows from smouldering rooftops. People are huddled together in one another's arms. Some are in uniforms. Some are not. They even show the Annex; though still standing proud, its walls are dappled in thick smoke marks. Its perfect spire now dented and black.

The death toll is surprisingly low.

'Most of them will have someone that amended for them already,' Fi says. 'These things never kill as many as you think. If any.' She is speaking to herself, rather than me. 'People will have amended for them.'

'Not all of them,' I say.

'No. Not all of them.'

We watch in silence as the images change to those of care homes. Over-crowded and cramped, they show minimal staff, all of whom are bedraggled and rushing around too much to look at the camera. Justification for Prop Six; the Cabinet's rationale. At this moment in time it is more than clear who owns the television stations. They show the patients too, muttering to themselves, arguing with the air, waving their hands in front of the invisible spectres that haunt so many of them. It was the same with our mother. Of all the people I don't need reminding of tonight, *she* is at the top of the list. I pick up the remote and the screen goes black.

'I was meant to be part of it, Em,' Fi whispers to the blank television screen. 'I was meant to do that, attack those centres.'

'But you didn't.'

'I would have though, and people died. They killed people. I could have killed people,' she says, as if this is her first time realising it. 'People weren't supposed to die.'

'You wouldn't have done that. You know you wouldn't have done that.'

She pushes her lips together.

'I don't know that,' she says. 'Not anymore. I've spent so much time thinking, thinking about the past, the future. What would have happened if I'd not amended? If I'd kept it for something good? But I don't think it would have mattered. I think I was meant to end up here.' She pauses and looks out the window. 'Do you think they'll forgive me?'

'Who?'

'The others.'

'The Marchers?' I don't disguise the anger that bubbles through me. 'Fi, you're not making any sense. What do you need forgiving for? You just told me they killed people. You just saw that for yourself.'

'I should have listened. I should have gone with him. Maybe I could have helped'

'Helped who? Who are you talking about Fi? Do you mean

Luke? Are you talking about Luke?'

'He went about things the wrong way —'

'The wrong way? Just listen to yourself. He has brainwashed you. They are a sick, murderous cult.'

'Aren't we all?' She twists around to look at me as she speaks. 'We never think of anyone but ourselves when we make our amendments. All we think about is bettering our own lives. Screw who we hurt in the process. How many people, how many *children,* have died because of amending?'

'Fi —'

'We think it's without consequences, but it's not. It never is. We just close our eyes to it all because we don't want to see it.'

She spins back to staring at the blank television screen. Once again tears roll down her cheeks, but she makes no attempt to wipe them away. A small cough crackles in my throat as I open my mouth to speak, but my jaw just hangs there, loose and empty. I don't know what I supposed to say. I don't even know who her tears are for this time. Gabe's drinks cabinet is calling me from across the room. I force my attention back to Fi.

'You've still got your second,' I say. 'You still have choices. Don't let them take that away from you, please.'

Her face contorts into a sour twisted pout which grates on my patience like sandpaper on vanish. It's not her fault, I try to tell myself. After all, she doesn't even know what I gave up getting her here.

'You need some sleep,' I say. 'You'll feel differently in the morning.'

I decide to shower, leaving Fi staring at the blank TV. The front door is locked and there's only one key, which I take with me. It's petty I know, but I can't risk the chance of her bolting. Afterwards, in Gabe's room, I lie on the bed and close my eyes. Through the wall I can hear Fi is now watching the broadcasts, flicking through channels from one scene of desolation to the next. I half expect to hear the door to the drinks cabinet go any second. Right now, I'm not even sure I'd have the energy to stop her.

The day circles through my mind, image after image. The harder I try to block it all out — the envelope, the announcement, Luke — the more keenly it all comes back.

There's another part of the day too, one I'm trying not to think about. The visions. They are real, I know that much. Deep down, even before seeing Luke's scars, I had my suspicions, but now the evidence is too great to ignore. I cast my mind back to the other moments: the silver snowflake necklace resting against my chest, Gabe and I on a snow-capped mountain, sitting under wisps of pink clouds, sipping wine from the bottle, while he fastens a bracelet around my wrist.

I jump up from where I am lying and start to scramble around the edges of the bed. I move dirty T-shirts and less dirty magazines, push the curtains aside and lift the mattress up from the bed frame. Then, as I move a lamp from one side of the bureau to another, I catch a glimpse of silver beneath the bedside cabinet.

It's the bracelet. I am certain of it. The chest is only small; three drawers and barely higher than my knees. I try to lift it, but all my strength barely budges it. Briefly, I consider emptying the whole thing, but that seems like a little too much effort, so instead, I lie on the floor, stretch out my arm and attempt to squeeze it into the tiny gap between the bottom drawer and the carpet. It's a tight fit, but after much wriggling, I manage to nudge the bracelet with my fingers. Millimetre by millimetre, I pull it towards me. Eventually, enough of the chain is between my fingers that I can pull the whole thing into my palm and clench a fist around it. My body goes limp with relief.

With a sharp tug, I try to remove my hand. It doesn't move. I yank it again and again. It's jammed, trapped between the wood and the carpet, with my knuckles scraping the base of the cabinet. I try moving it farther forward, then farther back, but nothing works.

'Fi!' I call through to the living room. 'I need your help. Fi, get in here.'

There is no response. I can still hear the television flicking channels though. She is still awake and I'm certain she can hear me.

'Fi! Can you get in here? I need your help. This is serious. Finola!'

Half-a-minute later the thump of footsteps reverberates through the floorboards before she appears in the doorways.

'What do you want?' she says.

'What do think I want?' I snap, my head only just visible from behind the bed. 'I'm stuck. I need you to get me out of here.'

'You're stuck?'

There is a moment of absolute silence between the pair of us, before she doubles over, folding into herself with laughter.

'Finola,' I try and snap again, but I can't. Her laughter is contagious. I'd almost forgotten what her genuine smile looked like. Still, while part of me may be happy to see her laughing, a full minute later — when she is still going — the rest of me desperately wants freeing.

'What were you doing?' she says, finally getting the hint and moving closer.

'I was trying to get the bracelet you gave me.'

'Why's it under there?'

'I threw it here after…you know.'

She sits down on the bed next to me. My pulse rises with a sudden spike. I don't like her sitting there, above me; it's too close, there's too big a chance of her seeing.

'Why are you sitting down? I need your help,' I say.

She presses her lips together as she picks at her nails.

'Fi?'

'Before I help you, I have to tell you something.'

'Seriously? Can't you do it after?'

'No, it has to be now.'

'Can you at least tell me quickly then?'

It takes her another minute of picking her nails before she speaks.

'The bracelet. It wasn't from me. Gabe, he bought it, he wanted to give it to you.'

I say nothing.

'I didn't want him giving it to you, so I asked him to let me.'

'Why?' I twist around, straining my neck to get a better view of her face.

She shrugs. 'Selfishness, stupidity, alcohol. I didn't want you to think I couldn't even remember your birthday.'

'Fi, you had other things on your mind.'

'Still —'

I have to cut her short. 'Fi, I understand. I really do. And if you want to talk about it in a minute, then great. But right now, can you please help me before I lose my arm?'

A strange tingling has started to spread from my fingertips up the length of my arm to my shoulder. I don't mind if I lose it, that's not the main issue. I just don't want her seeing the scar. Every time she steps towards me, my whole body contorts. The sooner she can do this the better. She tries lifting the chest the same as I did, but it has no decent handholds to grab onto.

‘Try sliding it?’ I suggest.

‘Where? Anyway, it’s too heavy,’ she tells me. ‘Perhaps we should just wait for Gabe.’

‘That’s ridiculous I’m not staying here. Try tipping it sideways.’

I crane around to see her distinctly bemused look.

‘Please, Fi, just put some clothes underneath one side to cushion the fall and tip it gently. Just use those.’

Following my instructions, she collects some of the clothes strewn around and packs them tightly against one edge. In a minute she has an effective hinge and landing pad.

‘You should just need to push it gently,’ I tell her. ‘Gently, gently!’

The chest topples to the side, landing with a crash and spilling its contents over the floor. My arm is free. I rejoice in its liberty and flex my fingers. I’m about to say something when I catch sight of Fi’s expression. That’s when I see them, and my stomach plummets. The floor is covered in envelopes.

Chapter Thirty-seven

WE STAND, turning in a circle trying to absorb them all. There's every colour here: green, blue, red, black, so many reds and blacks, hundreds of them. Some are opened neatly along the folds, others sliced with a paper cutter, more than half torn in haste. After the shock comes the numbness.

'Did you know about this?' I whisper when I finally find my voice.

Fi shakes her head and bends down to pick one up.

'Don't touch them!' I scream.

She looks at me but ignores what I say. She picks up several and sits on the bed.

'*Take the earlier bus*,' she reads, placing a blue one down next to her, and reads out more. '*Don't take the promotion. Ask Jessica to marry you today.*'

'Stop it, Fi. Stop it. It's —'

'*Take Evie to the hospital. Don't give her up. Forgive Clemency. Stop Jack getting on the plane. Leave him, start again, it won't get any better. Tell her you love her every day —*'

'Fi, please.'

'*Just walk away.*'

'What are you doing?' Gabe is standing in the doorway, bags of food by his feet.

Fi's eyes dart across to me before she places the envelopes on the bed and squeezes past him. 'I'll leave you two to speak,' she says.

The awkward silence lasts less than a second.

'What am I doing? *What are you doing?*' I scream, the moment she's out of the room. 'What the fuck are you doing? These are envelopes, these are people's envelopes!'

'I know that.'

'Then why have you got them?'

'Why are you screaming at me?'

'You have drawers full of people's envelopes. People's amendments!'

'I know. I've collected them. Em, if you let me speak, I've done nothing wrong here.'

'You've collected them? What the fuck does that mean? People collect stamps, not amendments. You collect the things that went wrong in people's lives, is that it? You get some sick pleasure from looking at these things, laughing at their petty little issues? Have you got mine in there somewhere?'

'Em, that's ridiculous. No, I don't get any pleasure from them, and of course I don't have yours. They're from the bar.'

'What? You ask for the envelopes? Don't worry about paying, just give me your life's biggest regrets.'

'Em, you're being ridiculous.'

'So you steal them, you steal people's amendments?'

'For crying out loud, Emelia, will you listen to me?'

He moves forward, but I step back, shaking my head, blocking my view of him.

'Em, you need to calm down.'

'What kind of person would do that?'

'If you let me explain.'

'I don't want to hear.'

I try to barge past him, but he grabs my arm.

'Please Em, think. Luke is out there.'

'Why should I believe he's any worse than you?'

I spit at him, and he drops my arms.

'Fi! Fi, we're going.' I run out past him. 'Fi. Fi? Fi!' I head back into the flat and swing open the door to the spare bedroom. She's not there. I try the kitchen, the bathroom; there's nowhere else she can be.

'Fi!' Gabe is doing the same, hunting all the rooms. He catches my arm as I run out the door. 'Em.'

'Fi! Fi!' I continue shouting, ignoring him.

'You have to stay here.'

'I have to find Fi.'

'No, I have to find Fi.'

I try shaking him off. 'Let go of me, Gabriel.'

'Not a chance. You're wasting time. Fi's taken my car keys. Please, we will do this later. But you need to stay here. I can't protect you both.'

'We don't need your protection.'

Gabe's eyes flash. 'Have you forgotten what just happened already? Have you that short a memory? Please, Em, please. You threatened Luke. What you and Fi know, about his amendments, that would destroy him. You think he's going to just let that go?'

'I, I —' I flounder under his words. Gabe's lies, Luke's lies; there are too many lies twisting around in my head. I can't make sense of them all. I can't make sense of any one them.

'Please Em, think about you. You believe that a man who almost certainly helps carry out attacks on the centres, who would brainwash a woman into abandoning her family, you think he's just going to let you be? After you threatened to expose him.'

'But he can't, he can't —'

'He can do anything, Em, anything he chooses. He has an army of followers all ready to hand their amendments over to him in an instant.'

He stops and his faces falls with the weight of it all.

'Think rationally. I need to find Fi. I need to find her before she finds him and you'll only slow me down. I love you more than anything in the world, but I don't have time for this now. Please trust me. I'll explain it all, but now I have to go and find Fi.'

He places a kiss on my hand which I wipe away as he slams the door. So much for not being on my own.

I listen until his footsteps are replaced by silence, waiting, as if Fi might suddenly appear like she used to when I couldn't find her playing hide and seek. Back in the bedroom I take in all the envelopes lying scattered all over the floor. I pick up the nearest one, a blue one. *Make more of yourself. Sing, dance, live, love.* And I thought mine were unspecific. How that would be of help to anyone I have no idea. I pick up another, a red. *Give A another chance, you'll never forget him if you don't.* Another red. *Your wife is the woman you love.* A black. *Make him go to the hospital.*

One by one, I pick them up and read them all. Like mine, some are scrawled in barely legible writing – these are mainly the black ones. *Don't let G go out tonight. You must stop her. You must.* Others, the blues, tend to be more precisely written. I linger on these ones. Mostly they are simply worded yet open ended. *Take more chances. Work to live, don't live to work. Have children. Have more children.* These people had lives, full lives. They had waited years, assessed everything, evaluated, re-evaluated, reflected, and this is what they had learned. A couple are blank. I lift the first one to the light trying to make out any faint lines or faded letters, but there are none. Inside, I yearn for a chance I'll never have, a chance to send a blue envelope, or better still, a blank one. However, when my piles are complete, it's clear; most of them are red. In them, I see the same things repeated time and time again.

Tell her you love her every day. Play with your children. Ask her for dinner. I sit reading each one over and over again, every time more carefully than the last. The gradients of colour vary greatly as do the envelopes themselves. The faded ones are on thicker paper, slightly larger, too. I start to rearrange them, this time guessing the ages and placing them in piles. I find one which I do not put back at first. It reads, *I want to do it all over again.* I imagine the smile of a toothless, shrivelled man, so content, so happy he would live the same life all over again.

Holding my chest, I feel strangely calm, like what is meant to happen will happen. An anger starts to slowly simmer inside. None of this explains why Gabe has them, however pleasant they may be to read. Hours must have passed since he and Fi left, and when the distraction of the envelopes is over, the concern starts creeping in. What if Gabe didn't find her? What would Luke do to her? Without a doubt that's where she's gone: to beg Luke for forgiveness for not being there tonight, for not helping burn down centres and murder administrators. I'd like to believe that after this morning Luke's had his twisted fun; terrifying me might have been enough. But somehow, I don't believe that. No telephone call yet though; that at least must be positive.

Chapter Thirty-eight

NIGHT PASSES seamlessly, throughout it all and into dawn and morning and I remain awake. My eyes are encumbered with tiredness but even when the first sounds of life rattle up from the streets below I refuse to let them close. Television, books, sorting clothes, washing: Anything to stop me falling asleep.

I'm back flicking through the envelopes when I hear the catch on the front door. My muscles weaken as tears of relief flood my senses. Gabe would never come back without Fi, and Fi would never come back of her own accord. I leap up from the bed, desperate to hold them both in my arms, but as I reach the door I catch sight of the envelopes by the pillows and stop myself. That anger towards Gabe is still fresh; the trust between us once again on tenterhooks. I think about shoving them away, back into the drawer, but what's the point? I need to hear him explain; maybe this time I'll be able to listen.

I listen for voices – to judge the mood of their return – but there are none. My guts begin to twist. The footsteps are heavy and stop outside the door. It must be Gabe. I strain to hear him breathing as I wait for him to come in, but he's waiting, too. I feel my pulse racing away every second I wait. He didn't make it, he didn't find her. I crumple the paper in my hand as I wait for the door to creak open.

When it does, it isn't Gabe standing there. It's Fi.

She stands in the doorway, apparently unable to move. Her eyes are red and her cheeks are stained with tear tracks. Her breathing is a shallow rhythmic hiss. I move towards her, but she recoils, every limb shaking, her legs, her hands, her whole body trembling uncontrollably. As I touch her shoulder, she flinches and pushes me away. When I look down, I see she has left a red stain on my top.

'Oh God, Oh God.'

Memories of a night, of her barely breathing body, lying on the sofa, flash in front of me. At least she got back here, at least she's with me now. I can fix this, fix her. I know I can. I gently force her down on the bed; she is compliant to the point of submissive, staying perfectly still and silent as I frisk her body. Kneeling on the floor, my hands cover every part of her from her calves to her skull, but I can't find it. My hands are sticky and red, the sickly odour making me gag. There is so much blood, but I can't find the wound. I lift her arms and start to pull off her shirt when she grabs my wrists. She stares at me, into me, and slowly shakes her head. As her eyes lock on mine, I finally understand. There is no wound, not on her.

There must be sound, there must be; my howls, my sobs, the tearing of the envelopes, the smashing of the mirror. All of these must surely make some sounds. All the screams and cries, yet I don't hear a thing. Perhaps that's what happens when there's nothing left that you want to hear. Sounds just cease to exist. I see the pain plastered across Fi's face, but I don't stop. She doesn't try to stop me, and she doesn't try to calm me; she knows there would be no point.

I don't know how long it lasts, the screaming, the throwing, the silence, but eventually it stops. Eventually sounds come again, and with them every pain is magnified. As she holds me, her trembling matches my own and her murmurings blend into my stuttering breaths. Each mouthful of air is coarse and jagged as I fight to keep breathing. She lays my head on her lap and mutters comforting words. That is what I assume; all I hear is the clanging of a distant gong signalling all I have lost.

Fi hands me a glass of water. 'I'm so sorry, this is my fault, this is all my fault. Luke. I didn't know, I didn't know he would… He needed you to know, Em. He needed your, your...'

'My silence,' I finish for her.

I sit up and take a sip of water, my head pounding as though all the hurt and all the tears may be able to escape through my temples if only they could beat their way out from under my skin. Fi murmurs gently as she wraps me back in her arms.

'Em,' she whispers. 'You can fix this. It's fine, you can fix this.'

I can barely make sense of what she's saying.

'Do you want me to take you to the centre? I won't hold it against you.'

My skin bristles; I must have heard her wrong. 'Hold it against me?' I repeat.

'If you want to amend this, I mean. I wouldn't hold that

against you.'

I sit up and push her away.

'Why would you hold it against me? How could you? All of your fucking marching is the reason we're here.'

'I didn't mean it like that, Em.'

I spring to my feet in shock. 'How did you mean it then?'

'Em, please, please, forget I said it. Let me take you to the centre. You can put this right.'

I shake my head in disbelief.

'Em, it's okay. Really. We'll get him back. You can get him back.'

'You still don't see it, do you?' I say.

'See what?'

I laugh. I don't want to, but it's all I can do. All that stops me from striking out and hitting her.

'What? What is it?'

'My amendment, Fi. It's gone. It's already gone.'

'What do you mean gone? When? How? You've barely registered.' She rises to her feet, her jaw tightly clenched, her chest puffed out, trying to force my eyes down with a glare. 'What do you mean it's gone, Em?'

'You need to do this, Fi. You need to put this right, for Gabe and for me.' My voice quivers just slightly, but I don't look away.

'When did you use your amendment, Em?'

'He was trying to save you. You need to fix this.'

'When did you use it?'

'You said you loved him, and you say you love me, Fi. Please.'

'When did you use your amendment, Emelia?' she screams at me, shaking me by the shoulders. 'When did you use it? When? When?'

Her nails dig into my skin. I choke on the tears and the air that refuses to stay in my lungs as she shakes me back and forth.

'Em, tell me? Where's the scar, where is it?'

'You need to go back.'

'Where is the scar, Em? I swear I will —' But she stops. She grabs my arms and twists me around, tearing the T-shirt from my back. Tentatively, she runs a finger along the line, tracing it back and forth. I can feel her hand trembling. 'It was me, wasn't it?' she whispers.

'Please, Fi. Please, go back. Just give him a warning, please.'

'Was it black?'

'Fi, listen to me. I can't lose him, not like this, not this way.'

But she isn't listening; she's rocking back and forth, the mechanism of her mind furiously whirring away inside her head as she tries to figure her way through it all.

'It was black,' she says eventually.

'Yes.'

'Can I see it?'

I want to refuse. Make her swear to help Gabe first. But I know there would be no point.

I fetch it from my bag and place it in her hand.

She huffs. 'So, I died,' she says matter-of-factly.

'It looks that way.'

'Why hide it from me?'

'I don't know.'

'Yes, you do. You knew then that I wouldn't want it, I wouldn't want you to go back for me.' She pulls at the dry skin on her lips as she rereads the line, over and over again.

I join her, kneeling on the floor, fighting the urge to scream and shake her. I give her a moment's contemplation.

'Fi, it's done and if I saved you when you didn't want that, I'm sorry. That's my mistake, I get that. But please, this is not Gabe's fault, none of it. After everything you and I have been through. I need him. I am begging you. Please, Fi, I need him. Please go back for me.'

She shakes her head. 'You knew I didn't want this.'

'Please, Fi.'

'It's wrong, Em. Everything about it, it's unnatural. It's has consequences'

'Everything has consequences!' I scream at her. 'We are here because of you, because of your consequences. Please, Fi. Please do this for me.'

With a sad sigh, she stands up and brushes her legs clean of dust. 'I'm sorry, Em. I can't. It's not right.'

She has barely reached standing when I slap her with the full force of my weight, unbalancing us both.

'You had a choice,' I say, tears streaming down my face. 'What choice did I have? Six years spent looking after her when you did what exactly? Occasionally frolic in with a pay check so that we could bow down and profusely thank the prodigal daughter? And when it went wrong, when you couldn't cope, what did you do then? She wanted to die, you knew that, or at least you would have if you ever saw her. And you wouldn't even let her do that? How dare you take the fucking high and mighty route with me.'

'You don't know —'

'What? What don't I know, Fi? What it's like to be you? What it's like to be a failure? Of course you're a failure, you never even try. Why would you when you play the hopelessly-hard-done-by tart so well? No wonder the Marchers liked you so much.'

This time it's me who falters under the slap. I bring my hand to my face to try to stop the stinging, though if anything, it makes me feel stronger.

'You have no fucking idea, do you?' I hiss. 'Everything I've done, everything I've done for you. Staying at home so you could work, my first amendment, my second, you took them both from me. And the only thing you couldn't take, sorry, you couldn't keep was Gabe, and you'd rather he was dead than with me.'

'It's not like that —'

'That's exactly what it's like.'

'I couldn't have looked after her, not the way you did,' she says.

'You never tried. That's all you had to do. Don't you see that? You just had to try.'

'I tried! You never saw what I did, the number of times I had to stop her. How I'd clear out the flat in the middle of the night of everything, everything, cleaning fluids, razors, long bits of string for crying out loud —'

'But you never asked her what she wanted. She was always going to find a way to end things. All she wanted was to stop the pain. You were wrong to go back for her.'

'A mistake I won't be repeating,' she says.

I slump to the ground, out of tactics. The screaming, the pleading, the guilt. Fi isn't me, she isn't driven by guilt or emotion; she's driven by her inane urge to do what she believes is right. And to her that isn't saving Gabe.

'Em, I'm s—'

I flick her hand away from me, lacking the energy to even truly strike her. I turn and crawl onto the bed, hearing her steps on the creaking floor; when they are almost out of earshot, they stop.

'I'm sorry, Em, but you're so strong. You're so strong and so beautiful and you'll never be alone. You know that, don't you?'

Her voice trails into the ether, and she waits just a moment before clicking the front door shut.

Epilogue

THERE IS A MOMENT when I wake up and I don't remember. I don't remember the screaming, the pain, the begging. A moment when I don't remember to search my mind for every memory, every thought, every moment we had together for fear of losing the memories altogether. But the moment is barely a second and it all returns with a sickening velocity.

I reach for a glass of half-drunk water by the bed before changing my mind and heading into the kitchen for a fresh one. My wrist has a dent in it where I slept with the bracelet on, the seal of the envelope charm has stamped an indentation in my skin.

Sitting on the sofa, I pull out the week-old newspaper and flick past the first few pages. With all the news, it's not surprising it wasn't front page; in some ways I'm surprised it's mentioned at all.

Heroine attempts to foil Marcher Attack, the title reads. I read it for the millionth time. It describes it all so succinctly: How the centre was set alight, how someone saw the young woman rush into the flames, trying to come to the aid of those screaming inside. It tells how the young woman pulled out three administrators, one of whom later died in hospital. It said that the young woman's death was as heroic as it was tragic. It was all so, so tragic.

A hand appears on my shoulder.

'Come back to bed.'

'She wanted this, you know. She must have.'

'I know.'

'But why?'

'She must have had her reasons.'

She had everything so perfectly planned, letting me think I had carried out my amendment, making our reconciliation easy, only to steal Gabe's keys and leave when the bar was too busy for us to notice. By the time I'd realised she'd left and we'd shut up the bar, the guards were manning every corner, and we had no idea where she'd gone. We had no choice but to wait for the phone call.

'I found this,' Gabe says.

In his hand, he is holding an envelope. I drop the paper in my hand.

'When did you find it? Where?'

'On the floor of the bar, last night; it had slipped down the side of one of the tables. I don't know how long it's been there. It may not even be hers.'

'It's black,' I state unnecessarily.

He gestures at it again, and with my hand shaking I take it from him. There are no markings on it, nothing to say it's hers. If I don't open it, it's like I've never seen it. I place my finger under the seal and then, changing my mind, lift the envelope and hold it beneath my nose. A sweet, musky honeysuckle smell wafts from the paper. It is hers.

I stare at it, my hands trembling as I pull apart the seals and unfold the paper. I gasp as I see her writing, so delicately looped from one twisted tailed letter to the next. I can't breathe, let alone read it through the tears. Gabe tries to hold me, but I brush him away, desperately trying to find some air somewhere in the room. He waits patiently, just a comforting hand squeezing mine.

'What does it say?' he asks softly when I am able to breathe again.

I try to wipe away the tears, but more keep coming and my sleeves are soon black with the unending flow. Surely there is a limit to how much one person can cry? If there is, I feel I am a long way off.

'It's okay,' he tells me. 'It's okay.'

I concentrate, chakra-like breaths rattle through me as I wait for the tears to stop. The envelope is still open on my lap; I don't need to look at it, but I can't draw my eyes away. It's as if the words might somehow slip off the paper, taking with them the only concrete and tangible thought I have of her.

It was such a simple thing to write, subtle. An eloquence that Fi tried so hard to hide, seeping through the lettering. My voice and I break as I say the words, but I say them all. Taking me in his arms, Gabe rocks me back and forth, until the numbness takes the place of the pain and I can speak again.

'What should we do with it?' I say.

He wipes more tears away. 'I have a place, if I can show you?'

The sight is outstanding; there must be a hundred of them and in so many colours: greens, blues, blacks, reds, so many reds.

'Whose are they?'

'I don't know.'

'Where have they come from?'

'The bar. People have left them in the bar.'

'All of these?'

'Over the years.' I tentatively pick one up.

'Have you read them?' I say.

'Just the once, then I put them away.'

'What are they about?' I ask, picking up more and more, turning them over in my hand. The papers are so different.

'Different things, but mainly…'

'Yes?'

'Mainly they're about love.'

I pick up another one, a faded deep red on the front only, made of thick heavy paper. 'Can I?'

Gabe nods.

Love her despite her faults.

I crumple onto the bed.

I open another and then another, reading the contents over again and placing each one back as delicately as the first.

'Why keep them?' I say.

'I can't throw them away.'

'Why not? They've done their job. They're worthless now.'

He removes the one from my hand and sits on the bed next to me. He taps his toes musically while he looks at the ground for the answers, and when he looks up, he brushes down a tuft of hair on the back of my head.

'These envelopes,' he tells me. 'They're more than one person's decision, one person's amendment. They're linked in so many ways that we couldn't possibly hope to see. How many lives were altered because they were sent? How many times has my life been altered so people can make one simple change? I'm not saying amending is wrong, but throwing these away, to me it's like dismissing the whole world of lives that were there before. Just forgetting everything. I think somebody should be there to remember.'

He picks another one from a different drawer, this one green, and hands it to me. This one I recognise. When I open it, there are only two words written.

Be better.

When we have cleared the envelopes away, we head down to the bar. Gabe has hired someone else, but for now they can only do the day shift, not that it matters much. I pick up a few empties and swill them under the tap before delivering more cold drinks which will be warm and flat well before they are half drunk. Art sits as usual, propped up on his elbow, plucking the stray wiry hairs from his chin. I place the glass on the tattered mat in front of him. As I move away, he grabs my hand.

'It will get better, Princess,' he says.

His tone and look cause a prickling sensation to run down the length of my spine. I nod politely and tug my hand free, aware of the presence of something foreign within my grip. Art's gaze falters only to indicate Gabe, busy serving. Instinctively, I head to the stock room and wait until I'm inside before switching on the light, gently guiding the door shut. I sit on a full crate and slowly uncurl my fingers.

Inside is a scrap of paper. A few numbers and words in scruffy writing spell out an address, somewhere I vaguely recognise, not a nice part of town. Below the address, the letters are little more than a scrawl, rushed or drunk, the style is familiar. The words are not.

There is always a third.

Also by **Hannah Lynn**

The Afterlife of Walter Augustus

-Winner of the 2018 Kindle Storyteller Award-

Prepare to fall head over heels in love with Walter and Letty. Overflowing with humour and wonderfully memorable characters, this emotional and heart-warming tale will have you laughing and crying until the very end.

Walter Augustus is dead. After decades stuck in the Interim he is ready to move on and be with his family. But just as the end is tantalisingly close, bad luck and a few rash decisions threaten to see him trapped for all eternity.

Letty is not dead. Letty Ferguson is a middle-aged shoe saleswoman who leads a wholly unextraordinary life; that is until she takes possession of an unassuming poetry anthology and the world takes on a rather more extraordinary dimension.

As Letty and Walter's worlds become more and more intertwined, how far will Walter go to cut his ties with the living for good?

Praise for *The Afterlife of Walter Augustus*

"The Afterlife of Walter Augustus is wonderfully written and I thoroughly enjoyed this creative read." – **Lorraine Kelly**

"A hugely uplifting novel, full of humour and intelligent observations about relationships and a deserving winner of the Kindle Storyteller Award this year. Fans of Eleanor Oliphant would love it!" – **L.J. Ross, Author of the international #1 bestselling series of DCI Ryan mystery novels.**

"Heart-warming, clever, and populated with a host of well-drawn and engaging characters, The Afterlife of Walter Augustus *will*

surely prove to be one of the stand-out releases of 2018." - **Joel Hames, Author of *Dead North***

"A fresh perspective on the classic existential question – what happens next?"

"Tears and laughter until the very last page."

"A cross between The Five People You Meet in Heaven *and* American Gods. *A great read."*

An excerpt from *The Afterlife of Walter Augustus*

Chapter One

THE AFTERLIFE smelt of cut grass and fresh laundry.

This was not an aroma that had been landed upon lightly. Countless alternatives had been suggested over the millennia, such as ground coffee, frankincense with a hint of lemon, freshly baked bread, sea air with a whiff of slightly soured buffalo milk, spiced cinnamon and ginger, morning frost, rhubarb and spearmint and, obviously, chocolate. However, when all had been decided, newly cut grass and freshly laundered linen were deemed the most appealing scent for the wide range of clientele that passed through this interim aspect of existence. After all, it didn't matter if you lived your previous life in the meadows of fourteenth century Eastern Scandinavia or grew up in a tower block in 1984 listening to Michael Jackson on your Walkman. Cut grass and fresh laundry smelled good wherever and whenever you came from. Unless you were Walter.

In Walter's defence, he had spent the first century of his afterlife revelling in the starkly clean comfort of the scent. Even now, the occasional whiff could still tickle his senses and unexpectedly transport him back to a more pleasurable time. However, lately those moments had become few and far between. In truth, it was not the dewing aroma that Walter Augustus had grown sick of in the last few decades, more the interim in its entirety.

Whilst alive, Walter had been considered an attractive man. His hair was sun-bleached to the colour of straw, and his skin was tanned and weather-beaten in the way that skin that dealt with the elements often was. His slight shyness — and acute awareness of his position in society — meant he often avoided eye contact, but in a manner that came across as endearing, rather than rude. He had been a reserved, hard-working, and appreciative man in life, and for the longest while, these characteristics had travelled with him into the interim. Unfortunately, like the love of his post-existence aroma, he could sense that within himself these characteristics were also starting to fade.

Walter's current abode was an exact internal replica of the house in which he had lived during his adult physical years, one up, one down, with bare stone walls and a hearth that occupied the majority of the downstairs. He had opted out of its original view — a large and unfeasibly pungent manure pile — and instead, selected a cliff top position, complete with winding pebble path and distant, cawing seagulls. The garden outside was home to a selection of vegetable patches and fruit bushes, while his trusted wicker rocking chair was, if possible, even more comfortable than it had been during his corporeal years. These decisions had not been a conscious selection, of course. The interim would have never worked in such a prosaic manner.

Walter pulled a cast iron poker out of the fire. He plucked the toasted bread from the end and took a bite then coughed as the bitter tasting charcoal covered his tongue. Spluttering, he swallowed and took another bite. Not until he was halfway through the slice did he remember that whether he ate or not would make no difference to his day. He sighed, opened the window, and threw the remaining toast outside.

Since his great-granddaughter had passed on, Walter had stayed almost entirely in his little corner of the interim. He kept no company, and his existence had become a day-to-day monotony of habit and routine. That said, he had ways to keep himself occupied and tried to mix things up now and again. Along with strolls down to the beach, sometimes he chose to rest in the long grass of the cliff tops and scribble odd verses into his little blue notebook. Occasionally, he would saunter over to the workshop and hammer out an odd piece of ironwork should it so take his fancy. He had no desire to see how humanity had changed since his passing or to see how his afterlife existence could be in any way expanded or updated. Walter had resigned himself to live out the rest of his existential life on his own, in his own way. Particularly now.

For the first time in half a century, Walter was genuinely excited. This was not the sort of excitement felt for everyday events — like the thought of a good meal after a strenuous day's work or discovering long-forgotten money in the lining of a seldom worn summer jacket. This was the type of excitement that only resulted from years, if not decades, of anticipation. It occupied every waking thought and continued to bubble through his intestines at night. Bigger even than the birth of his children or Edi's arrival in the interim after finally escaping her last years of physical pain on Earth. Walter's excitement was almost beyond containment.

A day, a week, one month at absolute most, and he would be moving on, leaving the interim for whatever awaited him in the next stage of the afterlife. It was just a matter of time.

One more week until he saw Edith again. His stomach somersaulted at the possibility. One more week until he saw his children. One week. The anticipation was too great to sit still.

***

Letty rubbed her eyes and groaned. Every muscle from her ankles to her wrists throbbed, but it was her knees and back that were the worst. They had been on dodgy ground for a while now, with too many clicks and aches to mention, but today, they were burning. Simply bending down to pick up one of the many discarded Welly-boots was enough to cause a shooting pain to sear right through her thigh, all the way up to her spine. No doubt the extra weight she had piled on in the last few years hadn't helped, but she was fairly sure that age — not Mars bars and millionaires' shortbread — was the overwhelming culprit. She groaned again, hoisted herself up using one of the low square seats designed for fittings, and placed the boot back on the shelf.

'Why don't you do the till?' Joyce said as she straightened up the sale rack. Joyce was a slightly vacant but sweet eighteen-year-old that had started as a Saturday girl and had a penchant for revealing more information about her relationships than Letty deemed necessary. 'I can finish tidying up. Might as well get the vacuum out too. I don't think we're going to get anyone else in now.'

'You're probably right,' Letty said and glanced through the open doorway. The afternoon sun had started to dip, and the sky had taken on an orange hue. After a moment's consideration, she nodded her agreement and started towards the till. On route, she paused to straighten up a size four patent girls' school shoe and two rows of men's loafers before continuing over to the counter. 'Let's see how we've done today,' she said.

Shoes 4 Yous was a small chain of shoe shops that provided mediocre quality merchandise at a slightly less extortionate rate than its nearby competitors. Set mid-town — equidistant from the swanky bistros with their oversized wine glasses and the kebab shop where meat was of an unspecified origin — it attracted a range of clientele, particularly at this time of the year. With the start of the school year only days away, the shelves were packed with sensible looking black footwear, from slip-ons, to triple Velcro and — for those parents who still had the patience to teach bunny ears or the like — old fashioned lace ups. The aroma in the shop was one of faux leather and carpet cleaner, and while the soft lighting had been intended to create a homely inviting atmosphere, Letty was fairly certain that it had also resulted in her need for reading glasses since the age of thirty-five.

Still, there were worse places to work, she reasoned.

Now fifty-four, Letty had worked as the senior manager at *Shoes 4 Yous* for the best part of three decades. Prior to that, she had worked in a Woolworth's store, which had been converted into a discount furniture shop selling cut-price sofas. There was nothing about insoles, insteps, and upper leathers that Letty didn't know. She could tell a child's foot width from a cursory glance, the condition of a woman's arches by the state of her heel, or whether a man wore a size nine or ten, regardless of which he asked for.

'Letty,' Joyce said, cutting the vacuum only minutes after starting it. 'You wouldn't mind if I skip out a bit early, would you? Kevin's taking me out tonight, and I wanted to go see if I could get my bits waxed first.'

'Oh. Course. You get off.'

'He doesn't like it if I don't, see. He says it's like kissing a hamster down there.'

'It's fine. Please just go.'

'I'll finish the 'oovering first.'

'Don't worry about it. Just go. Honestly, I'll see you Monday.'

'Cheers, Letty,' Joyce said, dropping the vacuum where it was and blowing Letty a kiss. 'You're a right star, you are.'

As Joyce disappeared down the high street, Letty turned the sign to closed, locked the front door, then got about balancing the till.

The day's takings were good. Other shops were finding it

hard now, with online shopping and supermarkets managing to undercut them at every corner, but shoes were different. People liked to try shoes on before they bought them. And rightly so to her mind. In Letty's opinion, one could never underestimate the power of a good or bad fitting footwear. So, while other clothes and retail shops were closing up all over the place, *Shoes 4 Yous* was about to open its fifth branch. Not that it affected Letty at all, just a few more trainees to get up to speed here and there.

After balancing the till, Letty went about the rest of the jobs. That night, it included restocking the shelves, pulling used tissues out from inside a pair of high-heels, and wiping off a dubious green substance from the underside of the mirror. Once that was finished, she picked up the vacuum to finish where Joyce had left off. The old red Henry growled as the nozzle pushed against the faded blue carpet, it's heavy thrum drowning out the sounds of the radio and every sound beyond that.

Due to the noise and Letty's concentration on the job in hand, it was a solid minute before she finally registered a heavy knocking sound coming from the front of the shop. She glanced over her shoulder towards the door and started at the sight of a face pressed up against the glass.

A second later, she offered a short wave of recognition. 'One sec,' she called, before craning over and switching Henry off at the plug. She scuttled over to the door, unlocked it, and opened it with a jingle.

A woman with frizzy brown hair stood in the door, rocking a stroller back and forth. 'I'm so sorry I'm late. He wouldn't settle.' She gestured the pushchair in her hand. 'It's like he knows I've got things to do.'

'No, not at all. Perfect timing. I was just off in my own little world, that's all. You hang on a sec. I'll go and fetch it from out back.'

Letty ambled across to the back of the store and through the heavy white door marked Staff Only. A minute later, she reappeared, a large white box in her arms.

'Do you want to have a look first?' she said. 'Check it's all okay?'

'Thank you,' said the woman, who then took to jostling the stroller with her foot.

Letty prised away a small piece of tape and lifted the lid. The woman gave a small gasp.

'Oh, it's perfect. Thank you so much. You are so clever.'

'Oh, it's my pleasure,' Letty said. 'How is he, by the way? Over that tummy bug?'

The mother rolled her eyes. 'Finally. Honestly, I thought it was never going to pass. Craig's come down with it now.'

'Oh, I am sorry. Will he be alright for tomorrow?'

'He doesn't have much choice.'

Letty offered a polite little chuckle then took one final peek inside the box. She was proud of this one, even if it was simple. The coloured triangles of the bunting were the neatest she had done, and the little blue bear and toy box were easily as good as some she'd seen in magazines. Two tiers. Hand cut letters too.

'It's forty pounds, right?' The woman took the box and carefully squeezed it into the base of the stroller, before slipping her handbag off her shoulder. After a moment of rummaging, she pulled out her purse and extracted two twenty-pound notes.

'That's great. Thank you,' Letty said.

'No, thank you. Honestly, you should open a bakery. You're brilliant.'

'Maybe one day.' Letty felt a flush of colour rise to her cheeks, although any possible embarrassment was averted by a sudden interlude of bawling that erupted from the stroller.

'Not again. I swear he never sleeps.'

'It's no problem. You get off. And have a lovely day tomorrow.'

'I'm sure we will. Thanks again.' Making a variety of shushing noises, the woman headed back down the high street. After a moment more watching her, Letty shut the door with another jingle and went back to the vacuuming.

Also by **Hannah Lynn**

Peas, Carrots and an Aston Martin

Eric Sibley has it all; great job, big house, beautiful family. Even when his estranged father dies, Eric can't help but dream about the luxuries he'll spend his inheritance on. Unfortunately, Eric's late father, had other ideas.

Life quickly becomes a chaotic kaleidoscope of grumpy pensioners, wellington boots and vintage automobiles as Eric is forced to juggle his hectic career and family life in London, with regular visits to the small riverside town of Burlam.

Plagued by heavy machinery mishaps, missed deadlines and drug raids, it's not long before his job, his marriage and his sanity are hanging in the balance. Can he get his hands on his father's treasured Aston Martin before he loses all three?

Praise for *Peas, Carrots and an Aston Martin*

"The story flows really well and the entire concept had me simultaneously laughing, cringing and crying. It's a brilliant mash up of people and places."

"I loved the characters within this book, they were so deliciously lovely, quirky and believable, even when at their most absurd."

"It's a book that oozes charm."

"Wonderful book to get lost in. Adored the characters and loved the way the book was written - very easy to read and I loved, laughed & cried in equal measures - great!"

"So many funny moments, the prose is witty and bouncy, and I can't wait to read more from the Author"

An excerpt from *Peas, Carrots and an Aston Martin*

Chapter One

ERIC SIBLEY sat across from the solicitor. He was unsure as to what the appropriate or expected response was given the current situation. He blinked a few times and rubbed the bridge of his nose, then shuffled around on the chair and tried to find a more comfortable seating position. The shuffling included a solid minute of switching his weight from one buttock to the other, adjusting his legs from crossed to uncrossed and sliding forwards and back on the cement-hard plastic. After which, he concluded no comfortable position could ever be obtained in a chair so cheap and badly built. It was simply not possible.

The chair wasn't the only thing that was cheap in Eric's opinion. The whole solicitor's office, from the blutacked A3 posters on the window to the laminate desk, worn blue carpet and instant freeze-dried coffee reeked of skinny budgets and cutting corners. There was no class, no style. On the other side of the desk, the solicitor looked equally as cheap, with his polyester jacket, comic tie and supermarket aftershave.

'Just explain it to me again,' Eric said. 'You're saying I get nothing? None of it? Nothing at all?'

'No —' The solicitor removed his glasses and rubbed his eyes. '— as I have explained, your father has left you the remaining tenancy on his allotment and his 1962 limited edition Aston Martin DB4 series four, affectionately known as Sally, on the condition that you fully tend to the allotment on a weekly basis for the next two years.'

Eric shook his head.

'But the house? Everything in the house. The paintings, my mother's jewellery all of that, it... it's...'

'It's been left to the church,' the solicitor finished for him.

'But he didn't even go to church!' Eric thumped the table with his fist. 'He was a bloody atheist!'

The solicitor — who was possibly named Eaves or Doyle, judging from the sign above the door — shuffled the papers in front of him, then returned his glasses to the end of his nose.

'I realise that this is a difficult time for you. But your father was very specific about his wishes. The car will remain in your possession, permanently, provided you adhere to the specified conditions.'

'And if I don't?'

'Then your father has made provisions for that situation too.'

Eric sucked in a deep lungful of air then let it out with a hiss.

'But Abi? He must have left something to Abi? She's his only grandchild for Christ's sake.' Eaves-possibly-Doyle massaged his temples with his knuckles.

'I'm very sorry, Mr. Sibley, I don't know what to tell you. Perhaps your father felt you would value these gifts more than the house or money.'

'Like hell he did.'

Eric pushed back the chair, snatched the papers from the table and strode over to the door. When his hand was on the handle, Eaves-possibly-Doyle coughed. Eric spun around.

'Mr. Sibley before you leave, I have to tell you that if you were to step on your father's property from now on, that would be considered trespassing.'

Eric's lungs quivered. 'Exactly, how am I supposed to collect the car without going on the property?' he said, through clenched teeth.

'Your father has seen to that as well.'

Stay in touch

To keep up-to-date with new publications, tours and promotions, or if you are interested in being a beta reader for future novels, or having the opportunity to enjoy pre-release copies please follow me:

Website: https://www.hannahlynnauthor.com/

Twitter: @HMLynnauthor

Facebook: @HannahLynnAuthor

To claim your completely FREE exclusive content visit the email address below:
https://mailchi.mp/72960b762d85/marcherposters

Review

If you enjoyed reading ***The Amendments***, please take a few moments to leave a review on Amazon or Goodreads.

Printed in Great Britain
by Amazon